"NOW IT IS REVEALED,"
THE LADY CALLAIN SAID HEAVILY.

"This power has been within you all along but you kept it secret. Then, with no warning, you use the Touch on Elisinthe, who is nothing but a servant! Well, your ploy succeeded. I will do whatever I must to have a child. Name your price: tell me what you wish and you shall have it."

Dara stood rooted to the spot. Power? Within her? Callain believed she had granted the gift of fertility with a single touch. Dara's first response was simple denial——then she looked at the emotion in Callain's face and the reality of the situation hit her. How she acted now was critically important.

"What I wish no one on Khyren can grant," she said truthfully.

"Insolence! While you are at Highfields you are within my power. Never forget that I command here!"

Dara recoiled from that passion. What Callain wanted, demanded, was not hers to grant. What Dara needed now, most urgently, was *magic*.

"I've waited a long, long time for a novel as complex and absorbing as *Dune. Khyren* is it. . . . Science fiction doesn't get any better." Gary Wolfe, author of *Who Censored Roger Rabbit?*

ALINE BOUCHER KAPLAN

BAEN BOOKS

KHYREN

A Baen Books Original

Baen Publishing Enterprises
P.O. Box 1403
Riverdale, NY 10471

ISBN: 0-671-72046-5

Cover art by Larry Schwinger

First Printing, October 1988
Second Printing, March 1991

Printed in the United States of America

Distributed by Simon & Schuster
___ Avenue of the Americas
___rk, NY 10020

To my husband Seth,
who is my friend, lover, teacher, partner
and who always supports me
in everything I do.

CHAPTER 1

The sun was hot, sweat trickled down her neck, and something moved sluggishly over her ankle. Dara swam up from the dark into dull consciousness. Light beat insistently at her eyelids but it took a concentrated effort to open them. After several attempts were defeated by the stabbing of a sharp, painful yellow light, she was able to open them. For long moments Dara lay staring at tall stalks of grass waving in a breeze that did not reach down to her. She did not know why she was lying there. She also did not know where she was. All Dara did know was that she hurt in every bone and muscle. Worse, her body felt as if it had been pulled apart and then put together again quickly but not very carefully, without regard for fit. It seemed that any abrupt movement might cause her to come apart. She tried moving a finger, then a hand, and they responded. When she could see the hand and determine that it looked as normal as ever, Dara tested the other parts of her body. Satisfied that it was all in one piece, she gritted her teeth and pulled herself to all fours. Her body protested violently and she had to close her eyes again until the pain subsided. Then she knelt and looked out over the grass.

The first thing she saw was the last part of a large, slow-moving reptile that was slithering off between the stalks and blades. It was bright red with tan dapples and was thicker than any snake she had ever seen. It took Dara's brain a long moment to provide the information that there were no bright red snakes or reptiles of any kind, in Massachusetts. Looking around in confusion, she saw rolling meadowland, a pale lemon sky with no clouds, and a band of purple mountains. She scanned the horizon for 360 degrees, searching for a sign of someone or something familiar—a car, a building, a landmark. There was nothing but grass, sky, and distant mountains. She knelt in a meadow she had never seen before, warmed by a sun that was, when she squinted to look at it, larger and more yellow than it should have been, smelling air that was subtly, vibrantly different.

With another disciplined effort, Dara stood up and then almost fell. She felt light. One step took her half again the usual distance and she lost her balance. Sitting down again abruptly, she put her head in her hands and tried to force her brain into awakening and overcoming the confusion and pain which overwhelmed her. Think. Fragments of memory returned slowly. Today must be Thursday because last night was Wednesday night; she remembered that. They had eaten dinner. She had cleaned up after dinner as usual, put her daughter to bed as usual, gone out to jog as usual. It had been a pleasant, cool night and a good run. She was doing five miles easily now and was planning to increase her distance again. She was even thinking of training for a real race, a 5-K or maybe a 10-K. Everything had been normal. There was the quiet suburban neighborhood with a few cars going by, people watching TV behind blue picture windows, rock music forcing its way out of Bobby Petrova's room and smoke from the Anderson's wood stove perfuming the air. She had been the only one out but that was not unusual. Dust devil. That's right, there had been a funny whirlwind spinning leaves and pine needles around at the corner of Oak and Thalia. She had run right through it, feeling a little giddy as it lifted her hair. After that? She did not remember going home or going to bed or waking up. After the whirlwind, there was a blank. Dara looked down. She was wearing her blue sweat suit, white socks, and running shoes. "It was more dramatic when Dorothy did it," she thought with giddy humor.

Dara stood up again, being more careful this time, and looked around. Nothing had changed: the rolling meadow stretched unbroken in three directions. Then she noticed, off to her right, a copse of small, dark trees that filled a hollow and spilled out of it into a larger wooded area. These woods followed a depression which wound through the expanse of grasslands, making a vivid green accent among the yellow and tan hills. Hesitantly, she started off toward the trees where there would be shade, possibly water and, she hoped, some people who could explain all this. She proceeded slowly and with a certain caution. If she did not know where on Earth she was, Dara also did not know who lived here. She had no desire to run into a strange situation with open arms and a trusting soul.

The walk was easier than it should have been, even compensating for the downhill portion. Dara put this aside, however, not yet ready to deal with the implications. She reached the woods in less time than she had expected and, entering them carefully, she made as little noise as possible. Winding through the woods in the center of the hollow was a road: pounded red dirt, summer dry. It followed a body of water that qualified as either a large stream or a small river, depending on the climate. Looking carefully in both directions, Dara approached the empty road. The dust held many tracks of animals, human feet, and wheels. After staring at them stupidly for a long moment, Dara found a concealed spot and sat down to consider what she had just seen. The human footprints were left by both bare feet and shod, and looked normal. The animal tracks, or at least she assumed they were tracks of animals, were like none she had ever seen before. The long narrow grooves looked like they had been made by wagons although Dara had little experience with wagons. Nothing even vaguely resembled a tire. All the tracks headed off to her left, down the road towards the forest, as if aligned with some great magnet.

While she sat concealed and thinking, a low rumble became noticeable and grew steadily louder. Dara knelt and parted the bushes so that she could see while remaining concealed. The rumble increased and, as it grew closer, separated into discrete sounds: the creak of a loaded wagon, grunts, marching feet, chattering voices. Excitement mixing with disbelief, Dara watched a small caravan emerge around a bend in the road. In the vanguard strode large men, obviously guards or soldiers, dressed alike in brown leather and all heavily armed. They were followed by a number of people on foot and then a vehicle that resembled a stagecoach. It was drawn by a large and ponderous beast with long legs and silky fur, an animal that Dara knew she had never seen before anywhere, even in pictures. There were bearers and supply wagons, and riders on other, rodent-like, alien creatures. Moving slowly but with its own momentum, the astonishing caravan passed before her and disappeared down the road.

Perplexed, appalled, and beginning to be very frightened, Dara remained in her leafy hiding place all afternoon, watching the road. Insects buzzed around her and crawled over her but she barely noticed them. The heat increased until it was uncomfortable even in the shade but she remained still. Her patience was rewarded with a procession of groups including large parties and small bands all moving in the same direction. She saw merchants and traders, nobles and peasants. The animals were unearthly and the people, while outwardly human, were also undeniably different. They had skins that ranged from gold to a deep tan, and hair in various shades of brown. What she saw gave Dara much to think about but after about an hour she found thought impossible. Her brain settled into a nearly catatonic state from which not even the most outrageous sight could rouse it. The sun dropped toward the far mountain peaks without her noticing the passage of time.

Finally the caravans stopped coming and she looked up to see the last sunlight in the tops of the trees. Evening fell quickly and she roused herself reluctantly, then emerged, stretching, from her blind. Now she had two more things to deal with: night and hunger, and she was not sure how to handle either. The simplest thing would have been to head down the road until she came to where one or more of the caravans had camped and then ask for help. The problem was that she had no idea what the trade-off would be and she was extremely reluctant to give up her independence until she had a better idea of the consequences. Unfortunately, Dara had to admit that she could not live off the land even in the woods of Massachusetts, much less here in this totally strange place. Worse, she did not even know if it would be safe to eat the same foods the native humans, or humanoids, consumed. But the alternative to finding help was staying alone in the dark in a place where people found guards necessary, and starving. Dara shook her throbbing head to clear it, ran her hands through her hair, and made a plan. She would stay close enough to the campsites to beg protection in case of danger. Watching what the people ate, she would steal food whenever possible. And she would stay on the fringes, remaining hidden for as long as she could, until the best course of action became apparent.

In the rapidly thickening dusk, Dara stepped out onto the warm red road, following her nose and ears to a large, well-organized campground that was situated on a peninsula at a bend in the river. Cooking fires glowed in stone fireplaces, colorful tents were pitched in groups, wagons were drawn off to one side, and animals of all types tethered in picket lines nearby. Some of the people looked familiar, having passed by her blind during the long afternoon. Dara also noticed that guards were posted and vigilant. Dinner was cooking on fires all around the campground and the smells went directly to her very empty stomach. Like most middle-class, well-fed Americans, Dara was unacquainted with real hunger. Her only exposure to it had been on a twenty-four-hour fast that she had voluntarily joined in support of some cause or other. So it was strange and difficult for her to remain quietly in the shadows, watching others prepare and eat meals that smelled wonderful but which she could not touch. It was an unpleasant reminder of her predicament, one which would make life significantly different, at least in the short run, and a great deal less comfortable. Admonishing herself not to cave in at the first hint of hardship, she settled back against a sun-warmed rock to wait.

Then full night enveloped her and Dara was diverted from her own problems by its beauty. The myriad crawling, flying things that had swarmed around her in the daylight disappeared and were replaced by the night shift. All around her, but invisible, they sang in a lusty chorus so loud that the woods themselves seemed to be in full voice. There were high, piping calls and deep rhythmic pulses and an uncountable variety in between. Once, off in the distance, there came a long bass note that hovered between a moan and a howl. It sounded like a great humpback whale swimming in solitude through the night meadows.

Pulling her eyes from the sociable glow of the campsite and letting them adjust to the darkness, Dara was rewarded by a spectacle that at the same time forced her to face the truth she had been avoiding. The sky was filled with stars but they were not the stars of Earth. A thick belt of blue-white diamonds flung itself in arrogant majesty across two-thirds of the night sky. The stars were large and burned with a relentless fire. If this was the Milky Way, and Dara could only hope it was, then the world on which she found herself lay far closer to the center of the galaxy than the tiny solar system that included Earth. There was no escaping or denying the glorious proof that blazed above her. The reality of being on a different world was impressed upon Dara with an incredible finality. She began to shake and tears formed in her eyes. For an unmeasurable time, she trembled and cried alone in the dark, filled with the anguish of someone lost to everything safe and familiar.

Many hours later, when the fires had sunk to embers and everyone lay sleeping, she crept closer. Thanks to her long reconnaissance, Dara knew the location of the midden heap where the remains of the evening meal had been cast. She also knew which bundle on which wagon contained food and that the closest guard could not see it directly. It was time to act before the rumbling of her stomach grew loud enough to alert the guards. Heart pounding, she carried out her planned approach to the midden heap, the least dangerous of the two goals. Creeping through the darkness, she passed two guards and many sleepers wrapped in blankets and scattered under wagons as well as out under the open sky. When she reached the midden, she found that all her caution was pointless as the guards seemed accustomed to visitors of the four-legged variety and paid no attention to noises from that direction at all. Working quickly, Dara foraged enough crusts and scraps to fill her stomach. Although it was not the most appetizing meal she had ever eaten, she decided that hunger and fastidiousness exist in inverse proportion to one another. Taking her dinner with her, Dara faded into the darkness as the glow of oddly-shaped eyes and rustling noises told her that the more familiar diners were growing impatient for their meal.

Concerned about becoming a part of some large predator's dinner, she curled up behind a clump of bushes not far from the wagons and tried to sleep. Dara was grateful that she had her sweatsuit to keep her warm, for the night temperatures had dropped and the air grown chilly. Disoriented, frightened, and still in pain, Dara wanted nothing more than to join the civilized group so close by and seek relief. She thrust down the temptation again and then, quite unexpectedly, fell asleep.

For days, she scavenged from the travelers, raiding campsites after the evening meal and again when the morning's travelers had departed. The experience was disgusting, the tastes were strange, and her stomach often rebelled, as much from stress and fear as from the fact that she was eating discarded alien foods. Dara grew thin and yet, as the days went by, she also became increasingly wary and suspicious. As she continued her observations of this well-traveled, one-way road, she saw many things that made her glad she had not approached the first people she had seen. Life on this world was primitive by her standards, hard and even brutal. She saw people cursed and animals beaten. The social structure appeared almost feudal, ranging from servants to nobles of great status. Some of the people worked extremely hard and others did noth-

ing. When she was not actively involved in just surviving,
Dara thought a great deal. Yet she remained perplexed
about how and where she could find a way out of this alien
environment and how to fit in until then.

As she traveled, Dara surveyed the surrounding landscape. No matter how far she went, or how the road
twisted, the topography remained simple to the point of
being monotonous. Trees and underbrush of a deep green-
ish blue lined the river on both sides, filling the shallow
valley and shading the road for as far as she could see.
Above the valley to the left curved the great meadowlands
on which Dara had awakened. Green where it met the
valley, the meadow rapidly turned to a dun color similar to
that of a ripening field of wheat. Like grain, it shimmered
and rustled in waves before the wind. Across the river on
the far side of the valley, the landscape was rocky and
barren. Sparse vegetation grew between striated stones
that rose in broken steps to a range of jagged hills. These
hills paralleled the road, rising higher as they receded.
Nothing grew on the heights which, rather than upthrust
mountains, appeared to be a jumbled collection of randomly fractured and weathered rock. They hid whatever
lay beyond them.

There were few remarkable forms of vegetation other
than the silky grass and a variety of tall, broad-leafed trees
that rose solidly from the watered land alongside the river.
The underbrush was lush in some places and almost non-
existent in others and offered a variety of sizes and shapes.
Dara avoided it as much as possible, hoping that none of it
was poisonous, irritating, or carnivorous. If it were, she
knew that she would find out the hard way and without
the assistance of antihistamines or calamine lotion. The
only other native plant that Dara found striking was a tall
stalk, very similar to bamboo except that it was blue,
growing in vigorous clumps everywhere, seemingly without regard for conditions of moisture, shade, or soil. There
were no flowers.

Gradually the procession of caravans and their strange
animals became familiar to Dara. She continued to follow
them along the road, growing even more curious as to

where it led. What could be the destination to which people traveled for days and did not return? Early one morning she was drawn away from the road to the edge of the grasslands by a curious low burbling noise, somewhat like a coffee pot percolating in a distant room. With her now-habitual caution, she sought both a vantage point and a hiding place in the thick branches of one of the many sturdy trees. From this lookout, she spotted an odd, dark creature that was wandering up and down the gentle hills. Slowly it approached, following no visible trail, attracted by a patch of hooded green plants with recurved leaves that resembled jack-in-the-pulpits. As it drew closer, Dara noticed that it gave off a faint, pungent odor with musky undertones.

No matter how close it came, however, its shape remained vague and almost fuzzy, seeming to change continually. When the creature reached the nearby pitcher plants, the reason for this volatile appearance became immediately clear. It stopped, the burbling stopped, and a horde of flying creatures like large insects lifted and flew away from the greater creature that had carried them. Still for the first time, the carrier resembled a beetle the size of a large dog, with three walking legs on each side and four smaller legs emerging from a shiny black head. These small legs clutched a waxy amber globe about the size of a grapefruit.

While its flyers burrowed under the green pulpits, the carrier turned cautiously in a circle, alert to approaching enemies. After several moments of frantic activity, the flyers emerged from the pulpits and returned to the carrier's back. Almost as soon as they had landed, however, the flyers were off again. This time they circled the carrier in a rapidly moving swarm. The low noise began again and rapidly grew louder, while at the same time the musky smell intensified. As it did, Dara felt her senses grow keener until they seemed to pulse with a vivid clarity. Her vision was enhanced at both ends of the range: she could observe every chitinous detail of the flyers and see for miles toward the horizon. Every footstep, squeak, and rustle from the trail behind her was unmistakable. Beneath her fingers the tree bark became a wondrous interwoven pattern. Then an additional perception opened to her, and another sensory experience unfolded. Emotions were suddenly as tangible as the tree in which she sat. Strongest of these by far was the wariness and timidity of the creature below, mixed with the unfocused group desire of its symbiotes to settle down again. Fainter, like a whisper, came a ragged fringe of feelings from the caravans: fatigue, desperation, hope, anticipation. Fascinated and delighted, Dara was just beginning to savor these emotions when the burbling noise subsided, the fragrance diminished, and the heightened perceptions faded. The flyers swarmed across their host's back once more and the creature turned away. As it did, she saw that the waxy ball it carried was now shiny, as if it had been coated with liquid. Then the strange animal wandered back into the solitude of the empty meadows.

In a drugged trance, Dara slumped against the tree's broad trunk. For what seemed like half an hour she remained immobile, drained by the experience and sedated by the fragrance's narcotic aftereffect. She felt as if every pore and nerve in her body had been hyperextended and now had shut down to recover. Only the solid girth of the branch she straddled saved her from falling. Finally she recovered enough strength to slide down from her perch but her limbs were weak and twitched spastically and it was a while longer before she could make her way slowly back to the road. She would spend a long time thinking of that strange and wonderful experience and, even after she had examined it from every angle, she would savor its memory.

Despite the nomadic, fugitive, and fear-ridden circumstances of her life, Dara imposed order on the days. Each morning she rose when the guards around camp were changed and observed the travelers preparing for another day on the road. Once the groups had separated and each caravan gone on its way, the campsite was emptied. Then she was assured of a lengthy quiet spell before even the fastest riders from the next group of pilgrims appeared. Dara took advantage of this period to care for her own needs. First she gleaned the garbage heap of whatever edible food remained. Although always hungry by this time, she would not breakfast until she had completed a full set of exercises. Her repertoire included warm-ups for running and judo as well as an assortment of other calisthenics. She imposed this discipline both out of a personal need to keep in good shape and an insistent feeling that she would have to depend on it sooner or later. The workout was followed by a swim in the river, which she tried only after watching others do it with no apparent risk. The water was clear and cool and, although it smelled of frogs, very refreshing. Her impromptu baths led to a losing battle between her thick, curly brown hair and a scavenged fragment of comb. Only the fact that her hair was short kept it from becoming tangled beyond hope.

Dara usually obtained enough food—unsanitary and unappetizing as it was—to keep herself going. Being always a little bit hungry was the least troublesome of the side effects of her diet: not all the local foodstuffs agreed with her metabolism. Some filled and nourished her while others left her hungry no matter how much she ate. A few items on the local menu spent very little time in her gastro-intestinal system before making a hasty exit. After some painful trial-and-error testing, Dara learned to identify the problem foods and avoid them. If fortunate enough to scavenge more food than she needed for breakfast, she stored the remainder in a rough piece of cloth that had blown, unnoticed, off one of the wagons. This would serve for lunch. Her morning preparations completed, Dara would wait for the next group of travelers to appear and then follow them to the next campsite.

The days were much the same in temperature—warm, dry and pleasant. Making the climate seem even warmer was a sky that was basically yellow, although it ranged over the course of the day from deepest gold to pale lemon. At sunrise and sunset it was often streaked with spectacular colors but the sky never approached the cool blue that Dara was accustomed to seeing. At night, the heavens were brilliant, illuminated by the proximity of the galactic cluster. This light was bright enough to see by, brighter than a full moon. There were, however, no moons circling this world. Although she watched, night after night, hoping to see one moon or more, the only natural satel-

lites were small, irregularly-shaped objects. These asteroids, or so Dara assumed them to be, followed a narrow
path across the sky, moving rapidly from horizon to horizon. Their appearances were unpredictable however: sometimes there were several in the sky at once and sometimes
none for two or three nights in a row. Dara often watched
the night sky for as long as fatigue allowed her to remain
awake. She searched for the point of light that marked
home even after she realized that such an effort was pointless. She had no idea where the planet on which she
stood was located in the galaxy, or even if it was in the
same galaxy. But even after accepting that bitter fact, she
gloried in the brilliance, variety, and number of stars
overhead and never tired of the celestial display.

It was an unforgiving life. Although Dara became hardened to the rigors of the day and familiar with, if not
accustomed to, the nocturnal sounds, she was always on
edge. Guarding against capture on the one hand and the
dangers of the night on the other, she could never relax
and never sleep deeply. Lack of nourishment and rest
combined with dirty clothing and soapless river baths left
her grimy, edgy, and depressed. Still, she felt there was
no alternative but to go on. So she drifted through the
undergrowth beside the road with a few "possessions" in a
tattered rag bundle. One day it occurred to her that she
had become a kind of cosmic shopping-bag lady. It was an
amusing thought until she realized that she probably looked
and smelled like one too.

The baggage she did not allow herself to carry was
insubstantial but much heavier—her memories. Dara kept
all thoughts of her family and her old life before what she
now thought of as "the accident" securely locked away.
She knew that if she dwelled on how much she missed her
husband and her daughter, what they were doing without
her, or how empty her life was without them, she would
be overwhelmed by grief, anger, and frustration. But giving in to her emotions and falling apart were luxuries that
she simply could not afford. Survival was all-important and
anything that distracted her from it, anything that got in
the way of staying balanced on the thin edge, was dangerous and possibly fatal.

Survival hinged upon learning enough about this strange, yellow-gold world to make her way in it safely. That meant following through on all the details of the difficult task she had assigned herself: observing a large and mobile group of people. To do it, she had to remain close enough to seek protection if necessary while escaping detection herself. Though assiduous, she was not always successful. Chance alone dictated that there would be mistakes. Once she was surprised by a single pilgrim and fled, in what the man who had interrupted her saw only as a flash of blue brighter than any he had ever seen before. Despite her best precautions, Dara also left footprints in the dusty campsites and on the muddy riverbank. Since she moved slowly, but continuously, in the prevailing direction of the traffic, travelers coming along behind her discovered these tracks. They might never have paid attention to them if it were not for the unusual marks left by the patterned soles of her running shoes. These tracks were unlike any left by the sandals or boots of the people in the caravans. Dubbed "phantom tracks," Dara's footprints caused much consternation and were the subject of imaginative campfire speculation.

The most serious lapse in her defenses occurred, however, when hunger got the better of caution. On that night, Dara raided the midden before she was certain that everyone was asleep. Crouched down, with her hand outstretched to snatch some scraps, she found herself face-to-face with a young and very frightened servant girl who was finishing the last of her chores. With wordless gestures, Dara pleaded for the girl to keep silent and then faded back into the night. At any moment she expected to hear a cry of discovery and the alarm raised. Although she hid, she knew that they could find her easily if they searched. Part of her hoped that they would. Instead, the encampment slept on peacefully and the insects sang undisturbed by the pounding of her heart. Hidden in the night, Dara had no way of knowing that her unusual, wild looks and sudden appearance had convinced the superstitious servant that a spirit, an aspect of the Lady, had appeared to her. No one with any sense would disturb such an apparition. Indeed, the wise person would placate it in the hope of earning good fortune and, like most servants, she was always looking for better luck.

Thus, Dara was startled on the following morning when the same girl hung back as her caravan departed. Stealthily, the servant approached the place where the "spirit" had appeared to her. Looking quickly about to make sure that she was alone, she deposited a neat bundle and made a brief gesture. Then, turning, she raced away into the cloud of red dust that hung over the road. Ever wary of a trap, Dara waited longer than usual, listening and watching carefully before daring to step out into the open. Even when she had the offering of fresh food safely in hand, she headed off to the grasslands to exercise and eat, rather than remain in the exposed campsite.

CHAPTER 2

Sunlight dimmed in the large tent, then disappeared as the orange disk sank behind the distant mountains. Within the spacious, peaked structure, servants moved to light lamps, stepping nimbly around the four officers of the Rangers sitting cross-legged on a well-worn rug. The officers ignored the servants bustling around them just as they ignored the cooking aromas spreading from braziers at the back of the tent. They were deep in conversation and, while each had strong opinions, none could agree on a plan. The words flew quickly and sometimes forcefully as the four men discussed what should be done about the odd "blue phantom" that had been reported by many of the travelers coming into the Festival grounds from the south pilgrimage road.

"We must track this phantom and capture it," stated the largest of the four as firmly as would be expected of someone with his height and bulk. He stroked the long, dark beard that emphasized his broad cheekbones.

"And how does one go about capturing a phantom, Haron?" inquired the man to his right, whimsically. Smaller and wiry, but no less tough, he cocked an eyebrow at the others and his light green eyes gleamed with humor. "Phantoms are notoriously hard to pin down. Perhaps we should consult an Oben for guidance."

"No need for their arrogant meddling!" snorted the third man, ignoring the jest. "This is no phantom. What spirit leaves footprints? They're strange ones, to be sure, but there they are, in the dirt along with everyone else's. Tracks are tracks and they belong to the living. This is a task for the Rangers, not the Obenan."

"You're right there, Tirnus," asserted Haron, still tugging his beard. "We will plan this right now just as we would any other manhunt. The four of us should be sufficient to take one man on foot: we can handle weapons as well as anyone else in the Rangers. We'll need fresh mounts and a small pack of coursers, well-trained and trustworthy. After all, we don't want this phantom torn to bits before we get a look at him."

"And what then?" The soft question came from the fourth man, who had listened carefully to all the arguments but spoken little. "When we have captured this 'blue phantom,' what then?"

"Why, he will be brought before the Justiciar, of course, Resar," answered the wiry one firmly, "and he will be judged accordingly."

"On what charge, Khitum?"

"Why, theft of food, naturally," interrupted Haron indignantly, "and disturbing the peace . . . and trespassing."

"Food? Garbage, you mean, left for the animals to dispose of. Nothing has been stolen. As for disturbing the peace, that happened after the fact and here at Festival as the story spread, not on the road."

"But . . . you . . ."

"And trespassing? How does one trespass on a public right of way during Festival? Your charges are the real phantoms, Khitum."

"He is gormrith and fair game. We need no charges," asserted Tirnus in a low voice. He used a word that described anyone cast out from a village or freeholding for any reason, from the grossly deformed infant to the psychopath. Some men sought it for the freedom to rob and plunder the unwary traveler. Occasionally, in a bad year, an old one would choose gormri and almost certain death rather than burden his village through a hard winter. Whatever the reason, anyone outside the protection of society was considered gormrith, and outlaw.

"Gormrith, Tirnus? You must be mad," interjected Theram, the wiry one. "No gormrith scavenges and hangs about. Once outside, they die, commit suicide, or seek out a pack of their own kind and turn to robbery."

"Nevertheless, this creature has neither village, nor freeholding, nor even tribe. Therefore he is gormrith by definition and the law is clear."

"Tirnus is right," affirmed Haron, "let us end this pointless debate and plan the hunt. I'm looking forward to it: this will be the most fun I've had since we cleaned up that mess down at Rhuannan's Crossing."

"Does this plan include a kill?" queried Resar. The rest looked at him in silence. Resar straightened up to emphasize his point and, while not quite as tall as Haron, he was well-built enough to convey an impact just by physical presence. Of the four, he had the noblest birth and that showed both in the unconscious air of authority he assumed and the willingness of the others to listen to opinions that seldom agreed with theirs.

"Always the same point," said Theram with a sigh. "This grows tedious. And why *not* a kill?"

"Because we do not know what we hunt. Because what is done in the heat of the chase may be regretted on the slow trail back. Because we should not start this without deciding how to finish it."

"Then we shall run down this phantom and hold him at bay and *you* can choose. The gormrith's fate will be yours to decide," said Khitum.

The others nodded in agreement and Resar, with a look of relief, accepted the decision. A servant placed a tray of hot spiced vegetables before them and they began to eat enthusiastically as they arranged the details of the next day's hunt.

The next morning, Dara sat on the far side of the river, looking down toward the campground and the grasslands beyond it. The sun had just risen and she sat with her back against a stone, waiting for its rays to take away the night chill. For a brief moment she closed her eyes and indulged in a fantasy of being on vacation. When she returned from her morning run a hot breakfast would be waiting for her at the luxury resort. Eggs, she thought, scrambled with cheese and scallions. Sausages. English muffins dripping with butter and strawberry jam. Cold orange juice. Hot coffee . . . Her stomach rumbled fearsomely and, with an effort, she pulled back from the seductive daydream to a reality considerably less attractive.

Dara reviewed the prospects for her future—it did not take long—and found all of them wanting. They reminded her of a line from an old rock song that frequently ran in circles inside her head. The first and most passive idea was to remain on her own in the woods, living uncomfortably and in fear. This was feasible only if the climate remained temperate and did not cool into winter, and only if she could continue to obtain food as she had been doing. The second strategy was to approach one of the caravans and throw herself on the mercy of its people. After remaining undiscovered for so long, however, Dara was reluctant to give up her independence and "come in from the cold." A major factor in this decision was that she had yet to see any travelers whose mercies she would care to trust. The third and most viable scheme was to continue along the road until she discovered what lay at its end and then make a more informed choice. The third way won out.

Dara turned over her decision for a long time while the sun grew higher and warmer, torn between the practicality of her choice and the temptation to just give up. She was bitterly tired of catnapping in the woods and eating cold garbage, tired of playing a dangerous but unrewarding game, tired of trying to beat the odds against survival in a strange environment. That she had had little choice in the situation did not make her feel any better. But even worse than the physical hardships was the impact of emotional deprivation. Dara had never been so alone for so long. Objectively it was not such a great period of time, a little over a week, but it seemed much longer to her. She yearned for the sound of a familiar voice but would settle for anyone who could speak in a language she could understand, or even someone who would speak to her at all. Dara's isolation was unique, compounded of culture shock, language barriers, homesickness, and even a form of jet lag. Yet none of these could even begin to describe the devastating effect of being stranded, solitary and friendless, on a totally alien world. After a while her emotions began to play tricks on her. She went from understanding that she could not speak to anyone to feeling that no one wanted to speak to her, although this flew in the face of all logic and reason. Each day alone diminished her. Dara began to feel insignificant and almost transparent; a spectre whose haunting went unnoticed and unremarked. A mystic, she thought, would probably use this as an opportunity to seek deep within for the strength to surmount the trial and understand life's mysteries. But Dara was not a mystic and the White Light of the Universe was not visible to her. So she coped with the loneliness, resisted the urge to give in, and hoped that whatever lay at the end of the road would provide the answer to her predicament.

As she watched the road from her perch on a slight rise, a crackling of underbrush told her that someone was coming up in her direction. As quietly as possible she moved behind the rock and then, using it for cover, slipped uphill for a short distance. The sounds kept coming. This was most unusual: in all the many days that she had skulked about the road, no one else had moved far away from it except to gather firewood or to relieve themselves at a distance from the aromatic latrines. The sounds came from upstream, in the direction that traffic was heading. Dara angled off again and waited.

She saw them first and was puzzled by the small party of mounted men and large, dog-like animals moving randomly about in a way that was totally different from any other travelers that she had seen. When they converged on the spot where she had slept the night before, however, Dara realized with a shock that they were casting about for her scent—and that they had found it. A humming rose from the dog-beasts and then stopped abruptly. Next they turned and headed up the hill. For a moment, Dara thought of just staying put and simply waiting for them to arrive on her trail. But she was not eager to lose what little control she had and she wanted the situation to end on her terms. Fortunately, there was the river between Dara and the hunters to give her a good head start. She also had the advantage of knowing that they were on her trail while they were tracking blindly. Thrusting down the impulse to rush headlong into the hills, Dara looked around to assess the possibilities. She would have to think fast and use every ounce of her depleted energies to lose the hunters quickly. There was no question of outrunning them or enduring a long chase. She would seek the cover of the high, rocky hills and go to ground. Dara thought with a grin that she would give them a fox hunt they would remember for a long time. Yet she prayed that the sinuous beasts were tracking by scent or sight and not some more exotic sense that she could not outwit. Moving at a steady jog, she headed uphill.

Seeking every advantage the terrain offered, every opportunity available, Dara jumped from rock to rock to break her trail as much as possible. She left several false trails and backtracked, although this tactic required too much energy and consumed too much precious lead time to do often. When fortunate enough to spot such traces, she confused her scent with piles of animal dung, jumping over it and spreading it around with a stick. Although the ruse was simple, Dara could not help wondering what kind of animal had left the manure and whether it was more dangerous than the ones following her. She could be running out of the frying pan into a lair. When she encountered a thin stream trickling down from the rocky heights, she waded up its course for as long as possible, then crisscrossed it, jumping back and forth. All the while she moved upward, away from shady stands of fern and blue bamboo to hot, jumbled rocks and sparse growth of scrubby vegetation. The growing heat of the sun, the constant climb, and the attempts to hide her trail left her depleted of strength by mid-day, less and less able to think quickly or to act on her ideas. Although she had taken a long drink before leaving the stream, thirst and hunger put a wobble into her knees.

Approaching the end of her endurance, Dara searched

for a good place to lose the hunters and then hide until they had gone. Her running had so far been successful enough that the humming of the pack remained distant. Still, Dara had no illusions that she had lost them. It was critical now that she use the time she had gained to her advantage and end the hunt on her terms.

Above her the trail sloped up to a plateau that seemed to be honeycombed with fissures and caverns, one of which might provide the right conditions for throwing the pack off her trail. Of course, there was the peril of finding herself outfoxed and at bay or encountering some hostile creature on its territory. Without an alternative, however, it was a chance she would have to take. Meanwhile the trail up to the plateau lay over a pile of stone and rubble that had fallen from the top.

Climbing slowly but steadily up the talus slope, Dara reached the cleft that was the entrance to the plateau. Sheer walls on either side left her only two ways to go. From where she stood, heaving to catch her breath, the right-hand path seemed to lead to a narrow pinnacle of rock that had split off from the body of the plateau and stood in isolation. Dara swung left where the way was less steep and there was no dead end in sight. She realized that this smoother path would allow the beasts to move more quickly also. Although exhausted, it was a relief to be able to run steadily again after the long climb. Without the assist she received from the lighter gravity, she could not have come this far. As quickly as possible, Dara negotiated tight turns between vertical walls that rose higher and higher. Each turn raised her hope of finding a place where the topography would offer her the advantage she needed. Then she came to a large outcrop that extended from the right wall almost over to the left, with only a narrow gap between.

As Dara slipped around the outcrop, the humming deepened behind her and became louder as it echoed off the stone walls. She had lost her lead. The hounds were closing in and she was spent. Desperately, she sought an escape route. On the far side of the outcrop she saw both the place she was looking for—and the end of the hunt. Here the path became a broad ramp that sloped smoothly downward to a maze of caves and myriad twisting passages. It was exactly what she needed. Bisecting the ramp, however, was a broad, deep chasm that was too steep to descend and too broad to jump. There was nowhere left to go.

Chest burning and legs trembling, Dara looked around for anything that might serve as a weapon. Against the mountain on her left grew a stand of the familiar blue bamboo-like stalks. Hard but light, one snapped off with a noise like breaking glass. Using it as a staff, Dara grasped it firmly in the hope that it would serve to keep the hounds from her throat. There was little time to think further. With the humming almost at a roar, the sinuous animals rounded the outcrop and spotted her.

There were three of them, about the same size as wolves but more massive and powerful. Their heads were broad with deep-set, intelligent eyes and sensitive ears. They had short wiry fur and no tails. But their most distinguishing feature was their teeth: large, sharp, and angled back toward the throat so that nothing they bit escaped. Dara stared in fascination as well as fear, trying not to imagine those teeth in her body. She raised the staff and braced for their charge. Instead of rushing her, though, the beasts spread in a semicircle around her so that the chasm was at her back. Dara thought she would rather jump than go down under those fangs, but the animals still made no move toward her. Instead they waited at attention, with their eyes fixed on her and their mobile ears pointed backward.

Then the hounds began to hum in an audible pattern that sounded almost like harmony. Although pleasant to the ear, the physical effect of the thrumming sound waves was astonishing. Dara's bones began to vibrate in the same rhythm and, as they did, what small measure of energy she had left drained from her body. She stood, transfixed, wanting only to slump to the ground but unable to move at all. These animals were more dangerous than she had thought. Their vocalization was a weapon in itself, a very effective one that immobilized their prey until the hunters could catch up to the pack.

Her theory was confirmed when the hunters rounded

the outcrop and the harmonic humming stopped. In the sudden silence, Dara had time to catch her breath and realize that she could move again. She tried to raise the staff higher and was surprised to find that she had been leaning on it. She wanted more than anything just to sit down. The hunters ranged their mounts out behind the pack and watched her for a moment. Their expressions gave no hint of their intentions but they did not look like easy men. Dara waited, keeping very still, trying not to give in to her pounding heart and quivering legs.

The men conferred briefly and then three of them dismounted. Each of the three took a weapon from his saddle pack and approached the hounds. The largest man, the only one with a beard, hefted what looked like a tomahawk. His thinner companion held an arrangement of lines and weights that might have been a bola. The third kept an easy grip on a slim lance. Once in position, they looked to the fourth man, who had remained mounted. He studied her intently, then dismounted and, unarmed, walked to the pack of animals. At a word from him they relaxed their vigilant stances but continued to watch her.

Dara knew that the sensible, logical thing to do was to drop her staff and surrender. Escape was, after all, impossible. But just to give up after the long chase and submit to being a captive without knowing her fate was unacceptable. She would fight as well as possible and risk a quick death instead. The beasts moved aside to let the hunter through and then closed the semicircle again. The hunter stepped forward softly, without taking his eyes from her. Gripping the staff, Dara waited as he approached. The first move, she knew, always went to the loser but if she waited too long she would lose the advantage of the staff's length. Quickly she brought it up and jabbed its end at the man's stomach. He dodged the blow without effort and gracefully caught the end of the weapon. With a sharp twist, it was wrenched from her hand to spin out over the cleft and then down.

More confident now, he stepped forward and reached for her arm. Dara dodged to the left so that all he grasped was a handful of shirt. His grip, however, was unbreakable and he moved in decisively to take her. As he did, Dara took one step toward him with her left foot. In a fluid motion, she seized his tunic with her right hand, planted her right foot in his stomach, and sat back. The hunter's forward momentum carried him down onto her coiled right leg. Completing the throw, Dara thrust him up and back, in an attempt to catapult him into the cleft, but her exhausted muscles failed her. Instead of arcing back, he dropped almost on top of her and when she tried to roll away, a hand closed around her wrist like a manacle.

Dara was pinned while hands bound her ankles and then she was rolled roughly onto her stomach and her hands tied behind her. Grit filled her mouth and choked her but she had no saliva to clear it out. When she was rolled back, sharp pebbles cut into her hands and arms. The hunter squatted next to her, the point of his dagger resting casually on her jugular vein. The other hunters had moved closer and were standing around in what seemed like great good humor. Dara lay very sill and looked into the piercing green eyes of the man beside her.

He asked a terse question in the native language. Dara remained silent and he repeated the query, accentuating it with noticeable pressure on the blade. Stretching her head back, away from the knife point, Dara tried to speak, to explain that she could not understand him, but no sound came from her dry, dusty throat. A water bag was thrown down and the hunter unstoppered it, sending a thin stream into her mouth. The water was very warm and tasted like wet dog fur but Dara swallowed it greedily. After only a few gulps the bottle was taken away and recapped. Instead of repeating his question, the man pressed more firmly on the knife and looked at her expectantly. The point had broken the skin but Dara tried to ignore it and the blood that trickled down her neck.

"I can't understand you," she said. "I don't know what you want me to say. I don't even know where I am."

The hunter murmured in surprise and above him the wiry one replied in a tone of complete incredulity. The face of the man beside her remained expressionless and the knife did not waver but he looked her up and down. Then the dagger left her throat and, in one swift thrust, sliced her sweatshirt open. His hard hand grasped one of her breasts firmly and Dara stiffened. Then he pulled her sweat pants down and she shut her eyes. Nothing happened. She opened them again and saw a look of astonishment on the hunter's face, and on the faces of the other men as well. Suddenly Dara understood: they had thought she was a man. Instead they had just discovered that their quarry was female.

Dara huddled close to the small campfire using as much self-discipline as she could muster to eat the wafer of dried bread slowly and deliberately. Wolfed down to fill her sore and empty stomach, she knew that it would come right back up again. Coming down from the hills had taken longer than the journey up because the riding animals had to pick their way carefully among the jagged rocks or risk breaking a leg. It had been a long, hot ride, excruciatingly uncomfortable for Dara, who had been slung belly-down over the saddle. Unable to brace herself against the piston-like movement of the animal's legs, she had felt every step directly in her stomach. Only the man's hand had kept her from sliding to the ground on some of the steeper stretches. The night was cool, as always, and a knife-edged wind swept across the small hillside where they had camped. In between bites, she pulled her torn and ragged sweatshirt as close as possible even though it did little to cut the wind. Around her, three of the hunters sat or squatted in the firelight eating heartily the flesh of a beast which the fourth man was browning on a spit. Loosed with a curt command, the hunting pack had soon returned with several, large lizard-like animals. The men had butchered one and thrown the others and the offal to the pack. Dara had received the small round loaf of hard bread taken from a saddle pack. Its very hardness worked in her favor because it was difficult to chew except in small bites that prevented her from gulping it.

After the scavenging that had kept her alive, the bread tasted delicious. Before she could finish, however, the cold overtook her and Dara's shivering became uncontrollable. The bread fell from her hands and she herself would have toppled into the fire had not the bearded hunter reached out a sun-browned arm. Quickly he pulled a blanket from his pack and rolled her up in it. Another man scooped up an armload of dry bamboo and threw it into the fire where it burned with a sound like wine glasses shattering. Dara soaked up the warmth gratefully even as she realized that the convulsive shivering was caused less by the cold than by shock. Gradually the spasms subsided and her muscles relaxed one by one. Finally, in spite of her empty stomach and almost against her will, she slept.

Resar chewed the tough roasted leg of ridge-hopper slowly as he stared over the yellow flames at the still blanket and its highly unusual occupant. Grease ran down his fingers and gleamed on his chin in the firelight but his attention was on the scrawny female that now was his responsibility. Starved, filthy, and scratched, she looked as sturdy as a dried soapweed. But that was a deceptive appearance, as he had learned. No frail, weak creature could have lived in the wild for as long as she had, scavenging for food and avoiding becoming a meal for the predators. Nor could such a one have led them on this strange chase or put up such surprising resistance. He wondered both where she had come by that inner strength and where she had come from at all. She had no look of either the lowland people or the mountain folk, not in language or clothing or customs. Well, he had taken her and he would have to learn more about her. But first, he had to keep her. Resar spit out a piece of gristle, tossed the bone into the flames, and reached into his saddle pack.

CHAPTER 3

The ruddy sun hung low in a niche between rock out-crops, and sharp black shadows stretched against the bleak landscape as it gained height. Dara woke with a violent start and gouged her cheek on a sharp stone. For a moment she was completely disoriented, unable to remember where she was or who the strange men around her were. Then memory returned and the surroundings settled into a rough familiarity. The hunters were already up, preparing to resume their journey, and Dara watched them for a while as she gathered her wits and her strength. When she moved to unwrap the blanket she found abruptly that her hands were tied. Next she discovered that she was barefoot and her running shoes were nowhere in sight. She sighed and asked herself what she had expected— tea with toast and a hot bath? She was a captive and the sooner she adjusted to that fact the better.

Once the realization sank in, she tested her bonds. They were tightly and expertly tied: she would not get free that way. Free! Free to scavenge garbage, free to fear becoming some animal's next meal, free to run and to freeze. Once more the old rock song drifted through her memory and her lips twisted in a bitter smile. "Freedom's just another word for nothing left to lose." It could not have been more appropriate. She might well be on her way to slavery, torture, or death but, for the moment, there was warmth, food, protection, rest. They were things she had always taken for granted in an easy life that might just as well never have happened. In addition, Dara had no strength left to run or fight, even if she were free. It would be a while before she had recovered and by that time she would either know what was in store or she would be dead.

The hunters untied her and allowed her to stretch and relieve herself. Dara tried to follow their example and do so without concern for the lack of privacy but it wasn't easy. It was one more adjustment among many. After a spartan breakfast of trail rations and stale water, they were ready to depart. The mounts, much larger in proximity than they had appeared from a distance, were rounded up and saddled. Then Dara's captor approached her with a leather thong in his hands. He looked from her to the beast and back again as if trying to decide the most efficient way of transporting his human baggage. Dara, who had no desire to spend another minute stretched over a prominent, jolting backbone, decided to take the initiative. Pushing down an atavistic fear of the alien animal, she walked toward it as firmly and without hesitation as her sore muscles would allow. The massive rodentlike head turned curiously toward her as she reached up for a stirrup that swung nearly at her shoulder level. She swallowed hard and concentrated on getting her foot into the stirrup, a task that would not have been easy even when she was in good condition. Dara had nearly succeeded when her captor came up behind and boosted her into the high saddle. Settled comfortably, if uncertainly, in front of him, she felt inordinately pleased with herself as they started out.

From this perch, she looked more carefully at the animal she was riding. Although it carried itself on two powerful hind legs like some of the carnivorous dinosaurs, it was furred and warm blooded. The front legs were thinner and less heavily muscled but long enough, as she would discover, to carry them in a swift, four-legged run for great distances. The tail was long but smooth and hairless. At the other end, its pointed face bore small dark eyes topped by round ears. If it was, as she suspected, a giant omnivorous rodent, she hoped that it lacked the cunning and viciousness of its diminutive counterparts on Earth. The musty smell it gave off was pervasive and something she would have to learn to live with.

Now down from the rocks, they traveled at an easy pace all that day, stopping only to eat and allow the pack to hunt. Dara grew tired quickly and hung on to the saddle bow with grim determination. As the day passed she was grateful for the broad, strong chest behind her and for an occasional steadying hand. The mood of the hunters was cheerful and there was a great deal of good-natured conversation to which Dara listened carefully in the hope of picking up a word or two. But the men spoke quickly and by the end of the day she had learned only two: sapeer, which was the beast they all rode, and the name of the man behind her in the saddle—Resar. They camped as they had the night before and Dara was once again tied firmly. They reached their destination the next day.

The small band trotted over a rolling hill as the sun approached its zenith and stopped to look down onto the massed tents of the Festival grounds. Silk and canvas structures of many shapes and colors spread over the valley, punctuated by the smoke of cooking fires. Dirt "streets" crowded with people and animals separated the tents. It was an exciting sight and Dara watched, enchanted, while Resar dismounted and rummaged through his saddle pack. Her brief reverie was terminated abruptly when Resar grasped her by the waist and pulled her from the saddle. The few words he spoke were as unintelligible to her as all the rest and she was surprised when he tied a lead line first to a saddle ring and then to her bound hands. When he remounted she realized that she was to be paraded into the encampment. She steadied herself to do it with style and dignity but the idea of being displayed as a captive or of having to run a gauntlet of hostile people was daunting.

They started off at an easy jog and Dara was relieved to

find that she could keep up the pace. Once again the lower gravity was a considerable help. Her bare feet, however, felt every stone, burr, and twig in the grass. Several times she stumbled in pain as her weight came down on something sharp that lacerated her foot. As they approached the city of tents, people hurried out to line one of the dusty streets. Instead of the jeers or laughter she had dreaded, Dara heard only low murmurs and surprised questions. Keeping her head up she looked straight ahead, trying to ignore the fact that she was half naked, scratched, and dirty. Faces and tents went past in a blur until the riders stopped in a large clearing among the tents. Dara stood quietly, catching her breath and mustering her strength.

Soberly she realized that she was about to confront whatever it was she had been running and hiding from. She was going to come face-to-face with the unknown fate that had driven her to hide in the woods. The hunters dismounted and people came from the crowd to hold their mounts. Resar unfastened the rope from his saddle and pulled on it. Dara stepped forward. Then, with a shock, she saw the stake planted firmly in the middle of the clearing. Iron manacles dangled from chains fastened to both top and bottom. Its length was marked in several places with suspicious dark stains. Dara stopped abruptly, her eyes fixed on the post, which rose before a low platform on which stood a single chair. For a long moment she stood frozen, aware only of her rapidly-growing fear and a tingling feeling as the blood drained out of her face. Then Resar gave a sharp pull on the rope and she stumbled forward, into reality. Pushing back the fear, Dara lifted her head and walked forward steadily. Whatever was coming, she would not be dragged to it, kicking and screaming. She would go with whatever scraps of dignity she could summon.

At the stake, Resar unbound her hands and pulled off her cut-up, stained sweatshirt. Then his hard brown hand forced her to her knees in the dust. Raising her wrists, he fastened them in the circlets which dangled from the top of the stake and Dara's body was stretched upwards with her back slightly arched against the post. She could feel its rough splinters against her spine and the hot sun on her body. Her ankles went into the bottom pair of manacles. Almost able to sit back on her heels, but not quite, Dara tried to brace her weight against the stake to ease the strain on her leg muscles. Without a word Resar dropped her running shoes on the ground beside her discarded sweatshirt and approached the platform. It was occupied by a tall man, slim, with white hair and trim beard. His face, wrinkled with age, held a grave authority and his demeanor demanded respect. Resar bowed before this elder, then drew his sword and held it blade-up before him. He spoke briefly, tersely. When he had finished he turned the weapon point down on the platform and stood with both hands on its hilt. The old man proceeded to question him and Resar answered with deference. Then the hunter stood aside as the white-haired one questioned the crowd. He fell silent and there was a long pause but no one either spoke or stepped forward. Once again the elder queried with no response. Then Resar sheathed his sword and stepped down from the platform. Without looking at Dara, he joined his friends and they led their mounts into the crowd.

Dara understood that a decision about her had been reached but had no idea what it was. Even if anyone around her could do so, no one seemed interested in telling her. Instead, the crowd circled her silently and fear stabbed through her again. Then the people began talking freely and their fascination was evident even to her apprehensive gaze. Dara closed her eyes, then opened them again quickly as people began touching her, stroking her hair and skin, poking her ribs, as if to reassure themselves that she was real. Gradually, Dara realized that they were interested in two things: her eyes and her running clothes, particularly the shoes. She could imagine why her sweatsuit and fifty-dollar Rabbitsfoot sneakers would command their curiosity but had no idea why they found her perfectly ordinary brown eyes of interest. As time wore on, she stopped shrinking from the strange hands on her body and began to look back at the people who were drawn to look at her.

Many of the men appeared to be peasant farmers, mer-

chants, some even had the appearance of country squires.
The women presented a more homogeneous appearance,
being mostly respectable dames in long dresses or riding
habits of subdued colors. Both men and women came in a
wide variety of heights and sizes and their skin colors
ranged from suntan to brown. After a while, however,
Dara noticed that they all, every one of them, had green
eyes. The green changed shades from person to person
but other than that the color was uniform. That at least
explained why they found brown eyes so intriguing. She
also noticed that there were no children. All of the people
who wandered in and around the small square were over
the age of puberty and would have been at least teenagers
on Earth. That meant they were all, as the saying went, of
marriageable age. She thought it over carefully while they
eyed her and she studied them. This was obviously a
temporary gathering, some kind of reunion or fair, perhaps even a religious pilgrimage. As such, it could easily
be limited to adults and even to certain types of adults. It
was a puzzle that provided some occupation for her thoughts
as the shadow of the stake, and hers with it, lengthened
slowly on the yellow sand.

After a while, however, no puzzle could take her mind
off the increasing discomfort her position caused her. Pebbles and grit bit into her knees but, when she shifted her
weight off them, the strain on her arms was worsened.
The hot sun lowered and the discomfort became intolerable but there was no relief. To pain in cramped muscles
was added the dry fire of sunburn and, at the exposed
stake, only sunset offered hope of eventual coolness. Her
thirst also grew but she did not realize how bad it had
become until the crowd had diminished significantly. Then
one young man came and sat cross-legged in front of her
with food and drink in his hands. The skewer of grilled
meat did not interest a stomach nauseated by pain, but the
flagon of liquid was another story. He absently took a long
pull from the large vessel while he watched her intently.
Dara's throat contracted. She decided that there didn't
seem to be much to lose.

"May I have a drink?" she asked and her voice rasped in
a hoarse whisper. The young man cocked his head almost

like a curious bird but otherwise paid no attention to her request. She tried again, "I would very much like a drink." Dara may as well have been addressing one of the tent poles. Methodically he finished his meal and then, both curiosity and appetite satisfied, rose and wandered off. Dara was outraged. A stray dog would receive better treatment on Earth, she thought—and then said so in unflattering terms.

"Perhaps," said a quiet voice over her shoulder, "but dogs may also get put out of their misery."

English! Dara twisted toward the speaker, who stood just behind her right shoulder. He had positioned himself, however, so that the lowering sun was behind his head and all she could see was the dark silhouette of a tall man. "Who are you?" she rasped. The man did not reply at first and Dara squinted in an attempt to make out his features.

"That is not important," he said finally, "Tell me who *you* are."

"Why?"

"You are not in a position to quibble. Just tell me."

It did not take much time or thought to realize that he was right. And perhaps he had come to help. "A drink first. My throat is too dry to talk."

"Of course." The man gestured to a young woman who was walking by with a water jar on her hip. After a brief exchange with her inquisitor, she approached Dara cautiously and placed the jar to her lips. The water was fresh-drawn, cool and sweet. She drank greedily and water spilled down her chin and onto her breasts. It felt wonderful. The woman withdrew the jar and Dara thanked her. She smiled shyly and hurried away. Then the man spoke again. "There, you have had your drink, now tell me."

"My name is Dara Murdock and I come from the planet called Earth. You must know it: you speak the language. I was wife and mother and I programmed computers. Or at least that is what I did before I came here."

"Why did you come here?"

"Why? I don't even know how. I was running down the street and there was a kind of whirlwind and the next thing I knew, I was here."

"Was someone chasing you?"

"What? No."

"Were you being punished?"

"No. Why are you asking such questions?"

"Why were you running?"

"I run for the exercise. I like it."

"I see. So you came here by accident?"

"Yes. At least it was an accident on my part. I don't know what happened on this end."

"This end of what?"

"This place, this world, whatever it's called. I don't even know where I am."

There was a long pause followed by a guarded reply. "This world is called Khyren, which translates in your tongue as both *life* and *tawny*. It is the fourth planet in the Khymeit system."

"Where does that leave me on this Khyren?"

"At the discretion of the officer who brought you in. You have committed no crime. Once this—formality—is completed, you belong to him."

"You mean I'm a slave?"

"You are subject to his will."

"And what will he do with me?"

"Whatever he wishes."

Well, that was plain enough. She was about to ask another question when the man's shadow disappeared and the sunlight glared into her eyes. Dara turned as much as possible in an attempt to catch a glimpse of him but green suns danced in front of her and by the time she could see again he was gone. She rested her head back against the post and closed her eyes.

Shortly after sunset, when the rajypt-ei wheeled in the cooling air and the smells of cooking food spread through the Festival grounds, Resar reappeared. Dara was slumped against the post, sunburned and semi-conscious. Resar stood, hands on hips, regarding her with a look of combined interest and disgust. The legal formalities having expired at sunset, he removed a key from its groove in the top of the post and unlocked the manacles. Dara's arms fell heavily, pulling her body to the ground. Without noticeable effort, he slung the limp form over his shoulder and strode off past a row of tents.

What in the name of Neldarin's Sword was he to do with this misbegotten wild woman from the gods only knew where? Taking her back to the officers' tent was impossible. His small mountain farm was weeks of travel away and manned by only two people in his absence. His honor as an officer of the Rangers would not let him just dump her behind some tent and walk off as he was sorely tempted to do. She was worse than useless to him, and half-dead besides. Of course! That was the answer: he would take her to the Healers.

Abruptly Resar changed direction and moved purposefully toward a large tent. Marked with a yellow diamond, it was raised by the shore of the Lady's Lake apart from the rest of the tents. This was only a temporary solution, he knew, but it would give him time to think while he attended to his responsibilities. Blood ran strong and emotions were high during Festival and he could not afford to be encumbered. Resar also knew that it was a costly solution for him—and in more than just coin. His fellow officers would ride him tenaciously about spending good money on some barbarian karait too scrawny to be worth bedding. Maybe in a few days he would think of some way out of this dilemma he had argued himself into. In the meantime, he had made enough money on the wagers to pay the Healers to put some salve on her skin and some food in her stomach. And maybe after that she would at least look better.

So Dara spent the next three days tossing on a pallet, drifting in and out of reality while her body recuperated from the effects of exhaustion, starvation, exposure, and assorted lacerations. Whenever she woke, the Healers did indeed feed her soup and soft bread and cool drinks infused with beneficial herbs. But mostly she slept and, sleeping, missed the sun's gradual movement into a notch between rounded stone pinnacles each morning at dawn. She also missed the games and contests of skill, the flirting and matchmaking, the bargaining and negotiating that were an integral part of Festival. Dara slept comfortably on the morning when the sun's first rays struck bright and straight through the notch, across the still lake and into the narrow gorge opposite it. There, it illuminated the throng of determined women who surrounded a great stone altar in the center of the cleft. Dara slept on, oblivious of the fact that this central event in the planet's celestial calendar would not occur again for another five of its years.

The next day, with Festival over and the encampment already beginning to break up, Dara woke. Both eyes and mind were clear, the sunburn turned to a golden brown that matched the native skins. She rose to be greeted by a thin man in a long white robe marked with a yellow diamond. His name was Kureil and he had been waiting to communicate with her for four days.

CHAPTER 4

Clean and arrayed in his dress uniform, Resar paused before the entrance to the impressive tent of his older brother. But for the order of the birth, the tent, furnishings, and the large fertile estate from which it had traveled would all have been his. Instead he held a modest farmstead in the high mountain foothills and a captain's colors in the Rangers. Resar had not seen or talked to his brother in over a year: there was neither need nor opportunity. He straightened up and moved forward. At his approach, the doorkeep leaned into the tent and announced the arrival of Resar ak'Hept Bentar, Captain of the Rangers, then held the flap open. Resar entered the opulent tent, which was lit on this bright morning by sun slits in its peaked roof. His brother and sister-in-marriage greeted him from the elaborate carpet where they took early refreshment.

"Our day is brightened by your presence, Resar," they said cordially.

"I am honored by your welcome."

Resar sat cross-legged on the carpet and regarded the pair before him. Amrith ak'Hept Bentar, like his younger

37

brother, was slightly above average in height, dark of hair and eye, and well-muscled by the hard work of running the large family estate. Although similar in appearance and quite apparently siblings, they had never been close and were happy with their present arrangement of visiting but once every few cycles. Nevertheless the three chatted amicably over the several courses of an excellent breakfast presented by attentive servants. Inevitably, the discussion came around to the news of Resar's successful capture of the strange barbarian woman and he was able to address the real point of his visit.

"I took her to the Healers' tent: it seemed the only sensible thing to do." His brother raised an eyebrow and Callain, his sister-in marriage, nodded. "What to do next was a puzzle and I thought long on it without reaching a decision. After the woman finally came to her senses yesterday, I spoke with Kureil, the Chief Healer, who had attended her. The story he told me was strange, like everything else about this woman, and almost unbelievable. When they had cleaned her up, and that was no small task considering, he found a long, straight scar on her belly. Kureil and the woman had a conversation of sorts, using signs and gestures. He was very curious about the scar, for it could only have come from a severe injury, and asked her how she had received it. If he interpreted correctly," he hesitated, "it marks the place where her belly was opened with a knife so that a child might be removed."

Callain gasped and made the Sign of the Lady. "But why?" she exclaimed, "What savages would act so to destroy an innocent child?"

"You misunderstand, my sister," Resar said quietly. On the subject of children he considered Callain highly emotional and he wished to avoid an unpleasant scene. "By her signs, it seems that the woman labored long and yet the child would not be born. Finally, a healer of her people took the child from her." He paused again, looking at astonished faces, "Both mother and child lived."

"But that is impossible!" Amrith said, in a tone Resar found familiar. "The child perhaps; but how could any woman survive such a thing?"

"That is exactly what the Healers wish to know. Kureil has asked me to see that she learns our language so that they may inquire into the details of this story. I cannot do so myself. My term of duty with the Rangers has a season yet to run, and I dare not send her alone on the long trip up to Wintersfoot. Besides, only Markin and Tubir are there to keep the house and they are too old for such a task. Therefore I have come to ask of you this favor. Take her back with you now that Festival is over. At Highfields she can be held safely without risk of escape. Surely there must be someone about the estate who could teach her to speak our language like a civilized person. Then, as soon as I am free of my responsibilities here, I will come and remove this burden from you."

Amrith chewed slowly on a tigga fruit and contemplated the details of his younger brother's request. One head, more or less, would make no difference either on the journey back or in such a large holding. It would be no great effort to keep her there since Highfields was always well guarded. Some old servant—and he could think of at least one—could continue to earn his bread by teaching. In all, this would be an easy favor to grant since it required no effort from him and yet the possibilities of gain were enormous.

"I have no objections," he said with a smile. "What about you, Callain, you may comment before a decision is reached."

"I am always pleased to help my brother," she responded in a low, clear voice.

Thanks were accepted and the formalities concluded. Resar stayed on for a while talking of many things. Since they had so little in common, however, the conversation lacked substance and eventually there was nothing left about which to speak. Once the tent flap hid Resar's departing figure, the couple looked at one another and smiled at the golden opportunity that had fallen into their arms. Callain was far from being the hysteric that Resar, who saw her seldom, thought her. Daughter of the powerful lord of Starshadow Pass, one of the largest holdings in the mountains, she had been carefully educated and cultivated. She was bright, determined, and quite used to getting her own way. Nearly as tall as her husband, Callain was slim and distinguished by a thick crown of auburn hair. Her looks and intellect were a powerful combination, at times more than her husband could handle.

By law, the Starshadow Pass estate passed on to her father's only other child, a contract-son by a courtesan. With that door to power and independence closed, Callain had set her goals at being full mistress of her own holding and for that she needed just the right husband. There were many men she could have married and several that her father had urged upon her, but she knew that she would have to choose carefully. Amrith met all of her qualifications admirably. Highfields, which he held unchallenged, was a large and bountiful estate and Amrith was dedicated to its success. In addition, he was full marriage-son of a father known throughout the mountains and beyond for his fertility. In addition to Resar, who was a full brother, there were several contract-children by courtesans who had been eager to prove themselves fertile as a step to better things. All this meant a higher-than-average chance that she would bear a marriage-son to solidify her position as lady of Highfields. After that, there was the definite possibility that she could bear other children and earn a rightful place in the Order. A final strong attraction was the fact that Amrith was not quite as bright as she but was too self-assured to think it important.

So Callain had wed Amrith six cycles ago and cherished bright dreams, all turned now to shadows. She was yet mistress of Highfields but there had been no children, not even a blighted pregnancy. Her position was as unstable now as it had been on the day of their marriage: she could be replaced at Amrith's whim, by another and more fertile wife. What was more, she had watched the two courtesans she had carefully selected arrive, stay through their contracts, and leave without even a false indication of pregnancy. For his part, Amrith was as eager as she to witness the birth of an heir but he would accept one by any mother. He was the son of a proven sire placed in a very awkward position. There was his personal reputation to consider. "By Bentar's seed" was a common expression in the mountains but no one used it any longer in his presence. More importantly, there was the status of Highfields to consider. The estate was his, had always been, and he guarded his birthright jealously. Without a son of his body, it would go to Resar or, worse, to one of old Bentar's contract children. There was a third factor. Though Highfields was productive and bore abundantly, there was unrest and unhappiness inside its walls. The general fertility rate had dropped as if barrenness were communicable. The Children's House was empty and had been for three full cycles.

Now they were given the care of a woman who had not only borne a child but carried upon her body the scars of a miraculous delivery, a sure sign of the Lady's grace. The dames of the Order had a saying, "One breeding woman breeds another," and it was true, as surely as the reverse had proved itself at Highfields. Even better, this great good fortune had come to them at the Lady's own Festival on the day after Callain had stood at the altar and been blessed by the light of life. Callain and Amrith knew that they had good reason to smile: their destiny had changed.

On his way back from the officers' tent, Resar stopped by the kennel where the Rangers' pack was housed. There he selected and paid for the most alert of the coursers. With the beast he made his way past families working to break down tents and load pack animals until he reached the tent of the Healers. The courser stretched out in the shade of the tent on sand still cool from the night while Resar entered. The woman was sitting quietly on a cot, watching while the Healers went about their work. Dressed neatly in a plain white shift and sandals, she looked very different from the woman he had carried in slung over his shoulder. She saw him at once and turned toward him apprehensively but Resar ignored her and went instead to Kureil.

"Greetings of the morning, Kureil."

"And a fine day to you, captain. Have you come to take our mystery guest with you?"

"Yes, although she will not be with me for long. But I have arranged for the things you wished. She will learn the language and our ways. When she is able to answer your questions, I will take her to you. It may not be until snowmelt, though."

"Excellent. I am a patient man but I look forward to that meeting."

"What do I owe you for your services here?"

They negotiated the price and Resar paid. It was cheap, after all, when he considered the trouble that the Healers had saved him. With somewhat less assurance he approached the woman, who stood and faced him. "Follow me," he said, gesturing. To his relief, she did. As they emerged from the tent, the courser rose and shook the sand from its rough fur. The woman stepped back with a short cry of alarm. Resar turned and looked at her and said firmly, "He will not hurt you." He gestured to the courser and it moved to her, then around her. When the circle was complete, the beast tasted her with its long, absurdly thin tongue and hummed in code (Learned). The woman, Resar noted, had stood completely still during this even though obviously frightened. Resar then pointed to her and said "Guard!" in the same code. The courser sat and hummed tersely (Accepted). Satisfied, Resar moved on and the woman followed, with the courser walking close beside her.

At Amrith's camp, Resar sought out the commander of the household guard. This was not, as he had expected, old Khivoi, who had been in command when he was a boy, but a new man, who was young and filled with enthusiasm. Resar gave detailed instructions to the man, whose name was Barrikehn, and then turned both the woman and her guardian over to him. Since Barrikehn had already received his orders from Amrith, the transition went smoothly. "Do not concern yourself, captain," Barrikehn said. "We will guard her closely and, with the courser at her heels, she will be doubly guarded."

Resar nodded. "I will be at Highfields before the snows." He turned on his heel and walked away without a backward glance.

Cold-blooded bastard, Dara thought, watching Resar as he disappeared into the turmoil of the disbanding camp. Then the officer took a firm hold on her arm and guided her to a place behind a baggage cart in the household caravan that was forming up. She stood quietly in the place he had assigned her and looked down at the great beast beside her. It was the same kind as those which had tracked her and might even be one of the same animals. It looked back at her directly with large dark eyes that were disturbingly intelligent. It seemed even bigger close up than it had in the hills and she could see that its dun fur was flecked with irregular black markings. Powerful muscles rippled under that fur and its legs had two knee joints instead of one. In spite of the beast's wicked array of teeth, it looked as if it might easily speak to her. The intelligence that she perceived disarmed its fearsome appearance and she decided to try some of the same techniques that she would have used on an Earth animal. It had smelled her already and filed that scent in its memory so she took the next step and spoke to it. Dara addressed it as if it were human and made simple small talk. The beast hummed shortly and twitched its round, flexible ears. "Well, Sandy," she added, "it's going to be just you and me, together in this wide world." Sandy hummed again as if in agreement.

There was no time for anything else; with grunts, creaks, and much excited chatter, the caravan set off. It wound its way through the Festival grounds and then out onto the North Trail, heading in the opposite direction from the way in which Dara had come. She soon noticed that this road was far different from the one that she had observed for so many days. No river ran beside this trail, nor was there the pleasant band of trees with its deep shade. Instead, the road struck out over the rolling grassy hills toward a distant line of purple mountains. Years of travel had cut a groove in the dirt so that the road now lay between vertical banks that rose nearly ten feet in places and sank to only a few inches in others. The biggest difference, however, was the dust. Leaf litter and humus had covered the South Trail, and the shade had kept the roadway cool. Here there was only grass and the travelers walked in the full glare of the sun. Others had started out ahead of their party and already a thin curtain of yellow dust hung like smog in the air. Each wheel, hoof, and foot kicked up more. Soon they were moving in a swirling, choking cloud of dust that settled all over them. Many of the travelers wrapped scarves or kerchiefs around their faces to make breathing easier. Dara would have followed suit but lacked any clothing besides her shift and sandals. So she walked and coughed and thought about wagon trains crossing the Great Plains while Sandy padded at her heels, seemingly unbothered by the fine grit.

At mid-day, the caravan simply stopped along the trail and everyone flopped down in the shade of the wagons to rest. Both Dara's hair and Sandy's fur were powdered yellow. She shook out her shift to loosen what lay on and inside of it but what had settled on her sweaty skin just smeared when she brushed it, so she left it alone. A group of servants worked their way down the column, distributing cold food and cups of water. Dara accepted her ration silently, as it was offered, but she was very grateful for the refreshment. After one long swallow to clear her throat she ate the food slowly and sipped the water to make it last. Buckets were set out for the dray beasts. Sandy rose, hesitated, and then padded out into the sun. Turning so that Dara remained in his sight, he drank in a few great gulps and then returned. After a rest interval that seemed much too brief, the servants collected cups and buckets. Then it was back out into the heavy sun as the journey resumed. Dara trod steadily behind the cart until mid-afternoon when her strength rolled away with the perspiration that soaked her shift. Since the sun was still far from the horizon, Dara climbed into a small flat space on the back of the cart. No one ordered her out so she made herself comfortable and watched the monotonous scenery drowsily while Sandy walked along and watched her.

The caravan stopped for the night at one of the established camp grounds on the trail. Other pilgrims had already arrived but the party in which Dara traveled was large and rapidly filled the remaining space. When the cart jerked to a halt, Dara slid down. The camping area was a wide circle of beaten dirt surrounded by waving grasses that gleamed red-gold at the tip in the light of the setting sun. The usual latrines curved around one portion of the perimeter with a picked-over midden nearby. Dara looked hopefully for a lake or pond where she could wash off the sticky dust but the only water in sight was a thin spout that leaped from the top of a rock pile at the hub of the circular area. It poured into a thick, stone watering trough that was clearly intended for drinking, not bathing. The overflow formed a small rivulet that trickled across the dirt and then vanished into the grass. She sighed. Dara found a place to sit that was out of the way while camp was set up and the evening meal prepared. No one addressed her even indirectly or acknowledged her presence. She noticed a few sidelong glances and heard a few whispers that she wished she could understand. Only the guards paid her any heed but their interest was strictly professional. As long as she stayed quiet and remained close to her four-legged guardian, she was left alone. Dara found it difficult, however, to just sit in the midst of all the evening's activity and take no part in it. Even the noblewoman who traveled in the caravan had descended from her conveyance and begun supervising the preparations. There was, however, nothing else to do.

Eventually the aroma of cooking food started her mouth watering and her stomach rumbling. When people began to line up in front of the kettles and wagon tail-gate that comprised the field kitchen, Dara decided that it was time to take the initiative. She rose, followed by Sandy, and took a place at the end of the line. No one said anything but they edged silently away, whether from her or from Sandy she could not tell. Ignoring the distance, she watched what everyone else did and simply copied them. She walked away with a bowl of hot stew, a piece of hard, flat bread, and a dried fruit. Balancing everything in one hand, she took an earthenware mug from a stack and filled it at the spring. Close up, Dara could see that the rocks from which the freshet emerged were not rough boulders; they had been cut into shapes and carved with runes and designs. But they were very old; the original shapes were split and worn. Blue-green moss crept over the patterns and covered what hieroglyphs had not already weathered into obscurity. It was, she realized, the crumbled remains of an ancient fountain, one that had once been large and impressive but was now eroded nearly back to the plain rock. But the water it gave was sweet and Dara returned with it to her seat.

The food had that special flavor imparted only to meals eaten in the open air and Dara had the excellent appetite that comes from exercise. She was wolfing the meal down when it occurred to her that Sandy had not been fed. She dug a large piece of meat from her bowl and held it out to the animal. Although acutely conscious of the strong jaws and sharp teeth, she steeled herself to hold it steady. Sandy sniffed her offering and then turned disdainfully away. Dara placed the meat carefully on the ground in front of him but he continued to ignore it. She wasn't sure whether he had been trained to reject food offered by strangers, as guard dogs were, or whether the meat was simply not part of his diet. With no way of knowing, she shrugged and finished her dinner.

After returning the mug and bowl, Dara claimed a blanket from a cart full of bedding and found a space beneath one of the larger wagons. It had not yet rained in her experience on this world but, as she well knew, the morning dew could be heavy and chill. She rolled herself up comfortably and Sandy flopped down beside her with a weary sigh. He did not lay his head on his paws, however, but remained alert. Other people joined them under the wagon but none of the sleepers came too close. Dara lay in the shadows looking out at the flickering firelight and listened to the chorus of night creatures in full throat beyond the perimeter of the campground. She thought simply how much better it was to be on this side of the guard lines, warm and with a full stomach, before she fell asleep.

Shortly before dawn, Dara awoke to sounds of ripping and chewing. Alarmed, she rolled over quickly and saw that Sandy had left his place under the wagon. He was crouched a few feet away, facing her, worrying a great joint, tearing enormous mouthfuls of the raw meat and swallowing them without pause. His curved teeth and strong jaws worked efficiently and soon nothing was left but wet bone scored with long furrows. The scavengers would get little nourishment from it, she thought, and then realized how quickly she had distanced herself from being one of them. The sleepers around her began to awaken with the new light and, rising, she again followed their example. Sandy shadowed her as Dara packed her bedding, ate, and performed a perfunctory toilette. She did what she could, considering that another long, hot day on the road lay ahead, and lingered by the old fountain more to allow Sandy a chance to drink his fill than to cleanse herself. The yellow sun was not far up in the sky before the caravan was once again upon the road.

That day she was able to walk further before climbing into the cart to rest, even though the road went steadily upward. As they moved higher, the meadow grass gave way to taller vegetation. First came scrub brush, then the familiar blue bamboo, followed by trees of increasing height and thickness. By afternoon, they outdistanced the dust and welcomed the shade that fell, cool as water, beneath the trees. The road twisted and dipped and climbed again but always it pointed towards the jagged purple line on the horizon. Dara found herself drawn to the silhouette of the massive mountain range that seemed to be their destination. From a distance it appeared exotic, awesome, romantic, and fearful, all at the same time. She wondered what the reality would be.

The next day she was stronger still and by the afternoon of the fourth day she was able to complete the day's trek without resting any more than the others did. By this time they were high into the foothills and Dara found the air invigorating: she felt healthy and alive again. To the ill-concealed amusement of her fellow travelers, she began to limber up each morning, stretching her muscles for the steady climb ahead. She would have liked to do even more but was prevented by her knee-length, loose shift and a concession to modesty. Dara tried to ignore the reactions of those around her, despite the fact that they were displayed quite openly. Although she had learned only a few words of the language, it was plain that they considered her a curiosity with strange barbarian customs. Of them all, only the noblewoman sometimes watched Dara with a closed face and unreadable turquoise eyes. Dara told herself that she did not care what any of them thought but still, surrounded by people, she longed for the sound of a friendly voice.

Only Sandy was always with her, linked to her in a strange relationship. Although Dara gave him no cause for suspicion, he remained vigilant. He was there at arm's length, alert, when she closed her eyes at night and when she opened them again in the morning. He walked steadily beside her during the day and sat by her side while she rested and ate. He waited doggedly by the latrines and on the shores of the two small lakes where the travelers were finally able to wash off the worst trail dirt. And, in a different way, he was as much an outcast as she: the only animal of his kind in this party, he was left to do his work alone and unhindered. No one got in his way.

Dara liked animals and had always gotten along well with them. Locked in an artificial relationship with this formidable alien beast, she set out to win his trust. He was fed every morning by one of the guards but Dara was careful to give him every opportunity to drink. She made no overtures, sudden gestures, or loud noises. She made no attempt to touch or stroke him. But she talked to him by the hour. She spoke in plain, friendly tones as if he were a companion who could understand every word. His round, intelligent eyes would often regard her with a bemused expression that said he did not know what to make of a human who acted so. Most of the time he listened stolidly to her chatter and walked in silence. On the rare occasions when he hummed as if in response, she was encouraged. Touch was the next step in establishing trust but Sandy was aloof and she was hesitant to strain the tenuous balance she had established.

Day blended into day and Dara lost track of how long they had been traveling. As they climbed higher, the air grew crisp and nights became almost cold. Eventually Dara found her lowland shift and sandals inadequate protection against even the daytime temperatures in the mountains. Lacking any additional clothing, she kept her sleeping blanket and wore it like a shawl during the day. One night a chill wind blew down from the peaks ahead of them and, half wakened by the cold, Dara instinctively sought the warmth of another body. When dawn came she lay curled against Sandy with one hand twined in his coarse fur. His expressive face looked pained but tolerant as she disengaged herself. After that, however, there was less distance between them and Sandy would occasionally suffer a light touch during the day. Theirs was a unique relationship for reasons Dara would not understand fully until much later: it would be longer still before she would comprehend its importance.

At about the same time, Dara became aware of a rising excitement among the people around her. This lift in mood seemed to indicate that they were nearing their destination. By this time she, like everyone else, was trail-weary and looking forward to the end of the journey.

Late one afternoon they crested a pass and Dara looked down on a scene of great natural beauty reminiscent of one of the spectacular paintings of the Hudson River School. Spreading for miles before them was a large valley girdled on all sides by the steep slopes and rock cliffs of the great purple range. Cultivated fields, neatly demarcated by irrigation ditches, filled the valley and ran up the lower slopes of the surrounding mountains. Long shafts of butter-yellow sunlight poured down from between the peaks at the valley's far end, lighting these fields red-gold, green, and burgundy according to the different crops they nourished. Orchards cast patterned shadows. Animals grazed in pastures and geometric paddocks. In the center of the valley rose an estate the size of a small town and made up of many outbuildings surrounded by a high stone wall. There were wooden barns, stables, sheds, and houses. All of it was dominated by an immense and beautifully-proportioned structure that could only be described as a great house. Built of stone and several stories high, it had towers at each end, many balconies, and a roof that was wonderfully gabled. Myriad windows glowed gold, reflecting the light of the setting sun. One end of the house gave onto a small, bright-green park or garden that flowed around a jagged outcrop of the same stone that had gone into the house. Speechless, Dara took in every detail of the idyllic scene as it was lit by the clear, vivid light. A collective cheer went up around her as the travelers came in sight of home. Although she could not share their feelings, Dara could appreciate the peace and beauty of the place she would come to know as Highfields.

Everyone hurried, unwisely, on the switchback road that led from the pass down into the valley. Both humans and animals were eager to be safely inside the walls before full dark. As they descended, the air grew warmer and softened into an evening that was summer once more. Filled with the scents of tilled soil and growing things it became heavy, almost intoxicating to breathe. Flocks of birds swooped above them in the darkening sky. As is often the case in mountains, however, the distance was deceptive and despite their efforts the travelers filed through the gate by torchlight. As the caravan disbanded, the officer in whose care Resar had left her appeared. Grateful for some attention at last, Dara followed in response to his gesture. Shadowed still by Sandy, they arrived at a modest but attractive structure not far from the big house. There they were met by a servant whose years and bearing radiated dignity. The guard spoke to him and then turned to Sandy with a terse sound similar to the ones Resar had used. After a single penetrating look at Dara the animal wheeled and followed him. After they had disappeared into the night, Dara felt oddly alone, almost abandoned; Sandy had been her closest companion for weeks. With a sigh, she faced the servant who looked her boldly up and down in a disapproving way that left no doubt as to her standing in his eyes. Clearly, this assignment was beneath him.

Moving stiffly, he led her to a room that apparently was to be hers. It was simple but clean, with whitewashed walls that gleamed between massive beams of dark wood. Three windows high up on the wall, closed now, provided light and ventilation. The room was chill with that indefinable atmosphere of having been long closed and then aired in a hurry. The furnishings were few, but adequate. A bed covered with a colorful quilt shared the room with a simple chair, a wash stand, and a plain chest of drawers. An oil lamp glowing on the dresser made the room seem homey.

While the butler, as she thought of him, stood guard at the door and Dara looked around, an older woman entered the room. She carried a tray of food and a pitcher of milk which she placed on the chest beside the lamp.

Before leaving she gave Dara a quick, curious look. Then the butler spoke a few words, still unintelligible to Dara, and closed the door. Numb with fatigue and the adjustment to a new environment, Dara was still looking at the meal when she heard the door click shut. Automatically she crossed the room and tested it. As she had expected, it was locked.

With a shrug, she turned away to deal with more immediate needs. Although the water in the pitcher on the wash stand was cold, she poured some out. Moving quickly in the chill room, she did her best to clean the dirt off face, hands, and feet. Then, covered with goose bumps, she put the tray on the bed and climbed under the puffy quilt. After pulling it up around her she ate slowly, savoring every bite of the home-cooked meal. By the time she had finished, she was warm inside and out. Placing the empty tray on the floor, Dara lay back to savor the warmth, quiet, and privacy. After a short while, her eyelids began to droop. She leaned over to blow out the lamp, pulled off her grubby shift, and burrowed under the warm quilt.

Sandy entered the kennel quite happily despite his overwhelming fatigue. Coursers were gregarious creatures and he had missed the company of his own kind. The six animals in residence welcomed him and he accepted their greetings submissively, in the order of their rank. As an outsider, he had no wish to disrupt or challenge the established patterns of authority. All he wanted was to find a quiet, comfortable corner in which he could enter dormancy. It had been a long tour of duty and he was bone-weary: weeks of vigilance with no sleep had worn him down. Despite the need for rest, however, Sandy was satisfied with his job. He had been ordered to guard and he had done it well. It did not occur to him that somewhere along the trail he had stopped guarding the woman against escape and begun protecting her from danger. With a hum so deep it was almost a grunt, he curled up in the kennel moss and sank into the trance-like sleep of his kind.

CHAPTER 5

Martus ak'Hept Mytanni, Wearer of the Braided Belt, Master of the Five Disciplines, and Counsel-Regent for Domestic Affairs, stood with hands clasped behind his back and surveyed the complex happenings from the curved window of his office. His portly stomach was nearly pressed against the glass and his round face mirrored the colorful view. Beneath his serenity, however, lay carefully-masked displeasure. "Well," he began, addressing the window rather than the tall, thin man who waited respectfully behind him, "have you completed your investigation of the malfunction?"

"Yes, Your Grace."

"And the result?"

"As we suspected, when the rods arced prematurely, a brief temporal warp occurred. Because the techs were beginning the countdown for a transmission at the time it happened, the malfunction affected space as well."

"You traced this warp, I presume?"

"Of course, Your Grace." The nuncio's tone was slightly testy. He disliked having his competence questioned in any way, even by a superior with the right to do so, and he had not yet mastered the Third Discipline, complete control of his reactions. "The task was time-consuming, however. Being totally uncontrolled, the warp could have had an effect almost anywhere within a very large space/time sphere around a focus in the Northeast Planetary Quadrant. A complicated series of computer checks finally isolated the coordinates of the focus."

"And where . . . ?"

"Here on Khyren, Your Grace. More specifically, it was in the Grasslands near the South Pilgrimage Trail. The timing was approximately ten days before the Feast of the Lady."

"Marvelous!"

"Your Grace?"

"I meant simply that a less propitious focus for an extremely unfortunate accident could hardly have been planned. Proceed."

"Because of the sensitive nature of the focus, I investigated it personally, as you know. Since I had no idea what, if anything had warped through, a long search may have been required. Fortunately, that was not the case."

"I'm delighted to hear it."

Scaure ignored this interruption. He stared at the Counsel-Regent's broad back with antipathy; the man might at least have the courtesy to face him during the report. He continued, "Quite soon after arriving in the vicinity, I became aware that a disturbance had indeed occurred. That meant that something large enough to be noticed had come through. Identifying it was simple enough but in fact complicated the issue immensely." He took a deep breath. "Rumors spread of a gormrith that left odd tracks. Others spoke of a spectre in blue haunting the trail. There was talk of a bad omen for the Festival."

At this, the Counsel-Regent turned and regarded his agent gravely. "Are you saying that the warp deposited some humanoid creature in proximity to the Festival Grounds?"

"Not quite, Your Grace."

"This report begins to be interesting. Continue."

"When several reports of this nature reached the authorities at Festival, the Rangers were sent to dispose of the creature and put an end to the rumors. Instead they brought back a disreputable but very much alive human." He paused. "A female."

Martus's round face became even rounder, in concealed astonishment and some delight. "A human female? Indeed. From what planet?"

"Apparently from Earth, Your Grace, in the Sol System. This female was brought before the Resident Justiciar who was, of course, quite unable to determine that she had committed any crime. He settled the issue quite wisely by deciding that a day at the stake would quiet rumors and put an end to the issue. After that, she was remanded to the captain of the Rangers who had brought her in. Since she belonged to no village and had no family, she was more barbarian than true gormrith and it was really the only sensible thing to do with her."

"From his point of view, certainly," said Counsel-Regent. "But what of ours? This accident could have raised some very awkward queries. Did anyone question where this strange woman had come from?"

"Of course. I 'suggested' to the Obenan at Festival that they spread a rumor to the effect that she was a barbarian from a remote tribe beyond the Singing Sands. It was not a strong story but it was the best one I could come up with at short notice and since thinking is not usually a strong point at Festival, the tale remained intact. As far as I could tell, the plan worked."

"Acceptable. But what of the woman herself? Was she unharmed? Sane? Lucid?"

"Unfortunately yes, Your Grace, although more than a little the worse for wear. I probed her, being careful not to let her see me, of course. She was virtually convinced that her arrival here was the result of an unpredictable natural phenomenon and I said nothing to change that opinion. There will be no problem of her spreading rumors about secret technology or hidden machines, assuming she learns to speak the language. On that score, we are safe." Scaure paused and weighed his next statement carefully. "On another issue she may still be a threat."

"A threat, indeed?" Martus raised one eyebrow imperceptibly. He wanted very much to sit down but he refused to crane his neck looking up at his taller subordinate. Since allowing Scaure to sit while he reported was unthinkable, the Counsel-Regent remained on his feet. "What is this issue?"

"I was not able to obtain the details, only that it relates to fertility and childbirth and that the Healers are extremely eager to learn more. Through the captain's family connections, the woman has been placed in the custody of Amrith ak'Hept Bentar, Lord of Highfields, where she has been sent to learn our language. She will then presumably be able to enlighten the Healers about a somewhat sensitive topic for us." Scaure paused and smiled. His superior recognized that smile from previous situations requiring intricate strategy. It was an automatic reaction and Martus doubted that Scaure knew he was indulging in an expression that gave away his motivations. He also knew that Scaure was most in his element when involved in complex strategy. That was why he had selected Scaure for the post even though they had little in common and even held a certain antipathy to one another. A master strategist was a valuable asset, and one to be used to the greatest possible advantage. He had never brought the smile to his aide's attention. Scaure continued, placing his words carefully. "I have a contact at Highfields, one who is ambitious and nurtures a grudge. A summons would not be unwelcome."

The Counsel-Regent nodded sagely. Experience taught him that Scaure preferred to reveal his plan only when he was satisfied that it was complete, down to the last detail. "Excellent. Proceed with caution and brief me when the next phase is ready." His aide bowed stiffly and strode out the door. When it had closed behind him, Martus moved over to the large comfortable chair behind his spotless desk. Then, with an undisguised sigh of relief, he sat down.

The sound of the bolt being shot roused Dara from the longest, deepest sleep she had enjoyed in weeks. Rolling over beneath the warm quilt, she watched the door open, spilling liquid sunshine into the room. With it came a young woman who carried a stack of folded clothing in her arms. Depositing this bundle on the room's single chair, she went out again and returned moments later with a breakfast tray. By this time Dara was sitting up, the quilt pulled around her, and watching with interest. The woman was petite, not more than two inches over five feet, with a graceful body and a delicate oval face. The omnipresent dark hair and green eyes were elfin and bewitching on her.

Looking directly at Dara for the first time, she smiled uncertainly and placed one hand on her own breast. "Neva," she said earnestly, "Neva." Dara duplicated the gesture and said her own name clearly. The two names were so similar in sound that Neva laughed delightedly, causing Dara to revise her first impression. Womanhood was new to Neva and she was not quite comfortable with it. She was far younger than she had first appeared. She presented the tray to Dara who was openly astonished at being served breakfast in bed. While she ate, Neva unfolded each item of clothing and held it up for inspection. First came simple underclothing; then a long dress; then a riding costume made up of loose breeches, tunic, and blouse; a night-shift; and, finally, a pair of high, gleaming boots. The clothes were all made of soft, homespun fabrics either bleached or dyed in natural shades, and unadorned.

When Dara had finished the last slice of bread and honey, she pointed at the riding habit and said, "Let's try that one." As she slipped out of bed, however, Neva took one look at her charges's travel-grimed body and exclaimed volubly. She started a long discourse in a disapproving tone and then broke it off abruptly when she realized that Dara could not understand one word. Substituting action for speech, she retrieved the filthy shift from the floor and handed it to Dara, who donned it obediently but with a grimace. Then, with the new clothing under one arm, she shooed Dara out the door. The morning sun had already taken the chill from the air and illuminated a glorious day. They walked through the compound to a simple building not far from the small green park Dara had seen from the pass. Inside, the hot steamy air reeked of sulfur and Dara saw with pleasure that they were in a bath house.

A row of large wooden tubs lined one wall of the structure but she and Neva were the only occupants. Everyone else was presumably hard at work on their respective daily tasks. Neva selected a tub and removed a block from a stone sluice that penetrated the wall above it. Hot, mineral-laden water that could have come only from subterranean springs poured out of the sluice, filling the tub rapidly. Neva tempered the bath by adding cold water from a barrel and throwing in a handful of scented herbs. Dara was out of her shift and into the tub as soon as it was ready. The water was hot enough to make her gasp and turn bright red but the sensation was exquisite. Neva tossed something like a small dried tumbleweed into the water and then pantomimed scrubbing. Dara immersed the weed and squeezed it until it became supple and produced a rich lather. As she set to work eagerly she discovered that the weed also made a coarse but effective washcloth, even in the hard mineral water. She was soon covered with lather from her matted hair to her callused feet. After submerging herself several times, she emerged red, tingling and feeling cleaner than she ever had before.

Neva was waiting to hand her a large towel and Dara saw her look at the scar on her abdomen and then quickly avert her eyes. The clean clothes came next and then Neva went to work on her hair. It had grown out from short and curly to shoulder length without receiving a great deal of attention. Lacking a real comb, the best that Dara had been able to do was tie it back with a scrap of cloth. It was now so full of snarls that Neva had to comb it one small bit at a time. The process was slow and painful for the both of them. A lot of hair came out with the comb and twice Neva had to take a small knife from her belt and cut away pieces that were hopelessly matted. She perse-vered, however, and finally Dara's hair was smooth. Neva dressed it simply in a type of chignon at the nape of the neck. The style was both simple and practical: if her hair did not blow around, it would not become tangled and dirty so quickly. When they were finished, Dara felt like a real human being for the first time since a red snake had slid across her leg.

Full of energy, she helped Neva to clean up and then they walked back to her room. After being guarded so carefully, it felt odd to have an escort who was little more than a girl. Then Dara remembered the high stone walls encircling the compound and the well-trained guards on duty at the gates. It was a security system designed to keep others out but it would serve as well to keep her in.

That afternoon Dara met her other "tutor," and this meeting was neither pleasant nor friendly. After Neva had gone about her other tasks, an old man summoned Dara from her room. He was of medium height and thin, possessed of a cautious dignity that had not been diminished by the disease that crippled his hands. It was the kind of dignity sometimes assumed by servants who have risen to the most senior level of their station. Purchased with great effort, it was carefully guarded against assault from any quarter. He reminded Dara of an English butler, brought down by illness but unbowed.

Although they could not understand one another's speech, the man made it quiet plain that he considered his assigned task to be beneath his dignity. Although he treated her like a ragged woman of the streets, Dara was able to deduce that his job was to teach her the language. She arrived at this conclusion when he, without preamble, began pointing at objects around them in no particular sequence or order and then reciting their names abruptly. He continued this behavior on a walk through the compound and through dinner in the communal dining hall. Although she paid attention and repeated what she heard, Dara was soon lost in a flurry of similar sounds. She resolved to try and obtain writing materials so that she could compile a phonetic dictionary. In the meantime, she trusted that sheer repetition would help her to learn the most common words. She hoped that the language was not too complex nor its construction too alien to her thought structure. Tired of being an outsider, unable to communicate the simplest thought, she planned to work hard at learning to speak the language of this world.

Dara's days in the compound of the estate called Highfields assumed a pattern quickly and smoothly. Each morning the old man, whose name was Lekh, came to her room and unlocked the door, then took her to the dining hall where food was available to all who worked in the compound. From the moment he said a gruff "Thrai-din," or good morning, he began teaching her the many things she had to learn. These included language most importantly but also manners and customs, modes of address, and the proper courtesies. As Dara grasped more of the language he would expand his lessons to include animal husbandry, agriculture, topography, and weather—some of the many disciplines which affected life in a large agriculturally-based community.

He started, however, by walking her around the compound and naming objects, activities, people, whatever was handy and caught his attention. After two days of struggling to remember a plethora of unassociated vocabulary words, Dara meticulously pantomimed a need for writing materials. Lekh fetched them with a raised eyebrow and an amused expression that indicated he considered her only an ignorant, illiterate barbarian. In this, Dara realized with dismay, he was not far wrong. On this world she could neither read nor write in the native language. She resolved to change that situation as soon as an opportunity presented itself. For the present, she set about constructing a notebook that functioned as a combination phonetic dictionary and book of etiquette. With its help, learning the language became somewhat easier although she still had to create an orderly product from chaotic information.

Dara took notes while they walked, visiting the laundry shed, kitchens, storehouses, gardens, workshops, stables, smithy, weaving shed, smokehouse, and all the places housing the myriad activities which supported Highfields. Often she would lay down her writing materials and join in whatever activity she had been observing. Dara was unused to inactivity and missed the work and the discipline to which she was accustomed. It took no great skill to wash or fold clothing, chop vegetables, or pull weeds. She was, indeed, quite used to doing these things for her family and it made her feel productive and needed to be helping. The people laboring in these jobs were almost always glad enough for the help and seemed to know without explanation who she was and what Lekh was assigned to do. Dara was reassured to find that the grapevine was as efficient on this world as it was on Earth. The laborers helped her as she helped them, adding to her store of words and phrases. Some of these expressions were quite colloquial, as Dara would learn, sometimes to her surprise, when she became fluent.

Another reason Dara enjoyed participating in the work of the compound was that for a while she could feel as if she had a place in the community instead of wandering, seemingly without goal or purpose. She knew that this feeling of belonging was a delusion even as she indulged in it. While they spoke with her, the workers would always keep a comfortable distance away, regardless of how she moved about. This "flight space" was far enough to be noticeable even though the others were unaware of it. Eventually, there came to be a space around her which no one entered. It was almost a part of her and moved with her, like an invisible shell or a force field, and even Dara grew accustomed to it. Only Lekh and Neva seemed not to be aware of it and were not afraid to approach her.

Meanwhile, Dara studied and learned, her dictionary grew thicker, and she became a familiar figure in the compound. Her help was appreciated by many at the same time as her unfailing courtesy helped to mitigate the unease caused by her mysterious origin and strange history. In short, Dara came to be regarded neutrally at worst and sometimes with genuine good feelings by the people around her. Neva's presence was less predictable, although Dara saw her often, because her duties were in the Big House and she was not able to get away at regular intervals. One evening there was a small, swift tap on the door and it opened to Neva's delicate face, flushed with excitement. "Come," she said simply and held out to Dara a folded bundle. It was a long shawl, undyed but hand-embroidered and fringed in bright threads; it matched the one Neva herself wore. Curious, Dara slipped it over her shoulders, smelling summer herbs as it enveloped her in soft warmth. As they moved out into the sharp mountain night, Dara felt a surge of excitement: never before had she been allowed out after dark. All her evenings had been in her own solitary company once she had returned from the evening meal. Summoning her rudimentary command of the language, Dara queried, "Where do we go?"

"The baths," Neva replied brightly. "It is the Night of the Lady and we do honor to her." She pointed up to the sky where Dara could see a number of the asteroids, or Wanderers as they were named, glowing through a fine mist. Never before had Dara seen so many of the Wanderers in the sky, and in full phase simultaneously. Drawing a bow of light across the darkness, they were as beautiful as a necklace of jewels that glowed with their own radiance. The Night of the Lady. Whatever that was, Dara was sure that it would be more interesting than another lonely night. As they walked, she pondered over their destination; why the baths at this hour of the night? She went to the bathhouse regularly with Neva, as did the other women of the compound. What could be special about these baths?

The two women moved through the dark compound which was lit sporadically by squares of yellow light glowing through a window or torches ensconced outside a door. Gradually they were joined by others, men and women both, all walking in the same direction. The groups mostly kept to themselves although there was a good deal of whispering and some subdued giggles. At the next torchlit entryway, Dara noticed that all the women wore shawls while the men had loosely-belted robes of the same material, but lacking embroidery.

Frustrated by a command of the language that was still halting, Dara framed another question, "How do we honor the Lady?"

Even in the dark, Neva's eyes twinkled. "In the baths," she replied enigmatically.

Dara decided to try a more direct approach. "Who is the Lady?"

Neva stopped and looked at her, shocked. "But everyone knows the Lady!" she protested. *Even barbarians*, were the unspoken words.

"Tell me anyway," Dara said gently.

When Neva started walking again her stride showed agitation. "She is Cyris na Khyrienne, she who brings life from the Source of All Creation. She is Taroth Sier who kindles desire. The Lady is Bel Teresim, she who nurtures life. She is the twin sister and opponent of Sah-Charis who is the bringer of death and opens the door of the Shining Road back to the Source. She is the enemy of Neldarin, Lord of War, and of Narokh, Lord of Disease. We worship the Lady to bring life to the soil and to our bodies. She is the Mother of all children and surely has she been angry with us, for the Children's House is long empty." She looked at Dara, troubled, and added, "But surely you know these things already."

Dara smiled and decided to be diplomatic, if not truthful. "About the Lady, yes. But it is always good to hear them again. I am strange here, and did not know about the Children's House."

Neva sighed and replied, "I should not speak of that. Not tonight." And she would not be drawn to speak further, so Dara gave it up and began paying more attention to where they were going. To her surprise, they and the others began converging on the jewel-like park with the great rock outcrop in its center. The two narrow paths into this area were already crowded and they had to wait their turn to enter what appeared to be a small cave. Once inside the rock entrance, however, the cave turned out to be a door with steps just inside it, heading downwards. Hewn from the rock mass, the steps were worn and grooved by the passage of many feet. Like dripping water, the footsteps of the descending procession echoed off torch-blackened walls, each one deepening the grooves invisibly.

She and Neva moved downward for nearly five minutes before reaching a small chamber empty but for two doors and a strong smell of sulfur. The men disappeared through the right door with smiles and waves. The women went straight into a long narrow hall in the center of which steamed a pool of hot water. Along the walls, women disrobed, then dipped buckets into the pool and scrubbed themselves. Dara and Neva went to a stock of empty buckets, took one each, and approached the small pool. Here the smell of sulfur was so strong that Dara's eyes watered as she filled her container with the steaming mineral water. Then they chose a quiet spot and undressed, placing their clothing and sandals on a ledge carved into the cavern's rock wall. There were soapweeds in abundance and Dara lathered lavishly. Neva began to giggle again as they washed each other's backs and even Dara joined in when Neva piled her lathered hair into two towering horns. When they were thoroughly scrubbed, even under fingernails, they poured buckets of hot water over one another until they were gasping. The water and soapsuds drained away through cracks in the stone floor. Then Neva wrapped her shawl around her like a towel and Dara followed suit. They walked, slipping on the wet rock, until they reached the far end of the hall.

Through a narrow passage, more like a cleft than a doorway, and they emerged into a great cavern, high-ceilinged and dripping with moisture. Almost filling it was a huge pool which bubbled and steamed from the hot springs which formed it. Dara looked and then stopped in amazement. Piled by the pool's edge were shawls and robes, and the water was filled with people. Heads, both male and female, bobbed everywhere. Neva giggled at her astonishment and pulled her along by the hand as they skirted the edge of the pool, looking for an uncrowded place to enter. Dara noticed faces turning their way and the hum of conversation ceased as they went by, only to renew when they were past. Almost three-quarters of the way down, Neva found an acceptable spot, shrugged off her shawl, and slid into the blue-green water. Trying not to feel self-conscious, Dara did the same. The moment her body was exposed, however, a murmur arose from the people in the pool and echoed from the stone walls. Cheeks flushed with an unaccustomed embarrassment, Dara nearly jumped into the water. She resisted a strong desire to hide underwater and observed while the last stragglers entered and joined the bathers.

Finally, Callain and Amrith entered and stood alone by the pool's edge next to a brazier that was chiseled from the rock wall. Silence crept through the chamber until even the water stilled and reflected the people who watched attentively. Dara glanced at her companion and saw that Neva's eyes were fixed on Amrith with an intense look. Then Callain raised her arms and spoke, chanting what sounded to Dara like a prayer although she only under-stood an occasional word or phrase. When she had finished, Callain flung a handful of herbs into the brazier and a pungent smoke quickly permeated the great chamber, pulled by unfelt air currents through the cave. As people threw back their heads and breathed deeply, the effects of the smoke became evident rapidly. Happiness and relaxation gave way to abandon. The holiday atmosphere turned to a physical celebration and an air of sensuousness spread over the underground room. Dara watched, untouched by the drug, as laughter became foreplay and both pool and the ledge around it filled with bodies embracing, kissing, fondling, and coupling.

She was jarred from her voyeurism when one couple approached her directly. The woman, a serving maid, leaned against a field worker's muscled body and both swayed languorously. The drugged smoke lent the woman courage while at the same time she had to fight its effects to keep her mind on the task at hand. Resolutely, she stood above Dara and gestured urgently. As Dara swung herself out of the pool, the woman's eyes fixed on her scar and widened. She reached out, then snatched her hand back apprehensively. Dara smiled, took the girl's hand, and place it on the C-section scar that ran from her navel to her pubis. A spark like static electricity jumped between them from fingertip to skin. Light fingers traced the scar's length, pressed against it briefly, then were gone as the couple bowed gravely and slipped into one another's arms. Dara returned to the pool but found the water too hot for her to tolerate. Neva was gone—vanished into the mass of bodies that was, in some inexplicable way, more a ritual and a celebration than an orgy.

Dara stood up and looked around her sadly. The brief moment of camaraderie with Neva was gone. The couple had treated her as what she really was here—a symbol; a thing to be touched but not a person to be felt. None of this was for her. The belief that allowed total abandonment in the name of religion was not her belief and she could not take part in its observance. Surrounded by people wrapped in the most intimate of embraces, involved in the most total sharing, she was alone. Again. She took a deep breath and the pungent smoke that still lifted from the brazier caught in her throat. Coughing reflexively,

Dara suddenly realized the source of her strange mood. To everyone else the drugged smoke acted as an aphrodisiac and a stimulant, but her metabolism was playing tricks again. Instead of becoming excited and leaving her inhibitions with her shawl, she was rapidly sinking into a depression. The only cure was to get out, away from the hazy chamber and into the clean air. Quickly she traced a path among the tangled figures until she reached the cleansing chamber, where she retrieved her clothes. Wrapped only in the long shawl, with her clothing clutched to her chest, she continued on into the antechamber. Then she was running up the steps and out into the still night. There she leaned her fevered head against cold stone and took deep breaths. As she stood shivering with cold or quivering with anger, tears filled her eyes. For the first time since awakening in a sunny meadow, Dara allowed herself to grieve for her own lost world and family and for the situation in which she now lived. At some point her weeping turned to a blank despair for the enduring loneliness in which she lived.

When finally her emotions wore down and the tears diminished, a hand touched her arm. Through a watery blur Dara saw one of the young guardsmen: an officer who had, it seemed, followed her from the chamber of the ritual. Although the drug was still fixed in his eyes, his face held concern and his touch was gentle. "I am named Vethis," he said. "No one should be sad on the Lady's night. Do honor to her with me and be happy." Deep within, Dara felt as if a light had been turned on. It glowed warmly and the yearning was strong to go with him, to join with him, to belong, if only for a few moments. But even as her body turned to his, she knew it was false. This ritual coupling with a stranger was no way to replace what she had lost or to belong in more than a superficial way. With a smile of thanks and a few words of regret, she turned away and wandered back to the small room that was her prison and her home. Wrapped up in her own misery and still under the influence of the drug, Dara had little thought for the effect her words might have on the guardsman. Behind her, his face stiffened with anger before he re-entered the cavern to find another partner.

* * *

From his post on the tower, Vethis watched as the barbarian woman and the old man walked past the kennels. Many passages of regular meals and steady, if varied, exercise had filled out her face and rounded her figure. Although considerably more attractive than when she had first arrived, the woman was not beautiful and Vethis doubted that she ever would be. Still, she was pleasant to look at and, he considered calmly, probably more so when unclothed. Vethis had lain with women who were more beautiful—and considerably more willing. In fact there were many women quite eager to please and be pleased by the tall, virile Head of the Household Guard. That this barbarian had refused his offer had angered him but he was willing to let it pass. She was foreign, unaccustomed to mountain ways. Perhaps it was that very strangeness which intrigued him. As no other woman had, she offered mystery, a sense of the exotic, an undefined power that spoke to his dreams and ambitions.

Vethis knew that his destiny lay outside the walls of Highfields and beyond the mountains. He knew also that it was up to him to set that destiny in motion. There was truth in the old saying, "He who waits for fate, waits forever." He was tired of waiting and he wanted the barbarian woman as he had wanted no other, for he felt that she held the key to his future. To take her, to have her would be to set it all in motion. She was not willing: that was a new challenge for him. He was quite confident, however, that in the end he would get what he wanted. Vethis had worked toward that end since he was twelve, when his life had crashed around him.

He had been born in happiness to a farmer with a prosperous freeholding that stretched along the northern boundary of Highfields not far from the village of Field's Crossing. His mother came to her husband from Highfields, proudly pregnant by Bentar, Armrith's father and then lord of the estate. The union of a fertile woman and a man of substance was successful even when the woman miscarried. Soon pregnant again and this time by her own husband, his mother gave birth to a son. Vethis, as do babies everywhere, accepted the love and dedication of his parents as his due. When he was five, a sister had been born, securing his mother's future regardless of her husband's fortunes. Life was not easy: both he and Meila worked hard on the farm with assigned chores expected to be done well and on time. But they were young and strong and there was always time left for playing games, hiking in the mountains, hunting, and riding.

At twelve, Vethis began to learn seriously the responsibilities of running a large farm. He did not mind the greater demands on his time and strength because he understood that eventually it would belong to him. He was tall and lean and suntanned, the bridge of his hawk-nose always peeling and his hair bleached to a pale brown. Then, one late summer morning, the innkeeper at the tavern in Field's Crossing had shivered, turned pale, and fallen to the floor of his taproom. Before he could be settled in his bed, his clothes were soaked through with his own acrid sweat. By sunset of the next day he was dead but the Sweating Fever ran through their valley like a brush fire through ripe grain. Within a passage, the village was decimated and bodies lay stacked by the score in common funeral pyres.

Vethis and Meila were orphaned by the epidemic although their own sturdy bodies rejected it. Grimly the boy carried the bodies of his father and mother to their own pyre: both children had worked hard to give their parents that last honor. Meila lighted the blaze and they both watched as the stink of death became the obscene smell of burning flesh and their parents returned to the elements.

Vethis snapped back to reality as the woman and her frail teacher/companion disappeared through the kennel doors. He spat the remembered taste of ashes from his mouth and strode off on his morning inspection. The small coal of anger that burned always in his gut had flared. He went from post to post so brusquely that his men stood straighter but resentful behind him. Vethis stopped abruptly when he came upon Amrith and his overseer supervising the construction of a new storage barn. Amrith. Just the sight of him twisted Vethis' mouth into a sardonic smile and brought a small secret gleam of revenge to his eyes.

The lord of Highfields would give half of all he owned to father an heir, regardless of gender. But Amrith had gotten no offspring, neither on his wife nor on his courtesans. If Vethis had believed in the Lady, he would have said it was her curse on the man for his grasping amorality. But Vethis had not believed in anything since the afternoon he had held Meila's hand and watched their future turn into ashes.

Alone and unprotected in the fever-ravaged community, they were easy prey. Young Amrith, assuming the lordship of Highfields after Bentar had succumbed to the epidemic, became the adversary. He was new to power and to the duties and responsibilities that came with it. Ten years older than Vethis, Amrith knew what he wanted and did not hesitate to go after it. As a gesture of goodwill and neighborly concern he removed both children from their isolated farmhouse and placed them in the Children's House at Highfields. It was not empty then and in it they could be well cared for and protected. Then came a series of explanations, justifications, excuses: right of way, security of the borders, unpaid taxes, protective regency. Bit by bit, acre by acre, passage by passage, the rich farmland of their birthright was absorbed into the vast complex of Highfields. By the time Vethis reached his majority it was all gone.

Frustrated and angry, he sought help but found none. Who would side with a stripling of no great importance, the son of a dead farmer, against a mountain lord wielding authority, power, and money. For all of his striving, there was no contest. Finally, an embittered young man, he turned away from justice and embraced revenge. Revenge, however, was a different matter, one that required time, careful planning, and preparation. While he undertook this effort and until he reached his goal, Vethis had to live and to protect Meila. That meant curbing his temper and settling into one of the few occupations open to him.

Farming, the skill he knew best, Vethis rejected immediately. He would not labor in the fields of the man who had stolen from him his own land and his heritage. After considering several other possibilities, he settled on soldiering as the profession that would be the most valuable to him in the long term. It would teach him all the skills he needed to achieve his goals and then to survive afterwards as well. A dedicated student, he worked hard until he had mastered a variety of weapons, riding, strategy, tracking, and patience. There were no wars to test his knowledge but continual skirmishes with bandits and scattered gormrith bands honed its edge. And a position in the Rangers was always possible. In the meantime, the Lord Amrith was well pleased to have such an excellent warrior protecting his large and sometimes vulnerable estate.

Amrith was a man who rarely looked deeper than the surface of an issue or a person, especially if there was a chance that what he might find might be unpleasant. While committing theft and fraud for years, he had made two great mistakes: stealing from Vethis and dismissing him as a powerless child. Now, long after Amrith had forgotten, a child's outrage still burned in the man's trained and hardened body. Vethis remembered—and waited.

Now he had a strong feeling that the waiting would soon be over and it drew him strongly to the barbarian woman. The beginning of the change had really happened at the five-year Festival. Meila had attended for the first time and had not returned. During the games, a Flatlands lord from an estate near Bittersea had noticed her and spoken. By Festival's end she had contracted with him for the usual span of time. He had one child and heir by his legal wife but wanted another for insurance. It had been an excellent opportunity and Meila had gone. He would almost certainly not hear from her again until the next Festival. Vethis missed her deeply, but was, at the same time, glad that she had gone. Now he was free: to choose a plan, extract his revenge, and then escape to join one of the bands that haunted the passes. Away at Bittersea, under her Lord's protection, Meila would be safe from any retribution for his actions.

It seemed as though Festival had taken his sister and returned instead this strange woman. He would approach her again and try to get an answer. Meanwhile, Vethis finished his round and planned the next move.

CHAPTER 6

Lekh opened the door and Dara shrugged into a quilted jacket against the cool wind of an early fall afternoon. As they left the room she looked around for Sandy but Lekh had come for her alone. Her spirits fell: she had been looking forward to going outside the walls of the compound but without Sandy they never went past the gates. She stopped. "Where's Sandy?" she asked, still hoping that their walk would not be curtailed.

"The coursers went out with the hunt at first light. It is the time for stocking the larders with game to feed us over the cold passages."

She sighed. "So we stay in the compound today."

Lekh looked her in the eye. "We shall walk, as always. I take responsibility. But understand you that my life is forfeit should you be lost."

Dara touched him lightly on the shoulder and smiled. "Have no fear." She found it amusing that they still expected her to bolt for the woods at the slightest slackening in their vigilance. What else would a barbarian do? The old man nodded solemnly and resumed walking. Two women passed them carrying baskets of soiled bedding to the laundry shed. The plump one on the left shifted the loaded basket on her hip and squinted up at an opaque sky. "The Lady is gathering much wuliveen this year," she remarked.

"It will grow cold early," her friend replied, "and then last long." They turned the corner of the building and the rest of their conversation was lost. She examined their words and tried to make sense of them. Wuliveen was the fine hair of a domestic animal called the wuliver and it was woven into warm shirts, cloaks, and pants. There seemed no connection she could see between that, the sky, and a being she understood as a fertility goddess. Giving up, she asked, "Is that good or bad?"

"Both," Lekh replied in his slow way. "The mists grow heavier each day now until the first snow. The heavier the mists become, the greater the snows. It means that the cold will be great and any who are unprepared will suffer. Some in other holdings will freeze. But when the cold has passed there will be much water for the grass in the pastures and the crops in the fields. The harvest next season will be bountiful. When the mists are thin and the cold passages are mild and easy, the crops will thirst afterwards and the people will hunger." As they left the compound, Dara could see that the ceiling of mist was lower. Wispy tendrils curled almost to the tops of the trees on the high slopes. She shivered.

As they walked along the lower slopes that rose from pastureland, Dara could see how each leaf and spike on the trees gleamed with the moisture it had combed from the air. The ground beneath their feet was wet and springy but clear: the foliage would not fall until winter was established and its moisture-gathering function had been fulfilled. Heading back to the compound they crossed the furrows where gleaners bent seeking the last grains and stalks to be bound for animal fodder. Lekh explained in detail how every scrap of food must be used and not wasted. Dara only half-listened to his lecture. Surrounded by an open field and unconstrained by Sandy's vigilant presence, she felt light enough to fly back to the compound. Running was something that she missed in the confined life she was compelled to accept and at that moment she missed it more than ever before. She could feel the damp air lifting her hair and the blood pounding in her ears while the field rushed past her. It took discipline to continue walking sedately alongside the old man when she itched to be off but she had promised not to cause any problems and so running was out of the question.

They were in mid-field, close enough to the compound to see smoke rising from the cookhouse and hear the mill grinding busily, when a flurry of sounds rose from the hills behind them. The hunting party emerged from a small rift onto the field, trailed by pack animals laden with game and the coursers pacing wearily alongside. Successful and in good spirits, the hunters let out a ragged whoop and spurred their mounts toward the gleaners. Upon hearing the yell, the gleaners straightened, looked, and then took to their heels, dashing for the safety of the gate. Only the older laborers stood where they were and watched the chase, shading their eyes against the bright grey-white sky and smiling. The fleetest of the gleaners reached the open gate and then turned to cheer on the others. Some of those, less agile or less lucky, were lassoed by the riders and immobilized. The men were released immediately but the women were pulled up onto the saddles and kissed thoroughly before being returned to their feet at the compound. Dara watched the sport with great enjoyment and even dour Lekh chuckled beside her.

Then the leader of the hunting party, who had remained with the pack animals, whooped and spurred his mount toward her. Dara looked and saw that it was the soldier who had approached her after the fertility festival at the baths. Like a bolt out of a crossbow, Dara took off, running at last with the moist air clean in her lungs and her pulse racing. If it was a chase he wanted, she would give him a good one and gladly. Instead of running straight for the gate, Dara held course until the sapeer was nearly within lariat distance, then zigged to her left. Caught off guard, the rider turned his mount but she had gained seconds on him. Once again, timing it carefully, she zagged to the right and then, after three steps, veered to the left again. Thrown completely off stride by her tactics, the beast dropped back and Dara reached the safety of the

compound gate. Flushed and elated, she was cheered by
the knot of gleaners and other people who had stopped to
watch the sport. When the man who had called himself
Vethis came in, however, he was not laughing and did not
share the good spirits of the people around her. Instead
his face was tight and drawn, his eyes narrowed in anger.
He dismounted not far from Dara and looked at her as if
he would like to strike her. "Karait!" he snarled and spat
into the dirt at her feet. Then he jerked at his mount's
reins and strode off stiffly. In the sudden uncomfortable
silence, the gleaners headed back out to the field, the
riders moved off to the stable, and the spectators drifted
away.

Clam chowder. For a moment the aromas that drifted
from the long tables in the dining hall combined to trick
Dara's olfactory nerve into thinking it had smelled clam
chowder. Scent was such a potent trigger of memory; she
was suddenly awash in the kind of homesickness that she
had worked so hard to keep at bay. The smells of dinner
took her back to a night on Nantucket when they had
eaten chowder at a restaurant overlooking the harbor. The
boats in the marina had been all lit up and bobbing gently
at their berths. Afterward they had browsed through shops
and art galleries before returning to the antique rooming
house for the first night of their honeymoon. Angrily Dara
shook her head to clear away both the painful memories
and the tears they brought. Looking fiercely down at her
plate through blurred eyes, she willed it to turn into a
bowl of steaming chowder fragrant with nutty clams, translucent onions, chunks of potato, and a thick, creamy broth.
This was not the first time she had experienced a longing
for some food unknown on Khyren. Usually it would be a
favorite like lobster with drawn butter, fresh spring aspar-
agus, shrimp gumbo, or corn on the cob. At other times a
craving would descend suddenly for strawberries or choco-
late chip cookies, which were foods she had never really
enjoyed. Like friends who had done a tour of duty in a
foreign country, Dara found herself wanting what she could
no longer have. There was no way to assuage these hungers, however, as there were no friendly travelers to de-

liver packages of popcorn or grapefruit. In spite of her concentration the plate remained pottery and the food on it was still slivered chingaree in an herb sauce. It was not that she disliked it—chingaree tasted good and was nourishing—but it was not clam chowder.

Of course, Dara had liked chingaree even better before she had found out what it was. One day, after she and Lekh had toured the cookhouse, he had taken her to an oval building with a domed roof. Dara had ducked through the low doorway, straightened up, and then almost bolted right out again. The structure had been filled by a huge papery hive. Crawling over every inch of it, over the keeper and each other, were the enormous insects that had built it. With carapaces nearly six inches long, the chingaree had grey shells mottled with green and a smell like paprika. They had six strong legs, large faceted eyes, and long flexible tails which they used to carry, build, fight, and mate. The hive keeper had explained that the tail muscles of these prolific insects were excellent food. Dara had watched in horrified fascination as he plucked one of the creatures off his shirt and flexed its tail to demonstrate the strong muscle beneath the jointed carapace. Because chingaree tasted good and agreed with her metabolism, Dara had forced herself to overcome her repulsion to the glittering eyes and swarming bodies. She continued to eat chingaree but she had never again felt quite the same way about it.

She was finishing up her portion when Neva burst through the door of the dining hall, flushed and out of breath. It was obvious that she had run across the compound and Dara rose, alarmed. Neva was always busy inside the estate house at this hour and something out of the ordinary had brought her here in such a hurry. Spotting Dara, Neva made her way around the tables toward her as quickly as she could. Faces turned toward them but both women ignored the curious stares. "What is it, Neva? Is something the matter?"

"The Lady Callain. She wishes to see you. At once." Neva stopped, took several deep breaths, and then continued. "Something of great importance has occurred. My lady is distraught and she summons you to attend her at once."

"What is it? Do you know?"

"No, I was not in her room to see. But she has also sent for Tai. That is all I can tell you." Neva half-turned, already on her way back.

"I'm coming!" Dara asserted and followed her.

Oblivious to the interrupted conversations and curious faces around them, the two women hurried out through the incoming diners into the damp night. Automatically Dara looked up but could see nothing through the thickening mist. She missed the blazing stars of the galactic cluster that were her single, fragile connection with home. The fog that grew lower and denser every day made her feel even more isolated. On their way to the estate house, Dara wondered what could have happened to disturb the regal Callain and generate such an unusual summons. The lady of Highfields had paid her no attention until now and only the arrangements she had made for Dara's keep proved that she was even aware of the alien woman's presence in her demesne. It was plain that Neva had disclosed all that she could or was allowed to say, so the rest of the story would have to come from her mistress.

At the house Neva led her to a small side door and they entered a plain hallway. The great house was warm and very bright after the heavy night air. Dara followed her friend down the narrow hall and then up a steep back staircase that was part of the servants' area. They went through a large paneled door and were abruptly in the main hall on the second level. Dara, who had only accompanied Neva around the austere servants' quarters on a few occasions, got a brief, vivid impression of colorful rugs, textured wall hangings, and exquisite furniture before she was ushered into the private apartments of Callain, Lady of Highfields.

The richness of the hall was nothing to what met her eyes here. A thick rug woven in an intricate pattern covered the stone floor. Soft cushions rested on delicate sofas of gleaming wood. A magnificent tapestry embroidered with a hunting scene covered a large crystal window against the night. In one corner a brazier glowed bright orange, sending its heat out into a room that was already warmer than the rest of the house. Before them a tall goblet of amethyst glass and a book, face-down, stood on a table as if they had been put down abruptly. In the midst of this luxury stood its mistress, straight, haughty, and wearing a look of impatience. She was not alone. Beside her stood Tai, the Healer, whom Dara had often seen about the estate stitching cuts, lancing boils, and otherwise tending to the welfare of both humans and animals. He looked both elated and disturbed at the same time. Hovering close to him, as if for protection, was a slim and attractive servant girl whom Dara recognized immediately. Although obviously in awe of the company and her surroundings, the girl was radiantly happy.

Dara hastened to make a formal greeting in the manner Lekh had taught her and Callain nodded impatiently. She was distracted, not the poised woman who went about the estate seeing to its welfare. Her aquamarine eyes flashed and she gave off waves of tension that were almost tangible and visible. Whatever was on her mind, Dara did not think it would take long to find out. No sooner had the thought crossed her mind than Callain came right to the point. "Do you recognize this woman?" she asked, gesturing sharply toward the servant.

"Yes, my lady," Dara replied cautiously. The temper of the room was confusing and disturbing. Still far from fluent in the native tongue, she went warily. "I have seen her before but I do not know her name."

"It is Elisinthe," Tai offered, but Callain cut him short.

"That is not important," she snapped. "Where have you seen her?"

"In the baths," she responded, not certain she had used the right words. "Not the Women's Bath House; in the cavern."

"When?"

"On the night of the ceremony, my lady. It was the only time I was in the cavern."

"Did you speak to her?"

"No, my lady, I did not."

Callain's eyes flashed. "Did you touch her?"

"Not exactly . . ."

"Then what did happen?"

Again Dara paused, seeking the right words and feeling as though she were walking through a minefield. Callain's agitation was creating a great deal of anxiety among the others in the room. "She wanted to touch me, my lady, here . . ." Dara could not recall the right word so she touched her own abdomen to demonstrate. "She seemed a little frightened of me so I smiled, to let her know that I was not angry."

"How long did she do this?"

"Oh, less than a moment. Then she went away."

"Was she alone?"

"No, my lady, a man accompanied her."

"Would you know the man again if you saw him?"

"Yes, my lady."

"Is that all? Are you sure nothing more happened?"

"Yes, my lady, I am sure."

Callain stiffened, her fists clenched by her sides, and gave a low bitter exclamation. The cry startled Dara and confused her further. She really had no idea what was happening and looked around the room for help but met only three carefully-controlled faces. The feeling of threading her way through an explosive situation intensified. "I beg your kindness," she said finally, "but many things are still not clear to me. What thing has happened? Have I done something wrong?"

For a long silent moment she thought no one would answer her, then two people spoke at once. In the same tight voice Callain exclaimed, "Not clear!" and Tai the Healer said calmly, "Nothing is wrong, quite the opposite," He nodded toward the woman beside him, who blushed and looked at the rug. Under the weight of Callain's mood she no longer smiled but her face still glowed as though it were beyond her control. "Elisinthe is with child," Tai explained finally. "She came to me this evening to make sure. She is the first woman at Highfields to breed a child in many years: the Children's House has long been empty. Perhaps others will now follow her example and fertility will be restored here."

"That is indeed cause for happiness," Dara commented in a neutral tone. It explained Elisinthe's expression, at least, but the lady's thinly-controlled anger was still a mystery.

"And the father?" demanded Callain. "Who is it that claims paternity of the child-to-be?"

Elisinthe looked up shyly but with pride in her eyes. "His name is Awlik: he works in the fields. We have partnered one another for two cycles. Now that I carry his child we can truly marry."

"In the fields," Callain echoed bitterly, opening another door to Dara's comprehension. Those three words carried all the envy of a barren woman for her fertile sister and all the weight of her position along with it. The gift she wanted so badly for herself had been given to another instead. Worse, it had been bestowed on someone far below her in station. If Dara's guess was correct, Callain had meant to be the one to restore the Lady's Blessing on Highfields. The confirmed fact of Elisinthe's pregnancy was a distasteful draught for her to swallow. The only thing still unclear to Dara was how she herself was involved in any of this situation.

Callain drew herself up, wrapping aristocracy around her once again like a robe of office. In a remarkable display of discipline the unfulfilled woman gave way to the great lady. "You may all go," she said, "except for this one," and she gestured at Dara. "Tai, have the Head of Staff order a small celebration for everyone. Drink and some music for dancing as soon as possible."

Tai murmured acceptance and then, almost gratefully, he escaped the stifling room with Neva and Elisinthe. Neva threw an apprehensive look backwards as she went out the door and Dara nodded reassuringly, reflecting a confidence she did not feel. Then she took a deep breath, squared her shoulders, and faced Callain. This was when she would learn her part in the domestic drama. All instincts told her that this interview would not be easy. They were right.

"Now it is revealed," Callain began heavily. "All this power has been within you all along but you kept it secret. Then, with no warning, not even a hint, you use the Touch on Elisinthe, who is nothing but a servant! What could she possibly have offered you?"

Dara stood rooted to the spot with a mouth that was suddenly dry while her mind raced. Power? Within her? The Touch? It could only mean that Callain believed Dara responsible for the sudden fertility of a woman who had but touched her. It was incredible and Dara's first reaction was to deny it all as the religious superstition she understood it to be. Then she looked at the emotion in Callain's face and the reality of the situation hit her and sent a chill down her back. What she believed, or even knew, was irrelevant. Callain believed what her culture and religion taught her to be true and that was the only truth she would accept. How Dara acted now and what she said was critically important. But what could she say that would not implicate her further or fuel Callain's anger? "Elisinthe gave me nothing," she replied simply and truthfully.

"Ah, yes! It was a test, then. I thought as much. Well, the test succeeded and you have found out what you wish to know. I will do whatever I must to have a child. The heir. Name your price: tell me what you wish and you shall have it."

Once again Dara responded with a plain fact. "What I wish no one on Khyren can grant."

"Do not negotiate with me, woman. While you are at Highfields you are within my power. Never forget that I command here!"

Dara's mind raced. She had taken a step in the wrong direction and made things worse. Now she would have to regroup—and still she had no idea how she could fulfill such a request and meet such an enormous need. She thought back on everything Neva had told her about the ancient religion of the Lady and the few comments she had made about her mistress. It was little enough to gamble with. She spoke quietly but with conviction. "You may command my very life but I am only a woman. You cannot bargain with the Lady and not even you can command her gift." She had hoped to defuse Callain's argument but she was wrong.

"Insolence! I have heard you called karait. Do not deny you have the Touch. When Elisinthe's belly swells, the proof of that will be plain for all to see. Now let us cease this pointless debate and do business. What is the price?"

The aqua eyes were as cold as glacier ice and yet they burned with her obsession.

Dara recoiled from that passion, beaten again by her disadvantage. She did not know, among many other things, what a karait was. Unfortunate timing, however, had placed her in a very difficult position. What Callain wanted, demanded, was not hers to grant. No one, least of all this arrogant woman, would believe the truth and yet her gamble had only gotten her in deeper. What she needed now was magic.

Magic! The solution to the quandary was literally right in front of her. If Callain's barrenness was psychosomatic, then what she needed to overcome it was the fervent belief that she was demonstrating so openly now. All Dara had to do was harness that. And yet, a little magic never hurt. Suppressing her misgivings, Dara became serious and assumed a dignified expression. "I remind my lady that what happened to Elisinthe occurred at the proper time and in the proper place, after all the ceremonies had been observed. The Lady chooses when and where to bestow her gift. Prepare yourself well before the next ceremony to honor her and I will consider what is needed before that night." Whatever that was, she though.

"And your price?"

"I have none. What the Lady demands in payment is between you and her."

Mollified, if not chastened, Callain's fury abated. "Very well. But if you disappoint me, you will regret it, I promise."

"The instrument is not the giver. Only the Lady chooses who shall receive her blessing." Dara walked to the door and waited for Callain's permission to leave. Exiting without it would have been an unthinkable insult and she had difficulties enough already

Out in the sobering night air, Dara thought back over the confrontation and shivered. Barring any physiological difficulties, she knew that Callain's obsession with becoming pregnant was almost certainly what was preventing it. At home, she had heard of women who had not conceived until they had given up and redecorated the spare room, thrown out maternity clothes, or even adopted a child. Callain's belief in the Touch was the first step toward breaking down that barrier. The next question was how to get Callain to free herself from the tension that kept her from achieving her goal. The answer was elusive and it could very well be dangerous.

Later, just before drifting off to sleep, she remembered the tiny spark of static electricity that had jumped between her skin and Elisinthe's. And wondered.

The next day when Lekh came to fetch her for their afternoon walk he carried her running shoes tucked under his arm. Dara was astonished: she had not seen them since her ordeal at the Festival grounds and had no idea where he had found them. Wordlessly he proffered the footgear and silently she accepted. A few moments later they set out for their daily lesson. With her lightweight, fifty-dollar Rabbitsfoot running shoes on, Dara felt as if she could outrun anyone, even Sandy. That afternoon they walked in the fields north of the Compound, past the gleaners bobbing and stooping, all the way to a group of large stone cisterns buried deep in the hills. Here Lekh explained the system of channels and aqueducts that collected rainwater and snowmelt and held them underground, away from the sun, for use during the dry months. So extensive and well-maintained was this system that the compound had never run out, even during seasons of light mist followed by thin snowfall and drought. Here the water was sparkling and pure and contained no hint of the minerals that saturated the compound's bath and wash water. She assumed that the cisterns were separated from the aquifer that fed the Pool of the Lady by a layer of impermeable stone.

Then came the walk back and, even though Dara and Lekh were on the opposite side of the compound from the previous day, the afternoon's ending was the same. Down from the hill crest swooped the hunting party, leaping irrigation ditches at breakneck speed and yelping despite their fatigue. She watched for Vethis's mount which ran, again, in the rear with the pack animals. Determined not to be surprised, she acted at the first sight of him, sprinting for the gate like a runner out of the blocks. For a while, with footgear made for the task, she felt as if she were flying. This day, however, her strategy worked less well. When she zigged and zagged his mount followed without missing a stride: she had badly underestimated the intelligence of the native mounts. She needed a new strategy and quickly.

Judging as carefully as possible the moment Vethis drew into lasso range, Dara flung herself into a running forward rollout. The momentum carried her through the maneuver and back onto her feet almost under the nose of the surprised beast, which had overtaken her and was just checking its stride. Improvising, Dara flung her arms into the air and shouted as loudly as she could. Badly rattled, the animal shied and reared, its eyes bulging and its round ears pinned back. By the time Vethis got it back in control and responding to his commands, Dara was through the north gate and catching her breath. This time there were no cheers for her achievement and she expected none. This group played the game for fun and were uneasy with someone who played it to win. An apprehensive silence settled over the small crowd and deepened as the furious Vethis paced his mount through the gate. He kept his head high and seemed oblivious of everyone, Dara most of all. But his mouth was drawn and hard and his face was pale. Dara stepped away and watched him go, wondering whether it would have been wiser to let him win.

"What I don't understand, karait . . ." Neva broke off in embarrassment and covered her mouth with her hands. Her cheeks flushed darker.

"What does that word mean, Neva?" Dara asked in a carefully neutral tone.

"You have heard it before from the Lady Callain, I know."

"Yes, and from others. When people thought I couldn't hear. Or when they didn't care if I did."

"It is the name we give to a person, it can be either a man or a woman, who sees the world differently from everyone else. Such as person often has a deeper understanding of the mysteries, a closer relationship with the forces that shape life. A karait lives apart but not isolated and people seek that person's help when they are in need. You seek her help when you want to get something badly or lose something, or keep it. Something or someone. She may make an ointment to keep you beautiful or tell you how to get a baby. Every karait has different skills or powers. Some are better than others. I'm sorry. I'm not explaining this well."

"That's all right, I understand you very well," Dara said slowly. Well enough; but it was important to know how the local witch or sibyl fit into the social order here. "Does a karait belong to the Order of the Lady?"

"Oh, no!" Neva replied, shocked. "The Order would not have such a one and they almost never have babies themselves, anyway. The Order changes things, too, but in a holy way. Besides, a karait lives alone always. At least, I have never heard of one who did not. Often a karait goes out to speak with the wild things, with the wind and the mist, or with the stars. Most are strangers but they can be your friend in time of need. A karait can be familiar but still a mystery."

"Then why do people call me this?" Dara asked. "I live here among the people of Highfields and I learn your ways. I have done nothing to earn this name."

Neva hesitated, choosing the words of reply carefully so as not to offend. It could be so difficult to explain these things to someone who had not always lived with them, she thought. "Because you *are* different. You came alone from somewhere far away and even here you seem always to be alone, except for Lekh and me. You just do not fit into a place as the rest of us do: there is not a place here for you to belong. It is hard for you to join in the things that are important to us. Like the Night of the Lady. And you *do* change things."

Neva's speech was a very accurate description of how Dara felt and it saddened her to hear it from the lips of her friend. "What have I changed?" she responded, the challenge gone from her.

"Why, you brought a baby," Neva replied softly, looking straight at Dara. "Elisinthe but touched you and now a child grows within her. What change could be more important?"

"Awlik had more to do with it than I."

But Neva would not be challenged. "You know what I mean."

She did. Dara could not refute any of it. Neither could she explain that she had not caused any of it, for not even Neva would believe her. Stick to reality, she thought. "Does anyone ever harm a karait?"

"Harm? Of course not; only gormrith would risk being cursed for acting so and we all run the risk of bandits. That's why there are walls and guards. A karait maintains the clan or village ties he or she was born with, even if they live apart." Neva paused and looked at the tips of her scuffed shoes. "Does it offend you when others call you by this name?"

"My name is my own," Dara answered with more feeling than she had expected. "It is the only thing that still belongs to me."

"I will not speak it to you again, then," Neva said emphatically, looking her in the eyes again. "And I will tell the others what you wish."

"Thank you, Neva. I value your help. And your friendship."

Neva ducked her head in pleasure and then a mischievous grin lifted her cheeks. "Then you must answer my question."

"Then you must finish your question."

"Oh! Yes. What I do not understand is why you are doing this. The Harvest Race is a custom and harmless sport. Had Vethis caught you, he would have given you a kiss, no more. And that's not so bad. At least, I wouldn't mind. Now you have made him look bad before the men he commands. Why?"

Now it was Dara's turn to pause and word her answer carefully. "The first time it was just a game. But I like to run, it feels good, and I like to win. Today I knew I should have let him catch me but it was a challenge. I am not a person who likes to give in, even for a kiss. It might have been easier to do so had I known how angry he would be."

The next day was a clear one for the harvest season on Khyren. The ever-present fog had thinned and lifted to the hilltops, giving a temporary reprieve from eyestrain.

Although the sky was still the same grey-yellow color it had been for weeks, Dara could see farther than usual and her spirits improved with the visibility. With Lekh, she walked to the west of the compound through a field that had lain fallow during the growing season. Drops of moisture clung to the tall grasses which brushed their knees and dried weed stalks snapped beneath their feet. Occasionally a seed pod burst, sending tiny black seed on a short but critical trajectory toward a clear growing space. In a drier autumn, she and Lekh would have kicked up clouds of dust and chaff as they walked but the damp air weighed everything down. At the same time, it heightened the field's pervasive smell of crushed herbs and sweet fern.

Lekh, who possessed a landsman's practical knowledge of the high valley's natural history, lectured her on the vegetation they passed. He named for her the different varieties of grasses and weeds and explained how each was used. Dara had learned quickly that each of Khyren's natural resources was accepted and any possible good extracted without being exploited. She made mental notes as they wandered through the overgrown field and gathered samples of the most interesting specimens to study later in her room. At the end of the field they came upon a stand of hooded plants like jack-in-the-pulpit that reminded her of another creature about which she had wondered. "Lekh," she said, gesturing with her hands, "tell me what you know about an animal so high and about this wide, all black and shiny. It wanders here and there and carries on its back small flying things about so large." She marked their size with her fingers. "It was a strange creature and I've not seen another like it."

The old man looked at her with startled eyes but said nothing. His crippled hands trembled for a moment by his sides. It was not quite the reaction Dara was expecting, but she continued. "The flying things remove something from plants like these and bring it back to the large creature. That one carried a waxy ball with a strong odor." She thought it best not to mention the startling effects that odor had had on her and found she was right when Lekh gave a disturbed cry.

"A dream beetle?" His voice was thick and suddenly old, as though the words were reluctant to come out. "You saw a dream beetle! Where?"

Dara was perplexed by the vehemence of his reaction. "It was far from here, by the edge of the grasslands near the South Pilgrimage Trail. Why are you upset? Is a dream beetle dangerous?"

His lips trembled while Lekh considered his answer. By themselves, his hands snapped a seed pod from a dried stalk and began to shred it clumsily. Their nervous picking continued as he spoke. "Yes, the dream beetle is dangerous. It is also very rare. Few among us here in the mountains have seen it and I have only heard it described in legends." He paused and an unspoken word hung in the air between them. Once again she was different.

Dara sighed in frustration. "Tell me what the legends say."

"They say the dream beetle is really two creatures living as one and only together can they survive. The small seekers which fly take what they can find from growing things—sap, pollen, nectar, seeds. They bring these things back to the builder which walks. That is their function and, unless the beetle is threatened or disturbed, that is all they do."

"What happens if it is bothered?" she asked, thinking of her perch in the tree.

"Then the seekers are formidable. They have snouts for poking their way into plants and these snouts also carry a strong poison. One would only sting you but the bites of many would leave you dead. If you saw a beetle and are here to ask me about it, then you did not disturb it." Lekh dropped the shredded pod into the grass and stilled his hands by clasping them behind his back. His eyes drifted out of focus and he settled into silence.

"What about the builder?" Dara prompted him.

He looked at her as if from a distance. "The builder chews the substances which it receives, mixing them with the juices of its own body. This produces a waxy ball that the builder carries with special arms. As the builder eats, it produces more of this fluid and adds layer upon layer to the ball. No one knows the purpose of the ball or why the builder carries it always, or why the beetle protects it so fiercely. Some say that it encloses a shining treasure that will make you rich and fertile if only you can take it for your own. Other legends say that the meaning of life can be found in it. But the beetle itself is a creature of legend and, of those few who have seen it, not one has dared the flyers to find out."

"The builder, does it also bite?"

"No, separated from the seekers it is quite timid and harmless. But the builder is wary and the beetle is a solitary creature. That is one reason why so few have ever seen it."

"Isn't there another reason? One that would explain why you were so frightened when I described it?"

Once again the old man fell silent, staring off toward the fog-draped slopes. It was quiet except for the muffled sounds from the compound and the call of a hunting bird high in the mist. Dara waited patiently, knowing that this time his attention had not wandered. The agitated twisting of his gnarled hands told her that he was thinking hard. When he finally answered, his voice was low and she had to strain to hear the words. "Legend also says that the dream beetle is a creature of the Brotherhood and shares its dreams with them alone. It is said that those who but see one risk drawing their attention. To hunt the beetle for its treasure would be to call down their anger. Perhaps that is as it should be, for the Brotherhood is as solitary and elusive as the beetle." He looked up at her and his face seemed older, more wrinkled with sadness. "I cannot tell you what is true. But you have seen one. Remember that the Brotherhood is far more dangerous than the stings of a hundred seekers."

"Why? What is the Brotherhood?" Mystified, Dara was suddenly filled with more questions. The stubborn old man compounded the mystery, however, by refusing to speak more of it. Like Neva, he could be as silent and unmovable as the mountains when he wished. Dara fumed in frustration and decapitated a row of innocent seed pods to vent her anger. Abruptly, she was startled out of her preoccupation by the fluted call of the gatekeeper's horn piercing the air. Someone was approaching Highfields.

Lekh peered first at the compound and then at the road, muttering disgustedly that his old eyes could not see further than the next clump of weeds. "Who is it?" he asked testily. "What colors are the banner?"

Dara had no trouble seeing the pennant carried up the road by the lead rider. The rider looked familiar but the colors meant nothing to her. "It is yellow," she relayed, "with a blue band across the bottom. Do you know who comes?"

"Oh, yes!" he responded brightly, all his fearfulness gone. "It is the Lord Resar. Long has it been since he rode out of Highfields and down from the mountains. Many will be gladdened to have him here again." Lekh stopped for a moment and his lips moved as the words struggled with one another in their haste to emerge. "He was always such a cheerful boy. Of course, he did not carry the responsibility for Highfields as did the Lord Amrith. Cheerfulness and good humor come more easily to a light heart. He could be thoughtful, though, and I remember that he flushed easily with embarrassment. Yes . . ." His voice drifted off as his weak old eyes looked back clearly upon the past. Then, with a twitch of duty, he turned to Dara. "But we must return quickly. He will be sending for you. Let us hurry."

Lekh took her arm as if to urge her on but then used it instead to steady himself. Together they headed down toward the gate as fast as his aged legs would carry him. Dara was filled with conflicting emotions. She was not eager to meet again the cold, distant figure who had washed his hands of her so casually at Festival. Yet there could be no denying that he had arranged for her care. And, as she was all too painfully aware, her future lay entirely in his hands. The period of waiting and learning was ended: a time of change was about to begin. It was exciting and frightening at the same time.

Dara's head was so filled with jumbled images and phrases and contradictory thoughts that they were approaching the South Gate before it registered that the rhythmic pounding in her ears was not just her pulse. Instead it heralded the galloping feet of a sapeer. Turning wildly, she saw Vethis bearing down upon her with a ragged grin of triumph on his face. A shaft of fear stabbed through her at the sight. Dropping Lekh's arm so abruptly that he staggered and almost fell, Dara was off. This time she had no more tricks and no time to improvise. Only Khyren's lighter gravity worked in her favor as she made an all-out dash for the gate. So much adrenalin was surging through her system that the running was easy, almost like floating. She was so charged up that, at first, outracing Vethis seemed certain. But the sapeer was faster and stronger and the gate was not quite close enough.

Dara was within ten strides of her goal when the open lasso settled over her shoulders with lazy finality. Instead of drawing her smoothly to the sapeer, however, the rope snapped taut and jerked her off her feet. Unprepared and unable to break the fall with her arms, Dara struck the dirt with a stunning impact that jarred her head and drove the air from her lungs. Dazed, she was barely aware of being dragged the last few feet into the compound. All her attention was focused on getting her breath back and fighting vertigo. Not until its hollow buzzing left her ears did Dara realize how quiet it was. She struggled to overcome the residual dizziness and sit up but her arms were still pinned by the taut rope. A saddle creaked and then the pennant-bearer leaned over her. First he pried off the lasso, slipped the loop over her head, and tossed it disgustedly to one side. Then, slowly, he helped her to sit up. Leaning with relief against the man's muscular arm, Dara became aware that someone was speaking. Looking up, she was suddenly mortified to see Resar mounted on his sapeer above her. He was not looking at her, however, but at Vethis and both his tone and expression were thunderous.

". . . how you treat someone given into the care of your lord?"

"It was but a game, my lord, only a Harvest Race," said Vethis tightly.

"A Harvest Race is sport, not an act of hostility. It does not usually end with someone dragged through the dust!"

"I admit I was too rough, my lord. I ask your pardon."

"Curb your temper, Vethis. Do not act so again."

"No, my lord."

Vethis coiled his lasso, turned his mount, and threaded it through the silent crowd. Despite the rebuke, his back was straight and his head high. As the crowd closed around him, Resar looked down to where Dara sat, rubbing the rope burns on her arms. "Is she all right, Tirnus?"

"She seems to be, Resar, although she'll probably be dizzy for a while."

"Then we must go on. My brother and sister are waiting on our arrival."

Neva slipped out from the circle of people around them. She knelt beside Dara and took her arm firmly. Eager to be gone, Tirnus relinquished his charge and remounted. As the small party of riders moved off, the crowd dispersed quickly. The diversion was over and much work remained to be done. Scolding quietly, Neva helped Dara up and walked with her to her room where she lay down. It was not until much later, when she knew him well, that Dara realized Resar had been as embarrassed as she.

CHAPTER 7

Lamplight gleamed on cutlery and along the rims of crystal goblets. It filled the room with a mellow golden atmosphere, softening the three figures seated around the dining table. Servants moved quietly around them, placing heavy platters on the smooth linen, offering savory dishes, and removing empty plates. The sharp scent of the herbs and the more heady aroma of wine mulled with fruit and spices drifted in the air. Resar looked around and sighed to himself. The Small Dining Room, a cozy and comfortably furnished alcove, had always been one of his favorites among the many rooms at Highfields. In some ways it was more like a gallery, displaying along its walls the artifacts, mineral samples, old pottery, and other interesting objects collected by their great-grandfather. The room also harbored warm memories of the rare, treasured occasions when he and Amrith had been summoned from the Children's House to dine with their elegant parents. Though they were often painful, he hoarded the remembrance of those times just as his great-grandfather had hoarded antique pots and pretty rocks. During those long, leisurely meals, Bentar had invariably concerned himself with his older son, either quizzing him about his activities, lecturing him on his duty, or berating him for some failing, whether real or imagined. Resar would sit, ignored and only half listening, while Amrith bore the heavy weight of their father's attention. Left to himself, the boy had let his imagination loose to daydream about his surroundings. After memorizing all of the collected artifacts visible from his chair, he had focused on the window tapestry artfully embroidered with a still-life of fruit and game. He had often explored its complicated design and carefully inter-woven shapes. In the play of light and shadow under feathers and leaves and in the sheen on fur, he had found faces hidden.

Once lost, only two things had pulled Resar from his daydreaming. A word or simple gesture from their mother could command his attention immediately. Resar had wor-shipped her and, if allowed to, would have adored her. But to the Lady Ythiel, children had two functions: to inherit and to confer status. Having produced two children to fulfill those functions and having ensured that they were raised properly as befitted her responsibilities and their station, she lost interest in motherhood. As first child, oldest son, and heir to the estate, Amrith claimed what-ever maternal impulses Ythiel possessed. By his birth, Resar gave her entree to the Order of the Lady and the possibility of a future outside of Highfields should she so desire. Obligingly he survived infancy and grew to where he could inherit in the event of some catastrophe. That was all she desired and was, in fact, what she thought due her. Accepting that, she devoted herself to conducting the rites of the Lady perfectly and to maintaining an endless correspondence with the Residence and with other ladies on distant estates.

Resar had been raised with great affection by many people whose duties lay in and around the Children's House and, later on, the training fields. He had in many ways been quite happy. But the Lady Ythiel, his mother, had never once looked at him in the way that he craved. He had tried myriad activities, good and bad, to make her regard him with maternal interest or concern. He would have been happy had she noticed him at all. But none of his attempts had been successful. A year after Bentar's death in the epidemic she had gone on pilgrimage to the Residence of the Order and never returned. By then it did not matter: Amrith had assumed his inheritance and Resar was preparing himself for a commission in the Rangers.

Resar had also roused himself from daydreaming when Bentar spoke of his own childhood. Then, listening respectfully, he had felt a part of Highfields, and he could indulge his own love of the mountains and the beautiful estate they sheltered. Although he never had the intensive training given Amrith, he had learned on his own all the parts of Highfields and how they fit together. It was a working knowledge that came from talking to and helping its people as they went about their jobs. He loved nothing better than listening to stories of its past and how Bentar had grown up in the same place but in a different time. It was easier than hearing his father plan a future for Highfields that did not include the second son. Whether lost in the tapestry's design or in his father's stories, Resar could forget that some day he would have to leave the valley and give up all that he had come to love.

The tapestry was still there, covering the window of the Small Dining Room. It was worn now but had been cleaned and repaired with loving skill. With a twinge of guilt he searched its faded colors for the hidden faces of his childhood. Then a question from Amrith drew him from his reverie. "We are pleased," he said, "to have you with us again so soon. Will you stay at Highfields until the snows have gone?"

Despite the distance between the brothers, Resar knew the offer was genuine. They were not friends because there had never been any ground on which to build a friendship. Trained strenuously by their father in the obligations of his heritage and position, Amrith had had little time to become acquainted with a brother thirteen years younger. The distance in their ages had also precluded any shared interests or activities. Secure in his position as the heir, Amrith had been unaware of Resar's love for the estate and thus indifferent to his brother's frustration. Resar had, in turn, worn a cool but proper face in front of the brother who had, by accident of birth, inherited the right to everything he desired. To stay here throughout the cold season, however, to observe but never be a part of the estate was intolerable.

"No," he replied, shaking his head, "I plan to leave as soon as possible. The woman and I must travel to Targhum on the way to Wintersfoot."

Callain's perfect oval face became very still. "Surely you can stay a little longer, my brother. Can we not prevail upon you to attend the Rites of Ingathering? You are a son of Highfields after all, and many would be glad of your presence."

Resar curbed his temper: Callain could not know the storm of emotions her well-meaning words had stirred up. "I cannot. The season grows late and we have far to travel. An early snow could close the pass to Wintersfoot before we reach it and strand us on the high road."

"Then you could return here. You know better than most that Highfields is a comfortable estate in even the coldest weather."

Resar opened his mouth to reply but Amrith interjected, "I must admit that I cannot understand your eagerness to spend the cold season in a house little bigger than a hunting lodge. The snows come earlier there and stay later. Besides, it shivers in the shadow of one of the most formidable peaks in the Spine."

Resar wanted to blurt out, "Because it is mine. It is all I have and my small heritage is as precious to me as yours is to you." He checked that bitter answer, however, and took a long swallow of wine instead.

"I was raised in a place like that," Callain stated flatly. "Even here in these heated rooms I cannot take the chill of those stone walls from my bones. How will you manage there alone?"

"The same way Markin and his wife have managed for years. Besides, I won't be alone. Tirnus is coming with me. But to reach Wintersfoot in safety, we must ride soon."

"Ride?" queried Amrith. "Surely you will take a caravan. I will make sure that it is fully provisioned."

"Wagons are too slow and would only hold us back. Our party is small and can move more swiftly by sapeer."

"The barbarian woman cannot ride," interrupted Callain.

"It never occurred to us that she might have to. I will arrange for lessons immediately but it will take at least two span of days for her to learn properly. That brings us almost to the Rites," she continued. "Stay until then, the woman will learn to ride, and I will make sure that your pack animals are provisioned as well as Highfields can provide."

"And when you are ready, I will take a troop of the home guard and escort you to Targhum myself," Amrith finished.

Grudgingly Resar conceded. He would be cutting it close although there was a little more time than he would have them believe. It snowed earlier in the pass than it did in the valley but there was no reasonable alternative. They finished the meal in good spirits but Resar's mind was frequently elsewhere.

After all the drama of his arrival, with Lekh's warnings and Neva's fussing, Resar did not summon her until the next morning. Neva had arrived early to help her bathe and dress carefully. The young woman had spent much time combing Dara's hair, plaiting it, and pinning it up. Then Dara had waited alone while the time inched by and the sun rose higher. Now she followed the messenger nervously. She was thankful that, at least this once, she would be able to face the Ranger Captain with some dignity. She expected to be taken to the great house but instead the messenger led her to an exercise ring near the stables. There she was surprised to find Resar dressed in old, faded riding clothes and waiting for her. With concealed distaste Dara performed the ritual obeisance in which Lekh had persistently schooled her. At least she could be grateful that there was no one nearby—even the messenger had already disappeared—to witness the act of submission. Her knees had barely touched the dust, however, when Resar said gruffly, "Get up."

Dara rose quickly, straightened her shoulders, and looked at him directly. It was his place to speak first but for a moment he surveyed her in silence. This gave her an opportunity to look at him from a different perspective. On first acquaintance, she had been too exhausted and confused to really see him. He had been one of several men, all of them much the same. Now she looked at the brother of the lord of Highfields with fresh eyes. He was big: tall, large-boned, and broad of chest. Skin weathered brown covered muscles that had been hardened by years of hard work and time spent on the back of a sapeer. His hair was black and straight, his eyes a deep moss green. Resar was not handsome; his nose was too broad and had been broken at least once, leaving it slightly crooked. His mouth was also too thin and tight for classic good looks. Yet there was a definite presence about him made up of authority combined with a very strong masculinity. It was a combination that was both compelling and somewhat intimidating. Looking at him, Dara decided that she did not wish to be intimidated. "I am told you now speak a civilized tongue," he said finally.

"I speak two," Dara retorted. "Mine and yours."

Resar was taken aback. Then his mouth twitched at the corners. "I see. Then perhaps you can use mine to explain what happened yesterday."

She flushed with the memory. "I am not sure I understand what happened yesterday, my lord. That man, Vethis, was attracted to me some time ago, at a ceremony for the Lady. I—discouraged—him. I must have done it badly, without courtesy or grace. Many of your customs are still not clear to me and I was ill at ease. The insult to his pride led him to read a challenge where none was intended. So the Harvest Race became much more than a game for both of us. He had to win and I don't like to lose. Twice before yesterday I reached the compound first and that only made things worse. Perhaps I was afraid to lose then. When he finally won, he did it with a vengeance. I did not mean to make him, or anyone, my enemy. Truly. But, as you saw, that's what he has become."

Again there was a slight smile. "I think you understand better than you realize. But he will not bother you again. While I am here you are protected and when I leave, you go with me. It's just as well. Vethis is an angry man and such men offend easily. They make bad enemies."

Dara was silent. His casual statement had changed everything abruptly. *You go with me.* When? Where did they go? Her thoughts churned and she was gripped by anxiety. For the first time she understood how completely he controlled her future.

Resar, however, was unaware of her turmoil. "How did you do that trick?" he asked abruptly.

"What?" Dara could not follow his mental leap.

"In the Shard Hills, when I moved in to take you. You rolled in a certain way and, had you been stronger, I would have gone over you into the canyon. How did you do that?"

"Oh! The *toemoenage*. It is not difficult. I can explain how it works . . ."

"No, show me here."

The paddock in which they stood stretched between the stables and the breeding shed. As it was not breeding season, the animals were all working or in fields outside the compound and there was no activity here. Dara reviewed the painfully short period in which she had studied judo. For the first time she wished that she had worked harder and studied longer. "I cannot begin the lesson with step five," she said. "You must begin at the beginning if you would learn to do it right and without injury."

Accepting the logic of this, Resar nodded. "Then we will begin now with step one."

First Dara demonstrated the correct way to fall by breaking the impact with a sharp slap of both hands. Puffs of dust rose from under her hands and arms as she struck the ground sharply. The she watched as Resar copied her, practicing first while lying on his back, then moving to a squatting position and then to a standing breakfall. By the time he could fall backwards or to either side and break the fall properly, the air was filled with dust and they were both coughing. At that point Dara called an end to the lesson. Her carefully-arranged hair was in disarray and her best dress was filthy. It did not matter. Resar ordered her to change into riding clothes and return to the paddock after lunch so she could begin lessons in riding.

During the following days they went together every day for practice sessions in the paddock behind the breeding shed. Dara obtained a pair of breeches that would fit her and wore them under her skirt. When they began working out she removed her skirt and had the freedom of movement she needed to teach Resar what he wanted to learn. Neva was scandalized but the first time he saw her in breeches Resar threw back his head and laughed. As she guided him through the basic moves, Resar became curious about how a woman could know things that even a warrior of the mountains did not learn. Dara explained about the martial arts and judo, how she had studied it for a year, and what masters of the art could accomplish. He listened in silence and then asked many questions, some of which she could not answer. The year of classes in the dojo seemed far distant. It was difficult to recall all the throws, holds, and chokes although the philosophy her Japanese *sensei* had imparted with them came readily to mind. She taught Resar all she could remember from her brief encounter with an art others studied for a lifetime. Resar paid close attention, absorbed it all, and practiced diligently. In the process he began to regard Dara in a different way. A person emerged where before he had seen only an illiterate ward and an unwanted obligation. The things she told him and taught him only confirmed the fact that she was alien and from farther away than he had first thought. The differences that emerged only made her more interesting in his eyes.

Questions about judo led to questions about her journey to Highfields and her experiences there before his arrival. He seemed content to listen to her accounts of daily life on the estate as she had observed it from an outside point of view. Resar was particularly interested in her stories about people, although he displayed no concern for any one individual. The only thing he never probed was her life before their tumultuous encounter in the Shard Hills. An unspoken rule declared that subject taboo and she was herself not eager to talk about her old life. Dara preferred to keep those memories very private as if sharing them would somehow dilute their intensity and make them fade away. Their talks were very interesting, however, and she enjoyed them. They gave her an opportunity to listen and learn something about the stranger who could change her life or her well-being with a command. He had a dry sense of humor and an easy manner that diminished the distance

between their positions. His sense of honor was deeply
ingrained and she sensed a strong ambition held so carefully in check that he did not seem aware of it. As he
became more familiar, her early dislike of him disappeared
and they developed a cautious friendship that each was
careful not to threaten.

Dara looked forward to their conversations for another
reason: it was exhilarating to have someone besides Neva
and Lekh with whom she could share ideas. For all her
eager helpfulness, Neva was young and inexperienced.
She had never been far from Highfields and her perspective was limited. Lekh, on the other hand, was old and
taciturn. Because he was poorly educated and had spent
much of his life in service, his conversation was limited to
first-hand experience and observations. Resar was someone who had traveled with the Rangers, had seen many
things, had developed opinions, who could kindle her
imagination. In their pursuit of an idea she could sometimes forget that she was subservient and nothing in his
manner, beyond an inborn acceptance of privilege, reminded her.

After they had practiced steadily for many days, furrow-
ing the dust of the paddock, Dara became increasingly
aware of his physical presence. From the beginning she
had been conscious of his hard, muscular body in such
necessary proximity to hers and that sensitivity increased
daily. She felt his strong hands moving surely in the grips
and lifts she taught him. Her own considerable strength
was as nothing compared to his arms which were as solid
and unyielding as stone. She felt the weight of his eyes,
green and cool as malachite, watching her. Even the earthy
smell of his body and the musky odor of male sweat
surrounded her. This purely physical reaction to him un-
nerved her. Survival on Khyren was no longer her primary
concern. The basic needs for food, clothing, and shelter
had been met. There was time now and room enough for
different needs, acutely felt but not so readily satisfied.

Between their practice sessions and intensive riding
lessons, Dara ended each day exhausted from non-stop
exercise and yet she often had trouble falling asleep. She
lay awake, aware of every pore in her skin, feeling every

curve and hollow of her body. When sleep finally descended, it was interrupted by vivid and confusing dreams. In them, her husband embraced her and smiled, only to become someone else when she returned the embrace. She found herself holding Amrith, Tirnus, Resar, Vethis, even men she had only seen. They responded ardently and she awoke from these dreams flushed, throbbing, and unfulfilled. Then, lying in the darkness and listening to the night sounds, a carousel of conflicting emotions whirled through her mind. While her emotions were still committed to a man separated from her by light years, her body sought more immediate gratification. A man in her position would not have had second thoughts about what to do. At the same time she was still confused about many of the customs in the mountains. The ceremony in the cavern had demonstrated that it was not an inhibited culture but memories of that night both excited and repelled her. Although she still had no need for the stack of soft cloths Neva had placed in the chest, she feared risking pregnancy on a world with such primitive medical facilities. A repeat of her first delivery could kill her here. She was drawn to a man who showed no attraction to her and yet had alienated the only man to seek her out. One by one the thoughts passed before her, each leading to the next until the first ones came around again. The circle continued without peace or resolution as the night drew on. Aching and confused, Dara rode the mad carousel of her thoughts until the pale light of dawn.

The instant the sky lightened, field birds awakened and began to sing a fluted melody. As their notes rose and mingled, a weary despair suffused her. It was the beginning of another day to get through. Another day to keep the mask of normalcy firmly fixed over the tumult within. Another day to work through with aching muscles, little sleep, and no chance of rest. For a while she dwelt in the hopeless state that slips so easily and so totally in between the last hours of night and the morning's first moments. In that awful time she felt most alone, irreversibly out of place, a stranger in a remote country. Always then she doubted whether she had the strength to make it through the coming day. She hated those birds.

Once she was up, the anomie receded and she could put it in its rightful perspective. It was the morning that she both dreaded and anticipated, however. There was Resar close by and touching her, yet seemingly oblivious to her as a woman. She decided that he must still see her as the skinny androgynous creature he had captured and not the woman who shivered with desire in his hands. That was the only explanation she could accept for his indifference to the heat that burned her and that she could not control even with the firmest effort of will. She was not an inexperienced girl trying to come to grips with her feelings. Dara knew exactly what she wanted and logic dictated that she make her desires known. Then he would either accept her invitation or not. Logic told her that over and over but she could not do it. There were too many other factors inhibiting her from taking such an action. He was a nobleman who could and probably did have his pick of any woman in the compound. Why should he find her attractive? Worse, he controlled her life and her future. How could she alienate him? Then came the most frightening reason of all: he might refuse her and she could not stand the possibility of rejection. It would be devastating. So she made no overtures and kept her desires as much under her control as possible.

Each afternoon Dara threw herself into the riding lessons as a safe and neutral outlet for her tensions. It was difficult to remember all the commands—head up, back straight, heels down, elbows in, lean back, pull, let out the reins, grip harder—but she worked hard and tenaciously until she had mastered the art of handling a sapeer moving at any speed on either two or all four legs. By day's end she was proud of her accomplishments, feeling the uncomplicated satisfaction of a skill learned and effort rewarded.

After approximately two weeks of their daily judo classes, Dara decided it was time to teach Resar *toemoenage*, the throw he had asked to learn. Step by step she explained the throw and how it used an attacker's own forward momentum against him. With complete concentration, Resar practiced the maneuver until Dara's own stomach ached and she was exhausted from being thrown repeatedly.

With determination, Dara thought that being *uke*, the partner who was thrown, was usually more demanding than being *tori*, the partner who practiced the throw. By the time they finished she was limp but Resar was showing proficiency. As she dusted herself off he spoke casually. "This must be our last lesson for a while. Tomorrow I must help my brother to assemble the tithe and we also begin preparing for the Rites of Ingathering. On the day after, we leave." Dara stopped brushing and stared at him. He looked back in surprise. "Surely you knew that we were leaving."

"Yes, my lord."

"Are you not even curious about our destination?"

She nodded. "I'm curious."

He turned to walk off and she hastened to keep up. "We ride to Wintersfoot, my holding higher up in the Spine. It has been so long . . ." His voice drifted off, then he collected himself. "On the way, we stop at the city of Targhum where lives Kureil the Healer. Do you remember him from Festival?" She nodded again. "When he tended you there he became curious about the scar you bear. There are questions about it he would like to ask you. And about some other things as well. I promised that I would help him do that. It is for that reason you came here to learn our language and the ways of the mountain people. Now I must ask you to help me honor that promise. Will you ride with me to Targhum and speak to Kureil?"

Dara gaped at him in astonishment. "Why do you ask, my lord? I belong to you. Surely you may do with me what you wish, take me where you wish!" She did not realize until the words spilled out how much that knowledge had rankled. "If you wish me to speak to Kureil, then I must do so."

Resar's emerald eyes flashed and outrage showed on his face. "By Neldarin's Sword!" he exclaimed, "that was only a legality. Has no one explained that to you? Perhaps your people hold slaves beyond the Singing Sands but we of the mountains do not! What slaves have you seen here? By my own actions I took upon myself responsibility for your welfare. In honor I could not have done otherwise. But no one here belongs to another. You are a free person and I ask you now if you will travel with me of your own free will."

"The Singing Sands?" Dara felt suddenly slow-witted, as if trying to converse in a dream where the subject changed before she could respond. "What have I to do with the Singing Sands?"

"Is that not where your people are?"

"No. Is that where you think I come from?"

Confused himself, Resar nodded. "Of course, but it would have been a great discourtesy to ask."

Dara looked up at the mistbound sky which now glowed with diffuse sunlight. She wished that it was a clear night with the Milky Way visible in its brilliant proximity. "My home is somewhere up there. I grew up under a different sun in a system far out on one of the galaxy's spiral arms. My world is the third planet from a small star that we probably couldn't see even on a clear night."

There was a long pause. Both of them now felt that the conversation had gone too quickly from the commonplace to the extraordinary. "The stars? A different sun? But how!"

"If I knew that, I might be able to figure out how to get back. But since I came here because of some cosmic accident, I don't think that will ever happen."

"How do you know it was an accident?"

"There was a man at Festival who spoke my language and he told me." Her forehead knotted in confusion. "I thought for a long time that he was an hallucination but he did tell me things I couldn't have known in a dream."

"If you come from the stars, how could a man at Festival have known your language? You must have been dreaming."

"Yes, my lord. You are right. And I do have vivid dreams sometimes. Where did you get the idea that I was from this place called the Singing Sands?"

"At Festival. It was wine talk; everyone knew. I wouldn't be concerned about it, rumors start easily at Festival."

"Festival. Interesting."

They stopped outside the approach to the big house There was nothing else to say but both of them had much thinking to do. "I must prepare," said Dara, "if I am to ride to Targhum on the day after tomorrow."

"Now, on this last item, Scaure, have you completed a strategy?"

Once again the aide delivered his report, but this time the two men talked as they strolled through the ring gardens. All around them—extending all around the city—stretched magnificent beds of flowers. Brilliant shades mingled with pastel hues, full disks with tiny starbursts, dangling bells with thrusting spikes. The perfume of the massed plants drifted heavily in the evening air, insinuating itself with every breath. Growing in seemingly wild profusion, assembled around terraced walks and leaning over rambling pathways, the flowers were in fact carefully nurtured and cultivated by dedicated gardeners. The wild effect was the result of careful planning over years of trial and observation. The ring gardens provided an environment designed for meditation and exploration of the mental arts. They were a spectacular sight and an invaluable resource and they would have been famous from one pole to the other had anyone outside of the Lost City known of them.

Martus had decided that if he had to stand while listening to Scaure's detailed reports, a walk in the perfumed twilight would make the task more pleasant.

"Indeed, Your Grace, a plan for dealing with the alien woman required no great thought. In three days Captain Resar ak'Hept Bentar will finish with his tour of duty in the Rangers. He will depart with an ultimate destination of his hereditary farmholding at Wintersfoot. On the way, he will most likely make several stops. During the first stop, at his brother's estate of Highfields, the woman will join his party. If my sources remain accurate, and I have no reason to believe otherwise, they will go next to Targhum where Kureil, Chief Healer of the Mountain District, waits to satisfy his curiosity. The road from Highfields to Targhum passes through some of the Spine's more unsettled valleys where gormrith bandits have been known to prey. A brief skirmish, an unfortunate accident, and the woman will never reach Targhum. By the next dawn there will be nothing left but bones."

Martus pondered this strategy for several long moments. A light breeze set the flowers stirring and nodding, loosening a fresh burst of scent. It bothered him that Scaure could speak so calmly of treachery and murder while surrounded by vibrant life and beauty. It was an illogical reaction, he knew, for the intrigues themselves were commonplace and flowers also have their time to die. But although he had killed, and arranged for others to kill at his orders, Martus had never accepted it with such impassive equanimity. "And how do your sources explain why the Chief Healer is so anxious to question this woman? Kureil is not known for an interest in comparative sociology."

"Quite so, Your Grace. One of the journeyman healers spoke freely to the Resident Oben in Targhum. Rumor says that the female bears upon her abdomen a mark left by past surgery, a straightforward operation for the purpose of delivering a child not exactly eager to be born. Since the secret of surgery has always evaded the Healers, as has the secret of anaesthesia, they hope to learn from her. For obvious reasons, we cannot permit this."

Martus felt a twinge of annoyance cross his brain but it never went as far as his expression. Then it was gone, dismissed along with any other emotions that could give away what was going on behind his deceptively placid countenance. "Quite correct, Scaure. But for less obvious and more compelling reasons, this woman may be far more important to the Brotherhood alive than dead."

Scaure stopped in mid-stride and faced his superior. For the thin space of a breath, unguarded, he was speechless. Strategy, with its accompanying grasp of detail, sequence, and execution, was his specialty. It was extremely rare for Martus to detect any flaw or error in his plans. Generally, he presented, Martus approved, and he proceeded with the execution. Scaure found the current situation unpleasant and more embarrassing than he would allow. He suspected that the Counsel Regent was enjoying it and he would have been even more mortified had he known that his surmise was quite correct. Despite the setback, Scaure recovered quickly. He had no choice; after all, he had missed something important.

"I beg pardon, Your Grace," he said stiffly. "Do me the

honor of explaining these reasons so that I may alter my strategy accordingly."

"Certainly. Rule 15 of the Code instructs us to make the fullest use of all available resources. Rule 9 admonishes us to waste nothing. There is no room in our philosophy for waste of any sort. This woman is, indeed, a threat to us but she is also a valuable resource in at least two ways. First, she is from off-world and holds none of Khyren's parochial superstitions and prejudices. Second, and far more important, if her claim to have given birth surgically is believed, it will make her unique on the planet—a person of great stature and even reverence. It is inevitable that the Order of the Lady will seek her out and use her to increase their own power. Think, Scaure, extrapolate! If she espoused our views, if she could be manipulated, if she could be planted . . ."

"Yes! How could I have missed it?" Scaure's irritation was banished by the sudden excitement of this brilliant concept. Once again he realized that for all his stodgy manner Martus had a first-rate mind. Periodically it rewarded Scaure's patience with a flare of genius. "With the right approach, the right techniques, she could do or say or be anything we wanted of her." His eyes gleamed with eagerness. "To do that—and to be sure we succeed beyond any threat of detection—we need to have her here."

Martus gazed benevolently at a large white blossom. He had known how Scaure would react to his idea and he had not been disappointed. The details of this plan would now involve Scaure fully and his aide would not be satisfied until every point of the strategy was examined, perfected and carried out flawlessly.

Suddenly the younger man looked up with a nearly imperceptible crease in his forehead. "We cannot bring her to the Lost City by the usual method."

With a serious but noncommittal sound, Martus acknowledged the concern. "I have the utmost confidence in your ability to turn that obstacle into an advantage," he replied. Scaure nodded briefly and returned to his silent plotting. The Counsel-Regent looked up and observed that the sun had long since slipped below the rim of the crater. It was nearly dusk; time to leave the gardens to those with greater need for them, those for whom the gardens had been created.

When preparation for the ingathering rites began in earnest the next day, everyone worked long and hard. Many of the critical tasks, such as hunting to add game to the larders, had already begun, but even so the pace picked up. Isolated and largely self-reliant, Highfields was normally a busy place whether in the compound or in the fields. Now, however, it was impossible to find a quiet place and wherever Dara walked something was happening. Domestic animals were slaughtered in the outbuildings amid a welter of grunts and squeals. Haunches of meat and wild carcasses were hoisted in the smokehouse nearby to cure over slow fires of tung-sat, an aromatic tuber grown in abundance for the tang it imparted. In the big kitchens, other cuts were ground finely, mixed with herbs and diced suet, then stuffed into sausage casings. Strings of them would hang from the rafter all during the cold passages, weeping fat and concentrating their flavor.

Root vegetables were carefully layered in beds of fine sand built into the storage sheds. Produce was stripped from the kitchen gardens and separated. What was not set aside for the feast to come was diced, chopped, shredded, sliced, or cubed before being either pickled, preserved, or simmered into sauce. Grain was threshed and stored away in huge pottery crocks. Fruit combed from the orchards was potted or pureed into jam. Thus is was possible to walk through the compound and smell the harvest, from the metallic scent of fresh-spilled blood to the sweetness of simmering preserves. The combined sounds were indescribable and lasted well into the night.

By the walls, barns were readied for winter occupancy and bales of fodder were stacked into their lofts. The hair shorn from animals in the spring and several varieties of fibrous plants were brought to the storage sheds of the weavers' hall. Over the snow-bound days ahead it would be cleaned and carded, then dyed and woven into fabric of all sorts. It was all the normal work of a large farm provisioning itself for survival until the next growing season. But the urgency that drove everyone through this advent

period had a religious motivation that contributed to the
fervor. Custom backed by religious law dictated that all
jobs had to be completed by dawn on the day of the rites.
Field and orchard must be bare, every task completed,
every board nailed down, every kettle scoured clean when
the sun rose. In addition, a sizeable amount of the harvest
had to be set aside for what Resar had called the tithe and
he spent all his time with Amrith seeing to this time-
consuming task.

Dara did not understand either the reason behind the
religious law or the emotion of those who obeyed it and
she doubted that anyone could explain them logically.
Neva tried but found it impossible. Dara sighed and reminded herself that religion is frequently illogical for,
when logic exists, faith is not required. It was no different
on Khyren than it had been on Earth. Even so, she
enjoyed the frenetic activity. A child of the suburbs, she
was excited and fascinated by the provisioning and helped
out whenever an opportunity occurred. That meant she
worked nearly as hard as everyone else. What thrilled her
most was knowing that all the work was necessary if the
people of Highfields were to be fed and clothed properly.
Any miscalculation would be felt deeply and could not be
remedied with a quick trip to the supermarket.

Now that all lessons were suspended, plunging into the
work also made it easier for her to ignore the frustration
that tormented her. She could forget, as well, that in a few
days Callain would expect her to perform a major league
miracle on command. Dara still did not know where that
particular magic was going to come from or how to put on
a good act when it did not appear as scheduled. While
kneading bread or up to her elbows in piccalilli, she reassured herself that an inspiration would come and she
would make it through the ceremony without a disaster.
But as the days rolled by and her body labored industriously, her mind seemed to work not at all. It was numb
and refused to consider the problem. As the time passed,
as she grew more worried and sleep evaded her, Dara's
appearance became haggard and drawn. Neva fussed at
her continually but could not help because she did not
understand the problem. How could Dara explain it when

it flew in the face of the woman's religious beliefs? Worse, how could she even mention it when her friend had come to accept what so many others believed—that Dara was capable of extraordinary actions.

Even in ignorance, however, the young woman's resourcefulness was surprising. When only two days remained before the rites, Neva approached Dara as she sat stripping rubbery husks off large black ko nuts. Neva's eyes were as sparkling as they usually were when Amrith was nearby, and she danced about lightly, unable to keep still. "Oh, Dara, guess what!" she exclaimed. "It's so wonderful, I can't believe it."

Dara put one hand protectively on the full basket of nuts at her feet to keep from losing the morning's work to her friend's restless feet. Then she smiled at her antics. "I couldn't possibly guess why you're so excited."

"I talked to my lady about you—you know how worried I've been. You're so thin and there are awful rings around your eyes. Oh, I understand why, you know. Going off to a strange place with no other woman for company. That would upset anyone."

Dara's mouth sagged open in astonishment but Neva was so involved in her news that she didn't notice. "So I explained the problem to my lady and she had the most wonderful suggestion: I'm coming with you! To Wintersfoot. Is that not truly wonderful? Of course, it's only for a year . . . even I know that I'm too young to stay there for a long time . . . but, still!"

Dara smiled incredulously, then giggled, then laughter began to roll out of her in waves. With no comprehension of the real problem, Neva had formed her own conclusion and then acted on it. While the idea was naive and reflected her own concerns, it was perfectly reasonable. She had obviously spent a great deal of time thinking it all through before taking it to a higher authority. At the sound of laughter when Dara had been withdrawn for so long, Neva became even more effervescent. To her, Dara's levity rose from the relief and delight she would have felt in the same circumstance. It proved to her the accuracy of her surmise and applauded her solution. That added to the considerable excitement she felt at the prospect of her first sojourn into the real world outside the valley.

When Dara caught her breath and wiped the tears of laughter from her eyes, she realized that Neva had analyzed the situation more accurately than she knew. The prospect of her company on another long trip across Khyren was indeed comforting. "How did you persuade the Lady Callain to agree to such an idea?"

"Oh, it was not as hard as I had expected," Neva replied guilelessly. "I just reminded her that no mountain woman of any stature can travel respectably without at least one female companion. You may not have had stature when you came to the mountains but you certainly do now. Besides, your position now reflects upon hers so she has an interest in seeing that you are provided for well.

"Also, I mentioned how lonely it can be spending the whole of the cold passages in a remote and unfamiliar house. My lady remembers only too well what that is like, having come here not so long ago from a holding far less comfortable than Highfields. When I had finished, she agreed that you need a companion and, since I've spent more time with you than anyone else has, she obviously thought of me first. She also mentioned that it would be good for me to experience life somewhere outside of Highfields before I go on pilgrimage for the first time. So she decided, and I'm going with you!"

To say nothing of getting you as far away from her husband as possible, thought Dara wickedly. She could not blame Callain for protecting herself, however; it was what she would have done herself, customs being what they were here. Amrith would eventually notice Neva's infatuation and Callain wanted to be safely pregnant with the heir when he did. A dalliance after the fact would be negligible to her.

"I can't stay with you too long," Neva rushed on, "only until snowmelt. I'll be needed back here as soon as the passes clear. Still, that gives us a long time. Right now there's so much to do. You'll have to help me pack, Dara, since you're almost ready yourself."

Dara nodded and listened with an amused ear to Neva's chatter and continued shucking nuts. Once she got through the ceremony in the cavern—somehow—she would be away from her awkward position here and off to a different environment where no one would call her "karait" and expect her to perform magic.

The days passed quickly until the morning of Ingathering dawned cold and murky. For the hundredth time Dara wished that it would snow and get it over with, if only to clear the air. She was tired of peering through the perpetually thickening mist, seeing less every day. Heavy frost rimed every roof, fence, and leaf and dampness lingered everywhere. Nothing dried or felt warm and even the trees drooped. If it weren't for the geothermal heat in the buildings, she thought that this season would be intolerable. Sounds were normally muffled by the heavy air but on this morning, Highfields was silent. After the weeks of noisy, hectic activity, the early morning stillness seemed unnatural. It stretched on past dawn as people, drugged by exhaustion, awakened late from the well-earned rest.

Gradually figures emerged, stretching and yawning, and gathered in the dining hall where steam heat and a strong fire at each end drove away the dampness. Platters of food prepared the day before were carried in from the larders by willing helpers. From johnny cakes to meat pies, cold roast fowl to fruit tarts, there looked like enough to last for weeks. Dara selected some, sampling cautiously the seasonal specialties which she had not tasted before. People came and went without the usual sense of purposeful activity. It was a quiet kind of celebration.

As the day drew on, however, musical instruments appeared and were tuned meticulously. Slow intricate melodies, love songs, and ballads drifted in the air. People sang or hummed along as the spirit moved them and the mood of the holiday lightened. In the afternoon, kegs of aged enzaitha were set out in the dining hall and in several other buildings as well. This dark and sparkling drink was fermented from the seed pods of the versatile zaith plant, then mixed with heady spices. Its brewing was an art jealously supervised by the master cook, who was justifiably proud of his product. Because it was so potent, enzaitha was reserved for holidays and for medicinal use. It was, however, one of the beverages that Dara simply could not keep down and so she avoided the mugs of it that were thrust in her direction. Instead she wandered quietly about, listening to sad songs and merry ones, watching the dancing when it began, and trying to keep her mind off the evening. No brilliant ideas had come to her and she was still as confused about what to do as she had been in Callain's chamber. When she spotted Lekh, solidly enthroned next to a fresh keg, she went and sat beside him for a while. He already knew she was leaving, as well as her destination, so they had little to discuss, but Dara wanted to thank him for his perseverance in teaching her and for his assistance. It proved difficult.

"Don't thank me," he protested grumpily. "I did what my lord told me to do, as I have always done and will do for so long as I am able."

"I understand that, Lekh, and I respect your loyalty. But no one ordered you to be kind to me and you were." Lekh humpfed into his mug and said nothing. "Without you, everything would have been more difficult. And it was usually hard enough." She took his twisted hand and squeezed it gently. That was as forward as she dared get with the old man although she would have liked to hug him. He turned and smiled at her in return and the smile was in his eyes as well as on his lips. Then a burly field hand came to fill his mug at the spigot and Lekh turned to speak with him. Dara rose and left the hall.

With one farewell out of the way, she went to take care of another. She found Sandy in the kennels with the other coursers, temporarily abandoned by the pack handler. While the rest of the animals slept or paced about, however, he stood motionless facing the door, as if expecting her. Dara was not surprised. Sandy slipped out of the kennel with her and they went to one of the stables where they could sit quietly together on bales of fragrant hay. As always, Dara talked to the animal as if he were human and he listened in the same fashion. As she explained the upcoming journey she regretted even more Resar's decision not to take Sandy with them. His reasoning was simple and logical: they would be staying for several days in Targhum where there would be no room for the beast. And if the snows fell early, it would be **hard** going for him through the pass to Wintersfoot. So he had decided that Sandy should remain at Highfields for the cold season and then accompany a supply wagon to the lodge after the thaw.

Dara wrapped one arm around Sandy's neck and pulled him close, unaware that even an experienced handler would have thought carefully before taking such a liberty. With her, the courser only rested his great head on her knee so that she could scratch under the thick fur on his neck. How much he understood of what was happening, Dara did not know. She suspected that it was more than most people would allow. She would miss his company and his protection and once again she wished that he was coming with them. When she took him to the kennel, Sandy went back inside easily enough but then he turned and watched her until she was out of sight. His vigilance made her feel uneasy, as if he could sense something ominous, something that was imperceptible to all the humans about him. With a sigh, Dara went to check her baggage and Neva's one more time. Tomorrow they would leave Highfields.

The ritual of fertility that ended the Feast of Ingathering was the same as it had been on the Feast of the Lady earlier. Following its detailed steps helped to lift the apprehension Dara had been feeling for days. The tenseness drained out of her in the anteroom as the hot mineral water loosened tight muscles and replaced the stress with a pleasant relaxation. When she was spotless and ready to enter the main cavern, Dara felt more at ease than she had for a long time. After days of thought she had finally come to terms with doing what was necessary and not worrying about the consequences. Having reached that point, it was easy to enter into the infectious good humor of the others participating in the ceremony. Neva, who had been suffering under the burden of her friend's somber mood, was delighted by the change and she encouraged it by assembling a group of happily chattering people to help them celebrate.

Dara's belated good spirits were bubbling when the group around her fell silent as Callain and Amrith entered the room simultaneously from their separate chambers. As usual, Neva's eyes lit up at the sight of Amrith and she sighed unconsciously. Behind the lord of Highfields walked his brother, Resar. At the sight of his solid figure, Dara's spirits rose even higher. His presence lent her strength and made her feel less vulnerable to Callain's imperious demands. It would be days yet before Callain realized how limited Dara's "power" was and Wintersfoot was far enough away from her almost certain anger.

At the same time, Dara found Resar's presence at this feast both exciting and unsettling. In spite of the fact that he had never done anything to arouse her, she had desired him for too long to react calmly when he stood nearby clothed only in a ceremonial robe. She was only too aware that he was courteous to her and friendly, but no more. He was a temptation to which she could not succumb and an appetite that she could not satisfy. While she stood daydreaming, Neva took her arm and together they walked closer to the nobles gathered around the ritual brazier. Three people awaited her but all she could see were the dark hairs curling damply on Resar's chest and the swell of muscles stretching his tanned skin. This infatuation is dangerous, she thought. His body was distracting her when she should have been concentrating on how to play a role well enough to convince the people around her, but she could not suppress the desire that rose inside her. She put aside the question of what she would do when the ceremony was complete and he partnered another woman.

The chamber hushed to total silence and Callain began her invocation in an archaic form of the language that Dara could not comprehend. When the chant was finished, she scattered a handful of dried herbs on the glowing coals and they went up in a bright flare of blue-green flames and a plume of smoke. As the familiar pungent smell filled the air, Dara turned her head to avoid inhaling it. She was so close to the brazier, however, and the odor was so pervasive, that it was impossible not to take it into her lungs. Within seconds, its medicinal tang cleared her head and expanded within it, making her feel light and exhilarated. A moment later she was filled with strength and determination, capable of everything. Her senses intensified. Blood raced in her veins and every pore of her skin vibrated with sexuality. Her breasts tingled and the nipples hardened.

She could feel the length of Resar's body nearby as if it were touching her.

Around them the chamber reverberated with the energy of the people it contained; each one looking, waiting, anticipating an encounter with forces beyond their understanding. Their barely-controlled excitement was like an electrical charge that made the hair on Dara's arms and neck rise. The drug, she realized quite clearly, was not the depressant she had supposed it to be. Instead, it was for her a mood enhancer—and her mood now was far different from what it had been the first time. She breathed deeply and her nostrils flared. A strange glow, more felt than seen, hovered on the very edge of her perception and she became aware of an unusual sensation. Without conscious thought, Dara knew that she had become a symbol and more to all the others participating in the ceremony. In this ceremony she was the personification of their urge to union, the embodiment of their compulsive search for fertility, the avatar of their collective desire.

Resar placed a hand on her shoulder and she shivered beneath his touch. He pushed gently, guiding her to where Callain waited, and Dara walked the few steps as if weightless, yet each one seemed to take hours. As she moved the glow became stronger. It was pure radiance pulsing with color and it was around and within her at the same time. While its source was invisible it could definitely be felt. Benevolent and nurturing, that source was both comforting and stern. In her altered state of consciousness Dara understood that only one entity could generate such a aura: she whom they called the Lady was present at this ceremony in her honor. Then Dara stood before Callain and in a perfect crystal moment only the two women and the unseen presence existed. The warm concern and the protectiveness that she had felt when pregnant surged within her, flowing down her arms and into her fingertips. All that she did then, unrehearsed, felt right and natural. Slowly, but without hesitation, Dara placed both hands on Callain's head, then touched lightly her breast and belly. For those few special moments she and Callain were held within the Lady's aura, outside of time and circumstance.

Then the glow faded, the moment passed, and Dara's hands fell to her side.

With absolute clarity Dara understood why during the previous days she had not been able to plan her actions. Thought was not required here and logic had no place. Feelings and emotions ruled instead. Now her task was done and her duty was discharged: she could see to her own needs. Dara turned toward Resar. Though her shawl had fallen unheeded to the floor, she was clothed in confidence and an ineffable, primal beauty. Her actions were sure and certain as she approached him. Dara neither knew nor cared how she appeared or what he thought. As she reached up to caress his cheek he grasped her roughly by the arms. His piercing green eyes were dilated and unfocused. They were all she saw before he pulled her to him.

CHAPTER 8

On the road to Targhum, Dara rode with Neva who was so excited to be going somewhere, anywhere, that she fairly danced in the saddle. Dara was also filled with an ebullience that made the misty day seem bright and glowing. Although Resar was riding out of sight with his brother at the head of the column, she could still feel him next to her. Just thinking of the night before turned her blood effervescent. She had forgotten how important it was to be close to someone else, to feel cherished and protected, if only for a short while. Everything is fine, she thought, feeling very much younger than she had in a long time. Everything will be all right. The words repeated themselves in her head in time to the rhythm of her mount's stride. All-Right. All-Right. Dara could feel the sapeer's rangy muscles working beneath her and its shoulder blades went up and down like organic pistons.

There was nothing beautiful about sapeers. They possessed none of the grace, intelligence, or nobility of the horse. They were ungainly and mostly out of proportion: ears were too small and dark, eyes were too big and light for the rounded heads and pointed muzzles. Even freshly

117

curried, their coats were coarse and ragged. Instead of the
healthy smell of sweat and hay they exuded a musty odor.
Sapeers inspired no songs or stories. They were not bred
for swiftness or beauty. Pride of ownership might extend
to the size of a herd but never to a particular animal. As
was typical of Khyren, they were not even named. Sapeers
were transportation, that and nothing more, and they were
basically interchangeable. Dara smiled and affectionately
slapped the shoulder of her mount, whom she had dubbed
Ratso. A small spray of water rose from his wet and un-
lovely hide. She laughed and Neva, not knowing the cause
of her mirth and not caring, laughed with her. Together
they rode into the morning of another damp fall day on the
flanks of the Spine. Ahead lay a home, a place for her on
this world, a friend, and a man who meant a great deal
more to her than she could even now admit.

Close to mid-day they came to the rim of a bowl-shaped
valley that resembled an enormous sink-hole or a weathered crater. The trail narrowed as it sloped down to the
bottom, where it wandered around great boulders and
between dense stands of trees. Then, only dimly visible in
the mist, it climbed the far wall and exited through a gap.
The bowl was an eerie place, still and timeless. The mist
was thicker here, as if trapped by the depression, but
wisps of it drifted sluggishly about, obscuring the trail and
then revealing it again. Even the air, which smelled of
vegetation, seemed dense and hard to breath.

As if by accord, they all stopped on the rim and looked
down into the ominous circular valley. Resar seemed less
concerned about the unpleasant atmosphere than the topography. Before they could proceed, he and Amrith dismounted and scouted the area thoroughly. It was quiet: no
beast called, no flying creature keened, no leaf rustled.
Even their own mounts stood subdued, as if listening.
Dara shivered in her warm cloak as she watched the
brothers take what precautions they could until, reassured, the men remounted. Resar issued a terse command
and the guards checked their weapons, making certain
that they were ready for use. The column re-formed with
the two women in the middle and Resar riding point.

Almost reluctantly he moved forward, leading them down into the sunken area.

They had all cleared the downslope and were winding slowly through the trees and rocks when the attackers struck. Muffled and hidden by the mist, they came at the column from all four sides at once. As Resar had suspected, it was the perfect site for such an ambush. The bandits hit them suddenly, with military precision, riding animals that looked like a cross between a horse and a gazelle. Brown, with stiffly bristled manes, they sported two short, slim horns on their foreheads. These mounts were lighter, swifter, and more maneuverable than sapeers and they gave their riders a significant advantage. Amrith's men wheeled to meet the attack with the same deadly silence: no energy was wasted on war cries. Then Neva cried out "Gormrith! Bandits!," the spell was broken, and the battle engaged. Immediately the mist-bound woods filled with the clamor of weapons clashing, animals screaming, and men grunting with exertion. From where Dara and Neva sat, closely reining their terrified mounts in the midst of the fighting, it was obvious that the bandits were truly gormrith. Their ragged clothes, mismatched armor, and unkempt appearance left no doubt of the origins. All were outcasts but one, whose face belied the dirt and rags. Neva spotted him first and exclaimed "Vethis!" in astonishment. "Vethis. But how? Why?"

The thin line of their defenders wavered, outnumbered. Dara saw it and cursed the fact that she was unarmed and helpless. Even less than being killed did she want to be taken captive by these hardbitten outlaws. As the fighting surged, Neva wheeled her sapeer toward a stand of trees and sehliki that would cover them. Dara spurred her beast to follow even though it needed no urging to seek safety. The fighting was now between them and the trail back to Highfields; they had no choice but to run for Targhum. As they reached the trees the mist drifted clear and, looking back, the two women caught a vivid picture of the battle. In that moment, Vethis was framed with his sword lifted over an unmounted and unarmed Amrith. Then the weapon sliced down and the lord of Highfields fell in a spray of blood. "My lord!" exclaimed Neva, pulling up her mount.

Dara reached over and slapped the animal's rump hard.
"Forget him," she ordered despite her own leaping fear
for Resar. "Ride!" They bolted off, riding low on their
sapeer's necks, dodging looming obstacles in a headlong
race to safety in a city they had never seen.

They dared not leave the trail to hide: getting lost would
have been only too easy. Besides, Dara suspected that
these men could find a fieldmouse in a hayloft at midnight.
Speed and a good head start were their only hopes. They
breasted the far end of the valley and headed upward
toward the next pass at a dead run. They rode until their
mounts were black with sweat and lather streamed from
the beasts' mouths. It was a hell-for-leather all-out effort
but it wasn't enough. Mounted on animals both swift and
fresh, the bandits caught up with them before they reached
the pass. Seemingly without effort, they paced the exhausted sapeers on their blood-spattered mounts and a
bandit grasped each bridle. Only too glad to stop, the
beasts staggered to a standstill and stood trembling and
heaving.

Dara sat on Ratso in grim silence. Until she understood
what was going to happen next she would draw no undue
attention. Above all, she wanted to avoid antagonizing
warriors still gripped by the heat of battle. Their eyes
gleamed with green fire and their hard smiles were trium-
phant. Neva, however, was outraged by what had happened and by what she had seen. She hissed defiance at
all of them and shook off Dara's restraining hand with fury.
Her greatest venom she saved for Vethis when he pulled
up his mount in front of them. The thin smile on his face
infuriated the younger woman. "Filth!" she hurled at him.
"Traitor! I should have smelled you before the ambush."

His lips twitched sardonically. "A pity for the rest of
them you didn't." Vethis was in an oddly buoyant mood
but underneath his elation lay a sharpened blade that Dara
had encountered before. She shuddered. The circumstances
were different now; the control lay in his hands. He was
unyielding. He was determined. He was death.

Neva was blind. "You've killed your lord. I saw it. And
he was unarmed when you murdered him."

"I revenged my parents and my heritage." His voice was hard. "Only a thief is dead."

"Revenge? He trusted you. You swore him fealty and you owed him your faith."

"I owed him nothing! But I killed him of a certainty. And his brother also." Dara gasped. Vethis looked at her and then turned back to Neva. "Now House ak Bentar is carrion. Without a legitimate heir, Callain cannot hold Highfields: it will be easy prey. When the time is right, I will take back my lands. I just might take her, too. She may be warmer than she looks."

"The Lady Callain is of noble lineage. She would throw herself from a cliff before she would submit to her husband's murderer."

"And how is she to know?" Vethis asked quietly. Dara caught the menace in his voice but Neva seemed oblivious. Dara seized her arm and squeezed but it was useless. The young and inexperienced woman was blinded to the need for caution by her desire for justice.

"I saw. And I'll dance at your execution. They'll throw your body to the kahn-dor-ei."

"Yes, you would like that," he responded in the same still, cold voice. "But I can't give you that opportunity. You're too great a danger to me. And to my plans." He looked at the ruffians around him, then added, "I bear you no ill will so I will make it quick." Before anyone could act, his sword flashed out and in. Impaled on the blade, Neva stiffened, her eyes wide with astonishment. Then the sword was gone and her hands clutched at a geyser of blood spilling from her breast. More blood ran from her mouth. There was a gurgling exhalation and Neva toppled from the saddle with gruesome slowness. As she struck the ground with an obscene thud, her back arched and her heels beat a spastic tattoo on the dirt. After long, silent seconds her body relaxed in death.

Dara screamed involuntarily. Then Vethis turned to her and she felt herself trembling uncontrollably. Never before in her life had she been so afraid of anyone. Not until now, not even facing the stake, had she ever really known what fear was. He wiped the crimson blade slowly on one leg of his filthy pants, then resheathed it. "Your lord is

dead," he said calmly. "I doubt if you'll mourn long but
don't think you're free. You have a new master now, one
who is far more demanding."

"You?" she whispered hoarsely.

Vethis smiled again. "No, not me. But when you meet
him you might wish that you had been friendlier to me."
He put one finger under her chin and raised it. Dara could
feel her gorge rising. "Not that it would have changed
anything: just look at the effort he went to on your behalf."

Appalled, Dara pulled away from his touch and gestured
back toward the valley. She could not bring herself to look
at Neva's corpse. "You mean all that," she asked in astonishment, "all that was to get me?"

Vethis gave a short bark of laughter. "No, not all of it."
He wheeled his mount and signaled for the men to follow.
The bandit holding the bridle of Dara's mount took her
reins. Then he headed off, leading her behind him. Infuriated beyond caution, Dara snatched the reins back and
glared at him with such hatred that he shrugged and
turned away.

They fled at full gallop as though the spirits of the
ambushed were in pursuit. The outcast warriors were too
hardbitten, however, to fear anything less threatening than
an entire troop of Rangers and only the mist swirled
behind them. For what seemed like hours they headed
steadily upward in a disorienting and terrifying ride through
deepening fog and darkness. Trees and boulders loomed
abruptly out of the greyness, avoided at the last minute by
a sudden swerve or leap. Only the riding lessons Dara had
received such a short time before allowed her to keep her
seat.

To minimize the hazards they rode single file, each
beast taking its cue from the one before it. Dara's mount,
nearly played out when they started, went on heart for a
long time but finally reached the end of its reserves.
Exhausted and faltering, Ratso was kept from dropping out
of the line by the relentless whip of the rider who followed
them. His sides heaved laboriously and foam dripped in
ropes from his muzzle. He slowed despite the whip and
became increasingly clumsy until finally he swerved too
late. The sapeer struck his foreleg against a rock with a

crack so sharp it seemed to pierce a hole in the mist. For a
second Ratso froze. Then he crumpled so slowly that Dara
was able to clear the saddle before it struck the ground.
The entire band reined to a stop while Vethis snapped
orders. One warrior dispatched the cripple animal with his
sword, putting an end to its pathetic moaning. Then he
removed all its tack and split it up among several riders.
He himself hacked a bloody haunch crudely from the
carcass and slung it from his saddle. Another man brought
up Neva's mount. Although tired, it had not been carrying
a rider and had some stamina left. Dara swung into the
saddle, wincing as her bruised and chafed skin touched
the leather. Then they were off again on their nightmare
ride uphill at breakneck speed.

It was sunset before they reached the top of the fog
bank. With startling abruptness they burst out of the mist,
emerging into air that was clear, dry, and very cold. Being
able to see again without obstruction was like a gift: Dara
felt as though a blindfold had been removed. Vethis pulled
up to gain his bearings. In the brief respite, Dara drank in
the beauty of their surroundings. Below, the ground fog
swirled like a sea of pearl-grey moonlight. Above them
rose the great range of mountains called the Spine. Jagged, hostile and breathtaking, their stone peaks flamed
gold in the dying sunlight. This was the range Dara had
seen on the way to Highfields as a purple line looming
against the horizon. It had long since been hidden from
the valley by the mists. Above the summits, stars long
obscured burned with growing intensity in the darkening
sky. As always, Dara searched the fringes of the galactic
cluster for the far-away sun of home.

But there was no time: Vethis pointed them toward
their destination. The top of the fog also marked the tree
line. A field of bedrock and boulders lay ahead. Over the
icy rock their mounts picked a way until they reached a
sharply jutting overhang. There, finally, they stopped.
Vethis dismounted and led his mount deep under the
looming rock. The rest of the band and Dara followed suit.
Out of the saddle, her legs trembled from the long hard
ride just as the tired muscles of her mount quivered and
rippled beside her. She was puzzled by the stop until she

saw their destination. Dwarfed by the overhang and hidden in its shadow was a shelter. It was roughly dome-shaped and the same color as the lichen-painted rock wall. When they drew closer, Dara could see it was made of a fabric she had not seen before, quilted and stretched over flexible framework.

They hobbled their mounts in a cul-de-sac to one side of the shelter and unsaddled them. Then each rider gave his beast a thorough rubdown. Dara discovered currying tools in Neva's saddle pack and followed their example, more for the animal's sake than for any logical reasons. When the men were done they stowed their gear carefully and replaced the saddle blankets on the animals for warmth. Then, one by one, they filed through the entrance flap into the shelter.

Within, the tent proved to be much larger than it had first appeared. In addition, Dara was astonished to find that it was bright, warm—and occupied. Although no trace could be seen outside, a fire burned cheerfully in a brazier at the center of the tent. Behind it a man sat cross-legged, watching them enter. He was stocky, brown, and hard-muscled. His clear green eyes were almost hidden behind thick eyebrows that blended into curly black hair. A close-cropped beard covered his chin. Despite her fatigue, Dara straightened up, wondering if this was the man to whom she was being delivered. He paid her no particular attention, however. Vethis stopped across the fire from the stranger and bowed deeply, as if to a superior. "I am Vethis ak'Hept Seveth," he said, as if that explained everything.

"And I am Portifahr," the man replied simply. "Your presence brightens my humble shelter. Be welcome."

"We are honored," Vethis responded formally. With a sigh of fatigue he sank to one of the mats scattered on the floor of the tent. Dara sat along with the others. Portifahr's eyes gleamed as the bloody haunch of meat was slung towards the fire. "Real food!" he exclaimed and busied himself locating and setting up a spit. Soon the spattering of hot fat and the scent of roasted meat filled the tent. While it cooked, Portifahr looked at Dara curiously. She returned his gaze with a steady neutrality. Without looking away he asked Vethis, "Is this the one?"

"Yes," Vethis replied, "that is she."

"And what is she called?"

"Karait," Vethis said shortly.

"Ah. That is most interesting."

Dara was fed up. Vethis was no longer running the show, that was obvious, and he was also not going to kill her. She saw nothing to be gained by sitting passively and letting them treat her like an inanimate object. "My name is Dara," she said coldly, "and I am *not* a karait."

Portifahr's bearded face split in a grin but he did not reply. Instead he turned his attention to the meat and they were soon eating ravenously. Dara had not thought she could eat a rodent of any size, particularly one that she had named and until recently been riding. After Neva's murder, she had not thought that she would ever eat again. But hunger won out and one bite convinced her: it tasted wonderful. For a while nothing could be heard but the sound of chewing. Then Portifahr cut another slice off the roast and looked up at Vethis. "It surprises me that you had time to hunt on the way here," he said smoothly.

"We didn't," Vethis answered. "One of the sapeers went down in the fog. We salvaged what we could."

Portifahr looked dubiously at the steaming meat on his knife, then shrugged and took half of it in one bite. "And the carcass?"

"We left it. In those woods, it will be bones by morning." He paused. "How do we go from here?"

"Carefully, my friend. There are mountains in our path and the cold to consider. As if that were not enough, there are signs that a K'thi is hunting these skies. For a while, at least, we have much to be wary of. Especially shadows."

"Until we reach the far side?"

Portifahr smiled again. "To a K'thi, the Spine is but a stone fence. One side or the other makes no difference: it is all the same sky. I meant only that for a while our path will protect us."

Dara's eyes widened in disbelief. From what she had seen of this range, it was high enough to require oxygen and precipitous enough for technical climbing gear. Crossing it would seem to require a major expedition. Then there was the lack of cold-weather clothing and the inexperience of at least one of the party to consider. That was aside from the danger of avalanche and the formidable-sounding K'thi. Were they mad? She refrained from asking and kept silent. Portifahr looked as if he knew what he was doing and she would find out for herself tomorrow. Meanwhile she had a more urgent need that required going back out into the cold. In another gesture of independence she rose without a word and moved toward the exit. Portifahr looked up and motioned with one hand. A warrior rose immediately to follow her. Dara sighed, but she had not really thought her try for privacy would work. In the frigid night they both relieved themselves without delay.

Back inside, the food settled comfortably in her stomach and warmth tingled in her fingertips. Gradually the need to concentrate on survival receded only to be replaced by hard anger. In one day the few gains she had made on Khyren were gone—because of Vethis. They were hard-won gains, each of them. Now the people who had meant something to her were dead and everything else was gone with them. Once more she was alone, the property of an unknown master who had unleashed Vethis to get what he wanted. As she thought it out, she wanted to seize the sword of the man beside her and strike out at Vethis.

As if he could read her mind, Portifahr turned his calculating gaze on her. They locked eyes and then he drew in his breath. "This one would appear as gentle as a sand burrower," he said evenly. "But if she could have your heart on a spit, Vethis, it would be roasting right now."

Dara stared at him incredulously. How could he have known? Her spirits sank. Whatever his secret, there would be no deceiving this man.

"I guard my heart well," Vethis responded.

If you have one, Dara wanted to add. It was a pointless comment, however. The Khyrenese did not confuse anatomy with feelings. Emotions originated in the brain. Hearts pumped blood.

"That is good," Portifahr stated. "But I will guard the

rest of us." He nodded at the warrior who had followed her outside. "Bind her."

Dara stifled her rage, carefully controlling it and then burying it deep where it could not break loose and threaten her survival. That was what was important now, survival and freedom if she could find a way. Anger was a luxury from this point on. While the man secured her hands behind her back, Dara fixed an icy stare on Vethis. He shrugged and turned away.

Rough hands shook Dara awake and sat her up before she had emerged from the dark tunnel of sleep. Unable to remember where she was, Dara looked groggily around the tent. Her hands were unbound while she oriented herself. Numb and bloodless, they dropped heavily to her sides, the pain of returning circulation rousing her from lethargy. To counter the needle-sharp pangs, Dara knelt with her hands in her lap and began a deep-breathing technique taught by her judo *sensei* as a remedy for fatigue. Across the tent Portifahr, alert as always, watched her without comment. When her fingers could flex normally once again, Dara stood and almost groaned aloud. The muscles of her legs were badly strained and bruised by the wild ride of the previous day. Worse, her rump felt raw and chafed. She breakfasted on cold meat standing up.

When the brief meal was over, Portifahr took a bundle from behind him and opened it. To each person he distributed a packet of folded material. Dara's, like the others, opened into a thin, flexible body suit made of a black silky fabric. The warriors quickly stripped down, donned their suits next to the skin, and then dressed again. Too weary and sore to care about modesty, Dara did the same. The suit covered hands and feet and was hooded, yet had openings for the necessary biological functions. When she was finished only her face remained uncovered: the rest of her body was quite warm, almost snug. Even when they emerged into the icy morning sunlight, the odd thermal suit kept her comfortable.

While the warriors set to work breaking up the camp and packing it away, Portifahr and Vethis disappeared beneath the overhang. They reappeared moments later encumbered by backpacks laden with supplies. Each member of the party, including Dara, received one of these. Hefting hers, she briefly considered refusing to carry it. After all, this was not exactly a voluntary expedition on her part. Then the flare of rebelliousness dimmed and reality won out. What else was left for her but to go with them— and on their terms? She shrugged resignation on again with the backpack. Besides, she was relieved that there would be no more riding. When even the tent had disappeared they were ready to move out. Stripped of tack and blankets, their mounts were released and sent on their way with a crack of hand on flank. Without hesitation the animals scrambled over the rocks and headed down into the mist. Defying their good sense, Portifahr turned and led the way up.

They went slowly, in single file, and four of the warriors climbed with drawn crossbows in their hands and their eyes half on the sky. Portifahr appeared to be leading them toward a sharply-defined notch between two crags. Behind this break loomed other, taller peaks. It was a barren and lonely landscape that made Dara wish suddenly for Sandy, padding at her heels, keeping silent company. She looked back over her shoulder as if to find him but a cluster of boulders hid the mist-covered valley from sight. They continued upward, the vapor of their breath vanishing quickly in the clear, dry air. The crisp atmosphere gave them a feeling of zest, however, and the exercise soon loosened up Dara's stiff muscles. For a while, concentrating on the moment, she almost enjoyed herself. But the climb soon became difficult, taking them over rocks of different sizes and erratic shapes. Although the degree of incline varied, their way led steadily and relentlessly upward. No level spots or downhill stretches eased the effort. Dara would soon have become overheated and started sweating, but the body suit adjusted for the added heat. Despite the exertion, her skin temperature remained constant. Not only did the suit keep her comfortable, it also prevented her from losing moisture through perspiration. Portifahr allowed periodic rest breaks but was always eager to have them on their way again.

Accommodating her slow pace, they reached the notch by late afternoon. At its base was a chasm, an unusual formation made of sheer rock walls rising at least one hundred feet but no wider than ten feet apart. These parallel cliffs began abruptly and wound on into the mountains. Portifahr herded them quickly inside the chasm like a mother hen guarding unruly chicks against a hawk. Two steps inside and the temperature dropped twenty degrees as if the rock walls generated cold. The body suit compensated immediately with a surge of warmth and Dara sensed that it had somehow stored up the heat produced during the climb and was now radiating it back. Two more steps and the warriors disarmed, then shouldered their crossbows. The chasm was dark and unwelcoming but far safer than the slope they had just traversed. Their guide had said, "For a while our path will protect us." This formidable trench must have been what he meant.

Rocks broken off from the walls littered the base of the formation, which was also stone. This debris ranged from fist-size chunks to some boulders larger than a loaded hay wagon. They would make the expedition's journey through the chasm more difficult. But the ground was also nearly level and to Dara's tired legs that compensated for any obstacles. Pressing forward, they walked quickly to take advantage of the remaining sunlight. Even so, it was not long before stars were gleaming in the narrow ribbon of sky overhead and Portifahr called a welcome halt.

With the setting of the sun, a wind picked up and then blew steadily through the chasm. In addition to making eerie noises, it impeded their efforts to set up camp but eventually the tent was pitched and wedged securely between the walls. The weary climbers crawled in gratefully and Dara collapsed. Once the entrance was sealed they pulled back their hoods and unpacked the dinner rations. While chewing a cold, dry meal Dara reflected on the rations and the body suits as well as on the tent which kept them protected and comfortable under adverse conditions. Although both were unobtrusive and appeared simple she knew that they were produced by a technology far more sophisticated than anything she had yet seen in her sojourn on Khyren or even on Earth. Dara was aware that she had been exposed to a limited segment of culture here, yet her observations left little doubt that such a technology was not only unheard of but unthinkable on this planet. She had also watched Vethis closely and in the morning noticed that he had been more surprised than she when the spacious tent had folded into a single compact bundle light enough for Portifahr's backpack. The others may have been familiar with these things or perhaps just taken them more in stride, but Vethis, at least, was experiencing technological innovation for the first time.

All the following day they walked through the chasm, scrambling over and sometimes under fallen rocks. The boulders had a way of twisting and rolling unpredictably underfoot and Dara soon learned not to step on anything it was possible to step over. In between obstacles she was able to look around and examine the surroundings. The walls were fissured and some of these seams held a kind of rock that was darker than that which made up the steep cliffs. Spotting a chunk of it on the ground, she scooped it up and examined it while she walked. It was smoother than the mass of rock around them, more finely grained, denser, and heavier. She thought it possible that the dark rock was of volcanic origin and had once filled the chasm. But the lava dike had eroded more quickly than the igneous rock around it, leaving the steep walls and a few traces of its presence behind. The water that might have accomplished such weathering was long gone, however, and moisture at this altitude was now in short supply. Ordinarily Dara would have expected walls of this kind to be dripping water and lush with moss, or hung with blue-white columns of ice. Instead the rock was bare and dry. Each person packed a supply of water but it was used sparingly. Perhaps, she thought, all the little moisture available was concentrated in the blanket of mist they had left behind.

After a while the path tilted upward again and the incline, combined with the multitude of stone blocks in their path, made for hard climbing. There were times when Dara felt like just sitting down and forcing them to carry her wherever they were going. Though such a rebellion seemed tempting when there was a stitch in her side and her calf muscles ached, she valued her independence too much to actually give in to it. She clung to whatever self reliance she could muster because it was all that she had left to cling to. Even the few possessions in her saddle pack had been abandoned back at the overhang. Whenever help was needed or offered she took it but otherwise refused to ask for assistance. Instead she trudged doggedly along, with tired legs and labored breath, yet taking some small pride in doing it herself. She might be a captive—again—but this time she wasn't helpless and would not be as long as she could stand and move.

The chasm wound its way through the notch but before they reached its end Portifahr turned aside abruptly to climb an even narrower crack. This new path pointed directly toward a double peak that had risen on their left. The path twisted tortuously, forcing the party to edge along sideways at times and to crawl at others. Finally its jagged walls terminated in a slender cave piercing the mountain's flank. Dara stood, chest heaving, and searched the cliff on either side of the cave for handholds or some other sign of the path. She found nothing: the cave was the only way forward. With this sinister gap before them, Portifahr called a much-needed rest break. One by one they propped their packs against the sheer walls and sprawled on fallen rocks. While resting, each climber nursed scraped hands, bruised knees, and torn nails, trophies of the difficult climb. Their thermal gloves protected only against the cold and were not proof against hard stone.

Dara rubbed a bruised index finger and stared avidly around her. The sun was high, sending a thin curtain of yellow between the dark walls. A sharp wind carried the clean scent of mountains and the keening cry of a raptor on the hunt. Bleak as her surroundings were, they vibrated with life in contrast with the blank mouth of the cave ahead of them. It was sinister, devoid of life and Dara did not want to go into its total blackness. The journey up the mountain had taken all of her energy and concentration, leaving no strength to chafe at being a prisoner. She knew that it is hard to rage at fate when each step requires all your thought. Now she was facing a place that forced captivity back on her. There was no alternative and no choice, she would have to go into the dark and minatory hole.

When they had rested, Portifahr stood and addressed them in his rough, matter-of-fact way. "Inside the mountain we will come to a big cavern containing a pool. It's large, more like a lake. Within that cavern you must make no sound if you value your life. Silence will be difficult but one noise—a cry, a grunt, it matters not—can mean your death. Prepare yourselves now; there will be no time inside." The outlaws listened to his warning without comment, then assumed identical postures. Backs straight, legs crossed, hands in their laps, they dropped into trances with what seemed to be practiced ease. Portifahr checked their rigid figures and then picked his way across the crowded ravine to face her. Looking down to where she sat, he said in a neutral tone, "You will need help. The Lake of the Silent River can make even the bravest man's resolve gutter like a candle flame and there is no room for error. Close your eyes and relax. I will make silence as natural as breathing for you." His eyes, a deep sea green, met hers honestly and that encouraged her. She had to trust him.

Portifahr laid his large hands, black in their thermal gloves, on her head and Dara leaned into their solid strength. She breathed deeply at his instruction, heard the wind hooting among the rocks, and then she was elsewhere. Deep within her being she traveled until there was a clear light and a place of quiet where there was no need for speech or sound. Relaxing further, she sank into the stillness and was filled by it. She became part of it, so involved in its slow rhythm that it would have been unthinkable to disturb the silence or interrupt the stillness. It was a wonderful feeling and Dara felt as if all of her consciousness had dissolved and yet been strengthened. After an unmeasurable span of time she disengaged from this inner refuge and slowly drifted back. Once again she heard the wind and the pounding of her heart. Portifahr removed his hands and she felt light, as if she would suddenly rise into the air and float out of the ravine. Dara opened her eyes. All was as it had been except that some of the outlaws were now awake and stretching, flexing their muscles.

Portifahr went to Vethis and repeated the same procedure. Watching them, Dara was amazed to find that it only lasted about five minutes of objective time. The bearded man then returned to his position at the head of the group and opened his pack. From it he removed a translucent cylinder about twelve inches long with a hand grip on one end. A gesture from him sent them all looking into their own packs. Dara located the rod without difficulty and fastened her pack again. Following Portifahr's silent example she twisted the grip and the cylinder glowed with a cold blue-green light. A reverse twist and the light faded. They were ready.

With Portifahr walking point they filed into the cave. Almost in unison the lume-rods glowed on. Dara turned for one last greedy look at the sunlight, then she was around a curve and day vanished as if it had never existed. Within, the air was cold in a still, dead way that was totally different from the exhilarating atmosphere of the slopes. It was suffused with a flat metallic odor that seemed out of place amid primal rocks, bare of any vegetation. Their lume-rods picked out outcrops and projections, making them cobalt, azure, and cyan. But their faces, set off by the thermal hoods, floated corpse-like in the darkness. Dara got a sick feeling at the back of her throat. She was not claustrophobic and no more than normally afraid of the dark. Something about this place made her nervous, however. As they headed deeper into the cave her eyes kept trying to penetrate the darkness and her ears became sensitive to every sound. Solid blackness lurked beyond their lights and threatened them with an ineffable menace. It breathed with the silence of the forest night when a predator stalks.

Despite her fears, they proceeded without any incident more ominous than stubbed toes until they reached the chamber Portifahr had described as their destination. Before entering it, he turned and made a sharp gesture that reinforced the mandate for silence. Stepping into the cavernous space, Dara knew with certainty that all her amorphous fears and suspicions were centered here. The underground chamber was so large that their lights reached neither the ceiling nor the far walls. Instead, their blue rods were reflected in shimmering lengths on the water,

illuminating all that she needed or wanted to see. The
lake's blackness surpassed even the utter darkness that
surrounded them. It transcended the black derived from
the total absence of light. The water was as liquid pitch
and Dara felt that, had she carried a glass vial of it out into
bright daylight, it would have remained so, extinguishing
any light that struck it. From the corners of her eyes she
thought she could detect faint wisps of mist just above the
lake's surface but when she looked for them directly the
air was clear. The metallic smell was stronger here, drifting about on air currents so that its source was impossible
to locate. She shivered, eager to be gone from this place,
and hoped that their business here would be brief.

With his lume-rod, Portifahr directed them to three
narrow boats lying on the rock shelf at the lake's edge. The
hair rose on Dara's neck in horror when she realized that
they were going out on the water instead of bypassing it.
The men also looked disturbed but they followed unspoken orders, sliding the boats into the water without hesitation and in complete silence. Portifahr took the bow of the
lead boat, Dara was seated in the middle of the second
craft, and Vethis commanded the third. Lume-rods went
into sockets to light their passage. When all were settled
in the boats, the outlaws took long poles from the bottom
and pushed away from the rock shelf. The slim craft moved
smoothly over the lake's fuliginous surface, which dimpled
and swirled around them as if gripped by strong underwater currents. Looking out across it, Dara could now clearly
see curls of mist rising in places. They could have been
crossing the River Styx. The men poled grimly in unison
as if determined to put the lake behind them as quickly as
they could. Dara was in complete agreement. The smell
increased, catching at her throat as if in an effort to make
her cough. A sudden suspicion struck Dara. Taking a
lume-rod from its holder, she raised it high. In the pale
light she could see that the mist was thickening, its wisps
reaching further into the dank air. The kneel of their boat
parted it and sent tendrils drifting back along the gun-
wales. She returned the light and took up a position as
close as possible to the center of the seat. The fear grew,
sending off alarms in her head.

One of the outlaws in the first boat caught his pole on an underwater obstruction. While clearing it he inadvertently knocked the pole against the boat's hull, giving off a hollow thud that echoed off the rock walls. Instantly a ghostly tendril twined up around the pole. The man moved his hands to the very tip of the pole and kept perfectly still while the mist quested upward and then subsided. Dara's fears were confirmed. As they moved further out onto the lake the mist grew bolder, seeking them before and behind. Everyone shrank instinctively from its clammy touch but could not move far in the narrow craft. Dara was grateful for Portifahr's help when a smoky finger brushed her cheek, and she did not cry out. The odor grew thick and choking.

When their lights picked out the ceiling and a promontory on the far wall, Dara knew they were nearly across. Her spirits leaped at the thought that they would soon escape this ghoulish chamber, leaving the fog to sink, unsatisfied, back into the black water. The first boat was but a pole's length from shore when Dara heard a strangled moan behind her. It echoed eerily about them as she whirled in dismay. She saw the man handling the stern pole frozen in his place with a thick tentacle of mist coiled around his throat. At his cry the fog swept quickly across the lake as if blown by a sudden sharp wind. It condensed around the horror-stricken outlaw until he was completely hidden from view. To the terrified observers he appeared encased in a gaseous chrysalis that pulsed in an awful parody of respiration. As it throbbed the mist grew viscous and colors coursed through it, sickening shades of yellow and purple and red. There was another cry, like that of someone in great pain but muffled and far away. They waited, transfixed by the macabre cocoon.

Then, in a manner more like a living creature than either gas or liquid, the color-flecked greyness uncoiled and slid with serpentine grace back into the water. The surface received it unruffled and closed over it into unmarked blackness. Dara stared, eyes wide and mouth open. Where moments before a man had stood, now only a skeleton wavered, still clutching the pole. The stripped bones reflected blue-green light, except for the dark eye sockets. For a terrible moment it stayed in place, then crumbled abruptly into dust. The pole fell in a slow arc and was caught by the nearest man before it could clatter into the boat. Dara became aware that a scream was gathering inside her, pushing against the wall of subconscious suggestion. Before turning again to the bow she saw Vethis staring fixedly at the fine grey powder dusting the water's surface. His face looked drawn and his lower lip was clamped tightly between his teeth.

Dara swallowed hard, put her head on her knees, and breathed evenly until she had regained control. She looked up, as if awakening from a nightmare, and saw that the boats were coming around the promontory. They cleared its looming mass smoothly and quietly. Expecting to see a landing place, Dara was astonished to find a sheer rock wall instead. Near the center was a low hole through which the lake's water surged and as the three boats entered the current they were lifted, as if by an unseen hand, and thrust forward swiftly. The men shipped their poles in unison and crouched in the vessels with their heads low. As the current carried them toward the chute she saw its edge approach with increasing speed. Dara made herself small and seconds later they shot into the pitch-black hole.

Although the tunnel cut straight through the rock, its narrowness forced the boats to bump against the walls and each collision boomed loudly around them. Dara clutched the seat to keep from being thrown about. The boat felt alive beneath her and kept pulling away from her grip until finally she sat on the wet bottom and wrapped her arms around the seat. The ride would have been exciting if it had not been so frightening. The walls rushed in by a blur of blue-green light and she was sickeningly aware that they had no control over speed or direction. With each hollow boom she expected a clammy tentacle to snake into the boat. All she felt, however, was the dank air and cold spray soaking her.

After a while they shot out of the tunnel into a second smaller cavern where the river broadened. As the boats slowed to a reasonable pace their passengers sat up gratefully. Dara flexed a painful kink out of her neck and stretched her muscles. She started to put a hand on the gunwale and then withdrew it from the jagged splinters of sodden wood. As they drifted on the slower current the cavern around them came to blue-green life. Light from the lume-rods just reached the walls, which displayed sharply-pronounced features. It was impressive, even beautiful, but different from the chamber of the lake. It was the atmosphere, Dara realized. Here the river was still black and still cold but it was just water. It made less noise on its way through the cavern than water should have, well earning its name, but there was nothing threatening about it to raise the hackles on her neck. No insidious predator lurked in its depths. No nightmare awaited them along its lightless course. No metallic smell choked her. Dara was confident that the mountains would place other powerful obstacles ahead of them, but now she had reason to hope that they would be natural barriers requiring only quick wits and strong muscles to overcome them. In that sense she felt that the worst was behind them.

With that realization, Dara's hands began to shiver in the aftermath of the massive surge of adrenalin her body had produced in the life-or-death confrontation. When they quieted she took up the abandoned stern pole and, along with the others, set to work keeping the boat away from obstacles and hazards half-hidden in the darkness. The activity kept her busy and also kept her mind off the bony hands that had last clutched the pole. As they traveled, the river changed size and speed, hazards came and went unpredictably, the walls closed in and moved back, but always the rocks remained perpendicular to the water. No shelves or beaches appeared, offering an opportunity for rest. When the river ran quietly they sat and stretched or took food from their packs and ate with their poles close at hand. Sleep was out of the question, despite fatigue, and they floated on in the timelessness that existed in utter blackness. There was no day or night, no time measurable by the height of the sun or the length of shadows. Even so, Dara's internal clock told her that it was late night outside. Above them the peaks of the Spine reached solidly into the night sky, blocking the bright streamer of stars. They were plunging through the heart of the range to its far side, evading the trackless slopes and unclimbable cliffs.

Eventually the pole grew heavy in her hands and her reflexes slowed. Still she worked at keeping the stern from rebounding on rocks or swinging into walls until, when she could hardly lift the long, wet pole, one of the men tapped her on the shoulder and took it from her. Then he pointed to a seat. Looking at him and the others, Dara could see fatigue circling their eyes but they were yet far from her exhaustion. They seemed to draw upon an inner strength that she did not possess. Behind them, Vethis looked worn but was hanging on, wielding his pole grimly. Dara shrugged and curled up in the center of the boat. Pillowing her head on her backpack, she was quickly asleep.

The sound of wood scraping against rock woke her and she uncurled from her wet, cramped, makeshift bed. Sitting up, she rubbed a numb hand, stretched and flexed her muscles. She was cold, the inside of her mouth tasted like mildew and it felt worse. The three craft still rocked onward down the endless black tunnel, encircled by a bubble of blue light. There was no way to tell how long she had been asleep but the faces of the men as they fended off yet another rock were haggard. In the boat behind them, Vethis sat, his pole shipped, fighting to remain awake. Dara felt a certain grim satisfaction at seeing his angry strength worn down. She turned and was about to take up her pole again reluctantly, and with stiff hands, when they swung wide around a curve. Ahead she saw a pale disc floating in the darkness. Her sleep-fogged mind took a slow moment to identify it as daylight. Her gasp added to the ripple of subdued excitement that ran through the group as the current surged ahead and the three boats ran toward the end of their underground journey.

The light spilled from a hole in the ceiling and cascaded down a rough slope of rock and dirt that spilled into the river, forming a curved beach. The men grounded their poles and heaved. One by one the boats slid smoothly up and nosed into the gravel with a crunch. Each bow man held his craft in place until everyone had clambered out, then they drew the boats well up onto the slope and stacked the poles. On firm ground once more, Dara covered her eyes against the glare. After the chemical light of the lume-rods, daylight seemed unnaturally clear and bright. She breathed deeply of the fresh air that cascaded through the opening. Looking back, she found a spot where the sunlight touched the water and was gratified to see that the Silent River was as black as liquid obsidian. Then, holding their packs, the group scrambled up the slope and out into daylight.

CHAPTER 9

Sandy watched the party of riders head up the road to Targhum and then began pacing the length of the coursers' run restlessly. The female had left with the other humans and he was unhappy. Being unhappy made him confused. Never before in the course of his work with humans had he encountered anyone like her. As with all the other coursers, he had always been identified only by the litter number tattooed on his muzzle. The female had given him a name and even though he did not understand what "Sandy" meant or whether it described his status in the pack, he liked its sound and the way it made him feel. Treated before simply as a worker, with detachment, he had not known what it was like to be scratched on the ruff or behind his ears. Baffled at first by receiving such overtures from a human, he had gradually learned to like them and to respond to them. When the female had thrown an arm around him while she slept, a strange disquieting feeling of warmth had spread through him, a sensation that took him back to being a cub being licked by his mother. There were no pets among the animals at Highfields so he knew only that she made him feel pleasantly different.

Now she was gone and there was something wrong. The scents of the compound told him nothing and, though he tasted the air repeatedly, no unfamiliar traces registered. The vibrations in both ground and air were also negative. Reluctantly, Sandy opened his empathic sense. As always, the proximity of so many people and animals hit him almost painfully but the sense of something not right—of danger approaching—was stronger. He hummed deep in his throat with distress. Gradually sorting the feelings that crowded this sense, he isolated the one that felt so wrong. Anger, fear, hatred, and anticipation surged in one human and the strength of the emotions was disorienting. The fact that these feelings came from a source very familiar to him was even more disturbing.

All that day he paced and balanced the rules, as he had learned them when a cub, against the danger that his empathic sense told him threatened the female. That he was no longer responsible for her presence or safety he knew well and had the human in peril been any other individual, he would have ignored the warning for just that reason. *Not* to ignore it meant taking action that violated the most basic rules of obedience and behaviour. The other coursers felt the vibrations from his conflict and turmoil and they moved away from him until he paced unhindered from one end of the run to the other. As he stalked back and forth the simple options open to him narrowed in the light of imminent danger. In the end his allegiance to the female who had befriended him won out and goaded him into action that would have been unthinkable under any other circumstances. At dusk, Sandy broke a hole in the wall of the kennel and, hidden by swirling mist, slipped out onto the trail.

Night and heavy fog obscured his vision but scent alone led him unerringly along the sapeers' tracks. It was a hard trail—cold, dark, and slow. Having decided on this course of action, however, Sandy kept at it doggedly. All night long he loped at a steady pace that diminished the miles and closed the gap. In early morning, when the sun's pale gold disk was sliding toward the tree tops, Sandy reached the scene of the ambush. He stood, panting heavily, on the rim of the bowl-shaped valley and looked down on the grim field. In the heavy silence and deepening chill he surveyed the death and confusion scattered before him and a high thin hum of anger built in his throat. Sandy shivered from the intense and chaotic vibrations that permeated the battlefield, then took command of himself. He was a worker and there was a job here to be done.

Trotting down into the valley, he went from body to body, nudging each and testing the vibrations to discern whether life remained. It was a discouraging task and one that drained all his energies but he had learned it early and well in his training. He labored now, moving methodically among the stiffening bodies that lay sprawled and tangled in a heap as though they had fought in close formation. There was blood all around him, matting hair, soaking clothes and the ground itself, sickening him with its stench. Grimly he persevered until he was rewarded with one form that still radiated life. It was not, however, the one he sought. Since his empathic sense told him that the man slept, he went on to complete his search.

When Sandy returned to the single surviving human he was still angry, but heartened. If all in this place were dead but one and the female was not here, then she could still be alive and need only be found. He could deal with that and was, despite his fatigue, eager to be off again. But duty and discipline called him to rouse the man from his senseless state first and logic added that he might, once awakened, be a help in the search. There was no certainty that this would be so but, since this was the man who had ordered him to guard the female and later had taken her with him, Sandy felt there was a good chance. First, he worked the man loose from the tangle of rigid limbs and weapons in which he lay. Then he turned the heavy figure over with his forepaws and used his curved teeth to loosen clothing. He licked and nuzzled and even bit as he would with another courser, worrying the man continually until he felt the life force surge up from the small place in which it had curled. Encouraged, Sandy renewed his efforts and was rewarded with a groan, a twitching hand, and a rasping breath.

It was dusk by the time the man was able to sit up. Watching him in the liquid darkness, the courser knew that he was hurt and needed food, water, and warmth before he could be of use. Those things, or their makings, could be found in a saddle pack. In full command of the situation, Sandy hummed code (Wait) and went in search of a dead sapeer that he had skirted earlier. Pulling off the saddle pack was far easier than he had anticipated since the sword cut that had dispatched the beast had also virtually severed the girth. With the prize gripped securely in his great jaws, Sandy returned to the man, who was sitting up with his head in his hands. Reassured that the man was all right, Sandy hummed another code (I will return) and left to hunt a live sapeer. Without one, tracking the female would be hard and slow.

Locating a couple of the pungent animals wasn't difficult, even in the dark. One of the well-trained creatures, still saddled, was munching twigs in a thicket off the trail. It smelled of the man. Although its small yellow eyes watched him warily, the sapeer followed readily enough when he took its dangling reins in his mouth. When Sandy returned with the mount, stepping carefully through the heap of bodies and upthrust weapons, the man was sitting before a small fire bandaging his wounds.

Resar rummaged through the saddle pack until he found firesticks wrapped in a waterproof lizardskin pouch. The specially-treated lengths were the only thing that would burn in the pervasive dampness and the travelers had brought a good supply. Soon he had a meager fire going. Its light and warmth helped to revive him but he was still chilled through and shaking. Resar got up, grimacing as flesh wounds and torn muscles made their presence known. In the flickering light of the fire he could see Tirnus's body contorted over the spear that transfixed his chest and lifted him from the ground. With difficulty, Resar wrestled the bloodstained but warm garment off the stiffened corpse of his friend. Tirnus, he knew, would have come back from the dead to track down the raiders and would not have begrudged his cloak if that was the only help he could give. Feeling light-headed and groggy, Resar wrapped the cloak tightly around him and then squatted by the fire to prepare hot rations. His shocked and drained body needed to rebuild its reserves before he set off at first light.

While the simple meal heated through, Resar probed his body from top to toe, learning the extent of his injuries. Besides the concussion there was a large gash stretching from his temple halfway across his forehead. Like all scalp wounds it had bled profusely and the left side of his face was caked with dried blood. Aside from the head injury there were some cuts that hurt out of proportion to their seriousness and a savage bruise on his right thigh that would hurt worse in a few days. The head wound must have saved his life by convincing his attackers that his bloody unconscious body was dead. *In the company of the dead, a sleeping man lies hidden.* He had never expected to prove the truth of that aphorism. With that thought he faced the next question: who *were* the dead? Resar grasped a firestick and stood, turning slowly in the still night. One by one the faces of his companions, his friend of many passages, his brother, leaped out of the darkness. There were no faces he did not recognize: if the raiders had suffered casualties, they had taken the bodies with them. That was strange, unlike the haphazard strike of a gormrith band. Then he remembered the face of Vethis, filled with a fierce triumph, and his smoldering anger began to glow. With that memory came the recognition that two other faces were missing among the slain— the women. With that, his spirit leaped and he was infused with a renewed purpose. At dawn they would begin tracking the raiders with even greater determination.

Resar sat down again and took a hot drink. The courser had appeared from out of the night, roused him from his stupor, dragged over the saddle pack, and then disappeared. That, too, was very odd. Where had he come from, alone, with no handler or hunting pack? Who could have sent him? No one at Highfields had suspected such an ambush. Had Vethis's treachery been discovered so soon? If so, why were there not people here from Highfields? There was something even stranger: although it was difficult to tell one courser from another, there was a familiarity about this beast. Resar was almost positive that this was the same animal he had selected to guard Dara on the way to Highfields. Several times she had spoken to him about this courser and how proud she was of having befriended it; as if it were possible to make friends with an unpredictable animal. Ludicrous as it seemed, she had even given it a name in her own language, There was some significance in the name but none of it made any sense to him. Sindu? Sander? "Sandy!" Resar had not meant to speak aloud and was startled by his own voice. Coursers were intelligent, sometimes intuitive, creatures. Was it possible that this one had sensed something and come on its own to help?

As if in answer, the beast appeared in the firelight. In his mouth he gripped the reins of a sapeer, which loomed placidly behind him. The courser dropped the reins with a satisfied air, then sat down and hummed code (Ride). Resar was not a handler and could not communicate as fluently with these animals as could the people who trained them and worked with them. Like all Rangers, however, he had learned the basic code necessary for tracking, hunting, and security work. He hummed back (Good work). Then, feeling faintly ridiculous, he repeated it out loud, "Good work, Sandy." The beast responded to this overture with a great yawning smile and hummed deeply (Yes). Gratified, Resar finished his food. Tomorrow they would hunt.

The sun rose pale and dim through the fog. Its faint yellow disk brightened the air and made droplets sparkle but gave little heat. It was time. Resar stood up and shook his head in a final effort to throw off the effects of the concussion. Around him the battlefield assumed a grey and grisly reality. He took a long look at the slaughter while Sandy made certain of the trail. He checked his sapeer's harness thinking that there was nothing he could do for the dead, not even a funeral pyre. Unseen in the mist a kahn-dor-ei called with a high clear keening and was answered by another of its kind. It would not be long before the scavengers assembled to do their work: the trail was waiting and the still bodies understood duty as well as he. Resar looked at the firesticks, still smoldering, then disregarded all his training and left them unquenched. In the dampness he had no concern that the fire would spread and it would serve as a memorial for the dead. Resar wheeled his mount to follow Sandy.

Sandy loped ahead eagerly, following a broad trail clear to both scent and taste. Of necessity he kept his empathic sense firmly blocked from the storm of emotions that permeated the area. They were too strong and painful for him to allow contact. The sapeer's feet pounded behind him and he could hear the rasp of its breathing over his shoulder. The blood surged in his veins at the pleasure of running free with the wind in his face, hard on the trail of the female he had to find. The long patient night of following his training had been rewarded. Not only had the man roused and entered into the chase, he had recognized that he, Sandy, was not just an ordinary courser. Now it was a matter of catching up to their quarry by reducing a lead of almost a day.

Sandy was running full out when the bitter taste of death struck at him. He slowed, then skidded to a stop over Neva's crumpled body. Although he knew instantly that this was not the female, he hummed distress in such a high frequency that it raised the hairs on Resar's neck. Coming up alongside the courser, the man swung from the saddle before his mount had stopped. Pulling the body over, Resar took in at a glance how Neva had died and the look of astonishment frozen on her blue-grey face. On one knee beside her, he tried to visualize what had happened but nothing he could think of explained why only one of the two women had been killed. If Vethis had wanted to protect his identity and hide his treachery he would have eliminated both witnesses. If the raiders wanted hostages, or rape, why not keep both women? Cursing under his breath, Resar dragged the pitifully small body off the blood-soaked dirt and placed it in a thicket of small trees. He could not protect it from wild animals without spending an hour hauling rocks, and once again it was more important to help the living. He mounted and rode on with Sandy leading the way, but this time they left the road and struck off through the underbrush. Ahead of them the Spine loomed unseen in the fog.

The trail was clear and open and they made good time despite the heavy mist and the steady upgrade. As Sandy zigzagged his way up the mountainside the murky air grew brighter but no warmer. He had no trouble slipping sinuously past trees and rocks only dimly seen but vivid to his other senses. He could have gone even faster but he had been trained not to lose the slower, clumsier animal thudding along behind him. Sandy had already discovered and circled the scattered bones of a sapeer when the man arrived. The skeleton was fresh but picked clean: some of the bones were cracked and gnawed while others were deeply grooved. Tracks of all kinds crisscrossed in the damp dirt around the remains, the only traces left by a horde of nocturnal scavengers. The man observed the scene carefully but did not dismount. They both knew that, had anything else been there to see, Sandy would have found it. The courser turned, skillfully sorted out the confusion of spoors, and loped upward.

By the time they reached the mistline, both he and the sapeer were winded and sweating. Sandy rested briefly in the lee of a boulder where he would not lose body warmth to the icy wind sweeping down from the peaks. He was thirsty but could smell no water anywhere near. While he regained strength, the man paced impatiently, frowning. As he strode he looked alternately downward at the pearly ceiling of mist and upward at the jagged rock summits. It was mid-afternoon, the days were growing shorter, and Sandy knew that humans did not often travel after dark. Once again the man scanned the slopes above them but they remained grey and chill and empty of movement. Sandy, to whom eyesight was only one of many senses, did not understand how important it was to the man that they sight their quarry. He knew too well that the female was outside of visual range. Beside them the sapeer blew out twin spouts of steam and shivered, its hide blotched and streaked with sweat. The man turned from the peaks, noticed his mount's condition, and took off his own cape. He flung it over the beast, then grasped its halter, and began to lead it upward. Sandy rose and slipped past, turning them back onto the trail.

There was still daylight when they reached the overhang, but just barely. With an excited hum, Sandy dashed past the looming natural formation into a small cul-de-sac that was hidden from sight. Resar dropped the sapeer's harness and followed the excited courser inside, where shadows were already gathering. Then he stopped abruptly and cried out at the sight of a cache of saddles and bridles piled up against the opposite wall. He reached them in three steps and, acting quickly, found twelve sets of tack for chammies and two larger ones for sapeers. That accounted for a dozen outlaws and the two women. Now that count was down by one human and one animal but he had no way of telling if any of the rest were wounded. Resar guessed that the animals had been loosed to find their own way down to wild herds in the valley. It was obvious that the men he tracked could only continue on foot if they were planning to cross the Spine.

He looked up and noticed Sandy standing protectively over two objects that were nearly indistinguishable from the shadows. When he approached, the courser moved obediently to one side and Resar identified the objects as the saddle packs of the two women. Now he was truly puzzled. Here were Dara's personal belongings, including warm clothing and everything she would need for protection against the snow and cold of a mountain winter. At this altitude, where could the outlaws be taking her that she would not need the fur-lined riding coat? Or the hat and gloves? In the Spine, warmth was survival and to leave it behind was to tease death. Unless . . . a chill ran through him. Were they transporting a corpse? And for what possible reason? Instead of unraveling, the mystery grew deeper with each discovery. Perplexed, he stepped back and saw that the cul-de-sac was nearly dark: he would have to make good use of what dim light remained to make camp.

Resar hefted both packs and returned with them to the shelter of the overhang. Not for the first time, he was grateful for the Ranger discipline of always packing a full field kit. First he unsaddled the sapeer, removing rolled sleeping bag and supplies. He lacked deep-cold gear but he was equipped sufficiently to continue the chase for a few more days. If the raiders eluded him or widened their lead, he would have to turn back and give up the chase. He stripped the rest of the tack from his mount and covered it with a blanket from Neva's pack. Sapeers were valley beasts, not acclimated to the cold peaks, and he would have to make sure that it did not succumb to the harsh winds. When he led it in under the massive overhang, the animal dropped its head in exhaustion. As the last daylight faded, he worked quickly to set up camp. It would be grim and comfortless but he had slept in worse and he did not plan to be there long.

Two days later, Resar sat heavily on a rock and stared in disgust at the black slit in the rock wall facing him. Despite setting a punishing pace in an all-out effort to make speed, he had failed to catch up with his quarry. His supplies were low and his mount was suffering both from the cold and the effects of a hard climb, yet he was no closer to success than before. Now the trail led directly into an ominous cave and he was ill-prepared to follow. His pack held a few fire sticks and no rope. Without trees he could not make a torch of comfortable size but he did have Sandy and that was his one advantage. The courser could navigate as well in the darkness as in full daylight but, even so, entering the cave would be a risk. Sandy leaned against his thigh and hummed unhappily in a range inaudible to human ears. Although he heard nothing, Resar felt the vibrations through his quilted pants. Neither of them liked the situation, it seemed, but the trail went in and they would follow it.

With a sigh, the former Ranger captain stood, removed his gloves, and made his preparations: there was no sense in prolonging the unpleasantness and he was only losing time. He unsaddled the sapeer, covered it with its blanket, and hobbled its hind feet to prevent it from straying. If they did not return from the cave it would die but it was beginning to look as if it would not survive in any case. He removed the items he needed from the pack and cached it behind a rock. He was ready. Squaring his shoulders, he grasped Sandy's neck fur firmly in his left hand. He would save the torch until it was needed. Side by side, they entered the cave.

Resar was deeply uneasy as they padded cautiously through the darkness. As a boy he had explored the many caves around Highfields, some of which extended far into the surrounding mountains. Some had been airy and exciting, others twisting and treacherous, but none had evoked the kind of deep dread he felt now. It seemed to fill him along with the strong metallic smell in the air he breathed. With the overwhelming alarm came fear of the darkness and what it hid. One moment he wanted desperately to light the torch and reassure himself that this was a cavern like any other, inhabited only by his imagination. The next moment he welcomed the darkness, content that he could not see his unknown surroundings. The mountain covered him with its weight and smothered him with its unseen bulk. Gradually the mountain and the darkness became one until Resar felt as if he were walking through rock itself. He became increasingly grateful for Sandy's solid body moving steadily beside him. That presence, alert but calm, quieted the worst of his fears.

As he walked blind and haunted, the journey stretched onward inside his mind, becoming, one step after another, the longest and most arduous part of his pursuit. After a period of time that could have been an hour or a day, the cave changed. The narrow, convoluted passages where their footsteps echoed back at them disappeared and even without eyes he could tell that they had entered a large chamber. The sound of their breathing went out into the dark and did not bounce back. The air was cooler, the smell stronger, and a draft almost like a breeze touched his cheek. They took a few paces forward into this cavern before Sandy stepped abruptly in front of him, blocking his path. Resar waited a moment for a hummed code and, when nothing happened, decided that it was time to look around. With a sharp snick he rasped a match against the rock floor and lit one of the firesticks he took from his belt.

Holding it aloft, he looked about him in amazement at the huge chamber and the lake of pitch that it enclosed. It was an awesome sight that held him spellbound and some time went by before he realized that the trail ended there, at the stone bank. He stepped around Sandy and went closer to the water but not even from just above the surface could his firestick pierce those inky depths. Resar searched up and down for tracks but found nothing. There were no scratch marks on the rocks to show where a boat had been dragged, yet they must have had a vessel to cross the lake: it was the only plausible explanation. Once again his gaze raked the lake's surface but this time wisps of mist were rising from it, masking the cold boil on the surface. The metallic smell was much stronger here and very unpleasant. Everything in this cavern was unpleasant. Had anything lived here, he would have assumed it was hostile. Chagrined as he was, Resar did not envy anyone a voyage over such a malignant body of water.

Once more Sandy stepped in front of him and pressed hard against his legs, as if trying to push him away from the lake's edge. Again Resar felt the vibrations of a hum beyond his ability to hear. Almost at once the mist that issued from the lake became agitated, appearing wind-blown even though the air was still. Abruptly the courser's vocal modulations dropped to an audible range and Resar identified the code for danger. Before he could react, a thin tentacle of mist snaked quickly onto the stone floor and wrapped itself around his left ankle. It whipped back viciously and Resar went over backwards. His skull struck hard and the firestick flew out of his hand, landing behind him. Green suns and white stars circled in front of him and blood roared in his ears. Semi-conscious, he was only dimly aware of being dragged irresistably toward the water. Spreading his hands wide, he tried to resist but had no strength to brake his relentless slide. He was struggling to overcome the dizziness when Sandy's strong jaws clamped down on his right shoulder. The courser braced his sturdy legs and began to pull in the other direction. In silence and flickering light the warm-blooded animal and the cold nebulous creature conducted a grim tug of war. As the vertigo faded, Resar could feel the damp rock moving underneath him, first in one direction and then the other. He summoned all his strength and, when Sandy dug in for another huge effort, Resar pushed also with one leg and both arms. For a long, frozen moment they strained to the utmost. Then, with a wet sucking sound, the tentacle gave way and he was free.

Lurching awkwardly to his feet, Resar turned and sprinted for the opening through which they had come, with Sandy a pace behind him. Together, man and beast plunged back into the darkness and began a headlong race to the outside. Behind them the firestick flickered and smoked on the rocks, illuminating the heavy mist that dashed furiously over the Lake of the Silent River. With a mindless rage it lashed out in one direction only to swerve abruptly and head off in another. It was still swirling in a frenzy when the firestick flared up and died.

The journey up and out of the cave was shorter and less harrowing than the trip in. Sandy, because he could see in the dark, emerged without problem. Resar did less well, bruising himself over and over although he did not feel the contusions until much later. When the pair finally burst from the cave's mouth they were as blinded by sunshine as the man had been by perfect blackness. Both man and animal stood blinking and gasping, filling their lungs with the clear, sharp mountain air. As soon as he could, Resar looked behind him to reassure himself that the sinister mist had remained within. Satisfied that they were alone, he searched among the rocks for his mount. Sandy found it for him, slumped against a rock close by and shivering uncontrollably. After some coaxing, Resar got it back on its feet, unhobbled it, and then loaded it for the return journey.

Because of the sapeer's depleted condition he chose to lead it until they reached easier ground. They were well on their way down when the sapeer jerked its head upward, pulling Resar's arm up with it. Only then did he feel the sharp pain in his shoulder and notice the rent coat where Sandy's teeth had pierced it. Once that pain had claimed his attention he felt another vivid pang. Looking down, he saw that his left riding boot and leggings had been eaten through as if by acid. Where they had been, swollen and blistered red skin encircled his left leg. He would bear the scar of that weird clasp as a permanent reminder of his unsuccessful pursuit.

* * *

When they emerged from underground a glistening winter greeted them. The egress was in a grove of tall trees spiked with rubbery needles and each bristling limb held an accumulated burden of snow. On this side of the Spine, heavy clouds bumped up against the jagged summits and dropped their loads of moisture. Drifts were piled up higher than a sapeer's head on the slopes beyond the protection of the trees. Piercing clear light from the mid-afternoon sun sparkled off every still flake, causing Dara to exclaim in delight. Portifahr looked carefully all around them, declared the grove adequate protection, and opened his pack. Within minutes camp was set up and the outlaw band sprawled in exhausted sleep inside the tent. After the initial flurry of activity, Dara was astonished to find herself in the middle of a silent landscape, alone and unguarded. She felt curiously light and giddy. Then came the steadying realization that they had no need of security here: the Spine was their guardian. She could not retrace their route and had nowhere to go on this side of the mountain range. She could always slip away into the woods but, alone, unarmed, and in the winter cold, she would not stand a chance. As usual, all the angles were covered and there was only one way to go—their way. She sighed and her breath rose in a white plume.

Dara had slept on the river and was somewhat rested but the men would sleep for many hours. What was there to do? After the darkness and damp confinement of the past hours, she felt the need for cheer, warmth, and coziness. Fortunately, they had emerged below the tree line with the majority of the Spine's mass looming above them. Staying well within the shadow of the trees, she wandered around the grove collecting a large pile of dead branches and twigs. She made several trips among what she thought of as floppy pines but what Lekh had called the taiga to ensure an adequate supply of firewood. Then she stamped out a place in the snow before the tent, moving methodically until it was well packed. She piled up a considerable stack of kindling and placed larger branches on top to make a blaze big enough to keep the melting snow from extinguishing the flames before they could really catch.

Her preparations complete, Dara unloaded her pack and laid its contents out neatly, something she had not had the chance to do since Portifahr had handed it to her. Then she examined each article before carefully packing it away again. Besides her sleeping bag, lume-rod, food, and a nearly empty canteen, she found a large cup, a folded sheet of the same thermal material as her suit, a compact first-aid kit, a coil of tough, supple rope, a small knife, and two metal tubes. Both were unmarked but one twisted in the middle while the other had several buttons circling an open end. She picked up the first one, aimed what looked like the tip at some sticks, and twisted. Immediately two of the sticks quivered and clung to one another. Cautiously, she picked them up and tugged but they would not come apart. She pulled harder and the sticks broke in two but still adhered to one another. Intrigued, Dara put them back down, reversed the tube, and twisted it the other way. The sticks quivered again and separated. Pursing her lips thoughtfully, Dara returned the tube to her pack.

Next she picked up the second tube, aimed it at the firewood and began pressing buttons. The tube emitted a pale but concentrated beam of orange light that deepened and became stronger with each button she depressed. Finally a deep red setting ignited the kindling. When the fire was snapping strongly she filled the cup with clean snow and set it to one side of the flames. To cook properly she needed coals and the fire was too young for that so Dara rose, her knee joints cracking in protest. Doggedly she began to stretch out, forcing herself to limber up, get her heart pumping, and banish the cramped muscles that came from confinement in the boat. It was difficult at first and awkward to do fully dressed but she persevered. After a while the exercise became easier and then satisfying.

She finished in a glow of work well done, drank the melted snow, and then tended the fire. Next she selected a crooked branch and raked out some coals. Refilling the cup with snow, she set it on top of the pulsing orange embers and went through the food supplies from her pack. Selecting some strips of dried meat, shriveled ko nut husks, and a tuber that was full of basic carbohydrates she put together a kind of stew. The sun sank closer to a tawny peak while the meal simmered and the sky flared into a multitude of shades. Sparks hissed sharply in the melted snow but aside from the sounds of the fire it was quiet, the muffled silence created only by a thick snow cover. When the food was ready, she ate slowly, savoring each hot bite despite the fact that it was flat and unseasoned. Portifahr's field rations were nutritious but not tasty. Regardless, the stew was hot and its basic warmth restored her spirits. While she ate the sun dipped behind the mountain, reminding her that it would soon be dark—and colder. Dara cleaned her cup with snow and packed it away. Then she rose fluidly and went out to collect more wood.

Her nose, an accurate thermometer and unprotected by her thermal suit, indicated that the temperature was dropping and the dry cold air bit at the mucous membranes. She gathered branches more swiftly this time as the darkness deepened and she was eager to return to the cheerful blaze in front of the tent. Once she jumped as a darker shadow passed silently overhead. Dara looked up apprehensively but could see nothing through the branches interwoven overhead. With her arms full she followed her tracks back to camp and built up the fire. The woods grew darker outside its flickering circle. She took advantage of the unusual privacy to relieve herself without an audience. Under her thermal suit she felt the dirt of days on a rugged trail. Her hair felt stringy even though she had tied it back to keep it out of her face. If she could have melted enough snow she would have taken a sponge bath in spite of the cold.

With her knees drawn up to her chin Dara stared into the flames and considered her position as a woman in the hands of very rough men. Portifahr had set the tone and their treatment of her had been businesslike and matter-of-fact so far. She might have been a head of livestock being delivered to a new owner for all the notice she received but that did not change biology. She had intercepted sideways glances when the men thought that Portifahr wasn't looking and the effect of her proximity to them was sometimes clearly visible. Even though suppressed, these reactions were frightening because what it all came down to was that Portifahr called the shots, the men obeyed his orders, and she went along. Her wishes or feelings were insignificant and she did what they commanded because she had no choice. The situation was actually not much different from many she had encountered on Earth, only more clear cut.

As the flames popped and sparks hissed in the snow, Dara's thoughts moved on to the women of Khyren. She had talked with them, watched them, laughed with them, and worked with them but never had she considered herself one of them. She had always regarded them as peripheral to her own very different needs. When examined in the light of their own culture, however, it became obvious that they were much the same as the women of Earth, but at the opposite end of the value scale. They, too, were in thrall to fertility but here the necessity was to achieve it, not avoid it. Except for the aristocracy where alliances were formed for political reasons, women were not even allowed to marry until they had proven themselves gravid. They brought their unborn children to the union proudly, like a dowery. Pregnancy was status, motherhood near royalty and possible entree to a power structure separate from the rest of society. Although Kyhrenese women were not worn down by repeatedly bearing unwanted children, giving birth was still the whole focus of their lives. It was also the only true way in which they could succeed in society as individuals, through the Order of the Lady, the only path to power and its benefits that was available to them.

Superficially the culture of Khyren allowed women much more freedom. They could work at any job for which they had an aptitude, seek to raise their position by negotiating a courtesan's contract with a nobleman, partner many men or be with no man at all. But all this freedom of choice was a false front. Behind it lay a single unalterable truth: safe delivery of a healthy child was every woman's greatest and only ambition. It was sad, she reflected, and that so few women attained this simple goal, even once, was pathetic.

And why? Infertility, while a problem in itself, was very often the symptom of a greater problem. There was no obvious reason why the population on Khyren was not flourishing. The people were certainly healthy and vigorous. The culture was stable, secure, even prosperous in her experience. Food was abundant. It was a puzzle and one that perhaps only a biologist or endocrinologist could solve. An answer would certainly not appear this night. Her own problems were far more serious and immediate. While she had sat thinking and the fire had burned low, fatigue had caught up with her. With a sigh, Dara banked the fire for the night. Taking up her pack, she slipped into the tent and sealed the entrance behind her.

Inside, the gamy smell of unwashed male bodies was heavy. Several of the sleepers snored richly and the rest appeared sunk so deep in exhausted slumber they might have lain in a coma. By the light of Portifahr's brazier she set about making a place for herself to sleep. Lifting heavy arms and pushing aside sprawled legs she gradually cleared enough space in which to lie down comfortably. Once settled, however, she found sleeping impossible. The man next to her began to snore and the ragged, rhythmic noise imposed itself on her consciousness. There was no escaping the sound and each time it pulled her back from the brink of rest her level of impatience rose. She tried pushing and shoving at him but nothing made him quieter. Then, when her frustration had turned to anger, he moaned in his sleep and rolled over nearly on top of her so that she was pinned beneath his unconscious weight. Dara stared at him in disgust and pushed his arm off her chest. Abruptly, her carefully-cultivated resignation vanished and was replaced with a fury that was more intense for having arrived suddenly and unbidden. Staring sightlessly at the sleeping man she saw Amrith go down again beneath a flashing blade, saw Neva falling in fatal surprise, saw Resar pivoting to meet the charge, saw her only hope for making a life topple in the mist.

Rage boiled out of the small dark place where she had consigned it only a few days ago in order to concentrate on her own survival. Once free it expanded, filling her with an explosive need for revenge. With a ferocity born as suddenly as her rage she imagined drawing the knife that jutted from the outlaw's belt into her hip and cutting their throats as they slept. They deserved it, all of them, Vethis first. In their nearly catatonic slumber the men were completely vulnerable and this was the best opportunity she would ever have. Dara's right hand curled reflexively as if it already held the knife and she thought exultantly that only a few swift strokes were needed and it would be over in seconds. There would be much blood but she had already witnessed that, thanks to this tentful of raptors. Working feverishly, her mind told her that she could make a sled afterward and haul the remaining supplies down the mountain. Then she would be on her own in the wilderness but at least she would be free again. Her impromptu plan was intoxicatingly simple: power lay, for once, in her own hands.

While the rage built to a killing peak logic flung up desperate arguments in the back of her mind. It was only the beginning of winter and cold and food would be hard to find once the supplies ran out. She did not know how to hunt or live in the wilderness. She needed the blood-soaked tent but it would attract every predator on this side of the Spine. And civilization was on the other side. She would end up in a more deadly situation than she was now and she would soon regret it. All these well-reasoned arguments were short lived, burned up in the flame of her anger and destroyed by its irrational momentum. Letting go of her careful control and indulging in the maelstrom of emotion felt wonderfully satisfying and it was compelling, almost gratifying, to dwell on all that she had lost and what these marauders had taken so callously from her. With one stroke she could take control, avenge the dead, and disperse the shadow of an unknown master over her future. It would be easy, almost predestined.

Dara turned the outlaw's body, reaching for the knife, when she saw the gleam of Portifahr's eyes in the darkness. He lay unmoving but there was no mistaking the fact that his eyes were open and riveted on her. The impact of that gaze was as strong and as physical as if he had struck her. Immobilized, her heart pounding, she looked straight into his sea-green eyes and understood: he knew. He had probably been aware of her intention as soon as the thought had occurred to her. Now he simply lay still in the darkness and watched, certain that there was now no chance for her to succeed. With her eyes still locked on his in a strange bond, Dara's anger guttered and died, sinking back into its inner cell like a living thing. With it went the wild strength that had fueled and reinforced her purpose and in its wake the fatigue returned, magnified several times. She felt suddenly drained and weak. Breaking away from that steady gaze, she sank down and pulled the blanket around her.

CHAPTER 10

They descended the mountain the next day. Even with
their thermal suits and high-technology comforts, it was a
hard cold journey. Groves of taiga trees were only scattered on the slopes and far apart. Sometimes they walked
side-by-side over rocks blown bare by a constant, relentless wind but mostly they pushed single-file across bright
fields of snow. Portifahr led, followed by half the men,
then Dara in the middle, the rest of the band, and Vethis
guarding the rear. On the snowfields, Portifahr used his
heat rod to vaporize a path and they walked on slush that
hardened as they passed and froze behind them. The trail
they left winding down the slope looked like the rust-
shadowed path of a huge serpent. Occasionally they slid,
roped together but cramponless, down frozen streams. Ice
rimed the men's beards and moustaches and they watched
one another's faces continually for signs of frostbite. Always the armed men kept up a steady surveillance with
crossbows at the ready and whenever they were out in the
open several outlaws scanned the sky. Although going
down was easier than climbing, the conditions on this side
of the mountains were more difficult. Nevertheless, they

slogged along until their shadows stretched thin and long across the snow. By the time they pitched camp Dara, at least, was grateful to stop.

The following morning they awoke to find the tent shuddering violently in a gale. When Portifahr looked out, snow was falling so heavily that visibility was virtually zero and travel was ruled out. They stayed in the tent all that short dim day, resting from the arduous journey. The men cleaned their weapons meticulously, traded tips on fighting, brewed strong herb tea, and massaged sore muscles. Only Portifahr and Dara remained silent on opposite sides of the tent and kept to themselves. The storm howled on without a break. Outside the tent, the temperature was daunting and made worse by a wind so strong it blew the snow horizontally. Inside the tent's thermal barrier, however, the air grew warm, heated by the glowing brazier and thirteen healthy bodies. As snow drifted against the walls, adding another layer of insulation, the warmth became uncomfortable and one by one the men began to shed layers of clothing. After a while some men stripped down to the skin on top, leaving only the thermal suit on below the waist. In this odd sudatorium Dara removed some of the cumbersome outside clothing but dared not even go down to the thermal suit. She did luxuriate in slipping off her riding boots and rubbing her sore feet thoroughly. Feeling both calluses and bruises, she wondered what her feet looked like beneath their black covering.

Hour after hour the storm bellowed and bullied the tent. A rope was set up so that, when necessary, they could step just outside the sealed entrance and find their way back in again. Dara watched the men absently and listened to their stories without really hearing them. A place within her was still in turmoil from the surging emotions she had so recently experienced. Of all the emotions she had ever felt, murderous rage was one that had gone unconfronted until now and she was astonished at how easily she had accepted it. In her busy, safe suburban life Dara had not spent much time dealing with the concept of murder. On a philosophical level she had always believed that any mother, when faced with a threat to her child, was capable of killing decisively and without a qualm.

But her child was across the galaxy and she had to accept the fact that she had come very close not only to killing but to murder in cold blood. Her brain churned on, examining the issue, but after several hours it began to work more sluggishly. She drifted into a drowsy state that brought home to her how bone tired she was and how good it felt to rest in warmth and comparative comfort. The day ended early with the snow still scything across the flanks of the mountain and Dara was asleep soon after.

She pushed her way impatiently into the cluttered, crowded walk-in closet, searching the shelf above the hangers for her snorkel and mask. Their suitcases were nearly packed and it was almost time to leave if they were going to get to the airport on time. Dara planned to snorkel on this vacation, however, and first she had to locate the gear. Gritting her teeth, she shoved past several feet of her husband's shirts, winter clothes, maternity clothes bagged in plastic, and coats in zipped storage bags. The closet stretched on, longer than she remembered, and she could not quite see the end. Roller skates and boots got underfoot, tripping her, and she clutched at the clothing to keep her balance. The light dimmed and the closet began to smell oddly like a locker room. Then, as she groped on toward a dim corner, light glinted off the glass plate of her face mask. Encouraged, she stretched to grasp it but something about the blue and red ski suit hanging underneath it made her pause. It was draped as if hunched up and its posture was somehow strange and alarming. Frightened, Dara edged closer and reached for the snorkel.

It wasn't there. She clutched at a shadow and then movement caught at the corner of her eye. When she looked at the ski suit again, it had changed and its appearance was different. It was no longer slack but filled out as if it contained something or was being worn. Dara backed up a step, afraid now to take her eyes off the suddenly alien garment. A moth blundered through the open door and began circling the weak light bulb that illuminated the closet. The insect orbited the light, its fluttering wings animating the shadows. Even as Dara watched, the ski suit took on a more solid shape. In the flickering light, hands and feet grew. A slumped head formed itself, obscuring the hanger behind it. Thickly she realized that what she had mistaken for a ski suit was in reality a body. Its dull cyanotic skin was streaked with rivulets of blood that dripped and puddled on the floor. Horrified, aghast that such a macabre thing had crept into her home unnoticed, she stared at the corpse in disbelief. The moth circled the light and the body's head began to nod and twitch like that of a marionette. It bobbed up and down, higher each time, until with a final emphatic bounce it jerked upright. The empty face turned and stared at her with sightless eyes, grinning. She could see the streams of blood welling endlessly from a ragged gash across its pale throat.

With a guttural cry of panic, Dara turned to escape. When she attempted to push her way back out, however, she found that the rest of the clothing had also metamorphosed behind her. In the fickle light each body writhed and bled on its own hook. As she struggled past they reached for her, their cold hands falling heavily on her shoulders, tangling in her hair, holding her back. The light grew dimmer and she looked up from her struggle to see the closet door slowly swinging shut. Terrified beyond reason of being locked in with the closet's ghastly inhabitants, she fought harder, pushing the cold limbs away from her. The floor became a pool of blood in which shoes and sandals floated and her feet slipped backwards. Despite her exertions she moved slowly, watching in anguish as the slice of light ahead grew smaller. She gave one last wrench, a desperate lunge, and then she was through. Dara fell past the door and out into her normal, peaceful bedroom. In the cheval glass she could see that she too was covered with blood. Behind her the closet door shut with a click.

Then Dara was awake, sitting up and staring wildly around the tent. Her heart raced and she panted uncontrollably. The brazier had dimmed so that there was little light in the tent and sleeping bodies formed mounds around her. On the other side of the tent, however, another figure was upright in the darkness. Although his face was

hidden in the gloom she knew that it was Portifahr, who
had wakened and caught the echo of her terror. Dara
shivered from the memory of the nightmare, so vivid still
that it could almost reach out from the shadows and recapture her. She was afraid to lie down again and even more
afraid to close her eyes. To banish the dream she needed
company, the presence of another human being, the sound
of another voice. Stepping carefully to avoid waking anyone else, she moved across the tent to Portifahr's solitary
silence. He accepted her closeness but did not speak
immediately. When he did, his first words confirmed her
thoughts.

"It was bad?" he asked softly and it was more nearly a
statement than a question.

She nodded, then remembered that he could not see
her gesture. "It was very bad."

"I picked up fear and much blood. Tell me."

Haltingly, as if her very words could summon forth the
grasping, dangling shapes, Dara related her nightmare.
Sometimes she had to reach for words that would convey
to him the objects that her dream had conjured from an
alien culture. Despite the inexact translation Portifahr
seemed to comprehend without difficulty. When she had
finished, he released a breathy ejaculation. "That is powerful," he said enigmatically. "Do you understand this
vision of yours?"

"No. When a dream is that vivid, I can see only the
images, not the meaning behind them."

"Then think of this. The storage room was part of you,
yet created by you. The monsters inside it were ordinary
things turned malevolent. And because you entered that
room voluntarily, you came near to locking yourself inside
forever."

Dara thought of her killing rage and how she had yielded
to it. She remembered how this quiet man had prevented
her from succumbing to evil and in the darkness she
flushed. He was right. Portifahr's interpretation robbed
the dream of its potency and it began to fade, leaving her
empty and sad and much in need of reassurance. She
reached out and touched his hand: it was warm and hard.
Portifahr neither accepted nor rejected her overture. She

grasped his hand more firmly and it tightened around hers. With an electric tingle energy began to radiate from him, moving into her hand and up into her arm. It was an unusual sensation and one that she had never experienced before. Dara was amazed at how the vibrations filled her with a sense of renewed worth, chasing away the residue of fear and despair left by her nightmare. Beyond that, she found his strength and vitality compelling and she began to respond to his nearness, his understanding, in a more physical fashion. As her body awakened she reached out with her other hand and touched Portifahr's face. Beneath the thick beard it felt as obdurate as stone. She wanted more of him but hesitated to go further without some kind of encouragement. Instead, he slowly took her fingers from his cheek and squeezed them. "I would help you with this loneliness if I could, for loneliness is a terrible thing. But I cannot. That part of being a man is lost to me."

"Lost? But why?" She could not comprehend his statement when everything about him was so virile and his masculinity without question.

"For everything there is a price."

Dara sat silently absorbing this cryptic reply. It occurred to her that in her need she had probably trespassed in a delicate area and would be wise to back away. "Why is the price always so high?" she asked with a touch of bitterness.

She could feel his shrug. "Without price, what has value? We may choose to pay it or not but to obtain what we desire, we must pay the price willingly."

"But what if you never had a choice? What if you never wanted any of it? If you find yourself paying without even knowing what for? When there's no point, no choice, not even a warning?"

Again there was a silence. "Then it is sehr-pei, what the mountain people call fate. It may not be pleasant but you may choose to make the best of it."

"What else can I do but protect myself in the midst of my enemies?"

"What indeed? Remember only that all of life is change."

The flow of energy subsided between them and Portifahr's

hands were as they had been before. Dara let go of them and sat back, feeling bruised and drained. With a sigh she returned to her blanket as carefully as she had come. Once she was settled, however, she lay awake for a while contemplating what he had said. Just before sliding into sleep she noticed that the wind had dropped. The night was still and quiet around them.

"I have failed."

Resar leaned over the table and pressed his knuckles into its worn and battered surface. His voice was hard and full of the bitter anger that had overtaken him at the Lake of the Silent River. His jaw was clenched and muscles stood out beneath the quilted sleeves of his shirt. "Those people depended on me as an experienced Ranger captain. It was my responsibility to get the party here safely. It was my duty to protect them from a rag-tag band of outcasts and I failed."

Kureil confronted his visitor's anguish from the far end of the table. When he replied, his voice was calm but he spoke with vehemence. "It may have been your duty but if you think that you were ambushed by gormrith, defeated by undisciplined outlaws, then you have fallen so far into self-pity that you cannot think straight." He leaned forward and his voice rose and sharpened. "If you want to salvage anything from this massacre, you *must* think clearly. Use your reason. Otherwise you are no use to the alien woman, to us, or to yourself."

Resar straightened at the rebuke and glared at the Healer from beneath his bandages. Then he wheeled and strode to the firepit that struggled against the chill of the stone room. For a long moment he watched the pulsing crimson glow of the coals and silence stretched out between the two men, punctuated by muffled footsteps and the cries of the sick outside the door. Kureil's office, with its thick walls and heavy draperies, was a well of stillness in the noisy and hectic hospital. Finally Resar turned and said tersely. "Explain."

"No. You can do that better than I. You were there." With a gesture he stifled the nobleman's cry of exasperation. "What kind of animals did they ride?"

"Chammies," Resar answered in puzzlement. "They all rode chammies that were fresh and well-fed."

"Rare mounts, are they not?"

"You know they are."

"How were they armed?"

"Tana-do, with razor edges."

"Armor?"

"There were breastplates under their rags. I found them in the cul-de-sac." There was less confusion in his voice now.

"During the attack, was it each man for himself?"

"*You* might have thought it was so but I saw discipline in the fighting."

"They looted corpses and stole pack animals?"

"Some of the pack animals were scattered and the bodies were untouched." Resar's voice became more animated as the thrust of Kureil's question became apparent.

"Did they rape the women?"

"Not Neva. Not the one I found."

"And what of their dead? Were there many? Did you recognize them?"

"If there were casualties, they took them away. I thought it strange at the time." He returned to the table and pounded it with his fist. "You're right. I've been acting like a stubborn child. The evidence was there all along—a fool could have seen it right away."

"Ah, but they did not plan on there being any survivors to put the evidence together. With their lead and the first snow only days away, who could have mounted a pursuit fast enough to catch them? Even with you right behind them, they still disappeared into the Spine. But all of these answers only lead us to the really important questions. If not gormrith, then who were they? Why did they want to kill you and your brother? And why the disguise?"

"Perhaps they pretended to be gormrith so that we would underestimate them and they were right. Your second question is harder to answer. If my brother had any blood enemies, he did not warn me of them."

"Then eliminating the alternatives may be the way to find the answer," Kureil said coolly. "We have dismissed gormrith. Could it have been Vethis alone?"

"He must have had a motive but he did not have the kind of money it takes to buy men who fight like that and don't take plunder. He could have organized the attack for someone else but I can't think of anyone who would have gained by our deaths."

"Could one of your father's contract sons have joined forces with Vethis to gain Highfields for himself?"

Resar pulled a chair away from the table, twisted it around, and straddled it. He rested his arms on its back. "My father was not by nature a generous man but he always took good care of his contract children to prevent that very thing from happening. Each of them was well settled when Bentar died. Besides, I do not think that any of them would have had the audacity to strike at both lord and brother. So where does that leave us?"

There was another silence. Outside, a fierce wind whipped snow against the hospital's pitched roof. Off in one of the wards a patient screamed and footsteps rushed toward the sound. Almost reluctantly, Kureil replied. "It leaves us with the Brotherhood," he said flatly.

Resar's head snapped back. "The Bhoma-San? Are you serious?"

"About whether they did it or why I think they did?"

"Both."

"As you said a moment ago, Captain, one question is easier to answer than the other. My years as a healer have not all been spent in this hospital. I have traveled to many holdings and villages and I have worked in great houses. Several times I have encountered the Brotherhood. More often I had to deal with the results of their actions—when the victims could still be saved. What I have not learned myself I have heard from others and I can tell you this: the surest sign of the Bhoma-San is when there is no sign at all. Look for them to be where there are no tracks, no clues, no reason. Seek them not in the shadows but in the absence of light, not in noise but in silence. When all the signs seem to point to someone else, or to no one at all, they are almost certainly involved. This is such a time. We can find no substance, no motive, no direction but there is order within confusion. I guarantee it. Now we must find out what they seek to accomplish and why." Kureil mas-

saged his lined forehead with the tips of his fingers and
then steepled his hands before him. "That will be the
hardest task of all. The Brotherhood keeps its secrets well-
guarded behind a triple wall of myth, isolation, and coercion. No one outside understands what they do or why.
And they are ruthless. If they knew what I have learned
about them, I would not see the sun rise tomorrow."

"Understanding that," Resar replied, "the question becomes, what do I do next?"

"No, there are really two questions," Kureil stated. "The
first one is, what do you do about the woman, Dara, whom
the Brotherhood stole from you and spirited away to the
far side of the Spine, perhaps to the Lost City itself. You
know the answer to that question as well as I." Resar's
mouth twisted but he said nothing. Kureil continued,
"The second question is, as the new lord of Highfields,
how will you protect it? I know that you would like nothing better than to assemble an expedition and go charging
off through the mountains in the cold passages to somehow
find the other end of the trail. But in your absence . . ."

"I know, I know. Highfields is my responsibility, one
that I will carry well and willingly. It's just difficult to give
up, to leave this thing unfinished, to admit defeat." He
sighed heavily.

Kureil looked at his patient with professional eyes. The
concussion was healed, along with the patches of frostbite
Resar had brought down out of the Spine. Beneath the
bandage on his forehead the scar was still red and angry
but it was clean and would heal without infection. There
was a good chance that, where it entered the scalp, the
hair would change color. The blisters on the odd burn
around his ankle had broken yet they still wept fluid.
Resar had strict orders to keep it covered and free of dirt
until scabs formed. That mark, too, would scar but was not
as visible as the other. There were marks inside as well;
Resar was no longer the man who had led his Ranger troop
free of all burdens but his own resentment. Resar would
manage Highfields well, perhaps better than his brother
had, but he would never be the same again.

Next morning the going was harder. First the men dug

out of the drift-buried tent and they emerged into a world
that was daunting. The dome of the sky was a clear, vivid
yellow that gave it a feeling of great height. But it was
empty. Nothing flew or hovered or cried in all its expanse
and Portifahr read that as a bad sign. Weapons were held
at the ready. The wind had dropped in the storm's wake
and the air was still, mitigating the cold. Around them the
contours of the mountain were changed, masked by high
drifts with knife-sharp edges. After freeing the tent from
its snowy shell and packing up, they set off down a glaring
slope that was featureless except for the sinuous drifts and
their own shadows. As before, they used heat to make a
path and and walked single-file behind the plume of vapor
raised by the melting snow. Whenever possible they kept
to where the snow was less deep but were sometimes
forced to cut through huge drifts and in those places the
snow walls on either side of the path loomed over their
heads. As the sun grew higher and brighter its rays reflected brilliantly off the surrounding snowfields and the
inescapable glare blinded them, even when they squinted.

At mid-day they rested in another grove of the fleshy-
needled taiga trees. The russet shade beneath the trees
gave some relief from the dazzling light but it was quite a
while before their eyes could adjust and they stopped
seeing green dots. The branches above them were bent
and bowed by heavy loads of snow. Now and again the still
air was pierced by the sharp crack of a limb snapping
beneath its burden. In the afternoon the visibility grew
even worse as they walked downward into the setting sun.
Their goal was a dark line in the distance that marked the
edge of a vast forest. Its mass furred the mountain's lower
slopes and blanketed the foothills beyond. The snow would
be thinner beneath the trees, which would also provide
both shelter and protection. Portifahr meant to reach the
forest by sunset but Dara, growing tired, doubted that
they could cross that much of the snowfields before the
sun touched the horizon. To speed their passage Portifahr
led them over a ridge of rock that had been scoured clean
by the storm. On its exposed ledges the snow lay only
ankle deep and they could move quickly. The glare grew
worse. To avoid it, Dara had learned to fix her gaze on the

back of the man she followed. Another day on the snow-fields, she thought, and they would all be totally blind. She paused on the crest of one ledge, preparing to slip down to the next when, without warning, a great mailed fist struck Dara's right shoulder and gripped it, knocking her backwards. Instead of falling onto the rocks, however, she was lifted smoothly upwards and carried away from the men. It happened so abruptly that it was unreal and Dara had the sensation of having dropped into a waking nightmare. Below her the ground pulled away carrying with it the line of marchers, frozen with astonishment. Above her a huge black shadow pumped rhythmically across the sky. Unable to get a good look at it, Dara was aware only of a sickening stench of carrion, fur, and ammonia that billowed around her with each massive wingbeat and of the inflexible grip on a shoulder that should have been in pain and was instead oddly numb.

The dream shattered when one of the men raised and fired his crossbow, followed almost instantaneously by the others. Dara flinched from the volley of arrows but found her body sluggish and unresponsive. The arrows, aimed expertly, struck the creature above her. The fist shuddered and she could feel something hard grating against her collarbone. Then the wings stopped their inexorable strokes and a frantic flurrying began. Another flight of arrows hit their mark and the animal began to fall toward the ground with appalling speed.

Then Dara lay bleeding in a drift, gasping for the breath that had been driven from her lungs on impact. The mailed grip was gone but above her stood a huge beast screaming raucous defiance at the puny men who circled it. It had a small head with dark, glittering eyes, a nose that was little more than ridged nostril slits and a short wrinkled muzzle, lined with carnivore's teeth, through which the creature snarled and hissed. It was an astonishingly ugly face, one that belonged hanging upside down in a cave. Leathery wings, fully outstretched, overshadowed her and whirled up clouds of stinging ice particles as the creature struck at its attackers. Both body and head, spiked with arrows, were disproportionately small compared to the awesome wings and the formidable talons, each nearly the size of her hand. Dara tried to crawl away from the hooked claws that shifted and jabbed around her, out into the open where one of the men could pull her to safety but her body would not obey. Lines of pain began to race down from her numb shoulder, surrounding her chest with bright bands that squeezed and sparked in pulses along with her heartbeat. Her mouth grew dry and her tongue swelled to fill it. Red patches eddied before her eyes. A high keening rose from the drifts and echoed in her ears, swelling and receding with the rhythm of the pain. The bands grew tighter and the pulses grew slower and Dara drifted away into a sea of red and burning snow.

CHAPTER 11

Resar stared fiercely out the great sheet-crystal window of the big house's central living room, fists clenched at his sides. The rippled pane looked out over the compound wall to a barren plot of ground. There, fat snowflakes fell heavily from dun-colored clouds, rapidly obscuring the charred and cold remains of a funeral pyre. "He will come back," he said firmly, his attention still fixed on the silent pattern of soft white on jagged black. Then he turned and spoke again, this time into the warm room. "He will come back and when he does, I'll be waiting for him."

From her chair by the fire, Callain's level gaze glowed aquamarine. The striking beauty of her face, framed by a mass of vibrant hair, was marred by ashes smudged in the traditional way across her cheeks. A flame-red sash was draped vividly across the dark wuliveen bodice of her dress, heralding her bereavement. No grief surged beneath the ritual trappings of her mourning, however, nor would it ever. When Resar had returned, alone, to tell her in blunt words of her lord and husband's death only anger and frustration had filled her. Outwardly she had performed all that custom required of her and if her eyes

173

were dry and her voice controlled, many would attribute it to the discipline of her rank. Then, silently and in solitude, she had raged at her thwarted plans and blighted future. None knew her rights better than she. None knew better that as a childless widow she had few rights at all. Callain could not even decide her own future; that was legally determined by the heir to Highfields. If Resar's decision was not to her liking, then her only recourse was to return to Starshadow Pass as a dependent upon her brother. In that childhood home, now ruled by her sister in marriage, Callain's position would be even worse. Most likely she would be married off again to someone of her brother's choosing and she did not care to wager the balance of her life on that choice. For once, therefore, Callain had reason to be grateful for Resar's strong code of honor. Sensitive to the delicacy of her situation, he had quickly reassured her that she would always have a safe and peaceful home at Highfields. She had smiled and thanked him with elegant courtesy and only the deepening green of her eyes had betrayed the burgeoning anger inside. A safe home and a quiet life had never been part of Callain's plans for her future. Yet, for now, they would serve.

Since his return, she had watched Resar very carefully. She watched him now and reflected, not for the first time, that fate might have handed her an opportunity instead of a crippling blow. If so, it was time to grasp that opportunity and shape it to her own ambitions. She was aware of his new moodiness, however, and thus she prompted him gently, "Who will return?"

"Vethis, of course," he replied, speaking at her without really seeing her. He was looking inward instead at his own failings and outward at alternate courses for the future.

"Why should he? I thought he was on the far side of the Spine." Callain knew well the reason for Vethis' return but she wanted to keep Resar talking, to draw him out.

"He is now. But he will come back here because he thinks that both Amrith and I are dead. That leaves Highfields open and vulnerable while my father's contract sons litigate their claims to rightful inheritance and squabble through the courts." He nodded at Callain. "While you might be able to put up a spirited defense, you have no legal claim to back it up. Besides, Vethis knows everything there is to know about this place, including its weak points. He'll be back. But he won't find what he expects."

"What will he find?"

Resar looked her in the eye for the first time and smiled grimly. "He'll find men he's never seen before deployed in ways he's never thought of. He'll find strength where he expected weakness. And where he anticipated a triumph, he'll find defeat. We'll be waiting for him and he'll be a dead man before he strikes a blow."

"How can I help you, my brother?"

Resar did not hesitate with his answer. "By staying here and baiting the trip. You may not have a legal claim but an alliance with you would appear to legitimize his actions. Then, when we've drawn him in, we'll strike."

"I would like to see that," Callain said with true feeling.

"Yes, I'm sure you would," Resar replied and Callain was startled by a sharpness in his voice that she had never heard before. In his face there was an expression that made her uneasy. It was like that white streak that had begun to grow around the scar where it entered his scalp: strange, eyecatching, disquieting. Callain reminded herself to be very careful around this man who was so different from the brother she had married. His simplicity and genuine concern could easily lull her into underestimating him. That was a trap and she would be wise to be wary of it.

The next day, two of Callain's messengers rode swiftly out of the South Gate. They stayed alongside one another until the road came down out of the pass, then separated, leaving tracks in the snow that pointed off in different directions.

Fiery red then freezing black, swirling together, advanced and receded, and both colors were part of a painful struggle for breath. The fight for each breath went on for years, accompanied by a ringing of the snow crystals that chimed in phase with the surging crimson waves. There was no end to the torment of sucking in air, knowing that with each inhalation the pain would blossom, the colors whirl, the snow ring and echo. Gradually the colors began to fade and the black became night, the red was the brilliant writhing of a fire. Faces separated from the flames and floated in midair, twisting and stretching into distorted shapes. When the fire flared, birds of flame soared into the night sky where they dipped and whirled in dizzying patterns.

Dara summoned her feeble strength and concentrated on what seemed the most real. She became aware that she was lying down and the men were scattered around her. The fire was the brazier, burning high, and the sky was the dome of the tent above them. She located Portifahr kneeling by the brazier with his back to her. The outlaws were talking but their words flew by too quickly for her to seize them and read their meaning. The birds were words and the words were pain. She closed her eyes tightly and a vivid memory of the K'thi's attack swept over her, bringing with it a flaring pain in her left shoulder. That was strange; it had been numb. Why should it hurt now? Dara attempted to move and found that her limbs, while responsive, were weak and not completely under her control. Her tongue, still dry and distended, foiled any attempt at speech.

Once she had absorbed all this information, Dara focused on what was going on around her in the tent. This was difficult because reality continued to mingle inexplicably with illusion and made her feel as if she were observing a surrealistic film that flickered right in front of her but had no substance. Then Portifahr stood and turned and Dara saw the long knife in his hand, its tip glowing white. The illusion vanished and she was abruptly in hard reality. When he moved toward her, Dara struggled to crawl away but strong hands grasped her and held her down. She was pinned to the blanket while Portifahr drew closer with the knife. Dara's screams were trapped by her swollen tongue and she watched with horror as the glowing knife descended. When it touched her already-burning shoulder, the firebirds plunged out of the blackness and exploded on her skin. Her body was rigid beneath the restraining hands and an agonized cry, more howl than scream, forced its way out. Before its echoes died she slipped back into the swirling red and black sea.

The boat was moving slowly through a light chop. Rigging creaked and waves thudded against the hull with monotonous regularity. A patch of sky overhead moved back and forth with an easier rhythm but the wind off the bay was cold and cutting. Why was she sleeping on deck? How long had she been asleep? Who was at the helm? Flushed despite the wind and thoroughly disoriented, Dara came up a level closer to consciousness and began to register details. The sky was yellowish, not the deep blue of the October bay and the craft smelled more like sweaty men than salt spray. She turned her head slightly to the side and the sail boat of her dreams disappeared, replaced by a litter slung between two of the outlaws whose steady marching produced the choppy motion. Right, left, back and forth . . . back and forth. . . . right, back . . . Nausea pooled in her stomach and Dara was suddenly and violently sick. Rolling to the edge of the litter brought her shoulder to flaming life but the queasiness was of more immediate importance. The litter was lowered and she crouched over the ground and retched until her stomach was knotted beneath her ribcage and she could not draw another breath. Still, she could not stop. Nothing more came up but the spasms continued uncontrollably. She gasped but no air came in. Then a large callused hand pulled her up.

"Now breathe! In. Push out. In again, deeper. Out."

Dara struggled to obey, succeeded, and drew in a shallow lungful of cold air. The next breath was stronger.

"Better, Karait, better. After surviving a K'thi, we would hate to have you cast your insides on the snow."

Dara looked up. The outlaws were grouped in a semicircle around the litter but Vethis stood apart, his hawkface watching her without emotion. Returning her attention to Portifahr, Dara moved her left arm and gasped at the pain generated by even this small movement.

"Is there much pain?" he asked.

Dara nodded. "More when it's moved."

He unslung his pack and searched inside it, then removed a packet of dusty green powder and his cup. Mixing the powder with water from a canteen, he handed the cup to Dara. "Drink. This will lessen the pain."

Dara sipped the mixture, afraid that her stomach would reject the vile-looking mixture. But the drink, which tasted musty, like the cool air of an old stone cellar, went down easily and stayed down. She finished it and handed the cup back to Portifahr. Dara wanted to stand up and walk on her own but before she could gather her strength the world around her faded and she sank once more into sleep, only this time it was free of pain.

When she awoke again, she saw the sun's great orange disk, framed by tree trunks, poised on the horizon and for a moment she thought it was setting. Then the bustle around her and the brightening sky told her that camp was breaking at dawn. She sat up, surprised at the effort it required using only one arm. Her left arm was in a sling. They were in the forest now but how far in she had no way of telling. From where he was packing up the tent Portifahr looked over and saw her move. He came to where she sat. "Well, awake at last and feeling better?"

"No. Wretched. What happened. Why am I so weak? How did I get injured?"

"You don't remember?"

"Nothing that makes sense. It's all confused, like just a strange dream."

Like a conjuror producing a coin from mid-air he proffered his open hand. On it lay a smooth object of what looked like stained ivory. It was thin, nearly as long as his palm, and curved like a scimitar, tapering to a wicked point. "The talon of a K'thi," explained Portifahr. "I removed it from your shoulder three days ago."

Gingerly Dara took it from him and was surprised by its weight. She touched the point cautiously and noticed a small aperture in its tip. "Is it hollow?" she asked.

"A K'thi has three large talons for striking and carrying its prey. The furrows on your shoulder come from them. This fourth talon is retractable and connected to a gland in the leg. At the strike, it extends into the victim and a paralytic agent is pumped through it. This poison is strong enough to immobilize large animals and kill small ones by stopping the heart. Your shoulder should have become numb almost immediately, yes? I thought so. The poison probably could not kill a full-grown man but you are considerably smaller. That you survived this attack . . . that you regained consciousness in such a short time . . . that you can move now, is remarkable. I have never seen such a recovery."

Unwilling to explain how her alien metabolism might have saved her life, Dara shrugged, unwisely, and wakened her punctured shoulder. It wasn't numb anymore. Portifahr checked the bandage over her wound and tested the sling. "It will take a while to heal," he said. "Let it rest until then. Afterwards you will have to exercise those muscles well and often if you want to regain the full use of your arm."

Dara grimaced and thanked him but she remained seated until it was time to leave.

After many days of marching through the cold shadows of an endless forest, they emerged from the foothills onto the last hilltop. It looked down onto a sloping floodplain where rain and meltwater from the peaks had carved a complex of braided streams. The streambeds were frozen now into city threads that curled and looped into an intricate design. For now, the riverbed would be easy to cross. When the snow melted on the slopes, however, the design and the sandy bed would disappear beneath one huge, surging river that would be a formidable obstacle to any traveler.

Beyond it stretched a landscape that caused them to stop in a ragged line and gaze in awe. Another type of plain, at once stark and breathtakingly beautiful, spread for uncounted miles. Its center and its source, a huge cone-shaped volcano, rose in dignity on the horizon. The top was wreathed in smoke or clouds and its bulk was reduced to human scale by the distance. From it had flowed great undulating streams of once-molten rock, frozen now in twisted and ropy patterns. Over the years these flows had accumulated into a vast basaltic plain. This black mass ended before them in stubby toes and sinuous tongues at the river's edge. Black sand in the riverbed attested to the age of some eruptions. The smooth surface of others declared that they had occurred too recently for weather to have touched them.

"The Plains of Thunder," said Vethis quietly. "I had thought them only a legend."

"And for good reason," replied Portifahr. "But they are real—and growing."

"What is *that* called?" Dara asked, pointing toward the distant mountain.

"The Splinter of the Sun," said Portifahr briefly. He looked about them and at the slope down to the river. "We'll camp here for the night," he added.

They set up camp while slanting bars of wine-gold sunlight streamed out from behind the volcano but it was dark by the time they finished eating. As if reluctant to enter the tent's confinement, the men built a large fire that crackled and spit, lighting in flares their tired bodies and drawn faces. Its cheeriness and warmth were welcome but could not dispel their deep weariness. Dara sat by the fire with the others, watching its leaping flames and looking up at the brilliant night sky. One of the Watchers rose into the sky from the rim of the basaltic plain and Dara's curiosity overcame her usual quietness.

"What is the legend?" she asked Portifahr.

"Legend?" He, too, had been staring into the fire and his mind was clearly on other things.

She gestured out into the darkness. "The Plains of Thunder, the Splinter of the Sun. Vethis mentioned a legend."

"Oh. Yes," he nodded. Then he sat quietly for a moment, searching his memory and assembling the story.

"In the legend," he began, "the sky goddess Darghiel left her windy home among the clouds to marry Therillin, radiant god of the sun. They lived together happily in the high dome of the sky until Darghiel conceived a child. Wanting a safe home for her baby, Darghiel left Therillin's side and descended to the peaceful grasslands, searching for a new home. When she had chosen just the right place, Therillin cast down a great splinter of the sun's fire. The bolt raised up a steep peak so that Darghiel could ascend to speak with him and let him know that all went well with her. Darghiel lived quietly among the grasses at the mountain's base while her belly swelled and in due time she bore a strong healthy son named Wyeast. He was a large child who grew quickly and learned twice as fast as he grew. To keep his strong body and nimble mind occupied, and to teach him the skills needed by a child with his royal lineage, Wyeast's parents built a city. They populated it with people and animals and this city became his kingdom, where he ruled with Darghiel's guidance while Therillin watched proudly from his duties in the heavens.

"Wyeast's city flourished and spread out around the mountain for, after its violent beginning, the peak remained quiet and its slopes nourished the inhabitants with rich soil. The air was warm, Darghiel brought plentiful rains, and no one went hungry. Wyeast's city became a place of great learning and greater prosperity, a city of science and magic. Artists and scholars created beauty and wisdom. The secrets of life were explored and mastered and many of those secrets once learned, are now lost. It is said that its wise men could even talk, through Wyeast, to the stars.

"Wyeast grew into a young man, full of the eagerness of the young, and in time he become impatient to join his father in his shining realm. But Therillin was not ready to relinquish any of his power over the sun, for in his years of watching the city prosper, Therillin had grown jealous of Wyeast's success and threatened by his strength. Again and again he refused his son's importunings until Wyeast turned angry and resentful. Then the mountain flashed with the fires of their argument. Darghiel pleaded with both son and husband, begging them to cease their fighting, but, in their fury, they barely noticed her. The dark clouds of her sorrow hung over the grasslands.

"Frustrated, she turned from them and beseeched the city's inhabitants to leave before they were harmed. Some—a very few—listened to her and set off across the grasslands to seek shelter in the distant mountains. The rest were concerned but saw no cause for real fear. They had been protected for so long that they did not fear anything, far less their god and patron who had given them such a good life.

"Finally, inevitably, Therillin and Wyeast came to a contest of their strength and wills. Then the mountain roared with the force of their conflict. For days and weeks they strove, father against son. Darghiel wept at first and then, ignored, returned to her home among the winds. The contest ended only when Therillin, in desperation, summoned the power of the sun and hurled it at Wyeast. In the cataclysm that followed, Wyeast was destroyed and his city with him. To ensure his victory, Therillin covered the land with liquid stone so that never again could people live there and prosper.

"The poison of their hatred spread from this place and that is why even now the women do not conceive easily. In vain has the Lady striven to undo his evil, or so the story says, and to return our people to fecundity. She is aided by Darghiel's tears, the rainstorms that bring life to the land. It is said that a woman who fasts for twenty days, and drinks only rainwater during that time, is supposed to conceive—provided that she has also honored the Lady with a suitable partner.

"But Therillin keeps watch from the stars and his mountain remains on guard here. It still throws out liquid rock, fire, and ash, warning all to stay away and not risk the fate of those who lived in the Lost City of Wyeast."

There was silence again, as deep as the night sky. Vethis got up and put more wood on the fire. It dimmed for a moment and then flared up. Portifahr looked up at him with a faint smile. "Do you believe the legend, Vethis?"

The other man brushed his hands off disgustedly and sat down. "I believe in nothing but my wits and my right arm," he replied grimly.

Dara snorted. He took everything too seriously, even himself; that was one of his problems. "It is a very interesting legend, Portifahr. I thank you for telling it." One by one they rose from the fire and entered the tent for the night. But before sleeping, Dara thought to herself that many legends have their roots in fact. She wanted to get another look at the Splinter of the Sun.

Before setting out across the frozen stream bed the next day, they each cut a stout walking stick of sehliki, the blue "bamboo" that grew nearly everywhere in Khyren's temperate zones. Dara removed her arm from the sling despite the wound's soreness and her stiff muscles. She would need both hands when crossing the ice and the treacherous black plain beyond it. The stream took just moments to ford and then they clambered up the lava's edge. Grimacing at the effort, Dara walked carefully over its eroded surface. The mountain rose ahead of them and slightly to the left, smoking in the clear morning air. As they walked, Dara observed the volcano and its lava in puzzlement. She actually knew quite a bit about volcanology: in the same way an average boy becomes fascinated by dinosaurs, her daughter had developed an intense, if transient, desire to be a volcanologist. Together they had read through every book on the subject in the children's library and several of the adult volumes as well. The following year Samantha's ambition had shifted to winning the three-day event but Dara remembered a lot of her enforced education. That was why what she saw did not make sense.

The Splinter of the Sun appeared to be a steep-sided strato volcano, the kind which lies dormant for long periods and then erupts violently with ash and cinders. Such volcanoes were frequently explosive and highly dangerous. That part fit well with the legend. Yet they walked on solidified lava that was thick, smooth, and ropey, the kind Hawaiians called *pahoehoe*. This usually flowed from the more active but less violent and dome-shaped shield volcano. The two did not usually go together. As she shifted the pieces of the puzzle around, Dara reminded herself in annoyance that Earth's geological processes did not necessarily apply on a different planet.

Through the day they walked in a more southerly direction with the sun off to their right as it sank instead of directly ahead of them. Portifahr used the volcano as a compass so that its symmetrical mass remained always on their left. Possessed of its own somber beauty, the Splinter of the Sun fascinated Dara. The geological anomalies she had already observed raised questions she wanted to answer. The more immediate problem, however, was how to traverse its petrified outflow without falling. The convoluted basaltic plain was rough going on foot and would have been impossible for a saddle beast to negotiate. Its surface varied from smooth, glassy stone that was slippery and treacherous to crumbling pumice that could lacerate the skin of a careless hand or leg. They moved slowly, each person placing feet carefully and using their sehliki staffs to brace themselves.

The air was less frigid at this lower altitude than it had been in the mountains but a strong cold wind bowled off the Spine and beat continuously at their backs. Although quite flat to the eye, the great rock plateau was riven with gullies that dropped away beneath their feet. Small plants grew tenaciously where the rock had weathered into black soil but nothing grew tall enough to break the force of the wind. It was still very much winter and their thermal suits continued to work hard.

In the late afternoon of the second day Portifahr led them into a steep gully. They followed its nearly vertical walls, walking single file, and stepping carefully on the narrow floor. It was not long before the gully ended in a rounded hole. Dara gritted her teeth at the thought of going underground again. This time, however, they made no special preparations and took no precautions against an arcane menace. They simply stacked their staffs against the stone, broke out their lume-rods, and stepped into a curving tunnel. Its walls and ceiling were smooth and yet patterned with what looked like frozen drops. Another product typical of a shield volcano, the old lava tube twisted erratically and after only a short while Dara lost all sense of direction. She plodded along, following Portifahr's light until the tube ended in a cave-in. A small patch of the ceiling had dropped in and a dim glow told her that the sun was setting. Another tunnel, smaller and obviously man-made, led off at another angle. They moved onwards and Dara placed one foot in front of the other mechanically as she fell into the numb fatigue that resembled walking in her sleep. She could have been doing it always and would go on doing it forever.

Giving herself up to the lethargy, Dara did not at first realize the significance of the door when they reached it. Then, at the sight of it gleaming in the blue-green light, she was jolted back to wakefulness. The door was round and solid, set heavily into the surrounding rock. Its machined metal surface reflected their lights dully, like the door to a vault of the entrance to an airlock. The unmarked portal was possessed of a quiet authority and radiated technology. Portifahr placed his hand on a flat piece of rock to one side of the door. A high-frequency whine sounded briefly, then the door slid quietly and effortlessly into the rock wall. Portifahr led them through and Dara noticed that only she and Vethis demonstrated any eagerness to see what lay beyond. As she had long ago conjectured, the others were familiar with such things. The door slid shut with weighty finality behind them, separating the darkness from the light.

CHAPTER 12

They stood in a long straight corridor whose walls and ceiling were made of an opaque and neutral-colored substance that was obviously synthetic. The floor resembled highly-polished obsidian yet cast back no reflection as the stone would have. Instead, it absorbed their images and appeared to be a window into infinity. It was like walking suspended over a black pit or looking down onto the end of the galaxy. Portifahr started off again immediately and Dara studied the details of their surroundings as they walked. She saw recessed artificial lighting and felt cooled and reprocessed air. She did not see wood or stone or hammered metal. It was like walking from a crude pre-industrial society into NASA headquarters and the change was abrupt enough to make her feel disoriented. She could only imagine what Vethis felt. He walked firmly with the others, however, his gaze fixed straight ahead and no flicker of emotion on his face.

The remarkable corridor also deadened the sound of their footsteps and kept them from echoing. It stretched far ahead, intersected at intervals by others just like it. Behind Portifahr's lead they turned left into one of these side passages, then right into another part of what rapidly became a featureless labyrinth. After their fourth turn, Dara abandoned her automatic attempt to keep track of their path. No landmarks or furnishings were visible to distinguish one hall from the other and she had the distinct feeling that a trail of breadcrumbs would have been discreetly swept up by the unseen environmental control system. Once, the floor rumbled beneath them and they stopped until the vibrations had subsided. Dara was glad that Portifahr had skirted the volcano and she would have been happier even further away from its power.

Finally they reached a corridor different from the others only because a series of identical doors punctuated its walls. There, standing in front of the first door, a man awaited them. He was large and stocky with a muscular build. His hair was light by the standards of Khyren and his eyes were an undistinguished green. His face was marked by stubbornness, however, especially around the mouth, and it combined with the solid body to create an air of permanence. He guarded the door with his arms folded across his chest. When Portifahr stopped before him, he saluted with one hand raised vertically. Then he opened the door and both men turned to Dara. No one spoke but it was obvious they wanted her to enter. She hesitated and Portifahr gestured graciously. "Do us the honor of being our guest. This room is yours." She chose to ignore the irony of his words and went in.

Behind her a change of air pressure more than any sound told her that the door had closed. She resisted the instinctive need to turn and test it: the door would be locked. Looking around she was pleased to find the room spacious, clean, and comfortable. A large bed stood at the far end with a clothes chest at its foot. To her left were a table and chair, to her right a softer, more comfortable, chair. A colorful rug, hand-loomed in shades ranging from burgundy to rose, brightened the room and softened its artificial, institutional appearance. There were no windows, as was to be expected if they were still underground, but there was a ventilation grille in the ceiling. At her right elbow was another door. Dara opened it and exclaimed in delight. There before her was a real, authen-

tic, civilized bathroom. Besides the necessary and welcome fixtures there was a shower cubicle. She tried it
tentatively, half expecting sonic waves or some other unfamiliar cleansing agent to emerge. Instead, wonderfully hot
water shot out in a tingling spray.

Exhausted as she was, Dara could not resist. She stripped
off her clothes, peeling off miles of trail dirt with them.
Then came the thermal suit with sweat and blood mixed
and crusted together on it. Leaving the dressing on her
shoulder she stepped beneath the water and closed her
eyes in pure luxury. In a recessed niche she found soapweed
and a vial of blue liquid that smelled like shampoo. Using
them both she lathered and rinsed and lathered again. She
scrubbed oil and dirt and tangles from her hair, grateful to
find nothing more animated in it. Then she removed the
softened dressing and cleansed the wound with its new
scab gingerly but thoroughly. It was probably the longest
shower of her life. When finally she turned off the water
she vibrated all over. It was an energizing sensation, as if
she had emerged wet and shining from a chrysalis. Dara
had not been this clean since the night of the ceremony. . . .

She pushed that thought away and took a deep breath.
There were no towels, only a mat in one corner. Curious,
she stepped on it and was instantly bathed in the rays of
what felt like a bank of heat lamps. In moments she was
dry and warm. Dara could not bear the thought of donning
any of her clothes, which lay in a grimy heap on the floor.
Investigating, she found a soft robe in the chest by the bed
and slipped it on quickly. It was large for her but clean
and comfortable and that was sufficient. Wrapped up in it,
she lay down on the bed to think.

Dara jerked awake abruptly when the door opened. She
sat upright, temporarily disoriented, her heart pounding.
The lights in her room had dimmed so that the two men
who entered were only black silhouettes against the brighter
lights of the corridor. They came closer and she saw that
one was the guard and the other was an old man. The
latter was small and walked unsteadily, yet when he stood
before her Dara saw that he burned with an inner strength
that radiated from his eyes. He carried a covered box
which he placed next to her on the bed. She stood quickly

and moved away from it. The vibrant green eyes regarded her directly and the lined face held a curious expression—almost as if he were confronting a refreshing change in a dull routine. "My name is Rathiyas," he said and there was no mistaking the touch of humor in his voice. "I am a doctor. Not a healer, a doctor. Please sit down again and loosen the neck of your robe. I must examine the wound." Dara looked pointedly at the guard and Rathiyas made an authoritative gesture. The guard moved back to stand by the door but did not leave.

The lights in the room brightened and the doctor nodded in approval. Dara slid the robe down off her shoulder exposing the long gashes made by the K'thi's grasping talons and the star-puckered scar left by the venomous claw. Rathiyas examined her shoulder thoroughly before giving his approval. "The wound is clean and healing nicely. The worst danger of infection is past." Since he seemed to be talking to himself and not to her, Dara did not bother to reply. With practiced efficiency he put a clean dressing over the new scab and continued his one-sided conversation. "A K'thi," he said. "Hmm, extraordinary." He had her demonstrate the range of movement that she could manage with both arms and then went on to examine the rest of her in much the same way as any other doctor would have. When he had finished, he warned her against using her arm for any strenuous activity and demonstrated a simple exercise for restoring flexibility to the damaged muscles. "And don't overdo it. A little exercise only, each day. If you do too much too fast, you'll re-open the puncture and have all the healing to do over again." He placed a rainbow-colored lozenge under her tongue and watched her carefully until it had dissolved with a taste of honeysuckle. Then he packed up his medical kit and was ushered out by the guard, who followed him through the door as silently as he had arrived.

Dara refastened her robe and lay back on the bed. So far, so good. There was no denying the fact, however, that this underground warren was Portifahr's destination and that she had been delivered. Sometime, presumably soon, she would be taken to the man Vethis had called her "new master," the man who had sent his trained killers out to get her. She searched for a way to prepare herself for this but found only that she did not know what to prepare for. The terror she had felt when Neva was killed rushed back unbidden but she got herself under control. Nothing in the way they had treated her so far indicated that she was under imminent threat to her life. They had certainly not brought her all the way here to kill her when they could just as easily have left her on the road with Neva. They, whoever "they" were, wanted her for something and perhaps that gave her a position from which to bargain. Beyond that, speculation served no purpose until she learned more.

The bed rumbled beneath her and she wondered how such a sophisticated complex could exist in proximity to the active volcano. They were underground in an area of unstable geology and she found it difficult to understand why anyone would choose to inhabit such a location. Her thoughts wandered around all the loose ends of this ongoing mystery, seeking a place where she could begin to knot things together. She wanted to figure out what kind of place this was, who these technologically-trained people were, what awaited her in the future. While she struggled with these questions, rainbow-colored sleep crept over her.

There was little time the next day—or perhaps it was the day after that—to spend thinking. Soon after she arose, the sullen guard delivered a large breakfast which Dara consumed totally. It had been a long time since she had eaten anything and even longer since the meal had been hot and ample. When he returned, bearing a suit of what appeared to be boy's clothing, Dara pushed at his shell of silence. "Thank you," she said, looking at him directly. "Breakfast was delicious." He gave her a brief, sharp glance in return and left. She had finished dressing in the slightly large, but clean, clothing he had brought by the time he entered the room a third time accompanied by another guard. Adjusting the full shirt, Dara felt a chill at the nape of her neck. The time had come. Moving with a casualness she did not feel, she walked between them out of the safe haven. Now she would meet the man who had shattered her carefully-constructed life for his own unknown purposes.

Once more she paced the long featureless corridors,

wondering at the system her guards and the other inhabitants used to navigate them. They came to a moving walkway and ascended several levels to another corridor filled with sunlight that poured from windows set so high in one wall that she could see nothing from them. They turned left and left again before leaving the sunlight and coming to the end of the passage. One door was set into it and her guard touched a sensor panel located on the wall to the right of this portal. The door opened on a plain, almost sterile, room occupied by two men. The one who sat off to her right was of medium height but carried above-average weight. His round amiable face was punctuated by piercing eyes of a darker than usual blue-green. The plain brown tunic and trousers that he wore were distinguished by a wide sash embroidered intricately in a many-colored design. Next to him stood a younger man, tall and slender. A gaunt face set in grim lines topped his figure. He also wore austere brown clothing but his sash had only a simple design in purple and red. Dara stopped and gazed from one man to the other, thinking that they were an odd pair but warning herself at the same time not to underestimate them. An almost visible tension in the room raised the hair on the nape of her neck. Behind her the door closed with one of the guards remaining inside. He stood to the right of the door with his back to it.

"You are welcome here," said the heavy man. "Please, make yourself comfortable." He gestured toward a contoured reclining couch in the center of the room. Dara looked around. The only other piece of furniture was a small table near the two men which held a cloth-covered tray. She did not like this chamber or its furnishings and she had no intention of lying down in it. And there was something else—a scent?—something she could not quite pin down that nagged at her memory.

"I am honored by your welcome," she replied civilly, "but I have only recently risen and I prefer to stand." She took a few steps forward so that the couch was between her and the two men.

"As you wish. I am the Counsel-Regent. You may address me as Your Grace." He waved one hand toward the tall man. "This is Scaure, my aide. We have looked forward to this meeting."

Dara thought of the circumstances which had brought her here and an image of Neva's surprised face flashed before her. "I am afraid I cannot share your pleasure."

"Regrettable," Martus said, "but understandable. It is not important, however. We have much to accomplish."

"We?"

"Oh, yes." He nodded toward Scaure. "The three of us. But first I would like to offer you an explanation."

"That would be a good start." Dara could not keep the sarcasm out of her voice even though she could tell that the Counsel-Regent was accustomed to authority and the deference that comes with it. This whole thing was his idea, after all, and she had no reason to cooperate. The intangible something tugged at her again. She tried to pin it down but it was too elusive. She gave up the attempt when the heavy man began speaking again.

"If you have not already deduced it, you are among the Brotherhood of the Bhoma-San," he began.

Dara drew in her breath sharply and reassessed her approach. He nodded slightly in acknowledgement. "You have heard of us, then. Good. I tell you now that whatever you may have heard was probably a lie—many are spread about us. We live, after all, in isolation and solitude. That is our choice but such conditions breed fear and fear breeds hatred. Few know us as we really are and appreciate what we do. The rest believe the lies and spread them. We are not monsters: do we appear so?" Once again he gestured toward Scaure, who remained silent.

"Appearances are often deceiving," replied Dara, choosing to answer the rhetorical question. "Is Portifahr of the Brotherhood?"

"Most certainly," affirmed Martus and Dara was somewhat reassured. Their guide had been tough but fair. He had treated her with more concern than many.

"And Vethis?"

"We are—testing—Vethis."

On this Dara reserved judgment. Much could be made of whether the ruthless warrior would pass or fail. And one must consider who had set the test.

"We of the Brotherhood pursue two goals: to help this world reach its full potential and to prevent the emergence of organized conflict—what you would call war." Dara wondered what he would call the bloody skirmish she alone had survived.

"Before you can comprehend our mission and its importance and join us in it, you must understand Khyren's ancient history, something on which we have a unique perspective. Are you sure that you would not rather be more comfortable? No? Very well. Two thousand years ago this world was densely populated. Millions upon millions of people clustered in great cities, living around and on top of one another. They covered the countryside from mountain peaks to the deep grasslands. Resources of all kinds were strained to their limits to provide clothing, shelter, transportation, tools, and weapons. But the greatest need was food, and agriculture was an overriding activity. Every square foot of land not covered by a building or a road was cultivated in an all-out effort to keep the massive population from starvation. Yet it was a job always perilously close to failure. A dry year, a blight, insects, or an early ice storm—any of these things caused a crop failure every few years. And that meant famine whenever it occurred.

"The overpopulation also caused social patterns to break down, leading to crime and deviant behavior. Wars proliferated. Empires were ruled by great queens and their noble warlords who rose to power on the strength of their armies. Each empire contested against the others for land, treasure, and power. When all of those were lost, revenge was a strong motivator. Hundreds of thousands, both warrior and civilian, died in each battle but that did not stop the fighting. Armies were easily replaced for, no matter how terrible the odds, there was never any lack of volunteers. It was, after all, better to die quickly and gloriously in combat than to starve slowly after battles devastated the fields and orchards. A warrior also had some hope of gain, whether recognition, advancement, or simple plunder. Wars were a necessary outlet for relieving the pressures of an overgrown population.

"Why, you might ask, was no attempt made to lower the

birthrate and eliminate the source of the problem. There were two reasons, both of them insurmountable. Socially, children represented status and wealth. The religion of that time guaranteed immortality in the afterlife for those who produced many worshippers to support the shrines. The cult of the Lady today represents a vestige of this belief. The queens, of course, were not about to dry up the source of their armies by encouraging smaller families. So people continued to fly in the face of all logic or reason and bear many children.

"It was a different world from the Khyren you know. The next question thus becomes: What brought about this enormous change? What could overcome the weight of religious tradition on one side and an economy based on a ready supply of people? If you know anything of history, you know that no one thing could possibly cause such a massive upheaval. Fortunately there was a critical convergence of two key factors: a charismatic man and a virus.

"The man was Bhoma ak'Hept Thusian, a Healer who left his profession to speak out against the ever-swelling population. He had seen enough misery to believe that only radical measures could cure it. He traveled all over Khyren, disregarding battles, disease, and famine. There were many roads then and they were well-maintained so that armies could move swiftly and be supplied in the field. He visited cities where now there is nothing but wilderness. He spoke to everyone from peasants in the field to merchants in their shops, even queens secure in their fortresses. No one listened. No one wanted to hear what he was saying.

"Then the virus struck. It started with fever and sweating, then muscle pain, convulsions, and death. Mercifully, it was quick and its victims died without ever becoming lucid enough to understand what they had contracted. No one knows how the virus developed or why, just as no one knows, even now, where it came from. Its first victims were in a metropolis called Sceptrinia, one of the oldest and most crowded of all Khyren's cities. Today Sceptrinia is just a low hill on the plains near Bittersea with all of its ancient grandeur turned to grass. Despite the exhaustive efforts of the city's healers, the disease spread rapidly.

Merchants and soldiers transmitted it to other cities, dying as they did so. And while people succumbed by the thousands, Bhoma of the Revered Memory preached his message of change, of hope. The Sweating Fever had come from the gods, he said, as both a judgment and a mandate for change. It was a chance for a new life. This divine instrument would bring the population down to a manageable level, from which to begin again.

"This thesis was revolutionary and contradicted everything the people of Khyren believed. Under ordinary circumstances he would quite likely have been beaten to death for heresy but the people were frightened. Although disease was common then and death an ordinary event, nothing like this plague had ever occurred before. The Sweating Fever was terrifying in its swiftness and the unpredictibility with which it took its victims. When people are frightened enough—and only then—they break away from familiar behavior. Some reacted by becoming devoutly religious and others by reveling in the pleasures of the flesh. A few achieved that most difficult of actions and changed a belief. They were able to accept the radically new idea that the Revered Bhoma expounded: once the virus subsided, the population must be kept from growing out of control again. Only in that way could the survivors attain the peace and prosperity the gods were offering. Those enlightened few who converted to his philosophy became the nucleus of the Brotherhood.

"By the time the Sweating Fever had run its course whole cities, like Sceptrinia, lay abandoned and decaying. Eight out of every ten people were dead. The lucky ones were returned to the elements on mass funeral pyres. Others simply rotted where they fell. Skies that had been dark with blowing ashes became thick with the smell of putrefaction and the cities were horrors, made unlivable by the presence of death. Those few who had been blessed with a natural immunity survived the plague and faced the awesome task of building a new society. They often found it hard to believe that they had been spared and were at the same time embarrassed at having lived in the midst of so much death. Unsure of themselves, uncertain of the future, they gathered in small groups to seek solace from one another. Forced from the empty reeking cities they moved into abandoned estates and country holdings left by the rich nobility. Such places were mostly self-sufficient and located in the mountains, by the water or in other isolated areas. Much of the old civilization was abandoned and the boundaries of human society on Khyren contracted sharply.

"Bhoma ak'Hept Thusian took advantage of this social disorder and the remoteness of the scattered settlements to further his plans. A charismatic speaker, he drew his followers together and filled them with the fire of his convictions. Then the Brotherhood spread out to establish a strong position among the survivors. In each location an Oben, an archaic word for leader, organized a disheartened group and gave them a sense of direction, set up the Guards, Healers, and Justiciars, all the structures a society needs for order and strength. They threw their support behind the strongest man who contended for leadership of the group. Strict loyalty to the group was encouraged and anyone who could not claim such ties became outcast, gormrith. The Obenan also established a system of tithes to pay for this structure and built tithing towers as a focal point of the new order and as a central resource. While all of this was occurring, Bhoma and his closest aides withdrew here to establish a headquarters. The Brotherhood has been here ever since.

"Life went on, for one really has no choice but to go on living. The sun rises, the body hungers, children must be fed, and animals cared for. The social systems that we established became entrenched until their origins, and the Brotherhood's part in them, were forgotten. Now each administrative area receives its share of the tithe and is content in its independence. That is as it should be, as it was planned. But behind it all the Brotherhood remains vigilant in its purpose. We continue to work in the interest of all Khyren and against the self-destructive influences that would quickly send the population spiraling upward. Never again will our world suffocate beneath the mass of its own people."

The Counsel-Regent generated warmth, sincerity, and good will. His attitude and bearing left no doubt that his intentions—and those of the Brotherhood—were beyond reproach; their only concern, for others. Questions had occurred to Dara as he spoke but now she found it difficult to recall them. Thinking back, it was hard even to isolate a specific issue on which to raise another point of view. Yet under the man's air of authority, beneath his almost fatherly mien, Dara sensed a reserve that strengthened her own wariness. If she could not contradict his admittedly-biased version of history, she also could not trust him.

And then there was Scaure. The Counsel-Regent's gaunt aide had not spoken once, had only listened attentively to his superior's lengthy explanation. Yet his eyes had been fixed on her as if they could see through skin and muscle to the bone beneath. Nothing about either man was openly threatening, but Dara's unease grew. "That is fascinating," she said. "I did not know any of that before. But what has it got to do with me? You didn't have me brought here for a history lesson."

"No indeed," Martus sighed lightly. "You are here for a very important reason although we have not yet reached that point. Please bear with me while I continue. Are you sure you would rather remain standing?" Dara nodded firmly and he sighed again. Once more, fleetingly, she smelled the phantom scent.

"As you wish. Well. The Brotherhood devised a method of artificially suppressing fertility that is simple, but effective, and it has worked well over the years. As must be expected, though, some women are naturally resistant to it. This immunity has allowed them to conceive and bear to term more than one child. Eventually such women came to hold a higher status in society than their less 'fortunate' sisters. That status became crystallized in an organization called the Order of the Lady. The multiparous women who formed it devoted themselves to undoing our efforts and returning Khyren to its former unbridled birth rate.

"At first they seemed a harmless group and, I must admit, the Brotherhood underestimated them. When finally we realized the danger, they proved very difficult to neutralize. Because it is open to any fertile woman, the Order permeates every stratum of society and thus cannot

be successfully separated from it. Moreover, its members
can travel openly to any location or estate, have access to
wealth, and can gain entry to the most private chambers.
They are stubbornly dedicated to their own concept of the
value of life and tenacious in their devotion to a primitive
fertility figure. For hundreds of years the Brotherhood has
sought a way to learn their plans and secrets so that we
could block them and thus prevent the chaos they would
bring about. Never in all those years could we find a
person with the suitable qualifications for accomplishing
this. Until now."

It took a long moment for the two quiet words to sink
in. "Let me make sure I understand what you're saying,"
Dara replied. "You want me to be your 'representative' in
a religious organization that opposes your beliefs?"

"In a manner of speaking."

"You want me to join this group."

"Yes."

"Learn what their plans and activities are."

"Yes."

"Then report back to you so that you can 'neutralize'
those plans and activities."

"Precisely."

"In essence, you want me to spy for you."

"That is a harsh word. Represent our interests is probably more accurate."

"But do it secretly so that no one else in the Order
knows what I am doing."

"Yes."

"I see. Tell me, what qualifications do I have that make me
your candidate for the job?"

"You are intelligent. You have a perspective on Khyren
that sets you apart from anyone else and lets you understand and appreciate the larger goals that we strive to
achieve. And, quite simply, you are a woman. This is not a
job that a man can do."

Dara looked at him, dumbfounded. In all the speculation she had done on the long trip here, never had anything like this entered her mind. Spying was something
that she felt might or might not be justified, depending on
who did it and why. To spy for men on the other women,

however, would require persuasion beyond anything she had heard in this room. She did not trust the Counsel-Regent's version of history, compelling as he had made it sound, and she did not trust his motivation. Nothing in the way she had been taken and manipulated for their reasons convinced her that she should take the Brotherhood's side and work for them, in secret or otherwise. His proposition went against her reason, her principles, her character, and her common sense. When she found her voice the words came out hard and tight but her voice was as unemotional as his. "I don't think so."

"Now, perhaps. We anticipated such an initial reaction. I am quite certain, however, that you will change your mind. Would you tell me why you feel this way?"

"Where do I start? First, my whole life was ripped away from me. Then, when I managed to piece together another life, you destroyed that, too." Dara's voice rose. "Your thugs murdered my friends and dragged me across a wilderness where I was almost killed and eaten. Now you want me to abandon my self-respect and be your spy. And for what? You haven't convinced me of anything but your own arrogance!"

"As I thought," Martus said equably. Neither man had reacted to her outburst or been fazed by her anger. "It is a pity, but unimportant. You'll do as we wish, when we wish. I did hope that my efforts would persuade you to work with us and I was prepared to reward you handsomely for that cooperation. Since you remain unswayed, well—the alternative is really quite simple." He flicked his hand, and Scaure moved for the first time. Dara looked around quickly: whatever their plan, they were about to put it into motion. The chair stood between her and the two brown-garbed men. The guard was to her right beside the door. Dara was convinced that this would be her only chance to act and the door was the solitary means of escape.

Scaure removed the cloth covering from the table beside him, revealing a slim metal tube and a vial of amber fluid. Inserting one end of the tube in the vial, he upended both and pressed a stud at the tube's other end. Instantly the liquid disappeared. The design was alien, the method of operation unknown, but what he held was without doubt a hypodermic syringe. Dara took a deep breath and with it came a stronger whiff of the scent that had been tickling her memory. It was strong enough so that this time the odor registered on her memory and she stiffened. It was suddenly more urgent that she flee from the sterile room and its sinister occupants. Pivoting on her left foot, she stepped forward with her right. Then, putting all her momentum behind the movement, she struck out and up. Palm rigid and fingers tucked flat, she aimed the heel of her hand at the guard's nose in a quick strike that was designed to drive the cartilage up into the brain. It was a deadly blow and it surprised the guard, who had expected flight rather than attack. If his reflexes had been a fraction slower or her shoulder muscles less stiff, she would have succeeded. Instead he blocked her attack at the last instant when her hand was only an inch from his face. Then one steel hand grasped her wrist, the other locked her elbow. A twist of one and pressure on the other forced Dara heavily to her knees. Immobilized by the painful armlock, she listened helplessly while Scaure approached. Behind him, Martus spoke. "So regrettable. I had hoped you would see things our way."

With one hand Scaure grasped her hair and tilted her head so that the left side of her neck was exposed and vulnerable. The fingers of his other hand stroked the hollow of her neck, probing the soft skin for the carotid artery. They rested for a moment on her racing pulse, then were replaced by the cool tip of the steel instrument. There was a slight tingling as Scaure depressed the stud. Dara held her breath for a brief second and then gasped as the drug's full impact hit her. With jolting force, the sensations she had experienced while watching the dream beetle flooded through her. This time, however, they were magnified a thousand times and her nervous system resonated dizzily as all five senses expanded and deepened.

Suddenly she could taste the air, touch the light, smell the colors. As the sensations bathed her and filled her, Dara luxuriated in their richness. Euphoric, she was barely aware of it when the guard lifted her unresisting body and placed it on the couch. Then, like a door opening on sunlight or the first surging notes of a symphony, the sixth sense she had experienced only lightly entered and illuminated her. Dara was suffused by emotions so powerful that they staggered her even though her body remained immobile. Then she "stepped" outside of them and exerted control, holding the new abilities carefully in check until she could flex them carefully. Dara felt complete and renewed. Within her was power beyond any previous experience, waiting for her to explore its limits. What she had felt long before in the tree had been but a pale reflection of this sparkling invincibility.

As both confidence and power deepened, Dara separated into two discrete entities. Her body, supine but tingling in every cell and fiber, remained on the couch. A casual observer would have thought her drowsing behind half-lidded eyes. Her conscious mind soared up and out, released from its confinement. After floating giddily, she hovered up near the ceiling to an invisible vantage point from which she could observe everyone and in some way experience everything that happened in the room.

Flex. Both the Counsel-Regent and Scaure were jubilant even though their faces remained expressionless. Their plan had worked perfectly and now they could concentrate on the second phase—conditioning the captive to their will.

Flex. Scaure, carefully re-covering the tray, felt that his ambitions were now closer to fruition. When this project was complete his abilities would be apparent to all. Yet he also harbored a new respect for his superior.

Flex. The Counsel-Regent, Martus, was deeply gratified and feeling expansive enough not to remind Scaure whose idea the plan had been. Dinner was also at the forefront of his thoughts, for food was the only reward that he allowed himself. Except . . . perhaps . . . Deeper feelings flowed in him like the black waters of the River of Silence. But they were professionally masked so that her raw new probes could not penetrate.

Flex. The guard standing once more in front of the door was impassive and distant. He had seen worse in his apprenticeship to the Brotherhood and would again. He did his job and looked forward to the end of his duty period so that he could enjoy the companionship of a special individual for the evening.

Flex. A handful of time had elapsed.

Scaure moved forward, positioned her head precisely on the low headrest, and lifted her eyelid. Watching from above, Dara could at the same time feel every pore in his fingertips. "She is ready, Your Grace," he said.

"Excellent." The heavy man arose, smoothed his wrinkled tunic, and looked down at her semi-conscious form on the couch. Satisfied, he transferred his gaze to Scaure. "Then begin, by all means. When you are finished, report to me in the refectory." The guard stepped aside and saluted as Martus left the room. Then he stepped back smoothly into position. Bending to his task, Scaure removed a patch of fabric from the back of the couch, exposing equipment and a complex control panel. Swiftly he attached a series of electrodes to her head and adjusted several switches. Immediately a voice filled Dara's head and a three-dimensional image leapt before her half-lidded eyes. The deep resonant voice spoke slowly and clearly within her skull. Its simple but emphatic statements vibrated in and through her while the swirling pictures mirrored what it said. Dara's body understood everything it saw and heard uncritically and accepted it as absolute truth. Most of the statements re-emphasized what Martus had already told her. It was fact, undeniable.

Floating in its euphoric state, her expanded consciousness experienced something totally different. That part of her knew instantly that the voice spoke a mixture of lies and innuendos carefully phrased to elicit belief and cooperation. The Brotherhood was good and selfless, working rationally towards a better future for all the people of Khyren. The Order of the Lady was a disorganized band of emotional women seeking mindless procreation without regard for the long-term dangers. Dara could help, should help, must help, or all would perish again. Critically she listened to the carefully-crafted fabrications and rejected them. After a while she grew bored with watching Scaure supervise the brainwashing of her body. The litany and accompanying holographs continued and repeated but she ceased to heed them. Why, she wondered, would they bother to practice such a transparent deception? Why would they choose a drug that only seemed to make their fraud more obvious?

Flex. She probed deeper into Scaure's mind and found in his complacency the answer for which she was looking. They did not know that she could experience anything beyond what they wanted her to know. With a disembodied smile she understood that, to them, the Dara on the couch was the only one that existed. Once again her metabolism had transmuted a native substance and altered its effects. On a Khyrenese, the dream beetle's essence would have induced a state of acute suggestibility in which dream and reality fused. Having obtained the information she sought, Dara drifted away from Scaure and the distasteful proceedings. It was time to explore the full range of her capabilities.

CHAPTER 13

"Mommy, Mommy, help!"

The piping cries of children playing in the back yard turned suddenly to terror and Dara rushed from the house in response. Samantha was there with the other children gathered in the bright sunshine but they were no longer sliding and swinging. Instead they huddled in a group, flailing at the air around them where small brown shadows swarmed, fluttering in a jerky way. It was the bats again, Dara thought as she ran. The miniature bats had grown bolder this summer; never before had they attacked in broad sunlight. She hurried to reach the panicky children across the small yard but the sunshine had the consistency of honey and her feet sank to the ankles in spongy green grass.

"Get awaayy! Help, Mommy!"

The bats were a temporary plague, usually descending on the neighborhood at dusk like mosquitoes. No larger than a quarter, they would drink a little blood from any creature they encountered and then depart. They were a nuisance and could be destructive but they were not really dangerous—except in a swarm. In such numbers they could cover a dog or cat, sometimes even a small child, and drain it of blood. Pets ran whining when the bats came and children particularly loathed the quivering little bodies.

"Get off! They're in my ears! Ugh!"

Samantha huddled in the thickest part of the swarm, bats covering her neck and arms. All the children were lightly clad in summer clothes that left shoulders, arms, and legs bare. I've got to get them inside, Dara thought, swinging sluggishly at the repulsive creatures that settled on her. Reaching her daughter at last, she scraped the clinging brown shapes off and picked Samantha up. "Inside!" she yelled at the panic-stricken children and led the way. More bats settled on them as they ran and she could feel their small sharp teeth scissoring her skin to draw the blood. The swarm was the worst she had ever seen and yet it grew thicker by the moment, nearly obscuring the house and the doorway she sought. Through the shifting cloud of bats she could see that the doorway was still far away, much farther than she had thought. Samantha squirmed and struggled in her arms, making it even harder to run. Dara was suddenly stricken with the cold fear that she wouldn't make it in time. Then Samantha grew still and very heavy in her arms.

With a sharp cry of anguish Dara woke up, looking wildly around. The flat walls of her cell gazed back at her impassively and seemed to hold her pinned to the bed. Her limbs were weighted down and unresponsive. Adrenalin surged through her veins in response to the dream's terror, however, and her extremities tingled as it met, then dissipated, the drug's aftereffects. Feeling and some control returned to her body while the nightmare was still raw in her mind. In the dream Samantha had been younger, little enough to fit comfortably in her arms. Dara thought the vision through again and again, cherishing her daughter's face and feeling still the solid small body in her arms. As often as she relived it, however, the meaning behind the powerful and terrifying images remained closed to her. Finally she sat up and, in doing so, discovered that she was crying.

The room's illumination was dimmed and there was a line of light under the door so Dara could tell that it was night, although she had no way of estimating how long she had slept. By the time she could govern her body enough to stand and move about, it grew brighter. The door opened and her guard entered bearing a tray which held fruit, bread spread with honey, and milk—breakfast. He was as brusque and silent as usual but this morning Dara could sense the emotions that lay behind his taciturn exterior. Her ability to "read" him was far weaker than when under the influence of the drug but she could still feel the stoic endurance with which he carried out a dull assignment. More dimly could she sense that his duty was punishment for an infraction of the rules and discipline for a volatile personality. He carried out his tasks meticulously so as to shorten his sentence. When he had gone she ate slowly.

Mid-morning found her strong enough to attempt a round of exercise. The warm-ups were difficult at first because her body was clumsy and unresponsive, but the movement helped. To get back into full control Dara worked hard, forcing herself through every exercise she could remember. She was sweating at the finish and her legs quivered with fatigue. She stepped into the shower, luxuriating under sharp needles of hot water and grateful that technology had left this vestige of sanitation untouched. Drying off under the heat lamp, she felt better and was more optimistic than she had been in quite a while. There was more to come, that was certain, but her metabolism had helped her to resist the persuasive effects of the drug once. Dara felt confident now that she could hang on through any further attempts to alter her mind. She ate a hearty dinner and then went to sleep early. It was fortunate that she did: the next morning they came for her again.

Martus walked wearily down the long corridor, his hands folded in the brown sleeves of his tunic. It was late and he was tired in a tense stressful way that worried him. He would have to do a full bio-control routine and meditate deeply before sleeping. He suspected that his weariness originated from the prospect of delivering another sector report to Rakal. These regularly-scheduled sessions grew more difficult for him as the Triarchal Master of the Brotherhood declined. It was obvious past comment among the superiors of the Brotherhood that Rakal could not survive his next scheduled treatment in the Yellow Room. This frailty of body and spirit came to them all eventually and was the price they had to pay for their artificially-extended lifetimes. The only question now open to debate was whether Rakal would nonetheless attempt the treatment or simply withdraw from life, entering the next phase quietly and with dignity. Although Martus held his peace in such discussions, he espoused the latter view. As he well knew, Rakal paid less and less attention to the daily activities of the Brotherhood and increasingly immersed himself in the study of interstellar poetry that had once been his avocation. Thus the sector reports were a trial to Martus who, knowing the organization's need for decisiveness and direction, was frustrated by the almost total lack of either that was the result of Rakal's frailty. He reminded himself that this hiatus would soon be over and a new Master selected. He suppressed firmly the ambition that surged unbidden at the thought. He reminded himself instead of the delicacy he had ordered and that was about to arrive.

At the end of the corridor Martus reached the doors that led to the Master's quarters. They were of an artificial crystal fired, molded, and colored into a radiant sunburst. The glory and artistry of the workmanship usually pleased him but tonight the doors went unnoticed. He passed his hand over a sensor and the sunburst parted in the center as the doors slid smoothly aside. After the brightly-lit corridor the room within seemed dark but his eyes adjusted quickly to the illumination cast by a few dim lamps and the lights of the city that glowed through the large window. The control chair behind the Master's desk was empty. Rakal sat instead on the right side of the room in a reclining chair that was tilted nearly upright in position for reading. An opened dispatch tube lay abandoned on the floor beside the chair while Rakal perused its contents, a fragile and antique scroll. The Master looked up, nodded absently, and waved Martus to a seat on the long, backless settee to his left.

As the Counsel-Regent for Domestic Affairs sat, he automatically noted his superior's physical condition. The man did not look old—no one who had emerged from the Yellow Room did. The muscles on his slim frame were still firm and his hair, though white, was thick above an unlined face. It was readily apparent that he lacked strength, however, and seemed both mentally and physically withdrawn. What fascinated Martus was that, as Rakal became more absent, his skin became more transparent, as if losing its ability to cover the diminishing life force within. On several occasions Martus had found himself unconsciously attempting to trace the flow of blood through the veins or detect an electrical impulse as it jumped a synapse. It was an illusion, he knew: the skin was not transparent. He suspected that when it was, there would no longer be a life force to cover.

Oblivious to his surroundings, Rakal read on in the darkened and silent room, becoming almost animated as he examined the parchment in his hands. Martus, who did most of his reading on a computer projection, grew exasperated. He knew better than to divert Rakal's attention, though. Waiting was easier. Gradually he relaxed on the comfortable seat, shrugging off the weight of the day's activities. He knew that his reflexes were dulling with fatigue and that his perceptions were no longer acute but he expected little challenge from this session. Thus he started and was unable to mask his surprise when the doors opened once again to reveal a figure silhouetted against the bright corridor. A quick glance at Rakal reassured Martus that his brief lapse in control had gone unnoticed. He pulled his composure together and greeted the last man he had expected to see: Estavin, Counsel-Regent for Internal Affairs. A small man, spare to the point of asceticism, Estavin made a formal bow and then perched on the other end of the settee. Like his larger peer he wore a brown costume and intricately-braided sash but, rather than status and dignity, his attire conveyed humility and an unassuming nature.

Martus was sure that behind the calm visage surged the same confusion he was feeling. Sector Reports were always delivered directly to the Master with no one else in attendance. There was no precedent for this action. What was Rakal thinking of? Was he about to make some announcement? Perhaps he had lost his grip on reality altogether. Then a voice from the shadows at the far end of the office interrupted his racing thoughts. "By the Beetle's Wings, can we now proceed? I'm exhausted and would seek my bed." Restobor, Counsel-Regent for Off-World Affairs, stepped into the light, his solid well-muscled frame clothed in the loose orange jumpsuit worn in zero gravity. It was adorned with pockets, loops, clips, and tethers designed for keeping objects from drifting away. He had obviously come in on the *Sigil* when it touched down at sunset and his angular, almost planed, face was drawn and tight with fatigue. This tiredness was all that the three men had in common. Martus was mortified at the realization that Restobor had been in the room all along, undetected. He had let his guard down more than he realized. The third man crossed the room and sat on a pedestal chair nearby. All three then looked expectantly at the Triarchal Master.

After an awkward pause, Rakal looked up and nodded at Estavin. Taking that spare gesture as a signal to begin, the Counsel-Regent began his report. Since he was responsible for the Brotherhood's organization and continued functioning, the facilities, recruitment, work assignments, administration, and discipline came under his control. Internal Affairs brought in some revenue since this group collected the tithes but, in comparison with the other groups, it contributed little to the overall assets of the Brotherhood. On the other side of the ledger it spent a great deal of money. Martus was astonished to discover how much overhead Internal Affairs consumed. Despite this, and despite the fact that Estavin spoke clearly and to the point, Martus found the report dull. Only one other time did he listen with real interest, during the section on recruitment when Estavin referred to Vethis. Martus's own network had found that individual and it was Martus who had gambled on the man's potential. Even now, Vethis was about to begin a new assignment, one that advanced Martus's plan. Rakal absorbed all the information in silence.

When the report was finished he stroked the antique parchment scroll on his lap and inclined his head in Martus's direction. The Counsel-Regent swallowed his distaste at revealing his organization's structure and finances before the others and began. He followed Estavin's lead and made the report as uninteresting as he could, reciting statistics and leaving the other two to draw their own conclusions. He refused to attract undue attention to his department's operations if he could help it. The strategy involving his use of the alien woman he glossed over as part of "ongoing surveillance of known activists." Let them make of it what they would.

Restobor, when it was his turn, seemed no more willing to divulge his area's secrets than the others had been. Martus listened intently and read between the lines whenever possible. Like his own department, Off-World Affairs was a center of revenue and profit for the Brotherhood. Between them, they brought in the wealth that built and ran the Lost City, imported the critical but expensive alien technology they needed, and underwrote the activities of the devout under Estavin. So it was with great interest that Martus heard and absorbed the report. He took in net revenues, return on investment, profit margins and capital expenditures, comparing the statistics to his own as he supposed Restobor had done previously. He found it all fascinating, the more so for having been kept secret. It was when Restobor came to the section on current business, however, that he really sat up and took notice.

"The authorized Trading Family chaired by Nashaum il Tarz demands that we increase our next consignment of Extract. The demand is excessive and cannot be met with current inventory. I fear that Domestic will be hard pressed to come up with the additional quantity."

Martus felt his weariness vanish in the face of a challenge. "How much do they want?"

"Ten packets over and above the regular shipment for the next five regular deliveries."

"Fifty packets? In less than a half cycle!" Martus calculated swiftly. "It's out of the question."

"Perhaps I did not make myself sufficiently clear. The il Tarz are insistent. And with good reason. The economy of Caris Minor is declining, which means that the government can be expected to purchase large quantities of Extract to keep the unemployed off the streets. At the other end of the Trading Zone, the G-class planets in the Veyik System are about to be opened for development. That means bribes for the officials, payoffs for the transport firms, and bonuses for successful labor recruiters. Any way you cut it, the il Tarz are in an excellent position to make substantial profits—as long as they have enough Extract. They are applying a great deal of pressure and we can't afford to anger them by not producing. What I need to know is, can Domestic increase shipments short-term?"

"The answer is yes, but not by that much or not that quickly."

"Why don't they take the unemployed from Caris Minor and ship them to the Veyik system?" suggested Estavin but the other two Counsels-Regent ignored him.

"If we lose the good will of the il Tarz Family," continued Restobor, "we lose their cooperation, their contracts, and a lot of money. Markets all over the Zone will be closed to us for a long time. It will have a devastating effect on revenues." He crossed his arms. "What do you need to meet those shipments? If it's manpower, I'll transfer some of my administrative staff to the assignment. Work them in shifts. Use up every flower in the garden. Just do it."

Martus replied quietly but forcefully. He did not like being told what to do. "Men condense the Extract but they do not manufacture nacre. Beetles do that and beetles do not work in shifts. If I use your men to step up refining I can raise the yield by perhaps thirty packets. Stripping the eggs we hold in reserve to replenish the swarm will bring that up to nearly forty. We can reach a few packets more than that if we terminate the eggs that are due to hatch soon. But that's the upper limit: beyond that we cannot go. As it is, each of those steps is serious and has important implications for long-term productivity. The end result is that our backlog will be gone and future production crippled. Those fifty packets will cost us any increases in profits on Extract for the next three full cycles— and that's only if our luck holds and the swarm remains healthy. A fungus attack or a drought would endanger our entire organization and the Master Plan. I find it hard to believe that the il Tarz are *that* important."

"Their enmity and opposition would bring us to the same point, only much sooner. And with less chance of recovery."

"Then the choice is between certain immediate profit and long-term risk. That is a choice that I cannot make. Only the Master can decide on an issue so important to the overall operation and direction of the group."

"Are you certain of your numbers?"

Martus looked at him evenly and did not reply. It was bad enough that this unreasonable demand was being placed on him by people who did not understand the difficulties of producing the Extract—Restobor included. His resources were not unlimited and he did not restrict them simply to control output. The beetles moved at their own rhythm and that was never fast. His men could monitor it and channel it. They could even do a few things to stimulate it. But under no circumstances could he or they control it. To be ignorant of this and yet to challenge his competence went beyond the bounds of the Brotherhood's ritual courtesy. His silence would proclaim his displeasure.

"Brother Martus, have you considered wild stock?" Estavin's question was reasonable and framed with respect. It had the desired effect of defusing the confrontation.

"There are some," Martus responded. Estavin at least understood the heart of the problem. "They are few and hard to find. Normally I employ them only as a control against inbreeding among the domesticated stock but this crisis is also a threat to the swarm. Restobor's men can help to search them out and the more they find, the better off we'll be. We'll show them the techniques we use to take the eggs without danger, although the wild beetles are unpredictable: there's always some risk in handling them. It's a good suggestion." He turned to Restobor. "Just don't count on too much. At best and with all conditions in our favor, they may bring us up to forty-six packets. I suggest you begin negotiating the shortfall with the il Tarz. The sooner they learn of this cap on their greed, the better."

Martus stood up heavily and faced Rakal. He bowed with full ritual formality. "Master, do you concur that I should take these drastic measures? Are you in agreement with limiting production for the next three or four cycles to meet this demand? We consult your wisdom, Master."

Rakal looked slowly from one man to the other as if considering the matter gravely. His face was calm but a pulse beat rhythmically at one temple. The three Counsels-Regent waited in respectful silence for his judgment. With the long practice of their discipline had come the ability to suppress their own opinions and prejudices so that they could deal most effectively with the decision of their superior. When Rakal finally spoke, however, his words shattered that careful impartiality. "Are you familiar with the poet Husnan of the Phoslirri System?"

His words were soft and spoken like an easy wind through the leaves yet they struck with great impact at the three men before him. Estavin said nothing but lowered his eyes. Martus stiffened with astonishment and thought: Is he that far gone, then? Only Restobor spoke, replying in a controlled voice, "Phoslir is a burned-out sun. Nothing is left of its system but a few balls of ice. Most of its civilization was destroyed with the star two hundred cycles ago. There is no life in the Phoslirri System unless you count an anthropological expedition on the fourth planet."

"Exactly," Rakal stated, as if Restobor had just proved his point. "And one of the reasons they are there is to discover what happened to a group of religious fundamentalists who chose to remain and die with their planet instead of evacuating. One of these people, Husnan, was a major poet, if not a popular one. This," his hand brushed the parchment in his lap, "was his last work. Attend.

" 'We have reached the end of light
    and the atmosphere is falling

into drifts around us.
The air we breathe condensing into flakes.
Quietly, the ageless cold of space seeps down
numbing what remains of holy warmth.

" 'We are all dead,
our bodies stiffened upright
in white satin coffins.
Only our spirits remain,
drifting like the last breath from blue lips.
Soon, they too will settle into white.

" 'It was a quiet end,
perhaps the easier way
and softer than God's fire.
Now the stars burn hard, without a shimmer.

" 'Should any follow after
they may find the mummies
of our towns and streets, buried
beneath a planet-wide Tsu-harri.
Still desert of crystal dunes.' "

Rakal looked slowly from one carefully neutral face to
another. "That is one of his most interesting works." He
sighed. "But it loses in translation and tastes in poetry
vary. I will not impose mine on you further. I shall retire
now." He closed his eyes and swiveled his chair away from
them. With a smooth hum it opened into a reclining
position and the room lights dimmed even further.

The dismissed Counsels-Regent rose abruptly and were
soon in the bright hallway on the other side of the sunburst door. There they regarded one another in embarrassed silence. Martus took the initiative and addressed
the issue "There will be no help from the Master. He has
left this problem for us to decide and it requires clean
thinking. We are all tired. I propose that we rest now and
meet tomorrow at the seventh bell when we are better
prepared to deal with the situation."

"I agree," Restobor said, and Estavin nodded. "Let it be
in my office, then, at the seventh bell."

The trio moved off down the hushed corridor, each man pondering his own thoughts.

Vethis sat up groggily and moaned. He rubbed his head but kept his eyes firmly closed. It was the wine: at dinner last night it had been potent and he should have swallowed less of it, he knew. Bright needles of light probed under his eyelids, sending warning signals to his brain. Darkness, Vethis thought, was what he needed to keep his head from exploding. Perhaps, if he moved very deliberately, he could turn off the light and keep the tumult inside his skull to a minimum. He raised his eyelids a fraction, just enough to orient himself and find the light control. All he saw instead was a tree. That meant he was outside. Outside! Headache forgotten, he opened his eyes and looked around quickly. He was surrounded by trees— tall trees with bare branches outlined in snow. Sunlight glittered like knives as the branches blew heavily in the wind.

Confused, Vethis looked down. He was sitting on a rock that had been dusted clear of snow and his back was propped against a large, rough tree trunk. He was stiff, as if he had been sitting in that position for a long time, and he was cold. His mouth was dry and felt as if it had been stuffed with foul rags. It tasted worse. Straightening up, Vethis looked about him more carefully. His eyes had adjusted to the bright light and this time he saw Portifahr leaning against another tree nearby and watching him. The man's face was expressionless behind its dark beard, giving him no clue as to what was happening. But then, Vethis thought, it rarely did.

He cleared his throat and gestured briefly. "This is not the Lost City," he croaked. "It's not even the Plains of Thunder. Where are we?"

"In the forest just east of Orrestai," Portifahr replied easily.

"Orrestai? But that's miles, hundreds of miles, from even the Spine." He paused, more confused than before. "I was in the City last night. Dinner was in the barracks mess. How did I, we, get here?"

"When it is decided that you should know, then you will learn."

Vethis digested that statement for a moment, then nodded. "As it will be. What is next?"

Portifahr's lips twitched in approval: the man learned quickly. "You have completed your first assignment successfully. The reward for that achievement is your next task." He folded his arms. "Do you know Orrestai?"

"Some." If Portifahr was giving away nothing, Vethis could also guard his words.

"Find the section of the city known as the Nine Chimneys. It should not be hard: many people can point the way but few will offer to accompany you. Seek there a tavern called the Dark Bird and frequent it until a man contacts you. He is called Zeched One Eye—you will know him when you see him."

"Yes, but why?"

"Zeched will help you to find all the men you will need to complete this task. His choice of fighting men is excellent and can be trusted. Use them to seize the estate called Highfields. Take it, and hold it for the Brotherhood. That is your assignment. When you command Highfields, we will speak with you again."

Vethis smiled. What more could he ask for? Highfields would give them a base on the near side of the Spine from which to launch their operations. Yet, tucked away in its hanging valley, it also offered privacy and few would see who came and who went. The fact that it was a rich holding and could supply them well was an added bonus. Once again the goals of the Brotherhood and his own were in complete accord. They would help him to achieve what he wanted most and, in succeeding for them, he would succeed for himself as well. When he had allied himself with the Brotherhood he had chosen well. Now he would take Highfields for himself and he would hold it for them against all the combined might of the Rangers, if necessary. After all, no one knew it like he did.

Portifahr stood away from the tree and, reaching behind its thick trunk, pulled a backpack out from its shadow. "Here are the things you will need to reach Orrestai and money for your arrangements in The Dark Bird. Use it well and wisely. You had best begin now: it's nearly midday and you have a long walk." Without a word of farewell or encouragement he turned and disappeared between the trees. A gust of wind soughed, swinging the branches above Vethis. Suddenly feeling the cold again, he felt beneath his coat and sighed. No magical black skin now protected him from the weather. The pack, when he opened it, held no mysterious tools, only objects common for cold-weather travel. Vethis knew without being told that he must not speak to anyone of the strange devices he had used on the trail to the Lost City. Not that anyone would believe him if he did. He mentally set aside those things into a closed and secret part of his life.

Taking the water bottle from the pack, he sipped carefully. Vethis knew better than to gulp water after a surfeit of wine that he now suspected might have contained another type of drug. He shivered, shouldered the pack, and set off. A long walk at a brisk pace would warm him quickly enough. As he marched toward the lowering sun, he hummed quietly. Everything was going well. There were difficulties ahead but he was already planning how to deal with them. Vethis breathed deeply as he walked, the clean air invigorating him after the short time spent behind the thick walls of the Lost City.

To one side of the trail a huge tree lay uprooted, victim of some long-past storm. Its roots, with frozen dirt still attached, reared up forming a shallow cavern. Within this shelter Vethis spotted a spray of frostfern curling up from the snow. Kneeling, he brushed the snow away until he had uncovered the long bottom fronds. Turning them over carefully he discovered two fat spores, brown against the evergreen fern. Deftly he pulled them off and popped them between his lips. As the spores crumbled between his teeth, an icy freshness burst out and tingled in his mouth, extending all the way up into his sinuses as he chewed. The spores were soft and quickly consumed but their effect, though brief, was refreshing. It dispelled the aftertaste of the drugged wine. He smiled. Vethis remembered when he had first known that his future was tied to the woman they called Karait, and how angry he had been when she refused him. Much had changed since then: life was different and his future was open ahead of him. Feeling alive and full of energy, he laughed out loud.

CHAPTER 14

When the door opened the next morning, everything was as it had been before. The same guard accompanied her. They took, as far as she could tell, the same path to the room at the end of the passage. It looked exactly as it had before except that the corpulent Counsel-Regent was not present. Only Scaure waited in the room, his eagerness humming around him through the mask of impersonal detachment on his face. Once again the other guard remained when the door slid shut. It was quiet. Dara stood perfectly still while Scaure approached the small table but a tug of war was going on inside her. One part of her was infuriated at being drugged and losing control of her body while the other experienced an intense desire for the blinding clarity of the drug and the power of mind that it created. When Scaure removed the cloth covering, she made a noise that might have been a moan of either fear or anticipation and the guard's solid hands clamped painfully around her upper arms. He would not be embarrassed—or reprimanded—again. Scaure approached, his features blank but his eyes glinting with a wolfish determination that was, for once, untempered by the watchful presence of his superior.

With practiced skill he bent her head backward and to the right. With her gaze fixed on the ceiling, Dara felt the hypodermic column's cold bite and the brief tingle as its contents entered the carotid artery. Then came an almost instantaneous hit, a sensuous rush of heightened awareness and the surge of mastery that accompanied it. This time she separated from her body more quickly and did not even pause to listen to Scaure's mechanical litany but set out instead to learn all she could. Her mind leaped, thrusting at the limits of its new capabilities. Unnoticed behind her, the guard swung her limp body onto the couch.

When, inevitably, the brilliant trance began to slip away like moonlight through her clutching fingers, Dara wailed soundlessly. She tried everything in her strange powers to prevent being drawn back, but failed. Caged once more inside her body, she pondered briefly the new knowledge she had acquired as she slipped through the enervation stage into deep unconsciousness.

Lazy afternoon sunlight slanted across the hillside where Dara sat talking. Many people moved quietly around her in the fresh, bright New England spring. All of them wore the antique, courtly clothing of seventeenth-century European aristocracy. Parading beneath the trees in stately rhythms and intertwining patterns, they quite formally observed the courtesies of their rank. The gorgeous full skirts of the women swayed like peacocks' fans against the vivid green of the new grass. The duke with whom she conversed was urbane, well-read, and thoroughly charming. Together they spoke pleasantly of diverse things while the court circled them languidly and the afternoon waned. Belatedly Dara realized that the sun was near to setting and it was time to leave. Looking about her for the first time she understood with a shock that she should, in fact, have left long before. It would be dangerous to linger any further on the hillside for, beneath their clothes and wigs, under their jewels and make-up, the glittering aristocrats were all vampires. She had known that all along and accepted it as part of their deceptive charm. But she could afford to ignore it no longer.

Murmuring her polite regrets to the duke, Dara rose and turned to go. His elegant hand restrained her. The duke spoke with great feeling of how her absence would desolate him. He pleaded with her to remain there among the elegant ladies and gentlemen of the court. Panic rose in her as the sun settled lower. She struggled to break away but, although his hand was bejeweled and soft, his grip was solid. The shadows lengthened while she tried to escape without being rude, for it was terribly important that he think of her as a lady and ladies are never rude. The last gleam of sunlight balanced on the horizon and Dara was ready to scream in terror when the duchess intervened. "Let her go," she said to the duke in a languid, dusky voice. "We do not need her here."

Free, Dara turned to run and stood instead transfixed. The lords and ladies had stopped their silent promenade and were gathered around her now with eyes grown huge and dark and compelling, with teeth that glittered like mother-of-pearl. She pulled her gaze away from those hypnotic eyes and saw, suddenly, a way out. It was a square black door in the grass opening directly into the hillside. With a wordless cry Dara flung herself through it and it slammed behind her, shutting out that pale ring of avid, hungry faces.

Then she was running through rooms that opened onto one another. They were all suites of bedrooms and attached bathrooms decorated in every period, color, and fabric conceivable. She fled blindly through Federalist, fur, Louis XVI, Oriental, marble, contemporary, and ivory. Dara raced from suite to suite, searching frantically for the exit. There was no safety here for she knew that, when their hunger overwhelmed them, the courtiers would forget the duchess's regal decree and throw back the door. Then the whole macabre pack would come hunting her without mercy through this opulent labyrinth. She had to find a way out. But behind each door lay other rooms until, tiring, she began to despair.

A hollow boom echoed behind her and terror spurred her on, moaning as she ran. Then Dara opened a small,

inconspicuous door and saw, not another room, but a
service corridor. Compared to the lush suites it was stark,
painted a dull institutional green and lit by dim naked
bulbs. It was the kind of place inhabited by silent janitors
with mops and wringer buckets; the kind where it was
always eleven-thirty at night. She lunged into it and the
heavy industrial door shut solidly behind her. Straight
down the hall she dashed, passing door after door, until
she reached the fly-specked EXIT sign at the end. One
more door, a final barrier, and she was out, free, safe from
the hunt and those glittering teeth.

Then, as she stood with her back against the door heaving for breath and feeling light-headed with relief, she
heard the small cry. High and thin and far away it called
her. "Mommy! Mommy!" It was Samantha, somehow lost
and wandering inside the hill. Warm and pulsing with
young life, her daughter was vulnerable and an easy quarry
for the ghoulish nobles. Again Samantha called out for her,
"Mommy, help me!" This time it was a shriek born of the
terror only a child can feel when alone and frightened.
Helpless before that summons, Dara turned back. She
knew as she opened the door that she had no choice but to
brave the evil, brocaded aristocrats. For if she failed
Samantha, they would find her daughter and relish to the
full her childish terror before destroying her. Worse, they
would turn her into one of them. As she stepped inside,
Dara woke with those dire words ringing in her head.

The reality of the darkened room was better, but not
much. Her heart pounded wildly inside the cage of her
ribs but it seemed the only part of her body that could
move. Once again the very air weighed heavily upon her
and she had to regain control of her body all over again. It
was harder this time, however, and until she could move
she relived the awful nightmare over and over again.

The door was plain metal of the silver-purple type that
proclaimed its origin as a starship's hull. Only hyperspace
would impart that distinctive color-that-was-no-color to

metal. There was simply no other way to create or even imitate it. Martus passed his hand over a recessed control panel and the door slid smoothly aside. Restobor was already in his office; Estavin entered moments later. The three men gathered around an input/output desk and, ignoring the formalities for once, got immediately to the issue at hand.

Restobor spoke cryptically and a block of light rose out of the table. In it revolved a still holograph of an old woman's head. Her face was pale and very wrinkled, her hair thin and white. She appeared petite but strength and will power virtually radiated from her pale blue eyes. "Nashaum il Tarz," he stated briefly. "She is a devious and greedy old woman of astounding determination. The Family she founded controls all commercial trading here in the Third Quadrant. She controls the Family. Nashaum is old but has lost none of her acuity. She can think three steps ahead of most people and is smart enough to spot any situation that may be to her advantage before it develops. Then she's amoral enough to exploit it, no matter what.

"Unless the Trading Family receives the Extract they demand, Nashaum has threatened to cut off our market, beginning with the M'Gwad Technocracy. Since the Technocracy is our main supplier of tools and equipment, to say nothing of spare parts for the geothermal diverters and turbines, the embargo would cripple our operations . . . both here on Khyren and off-world."

"Wouldn't it hurt them as well?" Estavin queried. "After all, we are the sole source of Extract and it's critical to their trade."

"Certainly," Restobor replied and his fingers moved again on the controls. A three-dimensional revenue chart replaced the holograph. "They could maintain an embargo indefinitely but after one Standard Temporal Period it would begin to cut into their own profits. The decrease could be subsidized by their other operations for nearly two more STPs before having a really critical effect here." His finger stabbed at a point on the chart. "My estimates are that they would be forced to resume trade then. But harbor no illusions: Nashaum will do it and damn the consequences if it suits her needs. Besides, with their enormous reserves of precious metals and their energy bank, they could hold out longer than we could. By the time the il Tarz are hurting, it will be far too late for us."

Martus, exploring the angles, said, "Are there sons? What of the possibilities there?"

"There are a few sons but Nashaum has no use for them or for men in general. If she could get away with it, she would probably hold them in reserve for breeding stock. Only daughters are allowed to work in the il Tarz Family. There are four of them whom my contacts know of who are part of the operations. Each is very bright, very well-trained, an excellent pilot, and a crack shot. I have spoken with two of the daughters personally but I learned little from the exchanges except that they have a tendency to condescend. Evidently they agree with the old woman's theory that men are the victims of their glands. She has stated publicly that men are good only in bed and battle, particularly in the front lines. In a tight spot she believes that men fight first and think second. In any dealings with women, thinking still comes last."

"What of the daughters you've met?" pursued Estavin. "Are they bribable? Is there a malcontent? Who's in line to run the Family when Nashaum is dead, and can she be reached?"

Restobor snorted, an undisciplined gesture that Martus assumed he had picked up off-world. "Who knows? Any il Tarz daughter fool enough to show such feelings would not live long enough to form an alliance with anyone . . . unless it served Nashaum's purposes."

Martus summed up the situation. "So the il Tarz Family can't be co-opted or penetrated. Not only do we stand to lose a great deal of business, we may even be forced to restrict *all* our operations severely."

"Are there any other alternatives?" asked Estavin.

There was a pause, then Martus interjected, "What about assassination? Every option is viable in this serious a situation."

No one reacted to this suggestion in any way, either verbally or physically, but the atmosphere became perceptibly tense. Then Restobor allowed a studied look of annoyance to cross his face. "The Beldame, Nashaum's station headquarters, is guarded like Lihntur's tomb with men, machinery, and the finest technology a fortune can buy. One of her daughters runs this security aparatus with a flextron hand and, if that wasn't enough of an obstacle, old Nashaum possesses strong psychic gifts. There are many who claim that she trained those talents among the T'Chu-Gourn. If only half the things that are rumored about her are true, that would seem likely. But no matter. Even if we succeeded in penetrating the overlapping layers of her daughter Gwynnym's security structure, she herself would find us out."

"Are you certain of that?" Estavin asked.

"Yes: I've already tried. This is not the first time that old karait has interfered with the Brotherhood's plans. My first operative 'accidentally' stepped into an open cargo bay without a flight suit. The Family shipped what was left of his body back along with polite expressions of regret about his lack of deep-space experience. The second operative didn't come back at all. What I'm saying is that, short of blowing up the Beldame and all our trade with it, there is no way to carry out a successful assassination. And time is limited: we must succeed quickly at whatever we decide to do."

The other two men assimilated in silence what they had learned. Then all three arrived at the same conclusion even though they reached it by different paths of logic and at different speeds. "So we negotiate," said Estavin firmly. "If we agree, let's proceed. When? What's our bargaining chip? And who represents us?"

"Let's take the last question first," replied Restobor. "We are at a strong disadvantage in this situation simply because we are male. As I've said, Nashaum il Tarz does not ever trust a man fully. To deal with them from a strong position we will need ideally a representative who is female, strong, intelligent, and cognizant of civilizations off Khyren. To get that, we'll probably have to retain an independent negotiator from the Third Quadrant Diplomat's Guild. That will make for a considerable expenditure in itself, and one that we can least afford now. But we have no choice. Unless, of course, you can think of someone suitable in this low-technology civilization." This statement carried a touch of irony since Restobor expected little more than polite concurrence from the other two.

He was, therefore, completely taken aback when Martus answered equably, "In fact, I do have someone available who meets those qualifications." Certain of their full attention, he then provided his fellow Counsels-Regent with a summary of the equipment malfunction that had brought Dara to Khyren. He went on to note her current presence in his Section, skimming over the events in between. The effect of this selective history was to make it appear that he had retrieved an unfortunate victim of circumstance and then provided her with refuge and care as a moral obligation. There was, he felt, no need for his audience to know any differently.

"Would she be willing to work with the il Tarz on our behalf?" queried Restobor.

"I am confident that, if the request were properly phrased, she would agree."

"Excellent!" said Estavin with satisfaction. "What a fortuitous accident. For us, of course. She qualifies for this task without a doubt but, if she comes from Earth's twentieth century, she is unsophisticated by today's standards. How do you propose to teach this interstellar waif all that she will need to know to negotiate successfully on our behalf with an opponent as difficult as the il Tarz?"

Before Martus could reply, Restobor queried, "What Earth language does she speak?"

"English, fortunately. It is archaic, of course, and she is unfamiliar with current idioms and technological terminology. A combination of hypno-study courses should eliminate that problem. But the negotiations present a trickier challenge. For her to be most effective, we should be at her elbow, so to speak, providing guidance and information during the talks. This is not possible."

"Not in person," replied Restobor. "What do you know about comlinks?"

"What everybody knows," said Martus. "They are standard equipment for two-way communications. They're used in the military, the space lanes, and many kinds of industrial operations, like mining and diving. But a hand-held unit would be ludicrous in this situation and we can't very well use the kind built into helmets."

"Of course not. But the M'Gwad have developed even smaller units that can be implanted biologically. These tap directly into the optical and auditory nerves so that we can see and hear what the carrier does."

"And she could hear us but no one else could?"

"Exactly."

"Excellent," said Estavin. "Is it possible to detect such an implant with a security screen?"

"The proper detection device, tuned to the exact frequency, would reveal one, yes."

"The il Tarz, of course, have such a device," stated Martus.

"They do. And even if they did not, old Nashaum could tell."

There was an unuttered sigh, then Martus said, "So even an implant would not pass their security."

"It would not have to," countered Estavin with an unmistakable note of enthusiasm. "If the il Tarz find the comlink as soon as our agent enters the Beldame, they will govern their actions accordingly. They will know, we will know that they know, and we can all proceed with the negotiations accordingly."

Martus agreed. "Yes, that should work. How fast can we get an implant here?"

"I can arrange a fast shipment via transporter." Restobor paused. "It will be expensive, though probably not even half what an independent negotiator would cost."

"That matters not," said Martus and Estavin concurred. "We have no choice but to make the investment."

"Then I can have it here tomorrow. When will our agent be ready?"

"Tomorrow will do."

"Then I will summon the Medical Subcounsel and we can prepare."

As the guards escorted her through the gleaming subterranean corridors, Dara expected to retrace the path they had followed twice before. Somewhere, however, they took a different turn and then entered a lift that brought them smoothly past many levels. Its doors slid open on a corridor that was still bare of ornamentation but brighter and warmer. Shafts of yellow sun punctuated its length, streaming from skylights placed at regular intervals, and from a distance they looked like shining golden columns. She craned her neck as they walked beneath a skylight but saw only an unmarked square of lemon sky. Dara found it cheering, though, to see daylight again after so many hours locked away below ground. At this level there were also people about, men in brown tunics belted with sashes of varying complexity and different colors. None of those she passed could equal the brilliant design of the sash worn by the Counsel-Regent named Martus but several equalled or outshone the one worn by Scaure. None of the men moving along so industriously paid her the slightest attention as they walked between sunlight and shadow. There were no women.

After several turns her guards stopped before a large door of burgundy-colored wood, wondrously carved in a geometric pattern and polished to a high gloss. In the otherwise sterile surroundings it stood out, dominating the eye. Dara appreciated both its artistry and its statement of human skill. The door opened silently and they entered a large room bright with daylight from an enormous opaque window in the wall facing them. To their left was a wall of roughly-dressed stone. The wall on the right was similar but covered largely by a tapestry. In the center of the room was a desk fashioned from the same wine-colored wood as the door. Its vast surface was interrupted by rows of buttons, banks of light, and several depressed areas. Even the smooth wood of the desk had a sense of impermanence, as if only temporarily at rest. Behind it sat the Counsel-Regent, wearing a placid expression. Dara stopped halfway across the room and stood straight, facing him. The guard laid a heavy hand on her shoulder and pushed. "Bow," he said. She staggered but remained upright. Martus waved indulgently and the two men turned and left the room to wait outside. Looking at Dara, Martus waved again, this time toward the chair closest to the tapestry. "Be seated, please." Dara hesitated and then lowered herself into the other chair so that her back was to the stone wall. The Counsel-Regent smiled and shrugged.

"I shall come right to the point," he began. "There has been delay enough. Have you changed your mind?" Dara shook her head firmly. Crossing his hands on the dome of his stomach, Martus leaned back. Looking directly into the strong opaque light from the window behind him, Dara found it difficult to see his expression but she could sense twinges of caution. "A strong dose of the Dream Beetle's extract is not usually a pleasant experience. In smaller quantities and dilute solutions the Extract is frequently used as a means of expanding consciousness. It can be quite useful and is often enjoyable when carefully controlled. But the dosage required to influence thought and alter memory has certain distasteful side effects. You are no doubt aware of these by now and you may also feel a strong craving for further usage of the Extract despite the debilitation it causes. If you continue to resist, there will have to be several more such episodes. Some danger is involved and we will have to be very careful not to cross over a very thin line and leave you with burned-out brain cells. I hope to avoid prolonging such unpleasantness." He paused, waiting for an answer. Dara said nothing but could feel that he was not as confident as he seemed.

After a moment of heavy silence, he continued. "I can understand your reluctance to enlist in our plan. Your somewhat emotional response to our first offer precluded a statement of the possible benefits to you. I decided to show strength but that was my miscalculation. I should have raised these advantages first. That situation is past, however, and things have changed since then. The offer I make you now is different and, I think, more acceptable." Martus made a sweeping gesture that took in the luxuriously-appointed rooms. "As you can see, we of the Brotherhood have access to technology unknown and unimagined elsewhere on Khyren. Some of it we manufacture ourselves and we trade for the rest.

"On this world, as on your own, trade involves business partnerships, negotiation, and contracts. A certain degree of trust between beings of commerce is necessary. Sometimes these things are simple and handled quite easily. At other times difficulties arise, perhaps unexpectedly. This is such a time: yet difficulty often uncovers opportunity. Our plans have altered to match the circumstances.

"The situation is this: one of our regular trading partners is demanding that we deliver more merchandise than we find reasonable. We have exhausted all normal negotiating channels but they remain obdurate. Now a representative must go to them and deal with them directly. It is not a difficult task but, for a number of reasons, a woman would be more effective in stating our case. Our new request, therefore, is that you travel to their trading station and represent us in the negotiations."

Dara thought carefully. Things had changed indeed. They needed her cooperation far more now than they had before and that strengthened her position. Still, she needed to find out more. "Why would a woman be more effective? Is there no 'degree of trust' between you?"

"There is, certainly, but only to a point. This trading group is essentially a matriarchy. It is a family run by an old and greedy woman whose lust for power grows stronger with her age. It is our experience that she will listen more closely to and deal more fairly with another woman."

"I see." This was even better. Although Martus was controlling very carefully the importance of persuading her, she could still sense his need. "But how would I know what to say on your behalf? How could I know what to offer? And how could you trust what I would say?"

Again Martus appeared to choose his words carefully and Dara knew that this was the crux—the issue that would most influence her decision. "To answer the first question, we would first brief you thoroughly with common learning techniques that allow nearly one hundred percent retention." He paused. "The answer to the second question involves the use of mechanical aids. The technology available to us here is far more advanced than that with which you were familiar on Earth. It is possible for us to place a tiny communications link smaller than your least fingernail on your person just beneath the skin. Although it would be invisible, this comlink would broadcast to us everything that you see or hear and allow us to speak to you without others hearing."

Dara shivered at the thought. "How serious a procedure is inserting this device?"

"Not very," he replied easily. "It requires a small incision using only local anaesthetic. You would be awake during the procedure and there would be no discomfort afterwards."

That didn't sound as bad as she had thought. "Where would it be placed?"

"On the back of your neck just below the skull."

"Could it be removed afterwards?"

"Quite easily."

"Would it transmit all the time?" With this device on her body she would have no privacy, have to consider every word.

"Not at all. You would activate it before the negotiations and de-activate it afterwards. At all other times you would be as you are now."

That gave her the basic information she needed. Now it was time to do some negotiating herself. "You're asking me to work for you, to submit to an intensive briefing, and to have a foreign device placed within my body. I understand the advantages to you, but why should I agree? What do I receive in return for my cooperation?"

Martus smiled thinly. "Of the many things we of the Brotherhood can offer you, only one will have any weight and that is the one you desire. Were you a woman of this world, that would be easy to determine. But you are not of Khyren and I cannot read minds so I will ask you instead. What do you hold valuable? Tell me what you desire—within reason, of course—and I will obtain it for you in return for your cooperation."

Dara sat up stiffly and leaned forward. A tiny hope that had been born in a thermal tent on the far slopes of the Spine, a hope that had burned unacknowledged in her subconscious, now flared. A shaft of excitement raced along her nerves and burst out before she could even formulate a sentence. "Home. I want to go back to my world, to my home, to my family. Can you offer that?" Even as the words emerged, Dara recognized the futility of her request. She was valuable to the Brotherhood here, not on

Earth. There was no possibility that they would let her go. Yet still, she had to know.

Martus seemed unperturbed by her request. She might as easily have asked for a glass of fruit juice or a new dress. "Can I send you back?" he mused. "To your world, assuredly. To your home, perhaps. To your family, impossible."

Dara gripped the arms of her chair to steady herself against the impact of what he had said . . . and what had remained unspoken. He knew where she had come from, but he also knew how. "Why not?" she asked tightly. "Tell me, now."

"Quite simply, the laws of physics prevent it. The accident which brought you here cannot be duplicated. That is unfortunate but it is also unalterable."

"Accident?" she interrupted, "what accident?"

"The transporter malfunction," Martus replied calmly, as if unaware of her agitation.

"Whose transporter?"

"Ours, of course."

Dara sat in the perfect stillness of shock while her mind raced to investigate the doors opened by this new information. Finally she had found someone who could fill in all the blanks and answer the unasked questions. Here was someone who knew. "Please," she said finally, "explain from the beginning. I want very much to understand this. I need to know."

Martus nodded easily, aware that this was an excellent opportunity to establish confidence, but mentally he protested the need for yet another lengthy explanation. He was by nature a taciturn man who preferred to probe and question, letting others provide the explanations. In the course of executing this particular strategy, however, he had been required to talk far more than was his norm. But there was no way around it; Scaure was simply not ready to assume the burden of running the operation. Martus hoped that there would, at least, be an interesting evening meal to compensate.

"I have explained that we trade for technology. Shipments under a certain mass can be handled quickly with a transporter which operates on the principal of matter-to-matter conversion. Larger amounts must be transported physically from one location to another. Just before Festival, our technicians were arranging for a shipment of goods by transporter when the conversion rods malfunctioned, arcing prematurely in an uncontrolled flare. Such an accident is, fortunately, rare. This one burned out an entire crystal of circuitry, requiring over one whole Standard ·Period of repair and throwing off the scheduling of more than one STU's trading. An incident of this magnitude has a negative effect on our profitability and the technicians who allowed it to happen were punished severely.

"Now, what has this to do with you? Because the transporter warps both space and time when the matter is converted, the results of such an accident are completely unpredictable. I checked the records. Anything unwittingly transported in the past has been either inanimate or dead upon arrival. Fortunately from our point of view, you were neither. I don't understand why, but it is so. You must be aware that no one on Khyren outside the Brotherhood understands that such equipment even exists, far less the principles behind it. And even our technicians cannot bend the laws of physics."

Martus pressed a button on his desk and a screen emerged from one portion of the smooth wooden surface, rising like a cobra's hood. Fully erect, it swiveled so they could each see a side clearly. He touched one side of the screen and numbers leaped away from its matte black surface. Dara examined the equations carefully but, despite her programming experience, they made no sense to her. Martus indicated the final group of figures. "As I said, the transporter warps space and time but only within rigid limitations. What year was it on Earth?"

"It was 1987."

He manipulated the screen again and the calculations changed rapidly. "On Earth now it is 2489—a difference of five hundred years. That's the extent of the time distortion caused by the malfunction. In normal operation, the equipment cannot reach so far back. Because the accident was uncontrollable, however, we cannot duplicate it. We could send you back to Earth but it would not be the Earth you know. It would not be home."

Five hundred years. The weight of his words was immense. Long ago Dara had tucked her family away in a small protected corner of her mind. She had kept all her memories there where they could not distract her with grief and longing, so that she could function every day. She had guarded those memories and cherished them against the day when, somehow, she would see her family again. She had never examined the logic of how that reunion would be accomplished because there was, really, no logic at all. Only faith. Now the faith that had become a part of her was exposed and undermined. She felt numb. Her husband was long dead and her daughter also.

There might be descendants but no one who would remember her or to whom she would mean something. There would be no one happy to see the woman who had disappeared return just as mysteriously, out of time and place. Nor could she adjust and fit into a society changed by five hundred years of technological progress. She would be a freak at first and then a burden, unwanted by her posterity. The hope that had burned deep within her and then flared so unexpectedly guttered and died, leaving in its place a black and shriveled cinder. For the first time, Dara was struck by the full weight of her isolation on Khyren. There could be no return. No hope. Ever. She felt alone and vulnerable and, in an odd way, very old.

After a while her brain started to work again and she blinked as if emerging from sleep. From this point her thoughts moved in a new and different channel as if a landslide had blocked her old way of thinking forever. Her future lay on Khyren and it was up to her to make the best of it. Until now she had been powerless, driven by circumstances, and subject to the will of strangers. With her new drug-enhanced insight, Dara knew that Martus's proposition was self-serving and corrupt. She understood that he could not be trusted. Yet he offered her an opportunity to take control of her life. She had no doubt that, given time, technology, and the drug, the Bhoma-San could break her to their will or destroy her in the attempt. Already she craved another experience with that bright super-consciousness regardless of the consequences. And she was only too aware that, while her mind was soaring,

her body was comatose and deteriorating. Far better, therefore, to go along with this new request, accede now,
negotiate whatever she could for herself, and maintain her
independence. Ignorant of her new talent, the Brotherhood might be duped into thinking that she was totally
under their control. Even now she could read Martus
who, sitting placidly once more with clasped hands, was
beginning to feel optimism yet tempered it with caution.
Although her ability to read emotions was not to be compared with what she had experienced with the Extract
surging through her veins, yet it was there where once
there had been nothing. Dara had no compunction about
using it on him or on any of the rest of them. Besides, the
alternatives were few and unpleasant.

Finally she responded by going back to the basic issue.
"If you can't give me what I really want, what can you
offer?"

"There are items of virtually universal value: wealth and
power. Knowledge. Even longevity."

"Wealth requires the freedom to enjoy it and a place to
spend it. Power is a function of position and usefulness.
What can you tell me of knowledge and long life?"

Martus allowed a faint smile to cross his carefully-
composed expression. "Look for yourself," he said, passing
one hand over a black strip on his desk. Behind him the
window flickered and then, beginning at the center and
moving toward the edges, its opacity disappeared. The
transparent material gave way to a panorama so vivid that
there might have been no window at all. With a cry of
astonishment, Dara was on her feet and across the room.
For long moments she gazed out on a scene of incredible
beauty and awesome accomplishment. An entire city rose
before her, its buildings seemingly grown from a seamless
synthetic material. Each structure bore many windows,
some opaque and others translucent. Vehicles of different
sizes and shapes moved silently everywhere. Some rode
smoothly but without wheels just above curving roadways.
Some hovered in mid-air or weaved confidently between
the towers. There were no stone buildings, no carts drawn
by dray animals, no cultivated fields. It was a sophisticated
urban landscape far removed from anything Dara had seen

on Khyren. She ran one hand through her hair and stared as if expecting the vision to disappear if she blinked but it remained, clear and solid.

Past the buildings, at the end of a straight road, a metal ovoid lay on a large platform that was bustling with people, crowded with containers and cables. The smooth shape was at once both gleaming silver and lightless black. Dara knew with sudden certainty that she was looking at a starship and a thrill ran through her. Beyond the ship a garden of luxuriant beauty encircled the city. It curved towards her and then disappeared on both sides of the window to complete its ring behind the building in which she stood. On the far side of the garden rose sheer cliffs that soared straight and dark, up and up and still further to an echoing circle of bright sky. Briefly the meaning of the precipitous cliffs that bounded the city eluded her. Then, with an almost physical shock, she understood: They, and the city, were inside the volcano! Dara whirled to face Martus, who had been waiting patiently for this reaction.

"Welcome to the Lost City," he said quietly. "It is lost, of course, because we wish it so. None can find it but those who are brought here. In this place you can have access to the wisdom and technology of half the galaxy. Imagine an open door to other civilizations and different cultures, both human and alien. Does that surprise you? There are humans in many planetary systems, on worlds with suns of many colors. We have a whole section in our library filled with speculation on how our species became so dispersed. Four times that space is devoted to studies of alien cultures. Think about exploring what has happened on Earth in the past century. Or researching your family's history. We offer knowledge open to no one else on Khyren outside the Brotherhood."

"It is fascinating," Dara said, tearing her gaze from the spectacle outside the window. "But what use will it be to me?"

"As our agent, there will be many assignments, some here, some elsewhere," he pointed upward, "and some out there. We will pay you a fair salary and you will be able to take advantage of our resources here in the Lost City."

"And longevity?"

"That can be yours before you leave us. It would be a necessary part of giving you the immunities you will need for the assignment."

"Then I have one condition."

Martus hesitated, not having expected conditions of any kind. Then he nodded, "What is it?"

"I will work on your behalf for a period of time equal to the normal span of years on Khyren. But I will not betray other women, no matter how 'noble' your cause."

He answered smoothly. "It shall be as you wish. You agree?"

"I accept. What must happen next?"

"Your briefing and background knowledge must be seamless, your conduct proper or the negotiations will fail. It will require much work to make this possible. We must proceed quickly so that you will be quickly on your way. Scaure will proceed with the preparations." He touched another button and the door opened. Dara walked around the desk as the two guards entered. With a bow of simple courtesy towards Martus, she turned and left.

When the heavy wooden door was again firmly closed, Martus turned toward the tapestry. It had been woven to his specifications by genetically altered bower birds on the artisan world of Dur-Iss and its designs flowed in soothing patterns. These designs were both pleasing to the eye and conducive to thought. Most of the time the tapestry was an aid to contemplation. Now its folds quivered as Portifahr slipped from the recess hidden behind it. He walked to the closest chair and sat without regard for the fact that the Counsel-Regent was still standing.

Martus did not show his annoyance by as much as a blink but he mitigated the insult by returning to his chair behind the desk. "Well," he said evenly, "how did you read her? Does she speak truth? Can she be trusted?"

Portifahr rubbed his beard, thinking it ironic that his superior should be so concerned with truth. "Yes and no. She intends to cooperate—for a while, at least, and for her own reasons. To that point she intends no betrayal and can be trusted. But there is something, a reserve, a wariness that I have not encountered before with the karait and I have spent much time in her company. It seemed as if, had I not kept my guard up, she would have known I was here. Granted she is an off-worlder but I never sensed it on the trail here. Only among the T'Chu-Gourn and those trained by them have I felt anything similar."

Martus crossed his hands on his stomach and stared at the tapestry. "Your analysis?"

"I cannot give you an analysis without reservation. As you said, she is not like the women of Khyren who can be swayed by a pregnancy or bribed by the birth of a healthy child. You know well that the humans of other worlds are deceptive to deal with. They appear as we but the flesh may conceal a mind and a culture as foreign as that of any alien. Then there is this reserve. My advice, for what it is worth, is use her—but take precautions. She bears watching."

"Your assistance is noted and appreciated."

"May I return now to my regular route?"

"Yes, but do not wander far. There may yet be another assignment."

Portifahr grunted as acknowledgement, then, ignoring the formal courtesies, he rose and left the room. Martus watched the polished door slide shut again before turning back to the screen. He touched its surface meticulously, calling forth streams of information. As the data appeared, he shook his head as though tasting something unpleasant. It was difficult to believe that such a man, blunt and ill-mannered, contemptuous of the formal courtesies and prescribed modes of conduct, had once been a Counsel-Regent. He had returned from the T'Chu-Gourn training, abandoned his position, given up all power and status, and taken on minor tasks. He went from village to holding, from mountain to farmland, carrying goods and messages for his superiors in the City, carrying out assignments similar to the one he had just completed—anything that allowed him to work outside and on his own, a solitaire. He was a paradox, working for the Brotherhood yet apart from it. Portifahr was also deceptive. Because he normally completed any task assigned to him, it was easy to overlook the few times he refused one. Because he worked alone and remote from any supervision, Martus was only dimly aware of time when he had acted on his own initiative to accomplish ends known only to himself. On those times, the man who had been Counsel-Regent displayed a strong streak of independence.

Once more Dara walked between the two silent men down corridors and through maze-like passages. This time she was less concerned with her surroundings than with the future she would have found unthinkable on the walk to Martus's office. Her preoccupation was to be expected; the agreement she had just made was worth only what she could make of it. It was possible that they would give her access to information deemed interesting but harmless, for such information would be a useful incentive and encourage her performance. It would also serve to distract her from the Brotherhood's true activities. The difficulty would come when her usefulness to them was over and they were under no obligation to honor a verbal contract. She had learned enough to know well how ruthless they were, and any number of outcomes was conceivable, from a convenient accident to a star voyage into slavery. She was as likely to receive a blade between the ribs as a "reasonable salary." Dara felt certain only of having bought herself some time. Now she would have to plan well and act wisely.

As they left the sun-pierced corridor of the Counsel-Regent's crescent, her mind worked furiously. Taking charge of the future would, in a way, be like writing an incredibly complex program: it would have to contain all the necessary functions and execute them in the proper order, from covering her role to getting free of their power. It would also have to be perfect for, in this set of directions, a bug could be deadly. Meanwhile there was an encounter with a device called a comlink to deal with and then briefing sessions to follow. By the time their footsteps echoed through the lower levels, Dara had braced herself for the events to come.

CHAPTER 15

The pass was nearly closed when Haron arrived with a troop of warriors and mercenaries riding at his back. Working quickly, he had assembled and armed his small troop, training them as best he could on the way into the mountains. Theram came in only hours behind him. Alone of their group, he had chosen to remain in the Rangers and had volunteered to answer Callain's personal appeal for aid and revenge. Thus the troops he led were well-disciplined and experienced fighters, many of whom had fought under and were eager to avenge the popular Resar. Callain welcomed them as they came through the gates, bundled in an enormous fur coat against the first flakes of another storm. Satisfied that her steward was settling their men comfortably, she led both officers toward the big house. Steaming warmth surrounded them inside the door.

"I am always grateful to be at Highfields in the cold passages, my lady," said Theram lightly. "It is one of the few holdings where one can be truly warm."

Haron, who cared little for comfort, snorted but Callain replied graciously, "That is very true and yet I, it seems, can never be warm enough." Her cheeks were now clear of the ritual ashes but she still wore the red sash and would for all the long time until the next Festival.

They chatted amiably together until they reached the entrance to the Great Hall. When the door swung open to reveal Resar standing within, both men stopped in bewildered astonishment. They entered the room as if in a dream and Resar could see undisguised emotion racing across their faces. Theram, the impetuous, spoke first. "The messenger said you were dead!" he blurted accusingly. "I believed him."

"As you were meant to do. As the leader of the raiders who attacked us yet believes."

"We are filled with gladness that you still live," said Haron forcefully. He started to embrace his friend but never went beyond the first step. Resar was different, unapproachable, no longer the Ranger captain they had lived with on such close terms. It wasn't just the long scar that puckered his forehead or the white blaze of hair that marked where the scar entered his scalp. Haron was familiar with scars and their effects. The difference was in Resar's eyes. They had a cold and barren look that echoed the white flakes now falling steadily outside the sheet crystal window. Even in this overheated room that look chilled him, for there was little in it of the friendship they had once shared. "But I am puzzled," he finished, "and I would like to know what happened."

"And I," echoed Theram.

"You deserve the entire tale, at least," Resar replied. He gestured toward a table which bore food and drink in quantity. "Take refreshment, my friends. You just came in from a long, cold journey and it's a complicated story."

The road-weary pair helped themselves to hot food and good ale and took their ease on the comfortable furniture. Callain settled herself in her usual spot by the fireplace and Resar was about to begin when there was a slight movement in the far corner of the room. Haron turned to it with a warrior's reflexes. Then his eyes widened and he straightened in surprise, nearly spilling his dinner. "By Gadman's Gizzard, Resar, when did you start kennelling the pack in your hall?"

"Not the whole pack," Resar replied with a wintry smile.

"Just one beast. This courser is special; in fact, he's almost as much a part of this war council as we are."

"All coursers are a little mysterious," interjected Theram. "Sometimes you almost believe they can understand more than the usual code. My father's pack handler swore that one of his could read minds. But don't you think this is overdoing it? They're still just animals—and dangerous ones."

Resar shook his head. "Not this one. Sandy followed us on his own and saved my life. I trusted him then and I trust him now."

"Sandy?" Haron queried, as if his friend had left his sanity elsewhere. "You have given a man's name to a domestic beast? Have you gone over the edge?"

Resar hesitated. "Well, not quite. I'm as level-headed as you are and I didn't give him the name." He looked at the other two men closely. "The best way to answer your question is to tell my story from the beginning. You'll see." He strode over to a chair and sat restlessly on its arm. As Resar began with his arrival at Highfields and the Harvest Race, his friends were not the only ones in the room who listened carefully.

Callain stared into the shifting flames and paid close attention to the narrative. Until now she had only heard fragments of the story blurted out by a man keyed up and too preoccupied to pay any attention to continuity. This recitation would enable her to put the pieces together. As Resar's words flowed through the room, Callain placed one hand protectively over her stomach. If the karait's arts had worked, she was safe. When she was Mother of the Heir she would remain the undisputed mistress of Highfields, with authority over any woman Resar might later take to wife—and Callain had her own plans in *that* direction. A child was not the heir, however, until he had lived a full year in good health. That time was far away and her pregnancy, if it truly existed, had yet to be confirmed.

Resar described the ambush and she shuddered. When fully pregnant, she could be in even greater danger should Vethis win in his bid to take Highfields. What value she might have to him as claim to the estate would vanish if he found her great with Amrith's child. After all, it is far simpler to dispose of an unborn heir than one crying lustily in his cradle. Back and forth her thoughts flew, uncovering both hope and despair in the condition she desired so avidly. If only she could be sure . . .

In his corner far from the fire, Sandy lay quietly with both sensitive ears perked up. He knew that Resar talked about the Woman even if he could not understand all the words. With his delicate sensory systems he could have told Callain what she wanted to know had he any way of communicating it. Tiny as it was, the almost-life inside her gave off its own vibrations. It was a good thing to touch, that little stirring, and it intrigued him. Sandy was learning to focus his empathic sense only on that flicker, blocking out all the other stronger emotions around him.

A skilled and tenacious tracker, he had never been defeated in his work until he had encountered the mist creature in the cavern. Worse, he had never known more of fear than that which created a reasonable caution in any hunter facing danger. But there beneath the mountain he had been filled with fear, so consumed by terror that he had not even thought of casting about for a way past the lake. He had abandoned the duty. He and the Man had both felt that overwhelming emotion and shared the failure. That was why he stayed in this sweltering uncomfortable room where he had to be careful of his behavior—that and the child-to-be. A new duty was calling to him, calling faintly, and he remained to listen.

The next morning all three men met with Barrikehn, former second-in-command to Vethis and now leader of the household guard for Highfields. Together they surveyed the fighting band that had been created by combining their troops. Barrikehn was hard and tight-lipped and eager, as if determined to wipe out the stain of treachery that Vethis had left. Under their direction he set about making arrangements for weapons drill and strengthening the fortifications. He was barking out orders to his second as they left.

With that critical first step accomplished, Resar directed his friends through the tracked-up snow of the compound while they discussed tactics. At the door to the main stable they were met by a small leathery man whose great age appeared to have shrunk him even further. What hair remained on his head was wispy and vivid white by contrast with his weathered face. The old man's eyes were deep-set, of a green darker than the deepest ocean, and they glittered with a ferocity that was out of place in such an aged form. "This is Khivoi ak'Hept Enkhi," introduced Resar. "He was Commander of the Guard for Highfields when I was brought to the Children's House. He knows more about this holding than anyone else alive. Khivoi knows its strengths and weaknesses—and he knows Vethis just as well."

The four men walked through the dim stables into a storeroom at the building's far end. When they sat on stacked bales of fodder, a faint scent of summer rose from the dried greenery. It floated around them along with bits of chaff that drifted lazily through the beam of light from a high window and spiraled down again. The clean herbal aroma offset the musty smell of sapeers and the more acrid scent of animal waste. Khivoi began speaking and, with the acute hindsight of the old, he began with the time when Vethis had first been placed with him for training. "He was an angry boy—insisted over and over that the Lord Amrith had stolen his land. I didn't know the truth of that and I still don't. None of my business. But after a while he settled down and concentrated on what he was there for, learning to handle a weapon. He had no trouble with skill at arms, either. Vethis was one of the best students I ever had. He picked up more and mastered it faster than anyone else I can remember.

"Then when he had learned one thing he pestered me until I taught him something else. Almost driven, I thought sometimes. He went quickly from being my star pupil to being my right arm. When I got past the age to continue as Commander, he was already my Second and the only one worth considering to take over the job. That anger of his, though, I guess it never really went away. It just got pushed deeper inside instead. Now that he's finally let it out, he won't wait long to take the next step. Too impatient. We've got to prepare to meet him as soon as we can."

"He waited long enough for his revenge," commented Theram blandly.

Resar answered him. "Yes, but as Khivoi said, the waiting's over now. Vethis wants action and that means Highfields. He'll move to take it as quickly as he can."

"I don't understand your concern with time," Haron said. "Yesterday's storm must have closed the pass. Surely no one can come through now until snowmelt. Before then, there can be no attack."

There was a small silence in which the sapeers could be heard munching fodder and scratching against their stalls. Then Khivoi spoke, "He'll come through the caverns when he's ready and that will be long before snowmelt."

"The caverns!" expostulated Haron, "What caverns?"

Resar asked a question by way of reply. "Have you ever thought about why Highfields is so comfortable in the cold passages?"

"Of course. Because of the water that's piped in from the hot springs underground," replied Theram confidently.

"Exactly. That water heated deep within the ground rises to the surface through cracks and fissures. Some of these are no larger than the hair on your head while others are bubbling springs the size of a barrel. Those are the ones we tap to heat the buildings and to bathe in and use for the laundry. The water is no good for drinking or for irrigation because it is full of minerals dissolved from the rocks. Over thousands of years the water has carved caverns which extend for miles beneath the mountains. Whether they connect with other similar caves, whether they are all part of one big cave or whether they just go on for great distances of themselves is unknown. Whatever the size of the caverns, one that we know of goes all the way under the Lesser Range. It was explored and mapped many years ago by my great-grandfather and several others. No one ever paid much attention to it, though, because it has no real use. So the maps have gathered dust among my grandfather's other papers and everyone has pretty much forgotten about the underground passage. Except Khivoi."

I used to go down when I was young," the old man continued. "I was convinced that the caverns could have some tactical use, some way of defending us better. But I never found one until now."

Theram was intrigued. "How does Vethis know of them?"

"He learned everything about them from me. Once when I was going down for another look he found out and kept after me until I took him down too. As I said, he was persistent. After that, he kept exploring on his own. Now he knows them at least as well as I do. As well as anyone."

"Where does this underground passage emerge?" asked Haron thoughtfully.

Resar answered him. "It comes out on the far side of the Lesser Range, by Smoking Springs. There are two ways to enter the cavern from this side. The first one is in the thermocaust, the building that houses the controls for the heating system. The Cavern of the Rites is the second way in. Both are inside the walls."

"And a way in is also a way out."

Theram smiled. "So, instead of pushing through snow-drifts in the pass and then throwing exhausted men against well-defended walls, Vethis plans to enter the compound by the back door and attack warriors who are looking outward. Very clever."

"Too clever by half," Haron said. He looked pointedly at Khivoi. "Vethis knows full well that you're still alive. Why won't he anticipate that you'll tell us about the caverns and then suck us into another ambush?"

"Oh, he'll anticipate it, certainly," the old man replied with disturbing nonchalance. "What he won't expect is that anyone here will listen. As far as he knows, my Lord Resar is dead along with the Lord Amrith. If his spies are what they should be, he'll know that a troop of Rangers was dispatched here. He'll probably also learn about a separate band of mercenaries thrown into the defense. But the leaders of both troops are strangers to Highfields and its people, confident of their own proven tactics. Barrikehn and the Lady Callain are unaware of the caverns. Who among all these people will listen to wild tales spoken by an old warrior too feeble to make one steady pass with a sword? More likely that old man will be dismissed. Not really coherent any more, you see. No, Vethis will count on having clear passage through the cavern."

"All the better. We'll have the advantage of surprise," said Theram.

Haron thumped one large hand down on the fodder, sending up a fresh eruption of chaff. "But can we win a battle in the caverns? If our men face them there, in close quarters and total darkness, can we best use that advantage? Or will the cavern still be used against us?"

Instead of answering them directly, Khivoi looked to his liege. Resar stood up. "We need a battle plan but we can't make one here without all the information at hand. Come to the office with Barrikehn after the evening meal. We'll look over the old map and put the strategy together." He turned abruptly and left them without a farewell. The others sat quietly in the dusty room, unwilling to comment on his brusque behavior.

The library of the estate house, long used also as an office, was a small chamber. With five men of solid build crowded into it, the room seemed even smaller and was very cramped. Shelves lined its walls from floor to ceiling, filled with books of many sizes, punctuated here and there by more of the odd objects collected by Resar's great-grandfather. A heavy table stretched along one wall and, aside from a couple of chairs, it was the only furniture in the room. Its top, a solid plank of wood two inches thick and five feet wide, had been cleared of all the paraphernalia needed to run a large estate. Now it held one item only: an ancient map drawn on yellowed vellum. The map was unrolled and weighted down at one end by books and at the other by ornate ink pots. The man leaned over it, scrutinizing its faded markings for anything they could use to their advantage.

"Here!" exclaimed Haron, stabbing the map with one finger. "Look at this stretch where the cavern narrows. It's marked 'The Funnel' so it's probably a very small passage. That means if it's difficult to negotiate, Vethis's troops may have to take it one man at a time. We could wait on the other side and pick them off as they come through."

"It is very narrow," admitted Khivoi. "They would indeed have to come through The Funnel single file and they would be vulnerable there. But fighting in the caverns is a knife with two points, as you said before. The walls are rock and sounds echo down there. The noise of fighting ahead would alert the men who follow. Forewarned of the ambush, all they would have to do is hold back the body of the strike force and give us the vanguard as expendable. Then we would have the unpleasant choice of either going through The Funnel after them—and being picked off ourselves—or allowing them to pull back and regroup. In either case we lose the surprise and the advantage. The next battle will be far bloodier because of it. And the outcome will be much less certain."

There was a long, uncomfortable silence. Then Theram spoke grudgingly. "He's right. We'll do better if we station our men above both the exits from the cavern. Then we can engage the strike force as they come out inside the compound. If we time it right and hold our men to a strict discipline, we can keep casualties to a minimum. They're mercenaries, after all, and once they know they're trapped they should surrender without an all-out battle."

Haron added, "That brings us to the next question, which is: How will we know when they're coming?"

"I've been thinking about that," interjected Resar. He turned to Barrikehn. "Do you have four good men, warriors with fast blades, that you would trust with your life?"

Barrikehn responded without hesitation. "Yes, my lord. And their loyalty to you is unquestioned."

"Good. Now listen carefully. Assemble the four tomorrow and have them memorize the map. While they are learning the way through the caverns, put together as many provisions as they can carry through The Funnel. We'll disguise all four as fur trappers and send them through to Smoking Springs. Instruct them to camp where they can command a good view of the trail up the mountain. They must stay far enough from the springs to avoid suspicion yet be close enough for fast access. When they spot Vethis and his warband approaching . . ."

"One will come back and warn us . . ." Haron interrupted.

"The other three will remain there until the enemy is all in the cavern," concluded Theram with dark glee. "Then they'll follow at a safe distance and hold The Funnel at that end. Once Vethis's troops are through, they won't be able to retreat."

"Exactly. Meanwhile, we'll drill our men and set up a regular watch at this end of the caverns."

"That should do it," commented Haron admiringly.

"It's as neat a plan as I've ever seen," added Barrikehn.

Khivoi chuckled. "All battle strategies are neater in the planning than in the fighting. But I think this one will work well."

Resar looked up from the map. "We'll have a mug of this year's enzaitha to seal the plan. Then let's get some sleep. Much work lies ahead of us."

Resar paced his room like a nervous animal, seeing nothing, while Sandy lay quietly in the corner and watched him. Haunted, the lord of Highfields kept hearing old Khivoi's voice saying, "He insisted that the Lord Amrith had stolen his land." Resar turned it over and examined it in his mind. Once again he realized that he had not known his older brother very well. Because of the thirteen-year difference in their ages, Amrith had left the Children's House when Resar was still very small. The differences in duty, in responsibility, and in training had kept a barrier between them and kept them from being friends as well as brothers. Afterward, Resar had left Highfields as soon as possible. He had lived long enough with Amrith, however, to know that his brother was used to having what he wanted and was not overly concerned about how he got it. Resar remembered several occasions when he had found Amrith's methods dubious and been uncomfortable with them. But there had never been anything he could do except look the other way. Injustice was a problem Amrith was likely to have worried about only when he was on the receiving end.

Muttering a decisive oath, Resar strode from his chamber, followed like a ghost by Sandy. Together they moved quickly down the long, chill hallways to the office. The small room was empty now but the map of the underground passage still covered the tabletop. Resar stared at it for a moment, then rolled it up quickly. Then he turned to scan the book-covered walls. Although the estate records had been kept neatly and in order, there were so many volumes that it took him a while to find the ones he wanted. First came an ancient map of the entire estate drawn for one of the regular census tallies long ago. Compiled shortly before the year of Amrith's birth, the map was simple and quite clear. On it, the northern border of Highfields ended well before a long rock outcrop that marked the southern boundary of the village of Field's Crossing. In between the two lay a large freehold farm that was labeled as the property of Seveth ak'Hept Artis. Although the next part of his search was not really necessary, Resar was determined to check completely. He turned to the map his brother had drawn up for the last census and, as he well knew, the farm was no longer there. Instead, Highfields spread unbroken from the pass to the outcrop.

Replacing the weighty census books, Resar next pulled down the estate records that covered the years after the Sweating Fever had ravaged the valley. One by one, page after page, they released the information for which he was searching. The dry statistics and unemotional entries held the complete story of how Vethis had lost his inheritance. There were even some records of payments scrupulously placed in trust for the orphaned children of Seveth ak'Hept Artis. No entry indicated that any of this money had been paid out, however, and Resar doubted that Vethis had ever been told of its existence. Amrith had held on, it seemed, even to conscience money. Resar closed the last book with a sigh and slowly placed it back on the shelf.

Although his new knowledge changed nothing, he was even more disturbed than before. Vethis had betrayed his fealty and his trust. He had murdered not only his lord and enemy but other people—innocent ones—as well. He had kidnapped Dara for his own devious purposes when surely she could have had no part in the way he had been cheated. He would attempt to seize Highfields and hold it in payment for the land he had lost. He had a grievance and just cause for anger but that did not mean he could now be shown mercy. His own actions had placed him beyond clemency and Vethis himself would be the first to admit it. Still, the fight was no longer as simple as it had been. The injustice existed and it gnawed at Resar.

The lamp on the desk guttered, casting long shadows flickering on walls and ceiling. It broke his concentration, reminding him of the hour and how exhausted he was. His eyes felt hot and swollen but, as he rubbed them with the heels of his hands, he was surprised to hear the door open. Resar was astonished when Callain stepped into the room, holding a candle and looking concerned. She wore a long, soft gown of the finest weave that covered her completely and yet emphasized her statuesque figure. "It is late, my brother, and you work too hard. Come now, and rest."

Resar nodded and then, on impulse, asked his brother's wife a question. "Did you know of any reason Vethis might have had to seek revenge against Amrith?"

Callain appeared puzzled and thought silently for a moment. The candle in her hand gave her skin a warm, translucent glow. "No," she concluded, "I know of nothing that could have caused his actions toward us. But Amrith did once say something strange to me. We were standing on the Long Balcony watching Vethis drill the men. My husband smiled and said, 'It is safer to bind your enemies to you than to cast them away.' I asked him to explain but he would not. Do you know what he meant?"

"Yes, I believe I do. Now." He blew out the lamp and walked toward the door. Callain stood aside so that he might pass but in the narrow doorway Resar could not help brushing against her. The scent she wore was soft and demure yet very noticeable. Was it the flowing gown, he wondered, that made her figure appear fuller and rounder? A sudden shaft of desire embarrassed him and then as quickly succumbed to fatigue. There was something different about his sister by marriage but he was too tired to do anything more than make a mental note of it. Side by side, with Sandy padding behind them on the cold stones, they walked back toward the sleeping quarters.

If it was possible for a head to feel stuffed and heavy, that was how Dara's head felt. After three days of having information loaded directly and indirectly into her grey matter, her brain practically throbbed. Worn out, she sat limply on her bed and stared at the blank wall, allowing thoughts from the last few days to run erratically through her skull. There had been lectures, learning machines, pictures in several dimensions, subconsciously-entered tapes, and countless data banks. After each session and at the end of each day there had been merciless drills to enhance her recall. Dara could now recite names, titles, and areas of authority for all the il Tarz women and the Trading Family's major officials.

Much of the data absorbed so far had been simple facts of no intrinsic interest or applicability that she could determine. Other information had caught her attention and appealed, for one reason or another. She liked, for example, the dry wit that had named the Family's headquarters and center of quadrant operations the Beldame. That thought led her on to the topic of language. Dara had assumed that the negotiations would be conducted in Khyren-ka. To her astonishment she had learned that English was not only one of the Ten Major Languages used in this quadrant of the galaxy but the one used primarily for business. Several languages originating from different worlds were most frequently applied to other specialized areas like politics and the fine arts. For that reason her briefing had included a session to bring her now-archaic command of English up to current levels of vocabulary and idiom. This process had proved both confusing and amusing.

The tape had told her that Heads-Up was now the name for a kind of zero-G, no-holds-barred rugby favored by entrepreneurs and that computer memories were now constructed at the molecular level and measured in weakforce bands and mil-links. She still chuckled at the knowledge that the Earth's major art museums and serious collectors were concentrating on "primitive" van paintings of the late 20th century. She remembered clearly a coworker's Chevy van decorated, sides and back, with fanciful scenes from Tolkien's ring trilogy. She mused that it would probably occupy a place of honor in the Museum of Fine Arts if discovered in A.D. 2489.

Another newly-acquired fact, less amusing, was the nature of the commodity for which she was to negotiate an agreement. Extract, a concentrated version of the same drug that had carried her to mental peaks and physical depletion, was highly valued throughout the quadrant for both medicinal and recreational use. Its effects could be modified with additives for alien metabolisms or changed completely by combining it with other drugs. Each race and species tailored the Extract to its own uses and biological requirements. She had deduced that it was never used in its pure form and she well knew why. Her scruples rebuked her for collaborating in drug dealing but Dara reminded herself that she had little choice in the matter.

Her thoughts drifting to the task ahead, she realized that she felt as prepared to begin the assignment as she ever would. Dara reached up and touched her neck gingerly, although Martus had reassured her there was no need for either caution or hesitation. In this case, he had been as good as his word: the implanted comlink could not be either seen or touched. As promised, the operation had taken less than an hour, start to finish, and she had felt nothing. What had hurt had been several of the many immunizations and inoculations which had preceded it. All of the medical operations had taken place in a formidable room filled with complex equipment of many sizes and shapes. Since none of this awesome apparatus had been used with her, she still wondered about its purpose. What puzzled Dara most was why, when the room was white and stainless, Scaure and the physicians had referred to it as the Yellow Room. It made no sense to her.

Dara grew more fatigued and less logical but her mind continued to circle without pattern or direction. The Yellow Room made her think of Khyren's bright sunlight. She had been shut away from all but occasional glimpses of the outside for so long that she ached to smell fresh air again. Dara had lost count of the days spent locked away underground, if indeed there was a correlation between the days marked off below ground and the rising and setting of the sun outside. She wondered if winter was still in full force in the mountains. Since she had no idea of the length of the seasons on Khyren, however, she could not tell how long it would be until spring arrived. She tried to picture Highfields in the spring with the early pink dayflowers Lekh had said bloomed first along the irrigation ditches.

She wondered who was lord there now and what had happened to the haughty and demanding Callain. And Sandy. She would not be back to get him after snowmelt as she had promised.

To keep from slipping into depression, Dara made an effort to re-focus her thoughts on the upcoming events. There was a lot to think about: the il Tarz Family, the frightening idea of negotiating for high stakes, what would happen on her return, space flight itself. It was hard to believe that she was really going up there. The stars had been unreachable in her old life but now she would get a chance to explore that frontier, to see for herself. Images of suns and planets, nebulas and asteroids kept her awake long past the time when sleep should have relieved her exhaustion.

CHAPTER 16

Dara stared out the forward view screen at the complex structure revolving delicately ahead of them. It was an intricately-organized sphere of geometrical shapes in layers connected to each other and to a hub by curved tubes and spidery lines. Each layer of shapes was a different color and connecting tubes were of gleaming naked metal. The whole construct turned slowly in its orbit and riding lights blinked evenly at places along its perimeter. She was marvelling at its functional beauty when Captain Andle raised her voice over the busy hum of the bridge activities and said, "That's the Beldame ahead."

Dara was startled. "That?" she asked. "I thought we were landing on the planet."

The first officer gave a dry laugh which the captain explained. "Thulin 2 is mostly ocean with nothing much in it but large ice packs and a few scattered islands. There's a landing station and trade compound on the largest one, but it's nothing elaborate." Dara looked more closely at the silver and dark blue globe with swirling clouds patterning its atmosphere.

"Besides," the captain continued, "it wouldn't make

sense to put a major trade center at the bottom of a gravity well. Landing the merchandise and then lifting it off again would raise the cost of the goods prohibitively. Be a real munger of a job, too."

That made sense but Dara was annoyed at her own ignorance. Martus and Restobor had briefed her quite thoroughly about some things while skipping over others that she considered necessary. They probably thought something like this was just a matter of common sense. Their orientation had also been incomplete in preparing her for the actual flight here. Dara had been excited even at the idea of space travel and had had trouble containing her enthusiasm when she boarded the *Sigil*. She had taken the crew's equally ill-concealed amusement as a reaction to her greenhorn status. It had been a crushing disappointment to discover that, in reality, space travel was immensely boring. Part of the problem was that the *Sigil* was a freighter and sported none of the luxuries offered by a passenger liner—or so the crew had informed her. Aside from the bridge, the crew's quarters, and a combination recreation room/cafeteria, its bulk was devoted to cargo. No portals opened onto awesome vistas of nebulas or gas giants. There were no meteor showers or asteroid belts, just blank walls and bulkheads.

The only place aboard ship where you could even see outside was here on the bridge. Although she had been allowed the web-chair reserved for deadheading staff, Dara was definitely out of place amid the working crew. Offduty, there hadn't even been any entertaining stories about hazardous assignments and difficult missions. The crew mainly slept or relaxed by playing long and very involved games with the ship's computers. The games were beyond her but she did discover that the computer network was, in fact, the only thing that was interesting. Tiny computers were scattered all over the ship, each one attending to a separate function while at the same time communicating continually with the master processor that coordinated all of the ship's operations. Dara had talked with many of them and learned that, besides having abilities far in advance of the archaic machines on which she had once worked, the artificial intelligences had their own "personalities," each suited to its specific task. In another time and place she would have been enthralled by the opportunity to explore the implications but now she wanted to experience space flight and was frustrated at having it elude her. Even free fall had become boring after a while.

Floating in the spare web-chair on the bridge, Dara looked at the Beldame, rapidly growing larger in the screen, with new eyes. To her, the trading center had assumed a shape logical to its function. Ships docked at the perimeter, cargo was held in the rings and personnel were housed in the hub. She tried to be unobtrusive as the crew carried out the synchronized docking maneuvers, yet at the same time watched everything they did with absorption. The *Sigil* spiraled in toward one of the brightly-lit docking bays, shuddering as its retro-rockets fired. Then the ship slipped neatly in to the bay and snapped against the gantry's magnetic grippers. The station's gravity field enveloped them and they all sank into their chairs. "We're here," said the captain brightly but unnecessarily. She unstrapped herself from the wrap-around command console and stood up. "Get your bag, Dara. I'll escort you to the receiving area."

Walking again felt slow and awkward after the gliding grace of free fall. In the reception room they were met by a three-person security team whose leader the captain introduced with deference as Director il Tarz. Dara's interest quickened as her briefing supplied her with background information. While smiling and shaking hands sociably, she was intrigued by the thought that the compact, athletically-built blonde next to her was one of Nashaum's daughters *and* was in charge of security operations for the entire station. Gwynnym il Tarz had lively blue eyes that reflected a contained but restless energy. Her personal aura was strong and, aside from a professional wariness, direct and friendly. Dara liked her at once.

Captain Andle departed in one direction while the team escorted Dara in another. Their destination was an area identified as SECURITY in the alien alphabets of the Ten Languages. While Dara followed the director into her office, the security guards remained in the anteroom. Dara sat in the chair indicated but refused an offer of refreshment. To put the visitor at ease, the security chief sat in an adjacent chair rather than behind her desk. "My name is Gwynnym il Tarz and I am responsible for security on the Beldame," she began. "Before you can proceed further into the station you must complete a series of tests which allow us to detect hidden weapons and other harmful devices. I will conduct you personally through these tests. Do you understand?"

Dara nodded. "Such precautions are reasonable and to be expected."

"I appreciate your cooperation. Everything has been set up so we can begin immediately. I'll explain each test as we go along so there won't be any unpleasant surprises."

The entire series required several hours and when it was completed Dara felt as if every part of her body had been scrutinized, analyzed, and evaluated—and with good reason. That was exactly what had happened. Cleared, finally, she proceeded with Gwynnym to her assigned quarters. Looking sideways at the other woman as they walked, Dara completed her own analysis. Nashaum's second daughter looked as if she would be most at home in a sweat suit or on a playing field. She was chunky and hard-muscled with a round face and short-cropped straight hair. She bounced instead of walking and radiated energy and good health. Dara warned herself to be cautious and not be deceived by an early favorable reaction. First impressions can be deceptive and nothing could be taken for granted in a high-stakes situation.

Gwynnym left her at her room, where she unpacked and then went to bathe. In the bathroom she confronted her own image in a full-length mirror, the only mirror of any size that Dara had seen since leaving her own home. She stared at her reflection, fascinated and appalled. Her hair was now long enough, when loose, to brush her shoulder blades but she wore it twisted into a heavy knot instead. It had once been auburn but now was shot through with white strands. Below it her face was gaunt, the eyes deep-set and the cheekbones prominent. Quickly Dara removed her flight suit and examined her body. In the bright light of the bathroom it was hard to believe that she had once jogged to keep her weight down: her frame no longer carried extra weight. Instead, her body was all spare and lean with no padding over the bone and muscles. The scar on her right shoulder looked like a white starburst radiating down her breast. Her body had toughened and weathered, showing that it had been through difficult situations, while at the same time it displayed a certain rugged strength. Dara thought grimly that there was little in her appearance that a man would find attractive. And it was just as well, for what man was there to attract?

SECURITY DIVISION
INDIVIDUAL SCAN—ANALYSIS OF RESULTS
STU 1487.6, Period 20

SUBJECT: Murdock, Dara T.
ORIGIN: Sol III, "Earth"
SPECIES: Homo sapiens

DESCRIPTION: Height—66 rods
                     Weight—12 standards
                     Hair—auburn & white
                     Eyes—brown
                     Reproduction—mammalian, multiparous
                     Sexual orientation—heterosexual
                     Esper level—normal, enhanced
                     Abnormalities—none
                     Note: tonsils missing (surgical removal indicated)

IDENTIFYING MARKS: 1) Scar—transverse abdominal (surgical origin)

                             2) Scar—starburst, right shoulder (puncture, origin unknown)

                             3) Mole—left ankle, normal

                             4) Teeth—dental repair on 7 teeth

                               1. bicuspid missing

                               2. adult molars missing

                               3. 1 crown

MEDICAL ANALYSIS:

Results are normal for a female of this species. All medical and psychological scans were negative for abnormalities as well. Surgical and dental procedures recorded are archaic for the level of medical technology on Sol III at this time. This would indicate procedures originating in an undeveloped geographical area or a remote timeframe. Subject is a healthy individual who shows no signs of physiological or psychological tampering.

SECURITY DEVICE SCAN:

Neuro-optical comlink (origin: M'Gwad Technocracy) imbedded in spinal column, filaments infiltrating cerebral cortex. Extent of infiltration indicates recent placement into subject. Device is designed to send aural and optical information and receive aural input.

SECURITY ANALYSIS:

Comlink is a common, if unusually small, device which allows instantaneous communication with the Brotherhood of the Bhoma-San, subject's sponsor. Knowledge of its presence renders it useless as a negotiating advantage. No other detectable security hazard exists.

ANALYSIS COMPLETE

Later, another of the security staff knocked politely on the door to Dara's room and escorted her to a different area of the station, one labeled SOCIAL. Gwynnym was already there, accompanied by a second woman. This individual was tall, slim, and graceful, with cafe-au-lait skin and shining dark hair. Her face was classically beautiful, with high cheekbones and large liquid eyes. Her simple green dress appeared so elegant on her that Dara felt for a moment underdressed. Then she reasoned that, on this woman, even rags would look sophisticated. Although she bore no resemblance to Gwynnym, Dara's briefing kept her from being surprised when the woman was introduced as Itombe il Tarz, the Family's senior daughter. Itombe's aura was a faint echo of her sister's but was definitely warm despite the reserve. The dangerous feeling of being among friends increased.

They sat at a beautifully-arranged table—something else that Dara had become unused to—and enjoyed an excellent meal. She savored the fine cooking, elegant flowers, and the pleasure of conversation with women of wit and education. As there is generally little charm in a guarded dialogue, they were all careful to speak only of neutral topics that had no bearing on the negotiations to come. Discretion was particularly important since Itombe was her mother's second-in-command. As Nashaum had grown older and become more reclusive, Itombe had become her functional arm, keeping the station's daily operations running. All the other station heads, as well as Nashaum's other daughters, reported to her. Here at this dinner, however, she put aside authority and all three women enjoyed themselves in a relaxed atmosphere. Then, reluctantly, they retired early. There was much to do the next day.

The negotiations that followed were worse than she had anticipated, generating stress in a way that Dara had never before experienced. The comlink activated easily at her command and she could hear Martus speaking to her directly. After that she had to remain alert at all times, even through long stretches where the talks were dull at best and sometimes incomprehensible despite her training. Not only did she have to monitor the il Tarz end of the verbal parrying, she also had to listen to Martus's voice inside her head and then rephrase his points in her own words. In addition, she was disappointed. Dara had looked forward to meeting the famous, or infamous, matriarch of the Family. Nashaum, however, never appeared. Instead, Dara faced the stately Itombe and four other members of the Family's staff.

Inexperienced in the finer points of negotiation, she had thought the issue straightforward and the dispute to be settled logically within compromise on both sides. The issue remained distant, however, with constant haggling over every word taking precedence and even proper accents subject to discussion. Progress was painfully slow and Dara became increasingly aware that different cultures have varied approaches to negotiation and even different concepts of what constitutes an agreement. There were times when she wanted to scream with frustration but the participants continued to inch along, each group testing the other's position for points of weakness. At the end of the day they were as far from dealing with even one substantive issue as they had been when they began. Dara felt weary in every pore and as bruised as if she had been beaten with sticks. Despite the comfort of the conference room, she was sore from sitting and stiff with inactivity.

As soon as the day's session was concluded and she could tactfully depart, Dara fled to her room. There she collapsed on the bed, wanting only to sink into sleep and shut out the entire day. She had barely taken a deep breath, however, when the call chime sounded. With a groan, she staggered up and punched the door release. Gwynnym literally bounced into the room and, looking around her, frowned at the dimmed lights. "What are you doing?" she demanded.

"Relaxing," said Dara, lying back down again, determined to have some time to herself.

"Relaxing! You've been cooped up in a small room with a lot of boring talk all day. Right?"

Dara sat up and regarded her warily. "Right."

"Then this is no way to relax. It's only your brain that's tired right now. You can't really rest until you're tired all over. Come with me."

"Where?" Dara had her feet on the floor but resisted being drawn any further.

"You'll see. Just come. I promise you'll like it." Gwyn's enthusiasm was contagious and, in spite of herself, Dara got up and followed.

They went around the ring corridor until they came to an area marked with the usual ten labels in different alphabets. One of them said GYM. Dara sighed. "I don't have enough energy left to exercise. I don't even have enough energy left to think about it."

"Exercise gives you energy and you don't have to think while you're doing it," Gwyn replied in a no-nonsense tone. In the locker room they changed into brief disposable sweatsuits, then stepped into the most impressive gymnasium Dara had ever seen. There were playing courts, pools, machines, and complete environments, most of which were unrecognizable but she was amused to see that there was a free-weight room as well as a weight-free room. She surveyed the facility and then turned to a grinning Gwyn who said, "I *knew* you'd like it. Let's go. I'll show you how it all works."

She did. They worked on flexibility, muscle strength, and stamina. Gwyn cheered and bullied Dara, always pushing her to the limits of her strength. After a tough workout, Dara jogged in an environment that reproduced a winding road on an alien planet. The simulator varied flat stretches with hills and straight road with curves. It blew winds at her from different directions and at varied speeds. It even provided sounds and smells to complete a true model of an outdoor run. When she finally stepped out she was sweating, exhausted, and happy. After they cleaned up, she and Gwyn went to one of the common dining areas where Dara surprised herself by eating an enormous meal. That night she slept more deeply than she had since first arriving at Highfields.

The following days repeated the pattern. As the negotiations dragged on, it became increasingly apparent to Dara that the il Tarz were stalling, although Martus's voice remained patient and he never became frustrated. When the delaying tactics were obvious, Dara adjusted her attitude. Instead of regarding the negotiations as a brief task, she came to view them more as a long-term commitment. This mental shift allowed her to be more patient, herself, and relieved some of the frustration she had been feeling. She grew adept at tuning out the long speeches and eloquent explanations as the tactical mechanisms they were. Dara also grew more skilled at balancing the voices in the room with the voice in her head and learned to pay close attention to the Brotherhood's reactions. In a short while, she became very good at anticipating some of the replies so that her answer was framed and ready before Martus or Restobor began speaking. She was always grateful, however, to return to silence and privacy at the end of each day.

Itombe and the other members of the il Tarz delegation
became well known to her. There was Tumi of the stocky
frame and square face, who was always tucking her fluffy
hair behind one ear impatiently. Her assignment was to
facilitate the sessions—to keep them moving at a predeter-
mined speed and according to the il Tarz script. Her aura
was neutral: she was a team player doing her job. Wasnohe,
the dark one, played devil's advocate. Her lithe black
body and blacker hair suited the role well but contradicted
her heart-shaped face. Her attitude was contentious and
contradictory. Whenever the talks seemed to be going
well, Dara could count on her to raise an objection. On
more than one occasion, Wasnohe drove Restobor's disembodied voice to break its studied reserve. Her aura was sly
and devious.

The third spot was filled by a series of women who
alternated as background resources, providing specialized
information as required. Finally there was Aurial, the
youngest of the il Tarz daughters, who spoke little but saw
much as she monitored the equipment which recorded
each session in case of dispute. Her aura was cautious and
uncertain. She was slim and yet somewhat awkward, as if
still growing and not yet comfortable with her new size.
Mostly her presence seemed to be a way of filling in her
education.

Dara grew to know them all better than she wanted to
but this was only during the sessions. After each day's
recess, the others vanished into their own lives and Dara
spent her rest and recreation time with Gwynnym. The
feeling of friendship she had felt right from the beginning
of their acquaintance grew stronger. She knew only too
well that the il Tarz had probably planned this relationship
well in advance as part of their strategy. They could not
expect to gain any specific advantage from it in the talks,
she thought, since Gwynnym did not participate in them.
They could, however, be seeking to draw from her a piece
of information that could later be used to their advantage.
That was one reason why, in all the conversations she had
with Gwyn, she was careful to limit what she said to
neutral topics and to think before she spoke.

There was another reason for this caution. Although

Martus had assured her that the comlink would be activated only at her signal and deactivated when the sessions concluded, Dara didn't believe him. Her own intuition warned her that the Brotherhood had turned on the comlink before she left the Lost City and that it had been on ever since. She was certain that they were privy to everything she saw and heard and said. Even though she couldn't prove her intuition correct, there were the headaches. On two occasions her conversation with Gwynnym had skidded dangerously close to areas that could have led to sensitive questions. Before Dara could extricate herself, she had developed a sudden intense headache so painful that she had been nearly incapacitated. Then, unlike any other headache in her experience, it had passed quickly, leaving no aftereffects. She could not believe that these attacks had been coincidental.

Dara therefore acted accordingly. She avoided all mention of her past life because it could have led too easily to how she had become involved with the Brotherhood and why she served them. She sometimes had to think fast to tactfully avoid answering direct questions. Gwyn, with her outgoing nature, seemed unaffected by the barriers Dara had raised. If she was frustrated or offended, she gave no sign of it. Even when a blunt rebuff led to an awkward silence her sunny good humor remained undimmed. Dara's reticence did not affect the quality of her companionship. She would change the subject easily, if necessary, and always stood ready to answer Dara's many questions about the Beldame or to cheer her out of a bad humor. As their friendship grew, Dara allowed herself to believe that a part of it was genuine and not all politically motivated.

Callain looked out her window to where the sun descended behind the mountain's flank. Darkness came to the valley early during the cold passages and stayed long. The brazier was burning low and the alcove in which she sat grew chill yet she had to stay and finish the accounts. While Resar and the other commanders planned their battle tactics, their men had to be fed three times a day and housed in comfort. Their mounts had to be stabled. It was her job to handle these mundane details and she had to allocate the stores so that food was consumed evenly. She also had to ensure that, while everyone was well fed, the supplies of food in the compound were not exhausted before the next planting. She had to make use of whatever decent shelter was available for housing without crowding the men so that tempers were aggravated and fighting broke out.

Callain looked at her fingers, stained blue with ink, and smiled. Her mother's hands had often borne the same marks that were the badge of being mistress of a large estate. In the cold passages, though, her mother's hands had also been blue with cold, for there were no comforts like heat from thermal springs in the house at Starshadow Pass. Callain shivered even though she knew that the room was chill only to her. Often her maids complained, when they thought themselves out of earshot, of being stifled in the heat of her quarters. Yet the warmth did not penetrate deeply enough, to the marrow of her bones where the cold resided. She sometimes thought that she could lie down on the Singing Sands at high noon on Festival day and not be warm. She would get used to it: being cold all the time was a small price to pay for what she had gained and the drain on her metabolism would certainly get worse before it got better.

Once again she looked out the darkening window. If Resar did not come before she finished the accounts she would have to seek him out. She had news that would affect her future and his directly and it was only fair that he hear it as soon as possible. She knew Resar well enough by now to be fairly certain of his response but there was always the element of his new unpredictability to cause her concern. In the main room outside the curtained alcove her women were sewing garments, doing the fine detailed work that required careful hands. She could not see them but she could hear the steady level of their conversation, punctuated now and again by laughter. Even with fine new troops kept under tight discipline there were flirtations and such behavior led inevitably to gossip and teasing. There was a knock on the door of the outer chamber and a chair scraped back as one of the women rose to answer it. Callain lay the pen down and straightened the papers before her.

A moment later, Resar was escorted into the alcove. Looking distinctly ill at ease in this feminine environment, he sat on the edge of the chair opposite hers. Callain dismissed the women: this conversation was not for curious ears. When the noise of their departure had subsided, she spoke. "My lord, how may I help you?"

Resar's eyes looked past her as he sought the right words. "I seek only a few simple answers, lady. Because I am not skilled with words I must be blunt. Did you send for Tai this day past?"

"Yes, I did summon him to my chamber."

"Is all well with you, then?"

"Yes, my lord, I am very well indeed."

"I am most pleased to hear it. Is there, perhaps, any particular reason for your state of well-being?"

Now Callain selected her words with care. Much depended on this conversation, for her future and her status deepened on how her husband's brother reacted to the news. "Yes, Tai confirmed what I had surmised, that I am with child."

"Then she did have the Touch," he murmured to himself. "I rejoice with you, as will all of Highfields. When will the child be born?"

"After snowmelt when the weather warms and the pass is clear."

Resar looked at her intently and Callain linked her eyes with his. "There are matters of consequence to decide," he told her, unnecessarily. "The law speaks plainly on such a situation: the heir must have a protector. Our duty is equally clear. The child will need a father. As the brother of your husband, and unmarried, it falls upon me to provide both. I am willing to accept my responsibility. I ask you now if you will have me to be your husband and to be a father to your child?"

Callain lowered her eyes demurely and controlled a smile. "I am honored, my lord, and grateful for having been offered the choice. Many men would have decided this without consulting the woman concerned." Resar made a gesture of dismissal with his hand and she continued,

"But I, too, would ask, what of your desires? Is there no other that you would rather take to wife?" She had not doubted that he would do as honor and duty dictated, even in the face of a blazing passion but it was best to understand the situation clearly. She preferred to know where she would stand in his regard so that she could respond accordingly.

He hesitated before replying, a pause that told Callain more than the words that followed. "At one time . . . perhaps. But no longer. I am content as things stand. You are already lady of Highfields, experienced in leadership and a symbol of stability to the people here. I am no longer free to choose a wife irresponsibly for love or for a pretty face. You bring to me all that I need in a wife and will be a partner, as you were to Amrith."

Callain was jubilant although it showed only in the aquamarine sparkle of her eyes. "When do you think the wedding should take place?"

He sighed. "Since we stand prepared for battle at any time, I think it best that we announce immediately the fact that you carry the heir. We can marry soon afterwards. I am sorry that there is no Oben here to perform a ceremony but the declaration of our vows before the people is all that is needed. And the period of mourning dictates a simple wedding."

"I am no inexperienced girl to need ritual and pomp. Our news will hearten everyone in these bleak days and strengthen their spirits. That is more important by far." Callain was gratified to see Resar regard her more seriously as he realized the good sense in her words. "But Oben or no and mourning aside, there must be some festivity and the cooks will need time to prepare. Five days should be adequate, if that meets with your approval." He nodded. "Then I will give the instructions tomorrow after the announcement."

"That is a good plan." Resar started to rise, then sat gingerly back in his chair. Callain grew apprehensive. Everything had gone even better than she had hoped and there was nothing else to arrange. "After the legalities," he said haltingly, "if you wish, or prefer, I will not trouble you . . . well, intimately."

"I do *not* wish!" Callain exclaimed indignantly. She was surprised to find that, for all her scheming, the words were sincere. "When I am your wife, I will be your full wife, not the shadow of one. While I would wish Amrith alive again, he is dead. We who still live must fulfill our destinies. Sehr-pei cannot be cheated or denied." She realized that she was speaking heatedly and softened her tone. "While there is now no love between us, I am not displeased to be your wife. Later, when I grow larger, well, that is different and soon past." And never, she thought fiercely to herself, will I give you reason to regret marrying me or cause to look elsewhere.

Resar stood and bowed politely. "It grows late, Callain," he said in a friendly and more casual tone. "May I escort you to the evening meal?"

She smiled ruefully and placed one hand on her stomach. "Unlike many women, I wake up hungry and full of energy but as the evening draws near I grow tired and cannot abide even the smell of food." That was certainly the truth; even talking about it made her queasy.

Resar smiled. "I thought that might be the case. Your absence at table these past nights is one reason I sought you out. Even so, you must keep up your strength to nourish the child."

"Oh, I eat enough for us both during the day and one of my women brings me something bland later in the evening when the discomfort settles down. I'm surprised the house cook hasn't started a rumor by now."

Resar chuckled, "Perhaps she has." Then they looked at one another and, to their joint surprise, began to laugh openly and spontaneously. It was a welcome relief of tension and, each of the two thought separately, a good omen.

CHAPTER 17

Vethis settled himself slowly into a chair at the back of
The Dark Bird's taproom for another long afternoon of
waiting. Although the time spent in expectation for his
contact to arrive was boring, it could have been worse.
Almost immediately after arriving in Orrestai he had discovered how well the Nine Chimneys district deserved its
evil reputation. For Vethis, who had lived with hatred all
his life and who served the Brotherhood, this was not a
shock. But a tavern in such a place usually reflected the
kind of people who were drawn to its shadowy attractions.
He had entered it expecting to find a filthy, disreputable
bar that reeked of spilled liquor and unwashed bodies. He
would have taken for granted vermin, bad food, and a
proprietor who cheated as a matter of course. Instead he
had swung open the door of a clean, well-run establishment that was like a beacon on a dark night. Its bar and
tables gleamed. The floor was covered with clean straw
and the air smelled of woodsmoke from a huge porcelain
stove and of damp wuliveen. The dishes were cracked and
chipped but scrubbed and they came to the table filled
with victuals that were good and filling. A regular patron

would grow tired of such plain cooking quickly but Vethis doubted that many customers ate here regularly. The clientele appeared to be the most disreputable people in the mountains and they drifted into Orrestai, then out again quickly. In the four days he had spent at The Dark Bird watching people come and go, he had not seen the same ones more than twice.

Vethis had also not met Zeched One-Eye. A few surreptitious inquiries had produced little except sideways glances and a quick departure. Only one man had offered any comment: You won't find him and you may not want him to find you. So he had swallowed his impatience and waited with his chair tilted back against the wall and his eyes on the door. This rendezvous was the next step in his instructions and, if waiting was a test, he was prepared to stay at the Bird until next Festival, or until his money ran out. He hoped it wouldn't take that long because he was going to need all the money to hire men. Vethis nursed his mug of enzaitha and watched the tap room fill up with strangers. After four days, only the bartender looked familiar. He was a big man, big enough to settle tempers before they could cause any damage to his establishment or any trouble with the Rangers. He also had the muscle to separate combatants and eject them if a disagreement got out of control.

The door opened and a group of men entered, slapping snow off their coats and stomping their boots. A gust of cold wind blew in past them. Two of the men went over to warm up by the stove while the rest went directly to the liquid warmth available at the bar. Orrestai was a crossroads town that attracted a variety of people in many trades and it was often difficult here to tell from a man's appearance what his occupation was. These men could have been anything, he mused, even gormrith down from the hills. Suddenly a chair was thrust next to his and a man appeared in it, startling Vethis. Despite his surveillance of the door this man had entered unnoticed and approached him undetected. At a disadvantage and not liking it, he surveyed the newcomer coldly. The man was of average height and weight and presented a nondescript appearance. He was the kind of man you could look at and not see, much less remember. Only one thing made him different and that was the rough leather patch he wore over his right eye. He sat facing the back of the chair with his arms folded across the top. "You must be the man who's been looking for me," he stated flatly.

"And you must be Zeched," Vethis replied.

"I am."

Neither one of them spoke then and they watched each other for several minutes. "Well?" Zeched said.

Vethis raised his eyebrows.

"What do you want?"

"Don't you know?"

"Look, I haven't had a hot meal or a full mug for days and I can think of better things to do than sit here and stare at you."

"Fair enough. I want to do business."

"What kind of business?"

"Before I tell you that, I need to make sure you're really who you say you are."

Zeched gave a short, harsh laugh. "You want proof? That's easy," He lifted the patch to show Vethis not the scarred empty socket that he had expected, but a smooth patch of skin that stretched from cheekbone to eyebrow, depressed where it covered the orbital hole. Vethis, who was long familiar with scars and the wounds left by sharp blades, recoiled from this natural deformity and Zeched laughed again. "Satisfied?" he challenged.

Vethis nodded and wondered if this was another test. "I need to mount an assault," he began. "I need men, good fighters who'll give value for their money. They'll need to be armed if they don't carry their own weapons. And I need provisions."

"Who sent you?"

Vethis looked around but the tables surrounding them were empty despite the now-crowded room. People here gave Zeched plenty of room. "Portifahr sent me," he responded.

"And then he vanished," Zeched stated.

"Yes."

"Where's the party?"

"In a valley on the other side of the Lesser Range."

"Then you're not planning to move until snowmelt unless you want to spend the rest of the cold passages in a drift."

"Not exactly. The pass isn't the only way to Highfields."

Zeched sat up straighter and waved one hand in the air. The boy who hustled food and drink to the tables appeared almost instantly. The one-eyed man ordered a large meal and a full jug of enzaitha and sent the boy speeding off to the kitchen. Then he looked at Vethis again and this time there was a sparkle in his eye. "This sounds interesting," he said, "and it's been longer than I care to think about since I've had a real interesting project. Keep talking."

The negotiations proceeded slowly each day, so slowly that it was nearly impossible to detect any progress. Not only did the agendas change and the positions of the participants fluctuate, but the issues themselves also moved as if there were no true facts but only a variety of opinions and perceptions built around a vacuum. Yet, with the quiet inexorability of the tide coming in or snowflakes falling, each small agreement, each minor consensus, added to the others made before it to achieve progress. It was not steady progress. Barriers rose and were either leveled or overcome. People took strong positions and then withdrew. An obstacle would be reached and then disappear without resolution. Almost without Dara's being aware of it the framework of an agreement appeared and then solidified. Issues were resolved and a consensus accreted. The process was not smooth; always it was a step backward for every two steps forward. This continual struggle disguised the growing structure even as it became stronger. Dara, listening to two verbal tracks simultaneously and juggling sometimes conflicting sets of information, was even more removed from the progress of the talks, so the end actually came as a surprise to her. After what had seemed to her a typically frustrating session, Itombe announced in a matter-of-fact tone that all the issues were essentially resolved and the agreement would soon be formalized.

"We will draw up the document tomorrow," she stated, "and conduct the formalities on the next day."

Dara sat frozen in a kind of emotional shock. Even the voice of the Brotherhood in her head fell silent. She almost missed Itombe's next words but jolted back into reality as they sank in. "Mother will validate the agreement for the Family. You, of course, will do so in proxy for the Brotherhood of the Bhoma-San. For validation we require a retina print, a chromosome pattern and, although it is archaic, a signature."

Dara nodded, smiling but dumb. She was finally going to meet Nashaum il Tarz. And then it all sank in: it was over. She found that simple fact hard to accept. After the formalities, what? How could she leave these friendly people, civilization, a goal in life, to return to the amoral sterility of the Brotherhood and the near-feudal society of Khyren. The prospect seemed suddenly very bleak. She could not think about it, would not. There would be far too much time to think later on.

In the communications lab where they monitored the comlink transmissions, the three Counsels-Regent regarded one another with careful expressions. The pressure was off and they had won. The Brotherhood would produce thirty-eight packets of Extract over the next half-STP, delivered directly to the Beldame. It would not be easy and there would be long-term repercussions but they could meet that commitment without seriously endangering the swarm. Martus knew that the il Tarz had never really expected to receive the full fifty packets. It had been a threat but it had worked: he admitted that and grudgingly admired their strategy. A season ago this agreement would have been counted a significant defeat for the Brotherhood. Now it was a success, if not quite a victory. Even so, he was not complaining. Their profits would increase and their relationship with the most powerful Trading Family in the quadrant was strengthened.

He looked around him. Estavin sat by the equipment watching Restobor, who had risen and was pacing across the room. Although all three men remained expressionless, there was an air of suppressed elation. Then Estavin broke the silence with his unassuming voice. "The outcome is favorable. And we reached the end only through cooperation. It was Restobor's idea and equipment combined with Martus's operative that achieved success. Without cooperation our situation would now be far different."

"Yes," agreed Martus, "it is a lesson well learned. Working together in the future we could accomplish much." *Whichever of us becomes Triarchal Master,* he added to himself.

"Surely you have considered another assignment for the woman when she returns? Perhaps she could be of assistance with the Order of the Lady."

"That has been in my mind," replied Martus smoothly. "And perhaps you could contribute to that effort."

"It would be my pleasure to help in any way. The Order is a burr in my operation and it would be gratifying to diminish their influence by using one of their own against them."

"My thought exactly."

The door opened on an attractive room, warmly lit and comfortably furnished with soft carpeting and chairs that were more like giant cushions. Gwyn had said that it would be a party, for just the two of them, to celebrate the successful completion of the negotiations. Dara had looked forward to it, pleased to be occupied so that she didn't have to think about her last night on the Beldame. They had just settled themselves and kicked off their shoes when the door slid open again to admit a very attractive man guiding a serving cart. He was blonde and his grey eyes were framed in squint lines above an honest face. His body was lean and strong, clothed in a sleeveless tunic that displayed the well-defined muscles of his arms. His skin had been darkened by a sun far from the Beldame's artificial light and he moved with the virile grace of a man accustomed to natural gravity. Although he was several feet away, Dara could feel his presence as if from physical contact. She wanted to run her hand down his arm and feel how the golden skin covered hard muscles. She was suddenly aware of how long it had been since she had been with a man.

Silently the steward set out a large green bottle enclosed in a thermal wrapper, along with plates of hors-d'oeuvres. Dara watched his movements almost in spite of herself, conscious of being rude but not caring about the discourtesy. There was a soft line of shining down at the nape of his neck. His aura was friendly and warm—very warm. "Thank you, Rolfe," said Gwynnym when he had finished serving the refreshments, yet it was Dara he smiled at before floating the cart ahead of him out the door. "Rolfe is part of my team,' Gwyn explained, "and he's very talented. Hilma—you've met my assistant—found him in an outback system and brought him in. So far he's proved valuable to us."

Gwynnym poured wine into delicate glasses where it bubbled like effervescent sunlight. Dara regarded hers dubiously: she had learned the hard way that alien liquor was not to be trifled with. Gwyn noted her caution and laughed. "It's all right. I was about to say it's harmless but that depends on how much of it you drink. It's only a sparkling wine from Earth, bottled exclusively for us at a gold-medal vineyard in a place called Little Compton." She unsealed the thermal wrapper and showed Dara the English label. "I prefer it to the more famous Brazilian wines."

Dara looked at her quizzically. "What about champagne?"

"Champagne? Never heard of it. Now, it's time, since you'll be leaving soon, that you told me what your life was really like on Earth. You've barely referred to it and I'm consumed with curiosity."

Dara's internal warning light went on automatically. She cast about for some way to dodge the direct question and avoid another "coincidental" headache. She thought furiously, but unsuccessfully, for a way out of the awkward situation. Gwyn busied herself with the food and said with a studied neutrality. "By the way, this room is more than just a pleasant place to have a party. It's also a clear room, protected against any kind of transmission either in or out. Whatever is spoken within this room cannot be monitored or recorded by any device obtainable in the Third Quadrant. I know; I've tested it." Dara sat very still as she absorbed the implications of this remarkable speech. Then Gwyn looked up at her with a steady forthright gaze. "I like you and I think that you're my friend but that friendship is between us and is no one else's affair. So relax, drink your excellent wine, and tell me the *whole* story."

Silence. It took Dara a moment to adjust to the idea. The Brotherhood had no way of listening to what she said or monitoring what she did. Silence. She would not have to worry about saying the right thing to satisfy two different audiences. No walking on eggshells. No invasion of her private thoughts. Silence. The comlink had always been quiet outside of the conference room but still, in some way, listening. This was different; a bond had been severed, if temporarily. Here it was only, as Gwyn had said, the two of them. It was a liberating thought.

To cover her lapse in attention, Dara tasted the wine. It was indeed excellent and she made a polite comment about its flavor. Then the bubbles went straight into her veins, rendering her blood effervescent. Her skin tingled and she shivered slightly, glad that Rolfe was no longer in the room. She sipped again, savoring the wine's sunny taste and the golden brightness that aroused memories of what she now thought of as her "first" life. It was a life which she had of necessity put behind her and which now seemed as remote to her as if another person had lived it. Responding to Gwyn's plea for openness she began to talk of that life and of the person she had once been.

Dara was not naive: she knew what the other woman sought to accomplish. On the other hand, she owed no loyalty to the Brotherhood and she trusted Gwyn's aura more than she trusted any of theirs. So, refilling her glass and nibbling a tangy cheese, she went back to the beginning and narrated what had really happened to her. It felt wonderful to finally confide in someone who could understand her story. Even so, she held back one thing: how the Extract had altered her perceptions. That information she reserved for herself. When Dara had finished the tale, Gwyn was wide-eyed and the bottle was nearly empty. Pouring out the last of the wine, Gwyn commented, "All things evaluated, you were pretty lucky."

Dara was flummoxed. "Lucky?! Tell me, what other sorts of things did you evaluate?"

"Just some of the alternatives. That malfunction could have happened anywhere a transporter station is located, and they're all over the quadrant. For example, there are many planets where slavery flourishes and you might easily have ended up wearing chains and up to your neck in some extremely unpleasant work. In the Melioru'us System you would have promptly become a rare and welcome addition of protein to the community food supply. Afterward, the Meliorans would have carved flutes of a unique tone and wondrous workmanship from your femurs. The flutes are always in demand and we make an outrageous profit on them. At least that's one kind of immortality."

She took another drink, ignoring the expression on Dara's face. "On several other quite civilized planets you would have been declared an illegal immigrant without status or rights of any kind. Your discrete components would have been placed in stasis in an organ bank for transplant into registered citizens. And those are the human worlds. Most non-human species operate transporters in an environment that would kill you in seconds. And a good thing, too. So, on the whole, you were lucky."

Looking distinctly pale and feeling subdued, Dara set her empty glass down. Gwyn pushed a button on the low table and added, "But that's not to say you had it easy. It wouldn't have been unusual if you'd just curled up in a ball for a whole Standard Temporal Period with a raging case of cross-cultural shock."

"I couldn't do that," replied Dara, regaining some of her spirit. "I was too busy."

"Oh? Doing what?"

"Staying alive. Besides," she giggled a little tipsily, "I haven't had a whole period since I ended up on Khyren. Or a standard one either."

"I'm not surprised," Gwyn commented. "First there was the trauma of going through a transporter. Then came adapting to a new planet with a totally different specific gravity, food chemistry, and diurnal rhythm. On top of all that, you were deprived."

"Deprived of what?"

"Of men, of course! You were on Khyren for over half of one of its years and in all that time you only had a man once. It's no wonder your juices are all dried up. That's no way to get your body back to normal. That's barbaric."

Dara sighed. She wanted to protest that she had been preoccupied with other things. It was not, after all, as if she had had a lot of options. But the words remained unsaid: Gwynnym was right. Then again, however, pleasure was not the only consideration. "I agree completely, but I couldn't risk getting pregnant. Too dangerous. There aren't any real doctors on Khyren. Outside of the Lost City, anyway."

Now Gwyn giggled. "That's right but you're being silly. First of all, if you don't ovulate, you can't get pregnant. Second, even if your system was working properly, it's impossible. Remember what happened with the food? The chemistry just doesn't match. For dinner you can get away with a near-enough link most of the time. When it comes to conception, though, the chemistry has to match precisely."

Dara set her glass down sheepishly. That explanation was simple enough, so simple she felt ridiculous. But it was one issue out of the way and she decided to try for the answer to another puzzle. "If you know that, perhaps you can explain why Portifahr turned me down. When I showed him I was interested, he said he couldn't. What did he mean?"

"Well, I can't be positive, of course. But from all that you've told me, I'd say he had studied with the T'Chu-Gourn."

"What, or who, is that?"

Gwyn gestured. "Rolfe can probably explain it better than I."

Surprised, Dara looked up and saw Rolfe standing just inside the door. This time the cart held steaming platters of food that gave off savory and intriguing aromas. Another bottle of "champagne" poked its green neck above the covered containers. Rolfe set out enough food for five people and refilled their glasses carefully. Then he sat down cross-legged between them. Dara watched all his movements carefully, noticing how he combined a boyish warmth and enthusiasm with a man's sure competence. It was a combination she found quite attractive. His muscular good looks did nothing to discourage her interest. She turned to the food, using it to distract herself while he spoke.

"The T'Chu-Gourn are a reptilian species who occupy a hot, dry binary system in the middle of the Second Quadrant," he began. "They have never made any attempt to colonize outside of their system, keeping pretty much to themselves and asking only to be ignored. Because their system is rich in several rare minerals, however, it attracted other interested parties—a few legitimate, most not. Some attempted to deal fairly with the T'Chu-Gourn, some tried outright theft. None ever succeeded in even entering their system. The T'Chu-Gourn wanted to be left alone and they were. The question was, how? To refuse trade is one thing: to police an entire system for smugglers and thieves is another. And they are a peaceful people.

"The secret they possessed was awesome. They are natural telepaths, the best in any quadrant. Wherever anyone planned to go, they were there first. Over the millennia of their history the T'Chu-Gourn had developed ways of enhancing and intensifying their telepathy. Eventually they discovered that these methods could be applied to other, less talented, species although these methods are of little use to anyone not already gifted with psychic ability. They began to accept students. The T'Chu-Gourn are very selective and the course is arduous. Many apply, very few are chosen, and some who go to study there never return. The ones who succeed, however, become matchless telepaths. The fee is prohibitive so most candidates are sponsored by some government or private organization. A few raise the money themselves and then sell their services free-lance for extremely high prices."

Dara thought of the times when it had seemed that Portifahr could see inside her mind. That part certainly fit with Rolfe's description. "But what has that to do with sex drive—or the lack of it?"

"Simple. Psychic effort, like any other kind of exercise, requires energy, only more of it. Energy levels that high do not simply appear. They can't even be built up through practice and a higher food intake. The channel must already exist. So the unfortunate side effect is that those who return from the Gourn System pretty much lack a sex drive. It's not that they want to but can't; they're totally uninterested. All that energy has already been channeled in another direction."

"How do you know?" Dara asked. Then an awful thought struck her and she blurted, "You haven't been there, have you?"

Rolfe laughed with infectious good spirits, joined by Gwyn. "Not I. There are several talents I can claim but telepathy is not one of them. No, I've never been anywhere near the Gourn System. Most of what I told you is common knowledge around the quadrant. Of course, you also hear stories out there that make good listening but haven't a mote of truth in them. People are always looking for myths, as if there weren't enough religions and cults to choose from. Too many people will believe uncritically anything they hear and invent the rest. Gourn-trained telepaths are very impressive and can sometimes seem omnipotent. But they aren't gods or demons either, just highly-skilled people. Gwyn and I can vouch for that. After we were all safely delivered, Mother made the journey."

We? Mother? Dara looked from one to the other in confusion. Both were attractive physically but in different ways. Gwyn responded to her unspoken query by toasting Rolfe with a flourish. "Oh yes, you heard right, Dara. Rolfe is my half brother."

"But you said . . ."

"Indeed I did, and it was true. Mother conceived several sons but chose not to bear any of them to term. Rolfe lived with his father and surrogate mother on an Outback system. That's what we call one that's so far out it's not listed on the quadrant charts."

"It was a tough place to live," Rolfe added, "but we liked it. Dad was an independent trader and didn't need much company. Mom was a geologist who spent most of her time hunting for gemstones—the rarer the better. All she wanted was one big find and we'd be rich, that's what she used to say. She died in a rock slide when I was ten, still looking for her big strike. Dad and I just kind of knocked around the Outback after that. There was a lot to keep yourself busy with if you weren't choosy and didn't mind working mungering hard. Some of it paid pretty well, too. We would probably still be out there if it wasn't for the Happy Worm."

"What's that?" Dara asked. She had the unsettling feeling that things were moving too fast for her and decided to go easier on the champagne.

"The Happy Worm is a parasite native to the Outback system we were on at the time. The adult, which flies, has gossamer wings of a beautiful purple and is harmless. Fortunately, though, it's not common. The adult lays several eggs in fruit, one to each piece, where they stay dormant, too small to be seen or tasted. The egg hatches inside the digestive system of whatever unlucky host eats the fruit. The larval worm grows by robbing all the nutrients from the host's food before they can be absorbed. The worm compensates for its theft by secreting a substance that stimulates chemically the pleasure centers of the brain. The host experiences every pleasurable feeling known from contentment to orgasm to ineffable ecstasies. Since these sensations become stronger after a meal, the host is motivated to eat as often as possible. The worm then gets bigger and excretes more happy juice. When it has grown large enough to require more nourishment than food intake alone can give it, the worm begins consuming the host's body as well. Eventually the victim is literally eaten alive, but in a state of euphoria.

"When Hilma showed up looking for me, Dad was just about a skeleton with a big smile. I didn't want to stay around for the chrysalis stage, so I let her convince me that it was time to come in from the Outback and try life as an il Tarz on the Beldame for a while."

Dara took another drink and let the bright bubbles erase the grotesque picture Rolfe had painted. "And do you like it here?"

"I certainly do. After the Outback, life on the Beldame can be confining, but it has its rewards."

"Such as?"

Rolfe ran one finger gently along the arch of Dara's foot, sending an electric current tingling upward. "Such as money. And challenge. And company. I didn't know much about women before I came here. There weren't many women in the Outback that I cared to spend any time with. The idea of being in the company of women—and enjoying that company—was new to me. I find it fascinating."

"In what way?" Dara asked. Even to herself her voice sounded shaky. She set her glass down and noticed Gwyn puttering around the serving cart by the door.

"In every way," Rolfe replied and she was drawn back into his gaze. His hand was tracing the outline of her foot and she wanted it to explore further. Dara flushed and realized that she had never thought of her foot as an erogenous zone before. As if in response to her thought, his touch moved to her ankle and he murmured, "Women think in non-linear ways that make their conversation intriguing. They are truly interested in other people and that is flattering. Their voices are musical. Their bodies are soft. I love to listen to them, to watch them move." Now his hand was stroking behind her knee. Shivers ran down Dara's back and gathered below her navel. Her nipples tightened and tingled. Her body felt weak. Rolfe gave a small throaty laugh. "You see? You are a woman and you are wonderful."

Dara looked around for Gwyn but both she and the cart were gone. It was a set-up but one she found difficult to resist. And why, she wondered dreamily, should she resist. As Gwyn had said, life without love or human contact was barbaric. She had come a long way from her silent, frustrated longing for Resar. Rolfe was here and he was fine in many ways. Dara tangled her hand in his fair hair and leaned back. At first she wanted only to enjoy his caresses. Later on she expanded his knowledge of women.

The next morning Dara felt relaxed and exhilarated, if a bit hung over. The depression that had sat on her shoulders was gone and she approached the formal meeting room surrounded by a warm glow. If this was truly her last day of friendship and of freedom, she would at least leave with good grace. Most of the people she knew on the Beldame were in the room when she entered: Itombe, Gwyn, Tumi, Wasnohe, Aurial were all there, as well as several other functionaries with whom she was not familiar. Rolfe was not present, nor were any other men in the room. After the introductions, Dara seated herself in the distinctive chair indicated for her. Unlike the other seats, it was larger, less delicate, and somewhat more cylindrical. She wondered if it was the seat reserved for guests.

Then they all waited for Nashaum. There was no light conversation or small talk. Everyone anticipated her arrival in silence. Dara looked around and made sure that she remembered everyone's name. She studied the equipment for verifying the agreement that was arranged in order of use at the center of the table. She watched the guards who stood impassively on either side of the door. All were silent. Even the comlink, which she had activated automatically when entering the room, was soundless. Then, without preamble, the door slid open and Nashaum il Tarz entered the meeting room. Without uttering a word or making a gesture she was immediately the center of attention.

Nashaum's serene face was crossed by thousands of fine wrinkles drawn on a skin so pale it might never have seen the light of any sun. Although of small stature and apparent great age, the matriarch moved gracefully. She wore a silky tunic over slim pants, both of a dark blue-on-blue pattern. This severe costume made her appear even more diminutive and yet she carried both dignity and authority about her like a numbus. Her true aura was strong, guarded, and so surprisingly cold that Dara recoiled from it instinctively. It seemed impossible that this distant woman could have mothered children like the ebullient Gwynnym or vital Rolfe, both so filled with unbridled life.

When Nashaum turned to her, Dara stood to make a formal greeting. As she rose, she felt an odd unfamiliar tingling in the comlink. Before she could gain her feet, she was surprised to see Nashaum's eyes widen and her thin lips open as the ancient face froze for a microsecond and then became animated. With a speed of movement and grace of action beyond anyone's expectations, the old woman whirled and slapped the control panel on the wall behind her, activating a circuit. At the same time she emitted a dry shriek. "Bomb!" she cried, her voice loud and harsh in the silent room. "Bio thermite. Put her Outside, immediately!" Then she was through the door, which slid shut behind her, and gone.

She left a room full of astounded people incapable of

either movement or emotion. For a space of a deep breath the group remained in a shocked stillness, then they burst into frenetic activity. Only Dara remained motionless and quiet, half-risen, immobilized by a bell-jar-shaped energy field. Barely perceptible, this field was projected by a mechanism hidden in the chair's base and activated by a circuit on the control panel. In the confusion, Itombe took charge, snapping orders at the guards, who had been alerted by Nashaum's sudden departure. "Get two carry-alls in here right away. Move!" She turned to Gwynnym who stood, stricken, staring at Dara. "We have an emergency here. Order your staff to clear the corridors from here to Sick Bay. Snap to it! She only has 80 STMs to survive the stasis field."

Gwyn looked startled but raised her communicator immediately. Itombe started to speak again but Aurial interrupted her with a blunt question. "Why Sick Bay? Dock A5 is empty. We could get her Out there in 5 STMs."

Itombe silenced the girl with a sharp look. "You call Sick Bay and alert them she's coming. That's an order, Aurial. They have to be ready to operate the micro-M as soon as we're in the door."

"Mother said Out," Aurial protested stubbornly.

"And I said call. We're wasting time."

Aurial stared at her sister, then bit back a reply, and put her communicator to work. The guards had returned with large powerized cargo-transfer handles and now they fastened them to the chair, pushing hard to get through the field's resistance. Activating the mechanisms, each man grasped a handle and lifted both the now nearly-weightless chair and its occupant. Then they moved out of the room and down the corridor with Dara suspended like a wasp in amber between them.

In the abruptly empty room Aurial lowered her communicator and looked at Itombe. "Sick Bay is ready," she said. After a pause she asked, "What happens after 80 STMs?"

"The protoplasm in the cells starts to jell," her sister replied shortly. "Then there is a complete breakdown of body functions, beginning with the nervous system."

"In other words, she dies," added Gwyn, in a ragged voice.

"Mother's going to be furious," Aurial began.

Itombe cut her off, "I'll handle Mother." The three women looked at one another in silent communication and then moved out of the room toward Sick Bay.

Inside the surreal dome of the stasis field Dara existed without thought. She was conscious of not breathing, of not having a heartbeat but these things meant nothing to her. She perceived movement around her as her chair was tilted forward so that she faced the floor of Sick Bay. There was speech, as well, but words were just random sounds that were absorbed by her entire body rather than heard through her ears. In her frozen world they carried neither meaning nor import and flew above her like birds, swift and untouchable.

"Move the light closer."

". . . brace it . . ."

"Med Tech here yet?"

". . . never worked in a stasis field before."

". . . unusual . . ."

". . . prepare micro-forceps."

"Think of it as a challenge."

"Clamp."

". . . like working underwater."

". . . did that either . . ."

"Give us a countdown to crisis, Tech."

"Laser scalpel."

". . . no suction."

"More light, aide."

". . . blood won't flow in a field . . ."

"Fifty . . ."

". .. there's the cord . . ."

"Incredible . . ."

"Get a ballistics rep, stat."

". . . mungering field."

"There it is."

". . . thing's fighting back."

"What?"

". . . comlink, then . . ."

"No, slowly."

"Where's the bomb?"

"Probe the sides . . ."
". . . no way that . . ."
"Thirty."
"Is anaesthesia standing . . ."
". . . slow, slow . . ."
". . . no choice."
"Wipe."
". . . little more . . ."
". . . couldn't hurry if I . . ."
"Wait!"
"Twenty."
". . . too small . . ."
"Definitely not comlink."
"Impossible . . ."
"Ballistics here."
"Don't let it slip . . ."
". . . smallest I've ever . . ."
". . . get it!"
"There . . ."
"Ten."
"No . . ."
"It's coming . . ."
". . . burn the cir . . ."
". . . can't, I . . ."
". . . have to cut."
"Here we go."
". . . anaesthesia . . ."
"Ready . . ."

Then the field was gone. For a nanosecond Dara felt incredible pressure, as if a cold vise had clamped on her neck. Then there was nothing.

CHAPTER 18

Kennistan waited until he was absolutely certain. Crouched behind a thicket uphill of the camp, he watched carefully the recent purposeful activity there. Then he checked the location of the sun once again. Its pale disk was lowering toward a bank of clouds that lay heavily along the horizon: more snow was coming. Although it seemed an unlikely time for it, there could now be no doubt that the warband was preparing to move out. He stepped into his snowshoes, removed his mittens, and bent to strap the frames on. His fingers fumbled with the straps, grown clumsy from the cold and his excitement. Then the gear was fastened, secured to his boots, and he was off through the forest.

He and the other three scouts who guarded the entrance by Smoking Springs had been observing the warband's camp ever since the men had cut their way up the drift-barricaded mountainside. Without the kind of cold-weather footgear he wore, their trek had been an enormous effort in the deep snow. As a result the warband had camped in a sheltered spot to gather their strength before attempting an assault on Highfields. Believing that the enemy was snowed-in on the other side of the Lesser Range, they had sent out no patrols and used guards at night only to protect against wild animals. Not even Vethis was aware of being watched by other, more dangerous, eyes.

Kennistan ran between the huge stippled boles of the taiga trees in a swinging, gliding lope. The shadows lengthening across the snow made him push a little harder. He and the others would have to move quickly to get the message through in enough time for Resar's strategy to be set into action. The fine edge had worn off their preparedness from waiting. Kennistan was one of the third set of scouts sent out to keep watch for Vethis and, like many others, he was surprised that the traitor had not returned more quickly. The lowlands men had become complacent enough to take bets that he would not return at all. Even some from Highfields had come to believe that the reinforcements would sit around for all the cold passages, eating up the stores until planting season came. Then, when the pass cleared and there was still no attack, they would all give up and march home. Kennistan, like the other men who had served under Vethis in the household guard, had laid his money safely on the man's return and was the richer for it. Now it remained to make sure that they won the battle with as few casualties as possible. As gamblers said in the barracks, "You can't collect a debt from a corpse." Not for the first time, however, he wished that he would be fighting freely in the open instead of lurking in the darkness to guard the rear against retreat.

Sweating from the uphill run despite the cold he reached their makeshift lodge and alerted the two men waiting there. Each was rested and eager to move but it had been decided that Alrin, who was most adept at making the underground journey, should carry the message. Now Alrin looked at the sky, brightening with a stark winter sunset, and calculated how long it would take the warband to reach the springs, then traverse the caverns. Stroking the frost off his beard he whistled in admiration. "What a plan. If they attacked in the daytime they would be blinded when they came up. And there would be people all around to raise the alarm. So they're going through at night instead, when the advantage is theirs both ways."

"The snowstorm will give them extra cover," Nicahr commented. "They'd have a good chance of winning if we weren't already two steps ahead of them."

"Good thing for us that we are," replied Alrin. He picked up the taiga branch they had cut two days ago and loped off toward the springs. The branch would sweep his tracks from the snow and rock around the spring. He would carry his snowshoes through with him.

While he and Nicahr waited for the fourth member of their team to return, Kennistan took down his long seidoh, wiped its already gleaming steel, and slipped the wicked blade back into its scabbard. When the sword was strapped securely across his back he checked the dagger in its sheath on his right leg. Both weapons were regulation issue. The slim, balanced throwing-knife in its scabbard on his left wrist was not. Most warriors had a favorite weapon without which they felt unarmed and that small but lethal weapon, made to his instructions by a master smith in Targhum, was his. Next he paid careful attention to his lantern, making certain that it was full and the wick trimmed. Kennistan was a big man, broad in stature and deliberate in manner. He was at home in woods and meadows or on any battlefield that let him face an enemy directly under an open sky. He did not like the dark damp caverns at all. The ceiling pressed down on him and the walls caught at his body. Skulking underground behind an enemy was not to his taste.

This assignment also meant that he would not have the chance to match blades with Vethis and that confrontation was what he desired most even if their fight could not be to the death. Kennistan was a veteran warrior, however, and orders, even if not what one might wish them to be, were orders. When his preparations were complete and Ovyan had still not returned with the traps, he took a mug of tea and squatted by the fire. The beverage he drank was one not well known in the lowlands. It steeped continuously in the pot until it was as black as the chirka pelts drying around them and nearly as thick. Drunk very hot and very sweet it was an effective stimulant.

As he sipped the scalding drink, Kennistan looked around the lodge. It was as cluttered and disorganized as a real fur trapper's base of operations, and with good reason. The first group of scouts had run a trap line to establish their cover in case advance scouts had gone out. The line had been maintained after that because it made sense to do so: the chirka on this side of the Lesser Range were plentiful and their pelts of a high quality. Each one taken had been carefully marked with its owner's sign. Once the fighting was over, several men would return to the camp and recover the furs. Many of the finest would go with the Oben in the tithe but there would be enough left over to make a pleasant bonus for the men who had guarded the spring. Kennistan had one pelt set aside for a certain young woman with clear eyes and a bubbling laugh.

His reverie was interrupted by a rattle of chains and a low whistle as Ovyan stooped through the doorway. "See how the Lady has rewarded us for our vigilance!" he exclaimed before he was into the lodge. "Here is the grandfather of all chirkas!" He held out the stiffened body of the largest such animal Kennistan had ever seen. Its lips were pulled back over long pointed teeth in a frozen rictus and its eyes glared fixedly. Beyond that fierce visage its fur was thick and soft and of a deep glossy black that was unrelieved by any shade or touch of another color. Chirka was the finest, most aristocratic of all furs on Khyren. Ovyan looked eagerly for his comrades' approval and saw instead that they stood battle-ready. The traps and chains slid from his other shoulder and landed in a jangling heap. "When did they move out?" he asked, suddenly serious.

"An hour past," Kennistan answered. "Alrin has gone ahead with the alert. Our job comes next."

Ovyan sighed and looked down at the animal he held. "I will prepare quickly," he said. Then a gleam returned to his eye. "But it's bad luck to turn down such a gift from the Lady and we need luck with us tonight. I will make haste." He slipped out his skinning knife and set to work.

*   *   *

It was quiet where she stood. Still. Silent. She was

alone. Dara looked up to where the elaborate plasterwork of an ornamental ceiling arched more than two stories over her head. Intricately scrolled, bordered, and painted it curved down to meet the walls on either side of a long, narrow hallway. They held the ornate facades of huge mausoleums stacked one above the other from the high ceiling down to the shining floor. The elegant work and rich detail of these tomb fronts was amazing in its Baroque splendor. Fronted with polished marble, malachite, onyx, and lapis, they gleamed in royal colors. Twisted columns and straining caryatids supported tall friezes and imposing pediments. Luxurious architecture for the dead, the tombs crowded one another in an abundance of imperious solitude.

Dara looked around at the solid door shut firmly behind her and then in the other direction at the long hall. Although it went on for a great distance, its details became vague and indistinct after only a few feet so that it was impossible to see where it led. She began to walk. No footsteps attended her passage and no other sound marred the cold perfection of the enormous mausoleum. As she walked, the tombs imbedded on the other side of the passage became simpler and smaller. As they decreased in size, however, the crypts increased in number until they packed the walls and it was impossible to fit so much as a handswidth between them.

Looking back to where she had started, Dara was surprised to see two men standing quietly, watching her. Startled and alarmed, she began walking faster but, no matter how quickly or how far she traveled, she could not see where she was going. Now the sepulchres were just flat black doors set into the wall. They had gone from ostentatious to simple to common yet, no matter what their appearance, they still enclosed only the dead.

Suddenly Dara was struck by the thought that she was here in this mortuary because she belonged here and that thought frightened her even more. Once again she looked back only to see that the two men were closer now and walking toward her with a determined stride. Panic rose out of her fear and she began to run. She ran past black doors and toward the constantly-receding obscurity ahead but her heart did not pound and her breath did not come faster. She did not breathe at all. Finally she came to the one door that was different, tall enough for a person standing upright, and she swung left, pushing it open.

She had gone through it and several steps beyond it before she saw, truly saw, what now lay around her. It was an extraordinary garden of an intense beauty, filled with flower beds and trimmed in borders of greenery. Paths wound away from her feet around and between massed flowers of every size and color, enticing her to follow them and discover new mysteries. Out of sight a fountain sang and birds echoed it with liquid notes of their own. Butterflies in gorgeous hues floated and dipped, illuminated by a nearly incredible light that bathed the entire garden. Brilliant light, almost overwhelming in its intensity yet strangely not blinding, it suffused every part of the garden. Its radiant glory also permeated Dara, filling her with great joy, contentment, peace, and love. She had a wonderful sense of having reached warmth after cold, food after hunger, rest after exhaustion, of having come home. Home. She smiled without being aware of it.

Dara was startled out of her ineffable reverie by the clasp of a firm hand on each arm. The two men now stood on either side of her and the one on her left said neutrally, "You must go back."

Back? To the cold hall, the tombs. Back to the darkness. Back to any place that was away from the glorious light? "No!" she protested, twisting away from the double grip, wanting only to be away from them and free to walk deeper in the peaceful beauty. But the men held her as firmly as the stone caryatids on the tombs held their pediments.

Then the man on her right said, "You must go. There is work yet to be done."

Without understanding the words she spoke, Dara responded, "I can't. They will mock me. They will fight me."

"That is your challenge to meet."

The other one added, "Yes. Your challenge. It is time."

"No."

Disregarding her protest, the men tightened their grip and then all three were rising weightlessly, past flowers and trees, beyond the birds wheeling in the light. As they floated higher into the encompassing dark, Dara strained for one last look at the fabulous garden below them, now no bigger than the head of a single flower. Then it was gone and they rushed ahead through total darkness and emptiness, moving faster and faster. There were stars and all the celestial majesty of galaxies around them but after the intoxicating light even space lacked the power to awe. Suddenly a dot appeared out of the nothingness ahead, growing rapidly into a tawny ball. Without warning her arms were freed and, instead of being propelled, she was drawn to the ball, pulled toward it like steel to a magnet. Falling, falling with a soundless wail, she went to meet the single point on the yellow globe that called her, and there was no escape.

When the world returned, she was lying on her stomach, arms stretched upward and head turned toward the left. She blinked and surveyed what she could see of the unfamiliar room around her. It was definitely not the conference room. There were no people. The chatter of voices was stilled. The chamber reminded her instead of what Scaure had called the Yellow Room. Dara was confused. One moment she had been preparing to greet Nashaum and the next . . . Nashaum! There had been a strange expression on her face. Something wrong. A shout. What was it? Startled into action by the fragment of memory, she tried to sit up but could not move her arms to brace herself. Although she could feel nothing on them, in some odd way they were pinned down. She tried to lift her head and found that also immobile.

Straining her eyes upward, Dara saw a red band of light beamed from a panel that was part of the bed on which she lay. The light streamed across her left hand and wrist and, though it extended outside her range of vision, presumably covered her right hand as well. The crimson band was transparent; she could see her hand clearly but could not make it even twitch. Her neck was a different story, seemingly encased in a wire cage that felt about two feet long. Why? There was a low pulsing ache at the base of her skull that brought back to memory a tingle in her neck. What was going on? A segment of time was lost to her and in that time something critical had obviously happened both around her and to her. Despite her hardest attempts to remember, however, Dara could not fill in that gap. There was simply nothing there.

Her concentration was interrupted by the sound of a door opening. A nurse entered her field of vision and looked down with professional concern on his face. Dara heard someone else walk to the foot of the bed. It annoyed and frightened her that she could not move to see who it was. The nurse spoke brightly. "Good, you're awake. Does your head hurt?" Dara considered the question and realized that the dull ache was flowing up into her skull. "Yes," she replied and was surprised to hear it emerge as a hoarse whisper.

"That's to be expected. I'll prepare some medication and be back in a few moments to keep it from getting worse. Don't worry about your voice—the laryngitis is caused by the stasis field. It will be back to normal in a day or two." He picked up a tube of liquid and held it to her lips. Water. It tasted wonderful even if it was distilled. When she had finished drinking, the nurse set the tube down where she could reach it herself. "Now, if you promise not to thrash around or roll over or touch the bandage on your neck, I'll turn off the restraint."

"No. Leave it."

The nurse looked back toward the unseen person, shrugged apologetically at Dara, and left. When the door was closed again, the other visitor pulled a chair up close to the bed and sat down facing her. Dara had thought she recognized Gwyn's voice but it was Itombe. "How are you feeling?"

"Not good. What happened? I remember being in the meeting room and your mother coming in. Then there's just a blank. What's the stasis field he was talking about?"

"That's right, you wouldn't know. Well, to put it bluntly, you were carrying a bomb."

"What!"

"Listen, Dara. You had to be aware that there was a comlink tied in to your nervous system, right?"

Dara tried to nod, failed, and whispered a hoarse, "Yes."

"Well, attached to that mechanism was a bomb. Bio-thermite. It was the smallest explosive device of any kind that our ballistics expert has ever seen. Gwyn's security sweep revealed the comlink, of course, but missed the bomb. Partly because it was so small and partly because we saw only what we expected to see. It was sloppy and careless. *That* won't happen again."

Dara remembered the tingling in her neck and her stomach turned over. In response a wave of pain surged into her skull. "I was walking around with a bomb inside me all the time and I didn't know it?"

"Didn't you?" Itombe's voice was quiet and reasonable but the two simple words were deadly and they had a nearly physical impact on Dara. The implications spread out from them like ripples from a stone flung into a pond. Pinned down on the bed, she suddenly felt helpless and very vulnerable.

She took a deep breath and tried to hold her voice steady. "No, I didn't. I agreed to work for the Brother-hood, to represent them here, not to be a walking death trap. I knew enough not to trust them but I underesti-mated how far they would go to get what they want. Doing something like that never occurred to me."

"How can I be sure of that?"

Dara thought wildly but could find no answer to that question. "Prove it!" she replied, "There is no way. No evidence, no testimony. Nothing. Unless you have ma-chines Gwyn hasn't already used and I'll go through any test you set up. If not, it's my word against the Brother-hood's. You'll have to decide."

There was a long pause and they looked at one another steadily. Then Itombe said in a matter-of-fact tone, "That's what we thought."

Dara, lying rigid, released her breath. "Thank you. But

if they could have set it off any time, why did they wait so long?"

"They—I presume you mean the Brotherhood—wanted Mother. Wiping out three other members of the family at the same time was a bonus but it was Mother they really wanted dead. They've tried it before, you know, and they haven't succeeded yet."

"Why not? How *did* she know the bomb was there when Gwyn hadn't found it and I didn't know it existed?" She looked alarmed, scared. "That's the last thing I remember."

Itombe smiled a great cheerful grin. "Mother trained with the T'Chu-Gourn. Her skills go far beyond telepathy and she is a formidable opponent. We who know her best underestimate her least."

"You mean, she just *knew* it was there?"

Itombe nodded. "She just knew. And acted immediately. It's a good thing, too, or we'd all be dead by now. We in the family have seen this kind of thing before and so we're accustomed to trusting Mother's insights. They're not usually so dramatic, though."

"There's something I still don't understand, Itombe. Why would the Brotherhood want to blow up the station? Killing your mother is probably logical from their point of view. And it's obvious that I was expendable. But destroying the Beldame would have hurt their trade and their profits. That's a pretty high price to pay for an assassination."

Itombe's smile faded and she leaned forward gravely. "Bio-thermite doesn't blow up anything. It only affects living organisms; inanimate objects remain untouched. You and I and every person in that room would have burned like solar flares. Oh, the room would likely have caught on fire as well but the fire control system could have taken care of that without much trouble. They wanted assassination, not destruction, and they planned it well. Much better, in fact, than any of their other attempts."

Dara, who had felt odd engaging in a horizontal conversation, comprehended why she remained under restraint. That she hadn't known about the bomb did not alter the fact that she had been, and might still be, a walking booby trap. Having nearly died in a particularly sickening way only made it worse. Once again nausea rose and she closed her eyes while she struggled to control it. When she opened them again, Itombe was waiting patiently. The expression on her face was unreadable: Dara did not even try. "Then what happened? The bomb was activated. Why didn't it go off?"

"The chair you sat in, and not by accident, has several fail-safe mechanisms built into it. One of them generates a small stasis field around the chair. That's what saved us all. The stasis field kept the bomb inert until we could disarm it. It also gave us a narrow chance to save you." Itombe's self-confidence slipped for the first time. All at once she looked embarrassed and slightly defensive. Her gaze slipped down and she sighed. For a moment she busied herself with the tube and gave Dara another drink. Finally she put the tube down and sat back but her eyes were still averted. "I don't like to say this but you must already know. There are problems."

An electric current of fear ran through Dara. Her imagination was only too ready to supply those problems for her. With an effort, she suppressed her racing thoughts and braced herself. Once again, Itombe sighed. "Mother is very angry. Her orders, frankly, were to put you and the bomb Outside where there would be no danger. Instead I sent you to Sick Bay, so right away I disobeyed a direct order. For the first time. As if that weren't enough, I put our best medical team and Security's ballistics expert at grave risk. And that doesn't include the threat of fire damage to the Sick Bay. That's just me. Right now, Gwyn is trying to explain how she and her crew missed the bomb when you first came in. Angry doesn't begin to describe Mother's mood right now. What I'm trying to say is that Mother has ordered you kept in restraint until Gwyn can do another complete sweep. I hope you understand."

Dara almost exclaimed in relief. "I'm not complaining. Especially when I could be drifting around one of your loading bays instead." She thought how close she had come to death without even knowing it, but couldn't believe in the reality. The headache pounding at the back of her brain was much more real. "Would I have burned up out there?"

Itombe gave her a puzzled look. "I don't really know. It's a vacuum, of course, but bio-thermite is more a chemical reaction than combustion. Even if you had, though, you would have been too dead to notice."

The door slid open and the nurse re-entered carrying a tray. Itombe looked over her shoulder at him and then leaned forward. "It won't be for long: Gwyn will be in as soon as she can set it up." She patted Dara once on the arm and then exited as gracefully as she had come. The nurse placed the tray on her empty chair and Dara saw a metal tube much like the one Scaure had wielded. Since her neck was inaccessible, he used the femoral artery. The medicine worked quickly, first dimming the pain and then sending her plummeting back into sleep.

Dara was sitting up when Rolfe came to visit her in Sick Bay. It had been several days since Gwyn and her staff, working meticulously, had cleared her of carrying any more concealed weapons. With that anxiety gone, the atmosphere had become noticeably more cheerful to everyone but Dara. She was depressed. If asked to put it into words she would have said that, although it was illogical, she had failed. There was no way she could have known about the bomb but her ignorance had betrayed her friends. Even the satisfaction of having completed her mission had been taken from her. She was very confused and her visitors could not lift her spirits at first. Rolfe looked weary when he came in and his hair was rumpled but a smile crinkled the little lines around his eyes when he saw her. Despite her unhappiness, that smile still caused a degree of internal turmoil. His good humor was infectious and his teasing and laughter gradually began to disarm the combination of anger and guilt that gnawed at her. By making light of things, Rolfe enabled her to confront those destructive emotions for the first time.

Dara began to speak tentatively of her feelings but they soon came pouring out of her as Rolfe listened attentively, offering sympathy without judgment. After days of anguished self-recrimination, Dara felt lighter, as if she were literally unburdening herself.

"I can understand your anger," Rolfe said when her outburst had trailed off. "We all share it. And guilt, well, emotions don't always follow logical patterns. But your surprise perplexes me. Surely you knew enough of the Brotherhood to have anticipated some treachery."

"Certainly I did! Treachery is second nature to them so I was expecting more than just *some*. The questions were, what kind and when? That's where I miscalculated. I thought they would do something *after* the negotiations were completed. Based on that assumption, I was planning to guard myself when the assignment was over and I returned to Khyren. Since I didn't know that assassinating Nashaum was at least as important to them as the agreement was, I was taken by surprise. It never occurred to me that the Brotherhood would jeopardize their hard-won contract and booby-trap their own negotiator to strike at her."

"Booby-trap!" Rolfe exclaimed in amusement. "What a wonderfully antique expression. What does it mean?" There was a tone of condescension in his voice that annoyed Dara. She was in a mood to be annoyed easily.

"A booby was an old name for a simpleton," she explained testily. "A booby-trap is usually something which appears innocent enough to fool a gullible person but which tricks him unawares."

"Thus, a trap for simpletons. To think, it almost worked in spite of all our precautions and equipment. The term may not be flattering but it certainly is appropriate."

"That's why I used it," Dara replied tartly. "My speech may sometimes be archaic but that does not give you the right to mock it."

Rolfe leaned forward with a conspiratorial twinkle in his eyes. His voice lowered even though there was no one nearby to overhear him. "Let me tell you a secret about the il Tarz—about everyone on the Beldame. They all deal every day with beings in every sector of the quadrant. They are familiar with other sentient races and species. They understand politics and diplomacy and play those games with consummate skill. They have available to them the finest art and culture, the richest of traditions. Yet, for all of that, they are quite parochial in attitude and their point of view is often narrow. Their way of thinking is the only acceptable way. Their way of life, their goals, and their language are the only ones they consider valid. All else, no matter how vital or exotic, lacks significance and, therefore, respect. It becomes easy to think of other forms of expression as quaint or humorous. Tell me, Dara, what's the 'archaic' term for people like that. What did you call them in your own time?"

"New Yorkers."

Rolfe thought, then shook his head. "I'm afraid I don't understand that either."

"Never mind," she chuckled. "It's an archaic joke."

He nodded. "Well, at any rate, I'm afraid an attitude like that can be contagious, even to someone from outside the Beldame like me. I apologize if I offended you."

"It's nothing. You got me out of my emotional funk and that's a lot more important." She took his hand and squeezed it. He squeezed back. "Just stay here for a while and keep me company. Recuperation can be lonely."

"I'll stay until the doctor chases me out. She's not to be contradicted in Sick Bay. I'll tell you about the time Dad and I were hired to bring back a live Shadow Bird."

When Dara was nearly well enough to start exercising again, Nashaum summoned her. Even with Gwyn as an escort, Dara was nervous. She remembered clearly the tiny wizened lady, with an aura of power so strong it was almost visible, who with a cold voice had ordered Dara dropped into the vacuum of space. She fingered the smooth claw of the K'thi, which Rolfe had set on a shining chain, as she and Gwyn wound their way deep into the station's central core until they reached the matriarch's apartment virtually at its hub. The room they entered was spacious, pleasing to the eye, and simple. Carpeting in different neutral tones ran across the floors, over built-in platforms and pedestals, and halfway up the walls. One pedestal held an exquisite vase made of an ephemeral opalescent substance from which sprang a single branch with three spidery white flowers. The effect was delicate, yet power-ful. Nashaum sat gracefully erect on a platform which gave her a direct view of the flower arrangement. She wore a dark tunic over tapered pants, a costume flattering to her petite figure. She motioned Dara to a seat at her right.

When Gwyn and Dara were seated, Nashaum began without preamble. "So, Woman of Earth, my willful children tell me that you were torn from your own place and time and cast into a foreign world, that you have found no rest or refuge since." She gestured at Gwyn, who was perched to her left. "This daughter has related much of your history to me. Yet I ask you to tell me one thing yourself. Speak only truth, for I will know otherwise. Why did you agree to work in the service of the Bhoma-San? Did the Brotherhood coerce you or did you choose for yourself?"

Dara's hand, on its own, went to a spot on her neck above the jugular vein and her pulse throbbed beneath her fingers. Gwyn nodded at her in reassurance. "There was coercion at first," she replied slowly. "Then I agreed of my own free will. There was nothing else for me on Khyren. This task at least gave me the chance to take control of my life and it gave me a purpose beyond just simply staying alive. My goal was not to serve the Brother-hood but to meet my own needs through them." She thought back to a snow-buried tent filled with the bloody twitching phantoms of her dream. "In the end, it is sehr-pei and you must make the most of your fate. You do what there is for you to do."

Nashaum gave her a parchment smile. "Sehr-pei. It has many names on Khyren and is known on many worlds. We all live with it. If you know sehr-pei, then you can under-stand my actions. The bomb had to be disposed of in a way that threatened the fewest people under my protection. I did not seek your death, although that would certainly have occurred. I did what I had to do. Afterward I was angered that my daughters had consciously disobeyed a direct order. Also I was angered by the hazard at which they had placed so many people, unknowing and uncon-senting. Yet I am pleased that your death was avoided."

She paused and her gaze drifted toward the vase. "The question we are here to discuss is not what will happen to you next but rather, what is there for you to choose? Obviously, there can be no return to the service of the Bhoma-San."

Before Dara could reply, Gwynnym interjected, "She can stay here and work on the Beldame."

"Oh?" Nashaum queried. "And what will she do?" She turned to Dara. "Are you conversant with essential gravitics or differential astrogation?" Dara shook her head. "Well, that eliminates working on the ships. How are you in xenobiology or molecular code imprinting?"

Gwyn began to protest that her mother was being unfair but Dara raised her hand to quiet her. "No, Gwyn, your mother is right. I'm a dinosaur here. You might as well be asking Marie Curie about her knowledge of computer operating systems. It's ironic: on Khyren they called me a barbarian because I could not speak their language when, to me, they were the primitive ones. Yet it's here on the Beldame that I'm truly uncivilized. My training was once highly valued but it doesn't have any relevance to your technology. And it's too late to catch up." Once again Gwyn tried to speak but Dara would not let her interrupt. "Oh, I'm sure that if you all tried hard enough you could find some small job for me to do here but filling time with busy work is not enough. There has to be a purpose to life. I need to feel like I'm accomplishing something and that's not possible here."

"Here? No, you are correct," Nashaum said quietly. "But look into the past and you will find the answer to your future."

"Back? The past? I don't understand?"

"That is because you are speaking out of confusion and without thought. Clear your mind. After all, you spoke of it first. If you are far behind the level of technology now, you are yet still far ahead of it on Khyren. Tell me, what is it that the Bhoma-San first wished of you?"

Dara hesitated and answered slowly, "To spy on the Order of the Lady."

"Why do you think that was—or is—important to them?"

"Because the Order opposes them and their goals on Khyren."

"What do you know of this struggle?"

"Not much. Only a few basic things. The Brotherhood seeks to limit the population of Khyren and control its society for their own ends. The Order stands for fertility and life."

"And what are their ends?"

"Those of the Brotherhood are profit and power. At any price. They rule in secret and trade only off-world but they have gained great power, knowledge, and wealth. The ends of the Order are not known to me."

"Nor to me. In supporting the Order, however, would you not be opposing the Brotherhood?"

Again Dara hesitated. "The enemies of my enemies are my friends? Perhaps."

"Would you be helping the women of Khyren?"

"That is more likely. The Order promotes the worship of the Lady and they place the well-being of women and children foremost. Its adherents nurse the sick and ease the dying but their greatest value is in assisting at childbirth. Beyond that, I know very little. Until I learn more, I cannot be certain what casting my lot with them would achieve."

Nashaum nodded. "It is good that you are cautious. What you do not know my researchers can find out. Suvoir, my advisor on the Bhoma-San, must already know much and will be a good resource." She looked sharply at Dara, who recoiled as if those grey eyes were drilling into hers. "My instincts have never failed me. Trust them now. Your fate lies with the women of the Order. Join them and you will find the work and the purpose that you seek."

"How can I join them when I know nothing of the things they do?"

She waved a hand in dismissal. "They are things which may be learned: midwifery, basic medical skills, nutrition, herbal lore. We can teach you all those things before you return to that world."

"Why?"

"Specify. I do not understand your question."

"Why are you concerning yourself with me? Why do you want to help me?"

Nashaum sighed, a delicate, nearly inaudible sound. "Must there always be a why?"

Dara's face hardened. "Once I would have said not but I am a different person now, in a different life. Yes, there must."

"All right, then. Because men have used you ill. Because through you I may aid other women. And partly because I wish to make amends for ordering your death."

Dara inclined her head in assent. "Thank you. I do trust your instinct and I am grateful for your help. If we may, I would like to begin as soon as possible. There is much to learn and I must become strong again at the same time."

Nashaum agreed and, after a few more polite words, Dara and Gwyn rose to leave. Dara was quiet as they walked back through the Beldame's circular passages. She had much to think about.

Resar stepped over the still-twitching body of his opponent and continued his search. Their strategy of ambushing the invaders had worked, without doubt, and yet, somehow, not everything had gone according to plan. The warning had come in time and torches had been gathered swiftly from storage. The warband had appeared exactly when expected, emerging from the caverns only to be blinded by the unexpected torchlight like eyeless spirits of the underworld. Surrounded immediately, they had been given the chance to surrender. Instead of throwing down their arms with the expediency of mercenaries, however, they had attacked. Resar thought grimly of how they had fought against great odds with a dedicated intensity, a single-minded purpose that made them effective far beyond their numbers. The struggle had occupied enough of the defenders to allow ever more of the warband to surface and join the battle. Their resistance was astonishing, if suicidal.

Now scattered groups of men battled one another, swords gleaming when they caught the torchlight and bodies steaming in the cold air. The sharpness of the night gave a bite to the strong smells of battle: sooty smoke, acrid sweat, fresh blood, and the stench of bowels emptied by death. Through the chaos of the compound Resar moved silently, examining the faces of the men who still fought, scrutinizing the contorted bodies of the fallen. Behind him, Sandy padded steadily, his fur matted with the blood of his victims. Resar's orders to the troops were firm and uncompromising: Vethis was to be taken alive. Despite these commands, he knew only too well that in a battle anything could happen. A man engaged in a fight to the death would strike instinctively to defend himself and think of the results later. Another possibility, which he refused to consider, was that under cover of the darkness and confusion, Vethis had escaped.

He was stooped over a reddened corpse, hand outstretched to roll it over, when a Guardsman ran up, excited and elated. "It's him!" the man gasped, his breath emerging in clouds. "By the granary . . . Vethis . . . they're holding him . . . come." Resar stood, with his sword still bared, and followed the man at a run. Sandy hummed vibrantly and kept pace with eager strides. Dodging the pockets of conflict, they arrived to find Vethis backed against the broad granary wall. Three of Resar's men ringed him and he stood, legs braced and sword level, watching them warily. His eyes were sunk deep above his hawk nose and the planes of his face stood out starkly.

Before they could stop, Vethis attacked the man on his right. By the power of his movements, the expressionless set of his face and the ferocity of his actions, Resar could tell that he was filled with the same battle madness that drove the others. The force of his attack was overwhelming, the viciousness of his strokes leaving no room for riposte. His quarry, ordered not to kill, was at a disadvantage. He could not parry quickly enough and went down, his neck nearly severed by the seidoh's wicked blade. The impact of the blow was also Vethis's undoing. His long sword lodged in the dead man's spine, and its hilt was wrenched from his hands as the body fell heavily in a gush of dark blood. The hilt of the sword vibrated in the air and then stilled. Vethis stood weaponless and, for a moment, quiet. Before anyone could move, Resar roared, "Vethis!"

The other man turned, trancelike, toward the voice that had called his name. For a moment he stared, unseeing. Then the berserk look retreated and recognition altered his features: his face changed but did not soften. "You. I left you dead, thief's brother." It was a flat statement of fact made in a hard voice that was full of hate.

"You were hasty, traitor," Resar replied. "You didn't make sure of your kill and it was your downfall. But for me, you would now be victorious. The new lord of Highfields." There was no answer. The two men faced one another in silence and even the sounds of fighting around them seemed to retreat. Resar knew that he should hate this man who had tried to kill him once and would do so again, without hesitation, now. He understood Vethis too well to hate him, however. Briefly he wondered how he had acquired this strange sense of honor when his brother, groomed from birth for leadership, had not. "You have failed, Vethis," he added more calmly. "Call off your men so that there need be no more killing."

For an answer, Vethis spat into the blood-soaked snow. His eyes glared from their deep hollows. Resar tried again. "I know that you had cause to seek revenge. Give up your fight and justice will be done, I swear it."

Vethis's voice grated, "I know all about how justice works here and I have had my fill of it. Your justice sickens me. Now I seek satisfaction."

"As do I, Vethis." Deliberately Resar sheathed his sword so that he, too, stood barehanded. "I have promised justice and it will be done—on my word of honor."

"Choke on your honor, nobleman."

Resar shook his head. "As you wish. We will talk later and I will find out then what I wish to know. Until then you will have time to reconsider." He gestured to his men. "Take him to a holding cell. Chain him and guard him well."

Vethis was moving before Resar finished speaking. He charged directly at his captor, reasoning that the best means of escape was overcoming the only unarmed man. Resar reacted almost reflexively to the attacker's onrush. He raised one foot, planted it solidly in the man's abdomen and sat back. He barely had time to reach for a handful of shirt before the impetus of the attack carried Vethis up and over in a smooth arc. The flawlessly-executed throw left Vethis sprawled in the red snow with Sandy standing above him, his two rows of formidable teeth poised inches above an exposed neck. Stunned by the fall, Vethis offered little resistance when two of the Guardsmen lifted him by the arms. They tied his wrists with leather straps and led him away.

Resar walked stiffly down the dim hall, his body hurting from myriad cuts and aching muscles. He was bruised by the battle they had won two nights past and bandages covered wounds he had not felt when they were made. He walked beneath a lantern fastened to a solid wall of pinkish-grey stone and passed through its circle of light. This was the lowest level of the great house, hewn and shaped from the rock outcrop. When a boy, Resar had called it the dungeon and on his few unsupervised visits to the house he had found his way down here whenever chance allowed. Creeping about in pretended fear of imaginary evil-doers, he had been frightened in reality by the shadows and the echoes and the massive walls, which almost seemed to breathe. His dungeon was really only a series of rooms, rendered more secure than most by the solid rock. Creeping insects might escape them, but nothing larger.

On the rare occasions when they were used, the cells held miscreants and petty criminals until weather allowed them to be sent before a justiciar in Targhum. Entering another circle of lamplight, he stopped before the well-watched door of the one cell that was occupied. Sandy stopped at his heels. The guards saluted, then one of them unlocked the door and swung it aside. Resar stopped, entered, and looked around the small space. It was a plain square chamber with walls of unbroken rock. One of the hot water pipes of Highfields ran through it and warmed away the clammy dankness that might be expected in a subterranean chamber. To the left was a low shelf covered with coarse blankets. The bed was unoccupied. A lantern hung on a hook to the right, providing the room's only light. In one corner a covered bucket provided for the prisoner's physical needs.

Vethis was against the far wall, squatting on his heels. His back was braced against the hewn stone and his arms were balanced on his knees. A manacle circled his left ankle. A chain depended from it, coiled on the floor, then ran to a bolt set in the wall. His wrists were cuffed in iron and connected by a shorter chain of no more than five or six links. His head leaned back, eyes staring straight ahead of him at a point in mid-air. He did not look up when the other man entered. Resar observed the prisoner. He could see that Vethis still wore clothes last seen on the night of the battle. They were slashed, grimy, and spotted with dried blood. His shirt was creased diagonally by the mark of the strap which had held the seidoh scabbard. There were blood stains on his body as well and Resar could not tell if the blood had belonged to him or to others. The small room smelled of his unwashed body mixed with the musky sevvet oil burning in the lantern. Resar drew a breath. "Unchain him," he ordered.

"But my lord . . ." began one of the guards in protest.

"Am I a child to fear an unarmed man with two guards and a courser between us?" he asked without looking away. "Remove the manacles."

"Yes, my lord."

Vethis uncoiled himself and stood straight while the guard removed the chains. He did not look at Resar, staring instead at the wall to one side of his enemy. Unfettered, he did not rub his wrists or otherwise acknowledge that chains had been upon him. His stillness was ominous, seeming to carry violence pent within it. When he was free, Resar began to question him.

"Why did you turn against the Lord Amrith?" There was no answer. "Was it the land, Vethis? I found out about the land."

Slowly the captive's eyes swung sideways until they engaged Resar's. Still he did not speak.

"Was it revenge you sought?"

"You might call it that."

"Revenge is a reason I can understand. There are other

things not so easily comprehended." He paused but once again Vethis showed no interest. "For example: what about the women?"

Silence.

"You killed everyone else. Why did you take them?"

"Why does any man take women?" It was more a sneer than a reply.

"I thought of that. But you left Neva dead on the trail. A dead woman cannot serve any man's lust. Or was it only Dara that you wanted?"

Silence again and Vethis returned to staring at a patch of wall.

Resar decided that direct questioning on that issue would not work. He would have to try a more devious approach. "What about the men you led? Even average mercenaries are expensive when you need to hire more than a unit. You had nearly a legion of the best. Where did you get the money for them all?"

Although Vethis did not respond, his smile tightened.

"For that matter, where did you find men who would do battle like that? They were fighters far above the average." A look of alarm appeared in the captive's eyes so Resar pursued it. "They fought as if each of them was possessed by Sporrenno the Bloody. Perhaps they were drugged. Or maybe they were trained by fanatics somewhere far from the mountains."

Vethis jerked and his eyes met Resar's again. He was fearful and could not conceal it. Resar decided that changing subjects abruptly would keep him off balance. "What did you do with the other woman—the one you didn't kill?"

The smile flickered back. "I sold her. When I tired of her."

Resar's voice was deceptively calm. "Sold her where?"

"To a gormrith chieftain who fancied brown eyes."

"You lie!" For the first time Resar spoke with some heat. "Do you think me so witless that I cannot follow a fresh trail?" Reflexively he reached up and touched the scar at his temple. "Even with my head split open I tracked you to the lake where the mist is alive. With a boat, I could have followed you over the water as well. Where did you take her?"

Vethis sidestepped the question with one of his own. "What was the karait to you that you seek her still? Was she your concubine? Has the great lord taken up with barbarians?"

Inwardly Resar was elated: he had managed to penetrate the man's cold reserve. Outwardly, however, he continued his questioning in a tone suitable for a man whose honor was being challenged. "She was under my protection. That's all." But as he spoke he knew that it was not true. "All of the others who placed their trust in my judgment are dead. If I can get her back, I can retrieve my honor, too."

"Your honor. Always your honor. It is sapeer droppings to me. Leave me alone."

"Not until I'm satisfied. Where is she now?"

"The karait is gone where you will never see her again."

"Perhaps. You've underestimated me before, Vethis. Tell me where."

"Follow our tracks over the lake and find her yourself. Better yet, ask the lake."

Resar ignored the jibe and returned to Vethis's weak spot. Deliberately he exposed the man's secret, hoping to make him more vulnerable. "The attack, your fighters, the battle here, all this smells of only one thing. The Brotherhood." There was an audible indrawn breath from the guards but Resar kept his eyes locked on his opponent. "I know that you attacked Amrith out of revenge for your lost inheritance."

"I didn't lose it; it was stolen."

"Also that you delivered Dara into the hands of the elusive Bhoma-San. Your fate is in the hands of a justiciar but I will speak to him of leniency if you tell me what you know."

The smile was gone and his mouth was set in a hard line across a face turned white and grim. With a sinking feeling Resar saw that, short of torture and perhaps even with it, there would be no answer. He had miscalculated but he would try again. And again. He turned and left the cell, barely hearing as the door thudded solidly behind him.

He would plan more carefully. He turned to a guard and gave his orders. "Send Tai in to look at his wounds. See that he gets water to wash and clean clothes. If he changes his mind, send for me." The guard acknowledged the command and Resar walked back up the hall. He felt wearier than before, but determined to prevail.

Walking alongside, Sandy hummed to himself in anger. He knew the scent as well as the taste of the man they had left. He had followed that track up the mountain, through the chasm, and into the cave. It filled his nostrils and vibrated in his senses. The man was their enemy: he smelled of blood. He had taken the woman away. Sandy's hatred was strong and he wanted his own kind of revenge. He craved the thrill of hunting, following the sharp scent of the man's fear. He coveted skin tearing in his teeth and the rush of hot salty blood. He wanted screaming—and then silence and stillness. His revenge was uncomplicated but quite satisfying. Yet it was not time. He yawned vastly out of stress and frustration: his chance would come.

CHAPTER 19

Dara sat, comfortable and happy, in the room where she had first confided to Gwyn and where she had first met Rolfe. Once again she sipped the good wine of Earth but this time, instead of reclining on cushions, she leaned against Rolfe's broad chest. His skin smelled faintly of his own special scent that combined fresh air with musky strength. She liked to feel his chest moving up and down in the reassuring rhythm of respiration and it felt good to relax in the company of friends. The training period was over: once again her head was stuffed with facts, skills, knowledge, statistics, all newly acquired. Tomorrow she boarded ship for the return trip to Khyren; this time, however, she did not dread the journey. She was leaving the Beldame to take up a challenge and to work toward a goal. She would miss her friends in the il Tarz family but they would not be gone from her forever.

Packed away in her bag was a brooch that was more than simple jewelry. Small and seemingly of little value, its crude workmanship disguised an extremely valuable molecular-electronic system that functioned as a sub-space communicator. She did not know if she would ever have

cause to use it but just knowing that she possessed it was
reassuring enough. The bag also contained a few long
dresses of good fabric, boots, and a warm cloak. In addition there were a comb and a few simple toiletries, all that
she would need: more ostentatious belongings would only
raise suspicion. Dara's one true possession was the K'thi's
talon that Rolfe had pierced and mounted on a chain. It
hung now between her breasts, its weight reminding her
continually of the need for vigilance.

The door slid open to admit the willowy Itombe, accompanied by Aurial and Gwyn. Greeting them with a smile,
Dara was pleased that they had come to bid her farewell.
She poured wine for them and they settled onto the cushions. "Are you set to return?" Itombe asked quietly.

"Yes. I'm as ready as I can be. After all that training I
feel like I could handle a breech delivery at zero Gs."

"You probably could," Gwyn laughed, "but I wouldn't
recommend it—for either you or the baby. Just in case,
though, I've had your bag taken aboard the *Grace*. Your
stateroom is all ready."

Dara made an unpleasant face. "Five weeks of boring
free-fall to look forward to. A ship that runs itself, a crew
that plays head games and no one but computers to talk
to. Feh."

"It could be worse," Itombe chuckled. "But if you would
like, you can take some tapes from the library to pass the
time. Help yourself."

Dara brightened at the thought. "Thank you, I will do
that before I board."

Gwyn proposed a toast and while they were drinking to
Dara's new career, the door opened again. Surprised,
Dara turned to see who else would be coming to the small
farewell party. She was not the only one to look astonished
when Nashaum entered the room, her petite figure draped
in a simple robe of subdued color. She was immediately
the focus of attention and her daughters quickly made a
place for her and filled a glass with wine. Although honored by the new arrival, Dara was apprehensive that the
matriarch's presence would dampen the celebration so, by
asking Nashaum questions, she began to draw her out.
Even if the others felt constrained by their mother's pres-

ence, the evening would go along smoothly as long as Nashaum talked. Fortunately, Nashaum cooperated by answering the questions unself-consciously and with good humor. Although Dara did not know it, she was being trusted with information that a number of people in the Quadrant would have paid fortunes to hear. Finally Dara summoned the courage to ask the one question that had always puzzled her. "If you don't think me impudent, madam, would you tell me why you trust only women? What happened to turn you away from the other half of the human race?"

Nashaum sighed heavily and put down her slender wine glass. Aurial immediately filled it again. "It is a long story, a terrible story, and I have not told it to anyone for many years. This is a party, a celebration. Do you really want to hear such a dreadful tale?"

"Yes, very much. If you want to tell it."

"Very well, then. Long ago, when I was a young woman just beginning my life away from my family, I had a friend. Her name was Virani. We had grown up together and been friends for many years. We began employment in a merchant trading company doing the kind of routine and boring work that gives you the drive you need to succeed and thereby escape it. One day an opportunity became available to us and to the others who worked there as well. The company was opening a new branch station in territory that was not quite the Outback but was certainly far from the more civilized systems. Both Virani and I had the chance to go and work on new accounts there. The new job offered more responsibility, considerably more risk, and somewhat higher pay. There were some who considered the new branch to be dangerous. Oh, the system had been certified as safe but, on a raw new world, distant from civilization, there is always danger.

"I was conservative then, as I am now, and so I chose to remain. Virani decided to go. Her decision was quite surprising to me and not only because it meant that we would be far apart for the first time. She was ill with a chronic and incurable disease that was controlled with periodic implants of medication. This illness had always been something of an embarrassment to her. Because of it she had always tried harder to achieve, to succeed. I think at that time it drove her to fill her life with all the experiences she could. It would never have occurred to her to use the sickness as an excuse or as a reason to back away from a challenge. So, perhaps I should not have been surprised. We said our good-byes, cried our young tears, and then she went.

"The branch station opened and Virani settled easily into her new position. The work there was not much less boring than it had been but the difference was enough to make her feel that she was moving ahead. A routine developed and the job became comfortable. Then, one quiet afternoon when she was concentrating on a problem, the door of the station was flung open with a crash. A group of men—at least they appeared to be men—burst in. They were tall, large of build, and most definitely male. Without hesitation they seized the women within their reach. When some of the men in the station, armed men, interfered, they were killed quickly.

"Then an intruder came after Virani where she stood, terrified, in her office. He wore only a short white tunic that did nothing to hide his powerful body. When this male saw Virani he laughed with harsh triumph and reached for her. Desperate, she backed away, then picked up her chair and swung it with all her strength at his head. He blocked the blow with one hand, as if the chair were made of paper but, although he made it seem easy, the shock of the impact jarred her to the teeth. Then the intruder wrenched the chair from Virani and flung it away. He stood in front of her and laughed that harsh laugh again and she, truly seeing him for the first time, saw that he was not human at all. At closer range his skin had a blue tinge and scaly texture. Six fingers on each hand sported thick sharp nails. His eyes were hooded, the pupils only small dots in a yellow globe. He had no ears and no hair, only a narrow crest. And his tongue, when he laughed, was round and bifurcated."

"Qestal," breathed Itombe.

"Yes, he was a Qestal male. He picked up Virani with one arm, as if she weighed nothing. His grip was rock hard and she found it difficult to breathe. By the time he reached his ship, Virani was seeing green spots and her ears were roaring. He carried her on board and flew her up to the Home Ship."

"Perhaps I should interrupt for a moment, Mother," said Itombe. "I can give Dara some background on the Qestal." Nashaum nodded, her eyes unfocused and far away. Itombe continued, "The Qestal are a nomadic species who travel from system to system on enormous vessels called the Home Ships. These ships travel alone, not in fleets, although a rendezvous is occasionally arranged. The males, known as Breeders by their own people, are solitary and spend most of their lives in one-man ships. They scout ahead of the Home Ship to trade whenever possible and to fight if necessary. They return to the main vessel for only three things: to unload trade goods, to be treated if they are hurt, and to breed when the biological urge is upon them. The Home Ships, as large as small moons, are run by the females, or Carriers. They navigate, maintain the ships and the economy, and run a society. The drudge work is done by a neuter sex, the Workers, who are by function a combination of crew and servants. But to get back to the story . . ."

"When the Breeder's craft arrived at the Home Ship, Virani was convinced that she and her co-workers had been taken by slavers. She might easily have been right; the Qestal are not above trading in slaves. Unfortunately, her surmise was wrong and it did not take long to find out just how wrong. The Breeder carried her to his cell and dropped her on the low pallet that was his bed. He stripped off her clothing before she could catch her breath and resist. Virani was aghast. She could not imagine what he was doing. Inter-species rape is pointless because the physical differences are too great to allow for any gratification other than a violent one. Sometimes it's actually impossible so she was totally unprepared for what happened next. When her captor removed his tunic she was even more puzzled. Instead of a typical male member there was only a short, thick tube, something like a rigid fold of skin. He straightened up and, while she watched, his organ emerged from the tube. It was more finely scaled than the rest of his skin, and long. At the sight of it she wanted to scream but her throat was locked by fear.

"He pushed her back on the pallet and entered her roughly. Then she did start to scream. He covered her mouth with his hand but other than that he did not move. Inside her, though, his organ thrust and writhed, taking her seemingly of its own will. Battered by that alien assault, Virani lay frozen by terror and pain. If the Qestal knew, he did not care. It went on for quite a long time although, under such circumstances, time is elastic. At the height of his lust two things happened. First, the pain increased beyond what she had thought bearable. Then he pushed his face against her shoulder. Two fangs swung out from their protective sockets and pierced her skin as he bit deeply. A fluid pumped into her, fluid that causes rapture in the Qestal females and stimulates the production of hormones that determine the sex of their young. In a human it generates what might be called an allergic reaction. By then, Virani was numb and beyond sound.

"When the male had finished, he left her and returned to his ship. She never saw him again, or wanted to. Virani lay in shock until Workers came and tended her. She was not aware of them or their ministrations. She became very ill, although she was not conscious of that, either. Finally her body cast out the egg that the Breeder had planted in her and she gradually grew better. I have always thought that this rapid miscarriage was caused by the reaction of her own medication with the fluid injected by the male's fangs. Whatever the reason, it saved her life.

"When finally she was well again, Virani found the other women who had been abducted and saw that they were growing large with the eggs within them. They, too, were cared for most carefully by the Workers and it was from these lowest and least valued of all the Qestalin that they learned the truth. All the females, the Carriers, aboard this Home Ship had been killed by a sex-selective virus transmitted by insects in a contaminated shipment of grain. The sexless drones were immune. As the females succumbed, one by one, their bodies were jettisoned. The Workers carried on without them, performing the routine functions of the ship as always. They also arranged a rendezvous with another Home Ship and set their vessel on course for the meeting. On the way there, however, the males had entered the breeding cycle and, in their compulsion, sought other female bodies in which to relieve their needs.

"No one, either human or Qestalin, expected any of the eggs to survive. After all, the hormonal and chemical differences between the two species were stupendous. At first, though, all that the eggs required was a warm environment and they were small enough to be marginally intrusive. After that early stage, the 'pregnancies,' if you can call them that, began to abort spontaneously. As with Virani, there was great pain and sickness, only worse because the eggs had grown larger. Although some of the women were stronger than the others, none of them survived. Their bodies followed those of the dead Qestalin females into space. A few truly unfortunate women lasted until the eggs hatched.

"You all know that the human fetus exhibits some of the stages of evolution as it develops. At one point during its gestation, it even has gills. Qestalin biology has a similar developmental cycle but with an important difference. The young of that species are still at a fairly primitive evolutionary stage when they are born, and even for a Carrier the birth can be difficult. The birth canal is well protected: the mother's skin is thick and contains few nerve endings. A special restraining basket is kept near to hold the newborn and nurture it in safety until it grows beyond this phase. The handful of women who carried their burden to term had no such protection.

"The Workers would have helped but for the fact that there was no way for anyone to know when the eggs would hatch. The small Qestalin emerged from their leathery shells into a hostile environment. No easy way out was available and no strong muscles urged them down the right path. They were trapped and dying inside a creature with an alien metabolism and there was no way in which they could truly be born. So, driven by instinct, they did what any primitive creature would do in this situation: they tore their way out. Virani knew all the women well by that time, helped them when she could, then watched them die horribly. After that, she was alone with the Qestalin.

"She did not stay with them for long, however. The Workers dropped her off at the next available station and gradually she made her way home. When she arrived, she was very nearly a different woman from the Virani who had gone off so bravely. Her face was lined beyond its years and her hair was streaked with white. At some point during her stay on the Home Ship her implant had run out, leaving her without medication. It was a long time before the implant was replaced. She was very ill when she returned to us and she never again was truly well. Never again was she the Virani I had known and grown up with. She may have been the only person to survive that awful experience but her spirit seemed to have died along with those other women. Without the spark that drove her to see life as a challenge and to overcome her illness, she just went on blankly from day to day. It was the spirit that mattered and the spirit was gone. Virani grew progressively weaker until her body could no longer hold off the disease she had lived with for so long. One day she, too, was simply gone."

Nashaum slipped into silence and looked at her quiet audience, everyone absorbed by her story. It was difficult to think of anything to say or any response to make to such a grim story. Finally Dara stammered, "But the Breeder— all of the Qestalin—are not human. Is it fair to blame humans for the actions of an alien?"

Nashaum smiled sadly. "A good question. It seems to answer itself. But what did the Breeder do that was different, really, from what men have done? He succumbed to the urgings of a biological drive. When the proper partner was not available, he took a substitute by force. He did it all without regard for her desires or concern for her physical safety. When he had gotten what he wanted, he left without even a thought for the consequences. Can any of you argue that this is alien behavior? Or say, truthfully, that men have never done the same? I grant that many men would never behave so but most are condemned to repeat history. And a long, sad history it is. If the male of the species—ours or any other—cannot control his mature drives by imposing intellect on biology, then it is possible to draw two conclusions. The first is that his reactions are not reliable because they are not primarily rational and thus cannot be trusted. The second is, simply, if you would not be sinned against, avoid the sinner. I have followed both these precepts since Virani died and I have never been sorry."

"But where does that philosophy leave those men who are able to sublimate their biological drives to the requirements of civilization?"

"I admit there is no room in my philosophy for such admirable men—excepting my sons, who keep turning up lately. I'm sure that these men do well and advance the cause of civilization. Elsewhere. And wherever that is, that is where they belong. I do not choose to trust them or the degree of their control."

"Then you have given up all chance of changing things. With your power and influence, you could work to defeat the behavior that you despise," Dara persisted.

"My dear child, you are quite right. I have abdicated that role. A long time ago I recognized that neither I nor any other individual could change what we call human nature, not in humans nor in other species. Regardless of wealth or power, it simply cannot be done. Only a fool would defeat herself by trying. Now, I apologize for spoiling your party. My only excuse is that I did what you requested."

"That's all right," said Dara. "It's time that I rested, anyway. The *Grace* lifts in only a few hours." After a round of farewells, she and Rolfe left for a more private leave-taking. When the door had closed behind them, Nashaum was alone with her daughters. Itombe turned to her with a query of her own. "You tell her story so well, Mother, almost as if you had been there."

Nashaum responded sadly to her eldest and most trusted daughter. "If I tell it well, it is because I heard it many times. Virani never told it quite that way, of course, such a story was beyond her strength. But I spoke with her many times before she died, I listened to her nightmares, and I saw her every day. I pieced it all together and after a while I felt as if I might have been there with her. Only I wasn't there to help her when she needed me."

"Who was Virani, really?"

"She was my sister. My twin sister."

Vethis lay still on the hard pallet but he did not sleep. Outside it was the depths of night. In his rock-walled cell, where it was always night, he watched the wildly-flickering shadows thrown on the wall by his single guttering lamp and thought of vengeance. He had begun, in the first days after his capture, by tormenting himself with the knowledge that Resar was right. Impossible as it was to admit, he had lost the battle and failed in his mission by his own oversight and complacency. In his mind he saw clearly, over and over again, the sword cleaving Resar's head, the rush of bright blood, the unresisting fall of his body. The picture was vividly imprinted on his memory and the man's death was plain in it to see. It had seemed to him then, and still did now, that survival was impossible. Yet, because of that certainty, he had not checked to make sure that the heart was stilled and that carelessness had undone him.

From that admission had come anger and the anger had bred hatred, so that now he was filled with the raging desire to revenge himself. Again. Each of Resar's interrogations had fueled his rage. There were endless questions about the Brotherhood, their motives and objectives. Then, inevitably, the questioning turned to what had become of the scrawny karait. Taking the safest course, he answered none of them and spoke little of anything. Having lost so much already, Vethis was determined to succeed at keeping his secrets and gaining a small victory thereby. So far, that plan had been easy to follow as Resar's justice did not include torture.

The rest of his captors were not so easy and it was another issue altogether how long Resar could hold off some of the seasoned officers, like Barrikehn and the menacing Haron. The first man considered the prisoner a rank traitor and the second saw the extraction of information as a purely practical task. Vethis knew well how tough these men were and knew also how eager they would be to pry from him the answers to Resar's questions. Realistically he knew that he was only flesh, and torture just might dislodge the information they sought. And that made him more eager for revenge.

The lamp flared, sending a black greasy curl of smoke spiralling upward. When it died, his cell would be black; the light from the hall torch did not reach so deep. The air was silent with the quiet that only rock can give. Had he not known better, Vethis would have suspected that the guards were dozing and, with any other prisoner, they might well have been. With bitter certainty, however, he knew that there would be no laxness in the corridor while he was in a cell.

Then, at the edge of his hearing, came a high-frequency whine. It grew louder. He swung himself upward, chains clinking dully, and stared at the empty corner from which the sound came. Already filled with shadows, the air there grew even darker. It took on substance, then form, then shape. When the whine ceased abruptly, a man stood in the corner and Vethis regarded with a thin smile the dark hair and swarthy face of Portifahr. For any other person or any thing to have appeared literally out of the air would have rocked him. Seeing Portifahr, however, had the opposite effect. What was impossible for everyone else was sleight-of-hand for the Brotherhood: technological magic was their stock in trade.

Before either man could speak, however, a metallic rattle came from the door as the key was fitted into the lock, proving the guards' vigilance. Portifahr stepped back behind the door just as it opened. Vethis pivoted to face the first guard as he stepped in cautiously, dagger in hand, careful to stay outside the range of Vethis's chain. Seeing the prisoner still safely manacled and unarmed, he entered the cell and whirled instinctively to face an intruder who could not possibly have been there. His quickness was his death as, the instant his back was turned, Vethis looped the chain connecting his wrist shackles over the man's head and around his neck. He twisted fiercely, turning the manacles into a garrotte, and dodged the desperate hands that clawed back at him. Then the second guard burst in with his blade out. Before the edge could reach its mark, Portifahr's arm was around him and his dagger opened the man's throat. In a moment, both guards lay dead in a spreading pool of blood that was splattered by their death throes. The cell stank of it.

For the second time, Vethis and Portifahr locked gazes. The captive spoke first. "Have you come to rescue me?" He was breathing hard from the fight but there was no conviction in his voice.

"I was sent with the Brotherhood's penalty for failure." Vethis snapped tight the chain he had just used as a garrotte. "That does not sound like a rescue."

Portifahr shrugged. "It is escape of a sort."

"And what does the Brotherhood gain from my death?"

"Security. You cannot now complete your mission and you are not valuable enough to bring back to the Lost City. You know too much for anything else. The Teacher said that he who strives and fails must be forever silent."

"With your help, I can still succeed," Vethis protested fiercely. "But only if I live."

"Do you fear death, then?" Portifahr sounded disappointed.

"No!" Vethis's knuckles were white from his grip on the chain and his eyes glittered. "I have looked down the few paths still open to me and death lies at the end of each. I do not seek to escape death, only a futile end."

"What, then, do you ask of me?"

Vethis stooped to the body in front of him and pried the dagger from the corpse's death grip. "Just this," he said, pulling his hands apart until the chain snapped taut again. Blood sprayed from the dagger's blade. "Just this—and the freedom to use it."

Portifahr gave a coolly appraising look at the man standing defiantly in front of him and smiled. "I did not think that you would bare your throat meekly to the judgment of the City." He stepped over the bodies and looked out the door. Reassured that they were still alone, he unhooked a key from where it hung on a torch bracket. Inside the cell again, he unlocked the manacles and removed them carefully and quietly. "There is your freedom. Take the sword as well: you will need weapons." He paused and his eyes grew hard, his face grim. "Have no illusions. I am going against my orders and on my authority alone. If you betray me, I will find you wherever you are or wherever you hide and I will kill you without warning."

"You have nothing to fear."

"Very well. In my report I will say that you escaped on your own before I arrived." He gestured at the two corpses, "They will not testify otherwise. In two days, meet me at sunset by the big split rock that looks like a mouth."

"The Howler. I know it." He brandished the knife again. "My thanks, Portifahr."

"Good hunting."

Vethis stepped cautiously out into the hall. It was still and silent. With no one to oppose him, finding his way out of the house unobserved and unhindered would be easy. His heart leaped ahead of him and he wanted to run, shouting, after it. Instead he slipped quietly out of the torchlight and into the darkness.

Behind him, Portifahr sighed and pressed a button on his belt. As the whine built and the cell faded, he thought of the disapproval he faced back in the Lost City. It would be unpleasant but, in actuality, unimportant. There was disarray these days in the City and little enough energy to spend on yet another breach of rules by a confirmed renegade. The difficulty would soon pass and the challenge here would more than compensate for it. He faded, leaving only corpses behind him.

CHAPTER 20

Dara lifted her head and breathed deeply while her eyes adjusted from the shuttle's bright interior to a dark afternoon in woods that were almost gloomy. It was spring on Khyren—just. Here in the lowlands a cold steady rain dropped from heavy clouds. The wind was strong but fitful, blowing from one direction only to pause and then drive the rain rattling before it from another angle. Fat drops splattered on the cobbles around her feet. Streams of water ran vigorously down from where the road in front of her stretched up the hill and curved into the trees. The rain left the blue-grey bark of these tall trees shining slickly. Although most of the ground beneath them was clear, lumps of dirty grainy snow crouched obstinately in the shadows. Wisps of fog hovered over these snowmounds like spirits of winter tethered unhappily to the ground.

Most people would have considered it a foul night, one to avoid by staying comfortably indoors before a warm fire. Dara reveled in it, relishing small things that those people, hurrying home to their snug hearths, would have ignored. Each fickle gust of wind brought the heady smells of wet soil and chlorophyll from new shoots too small yet

to be seen. It was the undefinable scent of life freshening
for a new season of growth and it was heightened by the
rain's cold freshness. After so long breathing air recycled
by machines and artificially purified, the natural atmosphere was rich and intoxicating to her. She inhaled it
greedily. The sounds of the forest were equally delightful
to her ear. Each time the wind gusted, it moaned through
the thin delicate branches and set the rain to drumming
on the ground. Around and above her, birds fussed and
settled sleepily for the night. Somewhere in the woods a
nocturnal carnivore yipped and then howled in preparation for the evening hunt.

The sounds and smells were stimulating. The air, if
cold, was fresh and clean on her skin. Dara felt vibrantly
alert, stronger and more alive than she had in a long time.
She took another deep breath and watched the vapor curl
before her face when she exhaled. Perhaps, she thought,
things would work out all right after all. The distant animal
howled again and Dara noticed that the dim afternoon was
growing darker. The wind shifted, puffing out the hood of
her cloak and blowing icy needles down her neck. She
shivered reflexively and drew the cloak closer around her.
It was time to move on; she had to reach the Residence
before it was too dark to see the road.

She lifted her bag and strode over the slick cobbles up
the hill. Stepping confidently along, she felt very much a
different person than she had been when last on Khyren.
Perhaps it came from the emotional support of the il Tarz
family and all that they had taught her. Perhaps it came
from being once again physically strong and in good health.
Perhaps, she thought ruefully, it simply came from once
again having new things of her own. Her running shoes,
the only remainder of the clothing in which she had arrived on Khyren, were still somewhere in her pack on the
lower slopes of the Spine. The fresh clothing supplied by
the Brotherhood had been exchanged for more suitable
garments on the Beldame. Those clothes had, in turn,
been replaced by outfits suitable for the role she was now
assuming. The only artifact she bore that had gone to the
Beldame and back with her, the K'thi's claw, hung safely
between her breasts. That was Rolfe's legacy. Gwyn's had

been more ominous. "Stay away from the Brotherhood," she had warned. "We took out the comlink's main mechanism but the bioelectronics infiltrate the nervous system to the cellular level. That means you can't remove them completely without destroying the nerve along with them. With the right equipment and in certain circumstances the Brotherhood could re-activate what's still inside you. So, for your own sake, stay as far away from them as you can."

Dara shook off the disturbing memory and trudged on. After the functional, comfortable clothing on the Beldame, she found the long skirts of Khyren cumbersome and heavy. It was impossible to keep them dry so that, after only a short distance, they were soaked nearly to the knees and swung against her legs like weights. She picked up her pace: the light was fading rapidly now and she had no desire to lose her way in the darkness. Fortunately, the shuttle had set her down fairly close to her destination and it did not take long for Dara to reach the Residence. Once she arrived, there was no question about its identity. It was an enormous stone structure that, standing in isolation, would have seemed both tall and massive. Its true size was diminished, however, by the looming outcrop of dark rock into which it was built. From where she stood, in front of the structure, it was impossible to see, or even estimate, how far the man-made edifice extended into the natural one.

The most immediate and impressive indication of the building's size was the huge door that rose before and above her. Fully twelve feet high and at least five feet wide, it was carved from one massive plank that must have come from a tree large enough to dwarf even the huge taigas of the Spine. This slab, gnarled and striped with the patterns of its grain, was banded by thick iron straps that added both strength and solidity. Dara faced this portal feeling both puzzled and a little intimidated. The idea of walking up and knocking on such a door was ludicrous. It would shed a sound so puny, as a river bird sheds water.

She looked around carefully, straining her eyes in the last remaining light. To her right she spied a knotted rope dangling from a small hole between two of the stones of the wall. She pulled it once, tentatively, and waited. The

wind gusted and hammered her with cold rain. She pulled
the rope again more strongly and there came the faint
sound of a bell ringing as if it were far away. Dara faced
the door and waited patiently, trying to ignore the growing discomfort of her wet clothing. Even the fur trim on
her hood was clumped into ratty spikes. She put her hand
on the rope again but a small noise from beyond the door
caused her to drop it.

There was a click, then a crack of light appeared on one
side of the door and quickly grew wider as the door
pivoted smoothly and quietly inward, belying its great
weight. Hefting her bag, she walked straight in and faced
the doorkeeper of the Residence, center of operations for
the Order of the Lady, home for its members, and pilgrimage site for thousands of ordinary women. Whatever
she had been expecting, what she saw was a surprise. The
doorkeeper was male and neither aged nor imposing. He
was, in fact, a very attractive young man with fine features, pale hair, and eyes the color of tropical water. His
aura provided the reserve and polish denied by his youth-
ful appearance. Closing the door behind her against the
rainy night, the doorkeeper scrutinized the late arrival
carefully. With great attentiveness he took in her fine
cloak of good weave and fur trim, her hair, still tightly
arranged despite the wind's best efforts, and her confident
bearing. Then he addressed her with the utmost courtesy.
"Greetings, lady. What is it that you seek here on such a
night and how may we serve you?"

"Greetings on this wet evening," she replied. "I require
nothing from you save shelter from the storm. In this
place I seek only one thing: audience with the Dame
Senior, she who does the will of the Lady."

"All at the Residence do the will of the Lady. Dame
Alasdare does not give audience at this hour. Yet, if she
has not yet retired, I will see that she receives your
message. Now, let us attend to your comfort. By your
grace, accompany me." He retrieved her bag from where
it sat dripping on the stone floor, then turned and led her
across a spacious foyer and down a long hall. It was cold
within the stone fortress, almost as cold as outside, but
brightly lit. What appeared to be gas lamps burned at

regular intervals on the walls. Dara smiled at this reminder of the way in which the people of Khyren used the local natural resources to their advantage. Dual shadows stretched before, then swung around and behind them as they walked. Their footsteps echoed off the bare stone.

In a large room at the end of the passage, a woman awaited them. Her thick dark hair, well-flecked with grey, was braided and wrapped in an elaborate pattern on her head and her generous figure was draped in a simple dress of pale blue wuliveen. She watched them approach with an air of authority that was undisturbed by a muted murmuring behind her. The noise sounded as if it was made by invisible people who were grouped somewhere out of sight, curious but too shy to show themselves. The woman inclined her head toward the doorkeeper without speaking and he answered her silent question. "This traveler seeks audience with Dame Alasdare. Will you see to her comfort while I convey the message?"

"It is my duty and my pleasure. Thank you, Terak." She smiled at Dara, turned, and gestured for her to follow. They went up a broad flight of stairs to a landing, then up again. The woman, whose name was Nestura, made polite conversation as they climbed. "It is a dismal night for traveling. The guest hall is empty, but then it usually is at this time of year. The snows are mostly gone here in the lowlands but still deep in some of the mountain passes. The first real group of pilgrims won't arrive for another two passages yet. Of course, some people do come all year round, like yourself. Were you long on the road here?"

The questions scattered through Nestura's homey discourse were not as casual as they sounded and Dara was glad that she and Gwyn had prepared a cover story carefully. She responded automatically now to the routine questions with a tale of traveling from a remote holding by caravan, and then accompanying other groups before completing the final stage of the journey on her own. The older woman accepted the story without comment and gave Dara a running description of the building as they walked through it. They went down a hall lined along the right side with bay windows against which the rain rattled and streaked. Finally they stopped inside the door of a large room that looked something like a dormitory.

It contained four beds, each accompanied by a chest at its foot, a scatter rug, and a small table with washbowl against the wall. There was a large fireplace on the wall opposite the door and a brisk fire burned there, adding cheer as well as warmth to the air. "This is the small guest room. I think it's the most comfortable at this time of the year. It's not fancy but it is warmer than most and it should be nice and quiet, since you'll have it to yourself. Unpack your things and I'll have some hot water brought up. Supper, too, if you haven't eaten. No? Good. The food here isn't fancy either but it will fill you up. Well, you just relax now and I'll be back in a few minutes."

She bustled out of the room and Dara set about removing her wet, cold clothing. Without Nestura's chatter the room was indeed quiet. The fire gusted and rain hammered behind closed drapes but those were the only sounds. Dara chose a bed closest to the fire's warmth and removed her sodden shoes. They went by the fire to dry and she spread her skirt across an unused bed. Then she skipped back to the rough rug's protection before the stone floor could draw all the warmth from her bare feet. After donning a simple night shift, she unpacked the rest of her clothes from the bag and placed them in the chest.

Nestura came back in with a bucket of hot water swaying from one hand and extra blankets tucked under her other arm. Another woman followed her, balancing a tray that held a steaming plate and mug. Nestura began talking as soon as she was in the door. "Such service as you're getting this night. Mind you, it's only because of the season and the hour. Put it down there, Fali." She took the washbowl and splashed water into it. "Tomorrow you eat in the dining hall with everyone else." She handed Dara a towel. "That's a lovely shift. Whoever wove that cloth certainly knew what she was about. Oh, good, your wet things should dry nicely that way. There'll be fewer wrinkles to take out later, too." She took the tray from the other woman and set it down on the chest. "Here's supper. As I said, it's plain cooking and there's no meat in it but it's hot and filling." The other woman, Fali, went and stood quietly by the fire. Dara was glad of the company; the room really was too quiet by herself. She cast around for a topic that would keep Nestura talking while the well-cooked meal went down and hit on the perfect question. "How long have you been here at the Residence?" she asked.

"Oh, going on three full cycles now. My husband, Beltran, and I ran a tavern down in Port Jaster. That's probably why I take to waiting on guests so easily." The air of dignified reserve with which she had first greeted Dara had been replaced by a homey warmth. Dara suspected that the woman missed the turmoil of the inn, the continuous activity, the gossip and rumor and news. The reserve was adopted because it was part of the discipline but with her personality she did not wear it well.

"The Cup and Ball was a fine place: twenty rooms, all cleaner than many houses I've been in, stabling for whatever kind of beast carried or pulled you in, and the finest food within three days' journeying. My oldest boy took it over when Beltran died." Nestura paused but Dara's mouth was full and she did not pick up on the cue. "I had four sons," she resumed, not as modestly as might be expected, "but fortunately only one of them was interested in the business. His wife took to the inn like she was born there and I decided to make the pilgrimage. There was work for me to do here and no need for me at the inn so here I've stayed."

Deciding that she was only going to hear Nestura's story and probably not for the first time, Fali stopped her puttering and left the room. Nestura saw her go but made no comment. Dara was finishing off an excellent bread pudding when Fali burst back into the room, a strange expression on her face.

"What is it, Fali?" Nestura asked. "Is something wrong?"

Fali put a hand to her breast as if to still her heartbeat. "Dame Alasdare requests that the new pilgrim be brought to her at once. She was most firm." For a moment Nestura was speechless. She stood up and smoothed her skirts with agitated hands. Her face was shadowed by rapidly-changing emotions of which astonishment appeared the strongest. "Get dressed and follow me, please," she said and turned

for the door. Dara delayed long enough to slip a clean skirt
and tunic over her shift. Then, accompanied by the curious Fali, they stepped back into the fenestrated hallway
that was filled with night and rain.

After another brisk walk through the immense structure, they came to a smaller section that, by its curved
walls, appeared to be a tower. Four flights up a cantile-
vered staircase, they reached a door of plain wood, no
larger or different from any of the other doors they had
passed. It was closed. Nestura paused a moment and drew
herself up straight. Then she knocked once, firmly. A low
voice bade them enter. The room inside was spartan, yet
comfortable and warm. Touches of color here and there
along with a few finely-crafted items lent the chamber
both charm and grace. Its circular walls seemed to embrace it protectively.

In a large, highbacked chair sat a woman with the
plump and rosy cheeks of a grandmother. Thick white hair
was woven skillfully atop her head. She sat erect except
for one small foot that was propped up on a stool. Her aura
was strong and almost tangible; shrewd, tenacious, steady.
It most closely resembled that of the formidable Nashaum
il Tarz. Like that other woman, she wore power as easily
as she wore her simple dress. Her eyes were strong and
could have held their own in the Lost City. Their gaze
analyzed Dara quite thoroughly and at length, yet she did
not feel threatened by it.

Nestura sketched a reverence and said, "As you requested, my lady, this is the guest who arrived just after
sunset."

"My thanks to you, Nestura. You may retire now." As
she turned to leave the room, Nestura gave Dara a small
secret smile. Then the voice came again, "You also, Fali."
The second woman exited as well.

Once again those eyes, more nearly hazel than green,
rested full on Dara. "I am Alasdare, Dame Senior of the
Order of the Lady's Benevolence," she said by way of
introduction. "This immensity of a building is my responsibility, along with all who live and work in it. Those who
travel about on the Lady's business are also under my
jurisdiction. Now, tell me who you are."

Dara "listened" with her mind for some traces of emotion but caught only curiosity and a certain eagerness. Once more she related her prepared story. Dame Alasdare listened attentively and nodded in all the right places but Dara knew that she did not believe a word of it. When the tale was over, that strong gaze held her once more.

"That's very interesting, but tell me, please, *why* you have come to Residence."

Dara looked back at her levelly. Many people would have been intimidated by that commanding presence but, she thought with an inner smile, it took a great deal more to intimidate her now than it used to. "I came to be of use to the Order. If you will have me, I will serve in any way I can."

There was a nod. "Well enough spoken and probably true enough. Now consider this: I am told that there was a bright flash of light in the valley not long before you came to our door. Perhaps you may have seen it. If so, can you explain what caused that light?"

Dara was taken aback. The shuttle was quiet and the engines shielded but there had been a quick burst of light when it took off. It must have been noticed in the murky evening. She decided that the best course was a modified form of the truth, since denial would only raise suspicion. "Yes, I did see a light such as you describe. It lasted only a heartbeat or two."

"Have you an explanation?"

"Why, no, my lady. I assumed that it had originated here."

"I see. I have another request that may seem odd, I know. Please humor me and step a little closer. My foot pains me in bad weather."

Now somewhat puzzled, Dara moved closer to the chair and watched Dame Alasdare slide a lamp across a nearby table so that it cast its pool of light in front of her. She peered up into Dara's face. "Your eyes. What color are they?" she asked abruptly.

"They are brown."

"Have they always been that color?"

"Of course they have."

"Isn't that unusual?"

Dara hesitated. The color of her eyes was unique only on Khyren but there was no way she could qualify her response without raising suspicion. "Yes, certainly. But it can't be changed."

"Excellent. Now, may I please see your hands."

Truly perplexed, Dara held both hands out, palms down, and then slowly turned them over for the Dame Senior's inspection. The older woman examined them as intently as she had Dara's eyes. Then she shook her head wearily and sat back. "I thought you were the one," she murmured, almost to herself. "I was positive you were the one." Then she opened her drooping lids and looked straight at Dara. "You *must* be the one. A coincidence such as this is impossible. And yet . . ."

"With all respect, Dame Alasdare, it would help if I knew who I am supposed to be and what you are searching for." She held out her hands once again and examined both sides herself but was no more enlightened.

"I was looking for claws," came the surprising answer.

"Claws! Claws? I am a woman like yourself, not a beast of prey. My eyes may not be green but the rest of me is as human as you are."

"Yes, I know. I beg your understanding. Please, sit down and I will attempt to explain. I can at least do that." She sounded weary and defeated.

Dara drew a chair over so that it was facing the Dame Senior and sat tentatively. Dame Alasdare sighed. "My scrutiny was rude and inexcusable, of a certainty. But the prophecy is clear and you fit its predictions in several ways. I merely sought to confirm my conjecture. It seemed impossible that I could be wrong about you. Nevertheless, I was misled by my own eagerness."

"My lady, excuse my ignorance. I come from far away and I am unfamiliar with the prophecy, with any prophecy. Of what does it speak? Perhaps if you tell me what it was that you were searching for, I can help."

"Help? Oh, yes, of course. My apologies once again. I have been inside these high walls for so long I have forgotten that those things which are an integral part of our existence here may be unknown to people outside. The Ine-Shail-Ruk is an ancient prophecy, spoken long ago in a trance by the Dame Shail, a venerable and revered member of the Order. There has been much speculation about it, in both the written and oral traditions. One school of thought has given it a detailed metaphysical interpretation that occupies volumes, with additional books of commentary. On the other hand, I have always felt that its message was quite literal and best understood when considered in that light. You may judge for yourself. The prophecy says:

> " 'By these signs you know a chosen one
> Who from darkness out of light will come
> With eyes like soil from which all life does grow
> Yet sees with other sight the way to go.
> Both star and claw witness Sah-Charis cheated;
> Though untimely, must the messenger be greeted
> With all the House can give, save only strife.
> To accept and listen honors me
> And honors life.' "

Dara sat very still and a shiver ran through her as she felt touched gently by a presence felt once before, mysteriously. That incident had had a greater impact on her life than she could ever have imagined at the time. Now this strong but gentle force affected her again and, though light, it was not to be contradicted. "What did you see in me to fit the prophecy?" she probed.

"Is it not obvious? First, you arrived untimely. As Nestura undoubtedly informed you, we do not expect the first of our pilgrims to arrive for at least a forty-span of days. You were unexpected, to say the least. Second, this dark dismal evening was pierced by that incredibly bright flash of light. I myself observed it, although I did not wish at first to say so."

"But why is that?"

"I wanted to know what you would say, and you could hardly stand here before me and deny what I swore to have seen with my own eyes. I am an old woman. Many places have I been and many things have I seen but never before have I experienced anything like that light. It was whiter than the deepest snow and bright as if a great constellation had swooped down to the clouds." She closed her eyes for a moment as if to see it again, flashing on the backs of her eyelids. Then Alasdare continued. "Third, your eyes are brown: that is unmistakeable and undeniable. It is a color I have never seen before, even though I have searched long for it. Your eyes are unique on Khyren. You are sure that they have always been brown?"

"Quite sure."

"So everything fit the prophecy well, but I was confounded by the star and claws. When all else seemed to fall into place, I thought that they, too, would be apparent. My enthusiasm outweighed my caution, though, and in the end I was mistaken."

Without replying, Dara moved slowly, as if in a dream. That touch, no matter how gentle, was not to be denied and it compelled her now. Dara knew that what happened from this moment was pre-ordained. She unlaced her tunic and lifted it over her head. Then she slipped the shift off her right shoulder. The scar stood out a vivid white against her skin. "What shape does the scar take?" she asked in a toneless whisper.

Sitting bolt upright in her chair, hands gripping the arms so hard that her knuckles were white, Dame Alasdare breathed, "It is a star."

Next, Dara drew the chain with its pendant from beneath the shift and held it out so that it dangled free. "The prophecy said claw, not claws," she commented. "You took that part of it too literally."

"Did this talon make the scar?"

"Yes."

"And from what manner of beast did it come?"

"A K'thi."

Alasdare drew in her breath sharply. "Then, indeed, was death cheated. The Lady's power is great, stronger even than we can imagine. You are her chosen one, her messenger, and I welcome you."

Dara replaced the pendant and arranged her clothing. Once again, she heard Martus saying that anything the transporter had conveyed from the past had been either inanimate or dead and that she was the only living creature to survive it. "I suppose I must be. It is a strange thought. Until now I had no knowledge of it."

"What, then, is your message to us?"

Dara thought of all that she had learned in the Lost City, what Martus had told her freely and what she had discovered when soaring out of her body. She thought of what the il Tarz had taught her and the mission she had accepted by returning to Khyren. It was a great deal. "My message is not in a few words given to me in a vision by the Lady. It is not another prophecy. What I have to teach you is neither simple nor brief and I am not sure of all of it myself. It is what sent me here to live with you. Let me stay here and work with the others of the Order. In time, the message will be heard and understood by those who are willing to listen."

"It shall be as you ask, for that is what the Lady wishes."

"I thank you for your generosity and your hospitality," Dara responded just as formally. Then she added, "It might be best if only you and I know what has transpired here."

Alasdare nodded in agreement. "Yes, it is difficult to listen and learn when such distinctions come between people."

Dara smiled, "Is there such great ambition among the Order?" she asked.

Alasdare sat back in her chair. "For many of the women who arrive here each year, just being part of the Order fulfills the ambition of a lifetime. Some among them actually think that the desire for power and achievement is peculiar to men. They expect to find here an organization that runs itself with the consent of all involved. Which is, of course, no organization at all. Most learn quickly that things simply run better—more smoothly and more quickly—if one person manages the decisions. Since very few people are willing to accept the kind of responsibility that comes with such power, there are not many problems. All have a place here and a job to do. We have found that people are happier that way."

Dara listened to this speech with well-concealed amusement. The last thing she had expected to find in this monolith was an unstructured, undisciplined, free-living commune. The thought of anyone with Alasdare's strength and sheer presence being part of such a thing was too incongruous for words and she thought it intriguing that the spiritual and temporal head of the Order had found it necessary to give her this little talk. She addressed the unspoken thought. "I agree with you completely, and I can assure you that I have come only to serve."

The older woman inclined her head. "By the Lady's grace. Now perhaps you should return to your bed. It has been a long day for you. Indeed, for us all."

CHAPTER 21

Snow crunched as Resar went down on one knee beside a drift-covered mound. As he brushed away light snow, the body of a large animal came into view, ice crystals clinging to its thick creamy fleece. He cleared more snow off the carcass until the long gash bisecting its throat was revealed, along with the dark frozen blood staining the whiteness around it. Resar cursed and the vapor of his breath clouded the clean morning air. Twenty more mounds of snow were scattered behind him, each marking the location of another dead wuliver. He and his men had already uncovered the body of the herdsman as well as the smaller corpse of his fast herding-courser. Standing, Resar wiped his hands on his thighs and surveyed the scene. Carnage had been masked well by the storm that followed it: Blood and death were smoothed and whitened into a deceptively peaceful meadow. Nothing, however, could hide the fact that Vethis had struck successfully again. Each time it happened, Resar was filled anew with his failure to protect his demesne against a renegade who should still be safely under guard.

Of all the devices they had tried to thwart his raids,

none had worked. Resar had detailed extra guards and doubled the number of patrols. He had sent tracking parties out and brought the wintering herds in closer to the walls. He had loosed packs of coursers at night and had Sandy track his prey by day. Still, in spite of all these efforts, Vethis struck at Highfields. His raids were random and their targets were unpredictable. The damage done, he vanished into the snow in the same way he had escaped from a cell of solid stone. Only stiffened animals and dead men testified to his success. Resar had put his best men and keenest coursers on the trail in a determined effort to run Vethis down and put an end to his marauding. Always the trail had vanished: into snowstorms, into the trees, seemingly into the air itself. It was not canny. Resar wished that Haron and Theram were still with him. He felt, irrationally, that if the three friends could hunt together, they would corner the fugitive. But his friends and the men they commanded had departed through the cavern and they had left while Vethis was still safely imprisoned.

Stiffly he gave the orders to bring out draft animals and haul back the carcasses. The wulivers would be butchered for meat and fleece and hide. The herder and his courser would wait with the other dead for a single pyre when the snow was gone. The people of Highfields were eating well this season . . . too well by far. The breeding herds would be smaller when they went back to graze the high meadows in summer. Because they would be even more vulnerable to attack then, it was imperative that Vethis be captured by snowmelt.

An icekit yapped its lunatic call in the dark woods and Resar walked across the meadow toward it. Only Sandy followed as he pushed hard through the drifted snow, punishing his body. Resar was filled with the sour acid of failure that had etched his spirit deeply over the past months. First he had found a woman who pleased him, even if he did not understand why. Dara was different from the other women he had known; she flung herself at life and drew him with her. She was a companion who stimulated and challenged him, an adult who still knew how to have fun. Sex, when it had finally come after some reservations on his part, had been better even than he had imagined. He had enjoyed being with Dara and missed her when they were apart. Then she was gone, stolen from him. If he had said that he sought to get her back out of honor, it was because his honor would not allow another man to steal away the woman he loved. Honor and all his effort notwithstanding, he had failed.

Now he had a wife, one far better suited to him by birth and station and training than Dara had been. Resar knew that Callain worked hard at being mistress of Highfields and wanted their relationship to go beyond duty and obligation. Yet, in his current mood, he could not see anything warm or loving in her. The warmth they had enjoyed and the support she had given him blew away on the chill wind. All he could feel was the bleakness that existed in his own suspicions as much as in reality. This Callain of his mind was cold and calculating. He saw his brother's relict as a woman who had married him for what it would gain her and not for love of her husband. The knowledge that love could grow afterward he dismissed. She was a woman who sought motherhood only as the means to an end. Once born, her child would be kept safe and healthy but it would grow up in the cold light of its mother's self-centered ambition. Resar knew well what that was like. Although he quickly banished the thought, this Callain was very similar to his own mother.

He stopped walking, ignoring Sandy, who strained toward the icekit's pungent scent. He had inherited Highfields, achieving his dream beyond all imagination, and everything had gone well. With Elisinthe and Callain growing larger, three more women were confirmed in their pregnancies. People said that he had brought prosperity back to the valley, that he had sent the karait with the Lady's touch to restore their fertility. Because this was a success that had always eluded Amrith, it seemed to many that his brother's death had been fated, necessary. Though Resar discounted such gossip, he understood the value of positive spirits and he raised them even higher by sending out a message with his departing friends. Theram had carried a letter for the Dame Senior of the Order requesting that they send an experienced midwife to Highfields as soon after snowmelt as possible to attend the birth of Callain's child. It was, after all, what the infant's rank and importance merited, as well as to be expected for a child born of the Touch.

Then Vethis had vanished from his stone cell, leaving behind two dead guards on a bloody floor. The coursers, with Sandy in the lead, had tracked him into the mountains and then lost the trail. Good fortune had departed with him. After that, the raiding began, leaving dead men, butchered animals, burned outbuildings, and at least one miscarriage in the wake of his carnage. People grew fearful and sought for an easy answer to their problems instead of working to help themselves. Resar tried to put an end to the fear and destruction but, once again, he failed.

What made it worse was that all his failures were the legacy of one man alone, one man who had slipped like a shadow through Resar's grasp. He wanted to crush that man and break him with his hands. Yet Resar was so eaten by failure that he now doubted his own ability to do even that. He was as close to despair as he could come and still function. He turned in the cold, bleak meadow and walked slowly back to his men. Behind him the icekit yapped once more and then was silent.

Dara lowered herself onto the bed and sighed with relief. Her feet ached and she was so tired that a pleasurable wave of dizziness swept over her. She lay still for a long moment, enjoying the touch and smell of clean, sun-dried linen as well as the support of a well-stuffed mattress. With eyes closed she reflected on the satisfaction of knowing that the bed was her own, that the room in which she rested, however austere, was her room. This place was her home and her refuge to which she could retreat whenever she desired. In it she could leave her clothing and few possessions without fear of anyone else entering unbidden. A room to herself at the Residence was a privilege accorded to her by Alasdare: most others shared a room with at least one and sometimes four different women. Dara did not miss her nomadic days of always traveling, going unwashed, and wearing the same clothes day after day. Even less did she miss the danger and uncertainty that came not only with travel through wild country, but also from living on someone else's sufferance or as an unwilling part of another person's plans.

Life was good here. She had a safe home and a useful function and was making a place for herself. She assisted in the lying-in ward as well as doing her part of the routine chores that were assigned to everyone living at the Residence. She spent some time working in each area of the community, learning the organization and its functions and the people who made it run. In the weeks since her arrival she had met many people both within and outside of the Order. During her conversations with them and as part of her work she had begun to share the things which she had learned and already some of the curious were coming to her with questions. It was a beginning for her most important task.

Flexing her toes, Dara let out a small groan as her feet throbbed in response. It had been a long delivery. Hour after hour the mother had labored, tiring gradually even while remaining in good spirits. All of the lying-in staff's best efforts to speed up her labor, or ease it, had not worked. They had coached her breathing, given her sips of herb tea, massaged her abdomen, walked her up and down, with no result. Finally, when everyone was exhausted, the baby had arrived in his own good time in an easy delivery. You could never predict these things. After weeks of working with the women who journeyed to the Residence to be delivered with the expert assistance of the Order, Dara had learned that each mother was different, each child unique. The expected was rarely what occurred. Even when the job had become routine, she did not think it would ever be boring. Her latest charges were now resting themselves, the baby firmly in his cradle and his mother on a glowing cloud of happiness and achievement.

Opening her eyes, Dara realized abruptly that she was hungry. While working, time tended to slip by unmarked and not until the task was done did her body reassert its needs for food and rest. Once asserted, those needs became insistent but, in this case, they were in conflict. She thought about going down to the kitchen, where one of the cooks on duty would always put together something tasty and nourishing but even the thought of standing up was more than she could bear. The growling of her stomach was preferable to being back on her feet. Perhaps Ejugah would look in after a while and let Dara coax her into making the trip to the kitchens. She had met Ejugah while they were both on duty rotation in the gardens supervised by Thunien, whose domain included the kitchen, herb, and ornamental gardens. They were a vital part of the community's resources, providing liqueurs and medicines as well as food. The Residence was self-supporting and famous for the quality of the products that came from its pharmacy and still-room.

Each area was overseen by a senior member of the Order, whose staff was made up of either junior members on rotation or people from the nearby village. Several of the functions were supervised by men, however, and Alasdare had laughed when Dara questioned this arrangement. "We use what resources the Lady provides. If no one in the Order has the skill or talent or strength to do a job, should we go without from pride? All are welcome here, regardless of gender or place of birth. We are not like the Brotherhood: I understand that they avoid women out of a sense of superiority but I cannot help wondering, if they are indeed superior, then what are they afraid of?" Dara had thought of Nashaum and Martus and laughed.

Ejugah, also new to the Residence, had attached herself to Dara. She was not young. Since all of the novices had borne at least one child and that rarely happened quickly on Khyren, all here were mature women with some experience of the world. Her enthusiasm and openness made her seem younger than her years, however, and she sometimes reminded Dara poignantly of Neva. Although they had little in common, the two women enjoyed one another's company. Ejugah was on duty in the laundry now and unlikely to have any free time at mid-afternoon. Dara's eyelids began to droop despite her hunger and she decided that sleep was the most sensible way to spend the next few hours.

A knock on the door roused her from her drowsy state. She bade the visitor enter and was astonished to see not Ejugah but Dame Alasdare. Equally surprising, though quite welcome, was the mug of hot tea and a pastie still warm from the oven that she set down on the bedside table. "Don't get up; you've earned your rest. They told me in lying-in that you had just completed a long delivery and I remember well how that feels. Just sit up so you can drink the tea and eat something. It will make you feel better."

Dara was only too willing to obey. The smell of the pastie had re-awakened her hunger and she had to restrain herself from gobbling it down greedily. Even with her best manners, however, the food was soon gone and she continued to sip at the hot tea. It was steeped from a tangy herb grown for its restorative powers as well as its taste. It made Dara feel a little high. Dame Alasdare asked quietly how she was getting along in her new home. It was a subject close to Dara's heart and she spoke with warmth of how easily she had adapted to the new and different environment, how well she had been received, and how good it felt to at last belong somewhere. "This is the first place I have had on Khyren that I can claim belongs to me because I earned it honestly. It was not granted on sufferance or on someone else's terms. It is not a prison or an overnight camp that I'll never see again. It means more to me to have this simple room than I can say."

Alasdare smiled and added, "Do not forget all that goes with this room. There is the support and protection of the Order, the friendship of good people and the Lady's blessing. When you have been here longer, your appreciation of these things will grow until it eclipses the rest." Then she looked exasperated, "Before I forget, as I do more often these days . . ." She reached into one of her dress's large pockets and produced a ripe tanglefruit. Dara set her tea aside to cool and bit into the fruit's cool sweetness. As she chewed, Alasdare continued, "I am glad to hear that you feel at home here but I am also a little dismayed; it makes the request that I have for you even harder than I had thought when the messenger arrived."

Dara stopped eating and looked at her with concern. "Then do not delay it, please. How may I be of help?"

Alasdare reached into her pocket again and withdrew a creased and stained roll of parchment. "This is a request for assistance: we receive many such. It was sent to us from an estate called Highfields, located on the far side of the Lesser Range. The message says that the lady of the estate will deliver an heir before the new grain is sprouted. Others are also with child and this after many years of barrenness. They ask that a trained midwife of the Order attend the lady's delivery and that of several other women who will reach parturition at the same time.

"For political reasons alone, we must honor the request. Highfields is a strong holding of the old nobility and one with which it is wise to be in good standing. More than that, I detect the hand of the Lady in this sudden burst of new life. Since you are her chosen one, come to us opportunely, it would be best if you go. As this would be your first journey for the Order, however, and an important one, I'll send Dame Lenti along for assistance and support, not to mention company. You will like her, everyone does. I have meditated on this request, as I frequently do, and I am now even more certain that it is the best course of action.

"It means that you will have to pack once again and leave your new home before you have had a chance to enjoy it. Once you are truly part of the Order, you will be sworn to obey such a summons whenever it comes and wherever it sends you. But for now, I present it to you as a request and ask for your cooperation."

Dara thought about being back on the road and sighed. Although she had not yet told Alasdare about her time at Highfields, there could be no doubt that the hand of the Lady was in this. Despite her reluctance to face the memories that Highfields would hold, there could be no thought of refusing. "When shall I leave?" she asked.

Dame Alasdare smiled warmly. "In two days; that should give you adequate time to prepare. We cannot wait longer than that for it is no small ride to the mountains and arriving too late would be a disaster. You and Lenti will be well-mounted and accompanied by four of our skilled guards to ensure your safety on the journey." She rose, grimacing slightly as her knees cracked. "Thank you," she said, and then added, "One more thing." She reached into her pocket again and took out a small cake iced in pink. She handed it to Dara, said, "From Cook," and was gone.

The next day, Dara walked by herself across an inner courtyard that would, in two more months, be filled with carefully-nurtured blooms. Now several people on rotation with Thunien were returning it to life. Deep in thought, Dara did not smell the rich scent of freshly-turned soil. Neither did she hear the tinkle of a wind chime set out to catch the warming breeze. Instead she sorted over the things that she would need for the journey and retraced the route in her mind. She was startled when a woman of the Order approached and placed a blue-veined hand on her sleeve. The woman was a stranger but Dara had been at the Residence such a short time that many of its occupants were still unknown to her, especially since they came and went with confusing frequency. An old woman, her hair was white and the fiery green of her eyes had banked to a duller shade. Her face had the quality of fine porcelain, delicate and valuable but unlined. It was remote, as though age had passed by but not touched her. When she spoke, her voice had the confidence that comes from good breeding and the directness of one who is accustomed to being obeyed. She wasted no time on amenities.

"Alasdare tells me that you travel to Highfields. Is it so?"

Dara looked at her, perplexed. "Dame Alasdare speaks truth, as always."

"Then you are fortunate. Almost do I envy you. Highfields is a place of great beauty, especially at this time of year. It is blessed by the Lady and by its people."

Now Dara was really puzzled. Who was this woman? Her reply was carefully noncommittal. "I am glad to hear that my destination will be pleasant after such a long journey."

The woman's eyes grew brighter and, tightening her

grip on Dara's arm, she began to walk beside her. "I am Dame Ythiel," she said, "and I was mistress of Highfields before you were born."

Dara stole a sharp look at the woman beside her. Ythiel. She had heard that name before, but where? And from whom? "I am honored to meet you," she responded formally. There was something about this woman that tied Dara's tongue and her aura, faded with age, was uninviting.

Dame Ythiel looked ahead of her at the past she saw clearly with unfocused eyes and her voice softened. "I came to it as a bride and it was like a gift from Bentar, my husband. He always did spoil me. It was a good place to live. Cool in summer and warmer in the winter than any other house in the mountains. Food was plentiful. We had to be careful with water but the cisterns seldom ran dry. Oh, it got lonely there after snow closed the pass, but I had Bentar and he was all the company I ever needed."

Dara made an affirmative sound, not wanting to interrupt the woman's rather astonishing monologue. Even had she remembered that Resar's mother had come to the Residence, she would probably have thought her long dead. Why that should be so she could not say, except that Resar had always spoken of his mother in the past tense. Face to face with the woman now, she had no idea why Dame Ythiel had chosen to unburden herself to an absolute stranger. She would have been even more surprised had she known Ythiel's well-established reputation for cool reserve and a solitary manner.

"Then, of course, Amrith came to us and he was all the son any woman could ask of the Lady. We were so proud of him, Bentar and I. He was tall and strong and graceful. He learned quickly all that he needed to know to take his rightful place as lord and he was always eager for more. The wielding of power and responsibility did not bother him. When the fever sent Bentar to the flames, Amrith ran Highfields well, as we knew he would." She paused and gave Dara an odd, sideways look. "It is a pity you will never know him. He would have given you guest rights that you would long remember. No one who met him could forget him. Such a waste . . ." She stopped as her voice thickened with emotion that sat uncomfortably on her.

Dara sought to distract her from her grief while encouraging her to continue talking. "Did you have just the one child, then?"

"What? One? Oh, no, the Lady treated us well, as I said before. There was another son later, but he did not inherit and he left." She stopped again, but this time it seemed as though she had nothing more to say.

Dara, however, was not satisfied: she needed to know more. Still she played the innocent. "Then I will not meet him at Highfields?"

"No," returned Ythiel quickly. "He is also dead and ashes. The Lady only knows who they will find there to offer you guest honors. For me, there is only my daughter-in-marriage left and the child she carries. My grandson. I know the Lady will reward my labors with a boy. He will inherit Highfields as Amrith did and perhaps, when he is older, he will avenge his father's murder." She stopped and looked at Dara directly for the first time. "They are all that are left to me and the Lady has placed them in your hands. Use all your skill and knowledge to keep them safe! I charge you with their well-being."

Dara's reply was on her lips when Ythiel turned stiffly and walked away. Astonished, Dara watched her until she disappeared from the courtyard. That Ythiel had sought her out was cause enough for surprise. Dara was still not certain whether the last statement was an entreaty or a threat. The truly remarkable thing, however, was how she had focused on Amrith while virtually ignoring Resar's existence. "But he did not inherit and he left." It was as though his death was an excuse that allowed her to forget that he had ever lived. Perhaps that omission said more than any direct statement could have done. Either way, the encounter gave her a lot to think about.

Something else demanded her immediate attention, however, and that was the reference Ythiel had made to "guest rights." From the woman's tone, these were something she was expected to know about and Dara inferred that she would do well to prepare herself. The difficulty was that she couldn't ask just anyone about a subject that was cultural common knowledge. It would be like asking whether people were buried or cremated after death: you were expected to know. If you did not, you were marked as strange. Dara left the courtyard abruptly and went in search of the one person to whom she could put such an obvious question. After checking with several people, she finally located the Dame Senior in a storeroom checking the supplies needed for the annual surge of pilgrims who were increasing in number daily. At the sight of Dara, Alasdare pulled her sleeves down, dismissed her assistants, and gestured for Dara to sit. Since the only chair in the room was under the older woman, Dara perched on a crate and phrased her question without mentioning Ythiel by name.

Alasdare cocked her head and gave Dara a look that blended curiosity with incredulity. She appeared to be searching for the right way to explain a perfectly obvious custom that had never needed explanation. "We of the Order have renounced husbands and other family ties," she began, "and yet we serve the Lady, who is Cyris Khyrienne, the giver of life. Are we to deny life or the desires of our bodies that were placed there by the Lady to create life? To do so would be an obscenity and a denial of the purpose to which we have dedicated ourselves. Still, those of the Order who travel find themselves often in strange holdings where there is no opportunity to develop *corzamijien* with others." Dara translated the word as friendship of the heart and it seemed appropriate. "Because the holding has invited them, and because of their position, the Dames are honored guests, offered the best and choicest of everything. All needs are seen to: food, clothing, shelter, and a companion of their preference. The more a holding wishes to gain favor, the higher the standing of the companion offered. This person is often the father of the child and it is not unknown for the lord himself to offer guest rights." She paused and a startled expression came and went on her face. "You need not accept, of course," she added hastily. "Especially at first. You may plead fatigue from the journey or the task at hand. Or you may simply say that you wish to be alone. No offense will be taken."

Dara realized that Alasdare had seen and misinterpreted her expression. Listening to the explanation with the thought of returning to Highfields foremost in her mind, she had remembered Resar's broad chest, the solidness of his body, how his skin had glowed in firelight. She was surprised by a wave of desire that made her briefly giddy and then receded. Ythiel had been right, although with the wrong person in mind. Who at Highfields was left to compare with that?

CHAPTER 22

At some point during the long journey, although she could not say exactly where, they joined the road Dara had traveled on her first trip to Highfields. The landscape became familiar and then she began to recognize landmarks. The moss-covered stone fountain still poured forth clear water when they camped around it, but now the glade was covered with delicate white and pink flowers springing from clumps of glossy dark leaves. Blooming in profusion, they transformed the campground from the dusty drabness of high summer to a place of mystic spring beauty. With her new knowledge she ran her fingers over the worn runes carved into the rock, comprehending for the first time how old they really were. For a while she lost herself in a daydream of what this place might have been like when Khyren was filled with people, before the plague had been unleashed.

Her thoughts drifted and she became aware how strange it felt to be returning along the same trail but as a very different person. It seemed as if years had passed since she walked this way, bereft of her past, homeless, illiterate, and unable even to speak the language. So much had occurred in what was really a short span of days, one cycle of the seasons, that she felt older than warranted by the simple passage of time. Now in addition to knowledge, position, and power she had something that was more important to her—a place of her own. While she had stayed in many locations on this world, it had frequently been against her will and often at a heavy cost. Now she worked honestly and hard for what she had and she valued it highly.

A late storm on the high trail held them up by forcing them into an early camp one night, so it was morning when they finally came to the high pass that gave entry to the valley and to Highfields. Once again her thoughts ran on ahead of her and she wondered what it would be like there now. She knew only that the estate had a new master which meant that Callain had married again. Still, Dara could not imagine another man taking Amrith's place as lord, save Resar, and he, too, was cold ashes by now. She pushed that thought away. She would find out soon enough what man would foster the child she had come to deliver.

They were climbing into the narrowest part of the pass when a bass hum sounded directly in front of them, echoing off the steep walls in a way that magnified both the volume and the danger. The guards unsheathed swords. It was a courser, they knew, but it was the wrong season for hunting and no riders were to be heard nearby. Such beasts were always half wild and too unpredictable for comfort, especially to those not trained to work with them. Dara pulled up her sapeer, elation surging through her, as she remembered the one friend left alive at Highfields. "Hold your weapons!" she commanded. "There is no danger." Such was her authority that the men immediately lowered their blades despite their quite evident alarm. Dara reined in her nervous mount, swung from the saddle, and turned quickly to meet the onrushing source of the throbbing hum.

A moment later both the guards and her companion were aghast at the spectacle of a full-grown male courser rearing to meet Dara and almost knocking her over with the force of its approach. Even more astonishing, Dara, face to face with those formidable jaws, was laughing. "Sandy!" she shouted with delight, "You sly old hound, how are you?" The rest of the greeting took place in a combination of hums and words, some in a totally unfamiliar language. Nevertheless, both human and animal understood one another perfectly and the emotion they felt was apparent to everyone. The guards were openmouthed but still cautious. The semi-domesticated coursers chose to live and work with humans but they were intelligent enough to enforce a reserved distance. This one could have destroyed their mistress with one bite. Yet, when the shouting and humming and laughter had died down, Dara simply looked up at them and said, "He's an old friend," by way of explanation. It was a statement that would be repeated often in the years to come. Then she swung back into the saddle and gestured them forward. The courser kept pace alongside her mount, staying as close as it could get without being trampled or kicked by the skittish sapeer. So they went on, up over the ridge to the first glimpse of their destination.

For Dara it was another step back in time. Unchanged but for the season, Highfields was spread out before them. Although well towards summer in the lowlands, spring was only recently arrived here. In spite of that, the season pushed forth with all its vigor, compressing the year's growth into a shorter time. Pale green tipped the orchards and mixed with the blue green in the fields. Highfields was as beautiful as ever, as elegantly laid out, as orderly and prosperous. More, it looked to her like home. Even at this distance she could see an honor guard arrayed before the gates, awaiting their arrival. Dara felt like clapping heels to her sapeer and whooping off down the slope at top speed. Instead dignity was called for. She pinned back a few straggling bits of hair, arranged her robes carefully, and raised the hood of her cloak so that the emblem of the Lady was clearly visible. They started into the valley at a stately pace.

Resar sat his mount easily at the head of the small honor guard and watched the delegation from the Order descend the slope. Wrinkles of puzzlement creased his forehead as he considered the most untypical way in which Sandy was behaving. Normally he stayed close to Resar, indoors or out, although lately he had spent more and more time by Callain's side. Today, the courser had slipped past him as soon as the gates were opened and then disappeared into the pass. Now Sandy had reappeared by the side of the Dame who led the delegation. Why he should suddenly attach himself to a complete stranger was as far beyond Resar's imagining as why that stranger had accepted the animal's presence immediately. It had taken Callain many spans of days to go from distrusting the huge beast to feeling safer when he was around.

He watched closely as Sandy paced alongside the lead sapeer. Only one other person had so commanded the beast's loyalty but Resar brushed that memory away just as he had carefully distanced himself from his recurrent feeling of failure. Looking beyond the vanguard he realized that the Residence had sent not one Dame, but two. That said a great deal about the importance of his request and the standing of Highfields among the major estates. It also meant that the success of their mission would be greatly enhanced. There were now at least five women due to deliver within a ten-day span. Both Dames would be kept busy indeed.

His mount jibed at the reins and sidestepped nervously. Resar quieted it with a few words and a firm hand and looked up again as the oncoming riders grew larger. They were down on the valley floor now and passing between the orchards. With the sun behind them he could make out details but, even so, he sensed something familiar about the lead rider. Quickly he looked over the rest of the group. There was no one in his party that he could question about the odd, impossible idea that was growing by the minute, all logic to the contrary. Scenes from the past ran flickering through his mind. It was not impossible. If anyone had been marked by the Lady, it was Dara, and the way in which this woman rode was too familiar. "Barrikehn," he said, "Can you see who the first rider is?"

The captain looked at him oddly, then raised one hand to shield his eyes against the glare. "No, my lord, I cannot make her out."

"Kennistan?"

"Not even a kahn-dor-ei could see so far, my lord."

Inside Resar, however, conjecture was turning rapidly to certainty and an undignified elation. He did not need to see her face to know that it was Dara. He spurred his mount forward so abruptly that he distanced himself from the rest of his surprised honor guard.

As they came down onto the valley's level floor, Dara looked up and surveyed the party waiting before the gates. The morning sun shone brightly on them, giving each figure a golden glow. She was delighted to recognize the faces of a few men that she had known briefly, if not well. One man rode out ahead of the others and she inspected with interest the new master of Highfields. Then, with a shock that felt like a blow, she recognized him, too. There was a hesitation only the length of a heartbeat before she slapped her hand down hard and leaned into the sapeer's jolting two-legged run.

A year earlier they would have followed their impulses to jump from their mounts and fling their arms around one another. Now everything was different. They both had positions and responsibilities that made them more than simply a man and a woman coming together across days of time and deserts of lost expectations. Instead they pulled their beasts up just short of crashing into one another and maneuvered them side by side. Then they sat, bodies touching from knee to thigh, and exchanged formal greetings while their respective escorts approached, watching curiously.

"Welcome to my home and lands, Mirendam," said Resar. "I and all who live here greet you and your companion and offer all that we have for your assistance."

"My thanks and those of the Lady, Lord Resar. We come in answer to your summons to give what is needed and assist as best we can the wellbeing of your domain."

Resar held out his hand, palm up, and Dara placed her palm on his. The electric touch conveyed all the warmth and longing they had for one another. For the first time Dara "saw" his aura and it was as she would have imagined it: strong, forthright, and sensual. She saw also the scar that ran across his temple and the streak of white hair that grew where it entered the scalp. Less dramatic but equally obvious to her were the lines carved on his face and the set of his eyes. He, too, had paid a heavy price for Vethis's betrayal. Her anger, long dormant for herself, surged up again for him here where it had begun. Then their moment together was over as her party and his met and the business of ushering everyone into the compound began. Dara played her role in it all, smiling both inside and out. Once she laughed outright when it occurred to her that the guest rights at Highfields would be memorable after all.

When the last travelers, beast and human, were safely inside the compound . . . when only a cloud of dust was left hanging in the mid-morning sunlight . . . when a solitary rajnor-ei had begun circling high in the golden sky . . . Vethis rose from his blind and backed cautiously away from the crest of the ridge. He had been in position since before sunrise, motionless and soundless, and he had seen what he needed to see. More than that, he had seen what he wanted to see. The Brotherhood was indeed powerful to have delivered to him the karait, and at just the right time to make his vengeance complete. Even had he never seen the woman before, Vethis would have wanted to kill her, simply because she was of value to Resar. The new lord had pursued her abductors and interrogated Vethis about her repeatedly during his captivity. And whatever Resar valued, Vethis was sworn to destroy. That he had known the karait before and would have final victory over her now made revenge all the sweeter.

He brushed a glittering insect off his sleeve and stood up. A smile curved his thin lips: Everyone was now sitting in Highfields like fruit in a basket, ready to be plucked—or crushed. All he had to do was choose the right time. Vethis could get into the compound without being seen as easily as he had gotten out. The only difficult part would be maneuvering close enough to the compound to gain entrance. Resar had his guards spread out in a wide net, looking for the phantom who struck and vanished. No one would be expecting him to hit them literally where they

lived. On the whole, Vethis anticipated little trouble achieving his goal at last and redeeming his futile first effort with
the Brotherhood.

He looked to one side where the guard's body was
nearly invisible, stuffed beneath a stand of sehliki. More of
the glistening blue-black carrion beetles were gathering
around it and the rajnor-ei was wheeling closer. Soon
someone would notice the bird and investigate. It was
time to leave. Vethis made his way down the ridge, moving silently and carefully. He did not hurry. It was not far
to the place where he would meet Portifahr and then,
using the Brotherhood's magic device, they would both
disappear as they had so often before.

Standing quietly on the stone-flagged terrace outside
the dining room, Dara watched as a marigold disk sank
toward the Spine's jagged violet peaks. Soon their long
shadows would bring a premature evening to the valley
but, as that moment approached, the sun compensated for
its flight by casting ribbons of ever more vivid colors. It
was quiet in the valley. The insects that sang in daylight
were resting from their efforts and the night chorus had
not yet awakened. The air was as clear and golden as the
finest wine and full of the scent of life.

Noticing a depression in the rolling lawn between the
house and the rest of the compound, Dara thought that a
lake should fill it, were there only free water in this dry
valley. In her mind's eye she could see its still surface
reflecting the sky and punctuated by the slim lines of tall
reeds. On such a late spring evening she could hear the
rumble of frogs and the secret plop of fish feeding. She
could see bright lilies and glittering dragonflies. She could
see long-legged birds silently wading . . .

. . . wading

. . . waiting.

Then she realized suddenly what this time was all about.
It was a moment of transition, of expectancy, when all
motion stopped. In this short pause, the present waited in
anticipation of the future. The valley waited for nightfall.
Callain and the other women waited for the moment of
delivery and fulfillment. The people of Highfields waited

for a sign of the Lady's favor. Dara and Lenti waited to do the work for which they had traveled here. Resar. Resar waited to meet his enemy and face his own fears. And somewhere in the darkening hills, Vethis waited to make his next move.

The sun touched the rim of the mountains, striking off long slanting shafts of light. Behind Dara the door opened and closed, letting escape a fragment of conversation like a bubble. The moment passed. Her imaginary lake shimmered and vanished. Resar came up to her back and Dara responded to his presence even though she neither moved nor turned. His aura was stronger to her than anyone else's, radiating feelings that were, at times, a mirror image of her own. He grasped her upper arms gently and she shivered.

"Cold?" he asked.

Dara shook her head, reluctant to break the sunset's spell of silence. Wrapping his arms around her, Resar pressed himself against her back. Desire for him flooded her abruptly and she leaned into his embrace. She wondered what it was about this man that made him so different. He was her friend and her lover, as well as protector, teacher, partner. Others had been one or another of those things for her but only Resar was all of them. She was vulnerable to his thoughts and emotions; there were times when she felt nearly lost in them. Yet that very openness made her cherish him even more.

"What are you thinking of, so quiet and alone?" he asked. Like most men, he was uncomfortable with a woman's silence and sought attention.

"I was thinking of the first time you spoke to me," she replied.

There was no response and Dara could tell that he was tracing their path all the way back to the Shard Hills. Then he laughed and the sound echoed off the distant slopes. "You were so scrawny and bedraggled, I didn't even know you were female. Here we had gone off hunting some wild thing, a bandit, gormrith, and I ended up saddled with a half-starved woman who looked good for just about nothing."

"Ah, but what was the first thing you said to me?"

"You don't remember?"

"Of course not. I couldn't understand you. I was just a barbarian, if you recall, who couldn't speak a civilized language."

"I recall perfectly well. I said, 'Who are you and where do you come from?' You couldn't tell me, either."

"Not at the time. Later on when I did, you had trouble believing it."

He laughed again. It was a sound she loved and heard far too seldom. "Is it my fault if I had never met anyone from the stars before? It was the first time I understood that you were special and not simply different. If I had known how special you were . . ." He paused. "If I had known that you were the only person who would ever love me for who I am instead of what I am or what I can do, I would have treated you very differently."

Dara fell silent and thought of Ythiel, cold and ambitious and obsessed with one son to the exclusion of the other. She recalled what she had heard of callous Bentar and Amrith wrapped up in his own plans and desires. It was no wonder that Resar had grown up feeling unloved. And then, receiving none, he had come to expect none, even when grown and away from the family that had belittled and ignored him.

She thought of his wife, big with his brother's child and heir, who had sought an alliance with him for the protection and status that he could give her, and not for love. Dara turned and held him tightly. "Sometimes only someone from far away can see the real worth of what has always been there for all but the blind." She kissed him. "After all," she added, "perspective is everything in life."

Resar squeezed her even tighter and whispered in her ear, "Let's go inside and look at it from a different perspective."

Dara laughed. "In a moment, when the sun is gone."

"Then we will wait."

She took a deep breath of the clear mountain air and knew herself to be happy. Despite all the dangers and worries, she was filled with a rare happiness that made her feel as bright and golden as the sunlight. It was a feeling all the more precious for being so hard to reach and difficult to hold. Like the sunset, it was glorious but transient. Like the waiting period, it would soon be over. The sun's disk vanished and dusk rolled across the valley. She turned to Resar and said, "Let's go in."

Sandy woke from a fitful doze and rose to his feet uneasily. All was quiet but for the rhythmic sound of deep breathing. The room's blackness was only barely relieved by a pale shaft of light from the window. It was overly warm in the chamber but Sandy was used to that: it was the sacrifice he had to make to stay close to the cub and strengthen the link between them as it developed. He padded over to the big bed and extended his empathic sense to the cub. It was awake and swimming placidly within the mound of its dam's belly. The mother was asleep and dreaming a good restful dream. Satisfied that nothing was amiss there, he moved over to the small trundle bed by the door. The maid, exhausted, was sunk in sleep too deep for dreaming. Next he crossed the floor to the narrow crystal window, stood on his hind legs and looked out. The lawn below and the compound beyond were still: a night guard walked his round steadily, with no sound of alarm. One of the Wanderers rose above the Spine and brightened the valley with its glow. In the stronger light, Sandy could see a kahn-dor-ei wheeling over the orchard, hunting its prey by the radiated warmth of their small bodies. The uneasiness grew upon him but it was not coming from outside. He would look elsewhere in the house.

Sandy moved to the middle of the room and sat facing a blank wall. Closing his eyes, he expanded his empathic sense and felt the immediate contentment, warm and reassuring, from the adjacent room. A variety of emotions filtered from nearby chambers but all were dulled and blurred by sleep. He searched further but found nothing. And then he touched it: anger, bright and hard. He recoiled reflexively from its impact, then re-established contact. There was anger, mixed well with hatred, but all controlled by one purpose and channeled into deadly action. Sandy hummed to himself in distress. He had tasted that anger before; he knew its shape and feel as well as he knew that this man was the Enemy. Already the man was in the house and moving quickly.

With a graceful leap, Sandy was at the door. It was bolted. He stretched up on powerful hind legs and worked the bolt with paws and teeth, but it was the wrong shape and defeated his efforts. After trying repeatedly, he backed down and looked around. The maid would be hardest to rouse but quickest on her feet. He nudged the woman repeatedly, bringing her from the black depths of her much-needed rest. When she was on the verge of awakening, he nudged once more and then stepped well back. Like all Callain's attendants, the maid had become accustomed to Sandy's presence. Since their mistress insisted that he calmed the child within her and made her feel safe, none dared protest. Yet they still generated more fear than friendship and stayed well away from him. If the maid awoke and found his face only inches from hers, the reaction would lose precious time.

The woman stirred sluggishly and propped herself up on one elbow. "My lady?" she queried. Sandy hummed urgently and went to the door. Reaching up he rattled the latch, then went back to her. "Well," she responded thickly, "I don't appreciate it but I'll be glad to get you out of here." With a stifled groan she rose, shuffled over to the door and lifted the latch. The instant the door was opened, Sandy shoved his way out and leaped down the hall to the next door. It was closed but not latched. As lord of the estate, Resar never locked his door, for need could arise at any time. He was needed now: the anger was closer and the Enemy was approaching.

Sandy butted the door open with his broad head and leaped over to the large bed. In it Resar slept curled against Dara with one arm flung over her shoulders. This time the courser wasted none of the remaining moments on caution. Bracing his forepaws on the man's chest, Sandy virtually roared in his face. The reaction was immediate and gratifying. The Man surged upright and his free arm reached for his sword before he was awake enough to realize what was happening. The Woman yelled and nearly leaped out of bed. Sandy hummed (Danger) imperatively at both of them and then added the code (Hurry).

* * *

Resar was already reaching for his boots before the second code registered on his half-wakened mind. He flung on a shirt and buckled on his sword. Then he turned to Dara, who was also fully dressed. "Get your dagger and go to Callain's room. Bolt the door behind you. Don't open it until I come back." Without waiting for her acknowledgement he went to the door. Peering out, he checked the dim hallway and then slipped out into it. Sandy was already ahead of him and moving cautiously. Not for the first time, Resar wished that he could talk to the beast and ask him what he knew. Instead he followed the courser down the hall with sword in hand. They had not reached its end when a shadow stepped from the stairwell in front of them. Sandy froze, one paw in the air, and Resar stopped. For the space of three loud heartbeats nothing moved. Then the shadow slipped forward into the flickering light of the hall torch and Resar stiffened. "You!" he breathed.

Vethis answered with a grim smile. "Who else?"

"I knew you would come. It was just a matter of time."

"I chose my time well, thief's brother, and the time is now." He lifted his drawn sword.

"Your quarry?"

"It is so convenient to have you all in one place. I'll remove you and the karait, then your widow with her unborn brat. Before sunrise all will be mine."

"Ambitious plans. Too bad I'm here to stop you."

Vethis sneered. "You? You never stopped me before. Not even with chains and guards."

Resar gripped his sword even tighter. "You have been clever. And devious. You sneak through the dark like the coward you are and strike from behind. But this is not an ambush or a raid on an unarmed shepherd that a coward counts as victory. It's a duel, face-to-face. It demands courage and skill, things you don't understand. That's why I'll destroy you."

"And if you fail? Again?" All emphasis was on the last word.

Resar nodded toward Sandy without taking his eyes from Vethis. "Then he will succeed."

Vethis ignored the courser's tense readiness. "Two on one? You always speak to me of honor but there is none here. Or is this a nobleman's idea of honor?"

"What has honor to do with this? I'm not going to treat with you, I'm going to kill you."

"Honor, my honor, has everything to do with this. Not that you would understand."

"I understand a great deal more than you know. True, my brother stole your land. Had you chosen another way of seeking redress, I would have helped you. But too many innocent people have gone to ashes because of you. No more will follow. Whether I stop it or Sandy does, your life ends here. Now."

Vethis shrugged his left shoulder. "But I am not dead—now!" He struck as he spoke the last word, sword gleaming in a deadly arc. Resar was ready for him and parried the blow. Then they settled down to fight in earnest. In skill and artistry they were as well matched as in their hate for one another. There were no extraneous movements, no diversions, only lethal concentration and determination. As attack followed thrust, the duel attained a simplicity of purpose and style that approached choreography.

Blood appeared on each combatant. It ran down limbs and stained clothing, unnoticed by either man. As the fight continued the noise of their weapons rang and echoed in the stone hall. Sandy circled them cautiously, careful never to get in the way and yet always seeking to be in the right place for a killing strike if one was needed. The torch guttered smokily as the adversaries advanced and retreated accompanied by their wavering shadows. They fought with controlled ferocity, eyes locked on each other. Sweat ran, mixed with blood, and dripped onto the floor in red spots. Stroke met parry over and over as each sought an opening and a chance to destroy his foe. They fought on and, although fatigue began to slow their strokes, it gave neither man an advantage. It seemed that they would fight all night without finding a fatal flaw. Not even if the torch died and total blackness fell would they cease.

Then, as Sandy shifted position again, Vethis's eyes flickered, drawn by the animal's movement. In that instant, Resar's sword sliced inside his opponent's guard and then into his body. Vethis stiffened and his grim face assumed a surprised look, as if his unpenetrable armor had proved faulty. Resar wrenched his sword out and redness spurted in its wake. Vethis tried to raise his weapon for a final blow but the sword was suddenly too leaden for him. He sank heavily to his knees and slumped in a widening pool of his own blood while Resar stood over him, heaving great lungsful of air.

A creak came from behind Resar and he half-turned toward it. As he did, Vethis summoned one final reserve of energy from his well of hatred and, clutching his blade with both hands, thrust it upward at his enemy's unguarded groin. Before the point could reach its mark, Sandy flashed in, jaws wide. When he stepped back, shaking blood from his paws, the dead man's neck had disappeared. Resar turned back toward the sound that had distracted him, so nearly with fatal results. The door to Callain's room stood open and Dara watched him from the aperture. Anger rushed in to fill the space left by battle fever and he strode over to her with his face a mask of fury. "I told you to stay inside and bolt the door!" he raged.

Dara was undaunted by either his mien or his words. "I was never much good at following orders," she replied calmly.

Then he saw the dagger in her hand and the sight of it brought the gnawing of failure back to undermine his victory. He suspected that she had opened the door because she expected him to lose and was prepared to defend herself and the other women against attack. The air suddenly became very quiet and cold swept through him as he groped about to find some way in which to deal with this ultimate failure. He tried to speak but no words would come. Then Dara's face hardened and she added vehemently, "Besides, I wanted to watch you kill him. I had to see it!"

Warmth returned to Resar and the awful, debilitating fear retreated in the face of her confidence in him. He knew that he could not fail in her eyes and that knowledge was all that he needed to become himself again. Resar smiled, cracking the blood that was already crusted on his skin. The grin broadened and he started to laugh. The laughter came from deep inside him, rising like bubbles of air. He felt light and free, as if he could float right up to the ceiling. Dara, however, looked startled. Putting a finger to her lips, she stepped out into the hall and closed the door of Callain's room behind her. Resar sobered at her action and asked quickly, "Were they frightened? Is Callain all right?"

Then it was Dara's turn to laugh. "They never even woke up," she replied.

Together they returned to Resar's room. He called for the house guard who came, mortified, and disposed of the intruder's gory remains. Dara ordered up hot water and took out her medical kit. When the steaming basin arrived, she removed Resar's shredded shirt and began washing him carefully. As gently as possible she cleaned the gashes made by Vethis's sword and wrapped the ones Tai would have to stitch. She smeared healing ointment on the other wounds and bandaged them. The light from the window was grey and brightening rapidly when she finished and they lay down together, as much for comfort as for rest. With her head against his chest, Dara listened to the sleepy twittering of birds as the rising sun called them to meet the new day. *I used to hate those birds,* she thought with a smile.

CHAPTER 23

Dara hummed a Festival melody under her breath as she assembled her things. It would be a long time until Festival but the Children's House was filled with babies and mothers and wet nurses. It smelled richly of warm milk and damp wrappings; the sound was indescribable. All the newborns were whole and healthy, even Elisinthe's twins, who had arrived undiagnosed but without complications. The waiting was over for everyone and the job was done. She packed her medical tools in a bag made of soft leather and tied it with a ribbon dyed bright yellow, the color of life. She felt curiously lightheaded and somewhat confused by mixed emotions. It was comforting to know that the Lady had blessed this place and brought it back to fecundity. It was a relief to know that all here were safe, that the Brotherhood's plans and its agent were defeated. It was satisfying to have a profession and a home to which to return. All those things were right and good and yet she felt that this uncomplicated happiness was wrong.

Dara took up her cloak, carefully laundered by the attentive servants, and set it aside in case the morning was cool as it so often was in the mountains. She decided that her ambivalence was puzzling but understandable. She began folding a tunic but was interrupted when the door opened and Resar entered the room. He took in what she was doing and stopped before reaching her. "Is it tomorrow, then?" he asked.

"Yes, just after sunrise," she replied. Dara placed the tunic in her pack. "It is a long journey to the Residence. Everything is settled here but others have need of our services."

"Do you go straight there?"

"Certainly. After that I go wherever and whenever the Lady sends me."

Resar clenched his fists, fighting with the words inside him. They had never discussed this openly, had never talked about what she would do after the children were born and the task completed. Dara knew what he wanted to say: he had not allowed himself to say it because it was not his place to do so. But things were different now. Time had taken them inevitably to this place where it was no longer possible to pretend. Taking a deep breath he said the words that he must let out. "Would you stay?" Having spoken the three important words, he relaxed his fists and went on. "We belong together. You know that as well as I. We have been separated long enough, through no fault of our own. Stay and we will have joy of one another. We deserve some joy."

Dara let the words go by as she watched his tight face and anguished eyes. The strength and immediacy of his feelings radiated from him and her heart ached for the both of them. "Once I wanted nothing more than to be with you," she replied. "I still find my greatest happiness, my joy, with you. And I am filled with delight to know that you want me here. But we have changed and the time when I could have stayed was very long ago."

"Not so very long. Only one cycle of the seasons."

"Not much time, perhaps. Still, time can be the least important measure of a journey."

"Have you traveled so far from me, then?"

"It is more that we have moved away from one another."

For a moment there was a pained silence in the room as they held one another's eyes. Resar was tight and controlled. Dara wished that he could feel her pain as she felt his. She wanted to go to him and comfort him but could not. There was duty and discipline and obligation to rule her and she stood, finely strung, watching him. Love was the tension between their two wills and two goals but they both knew that it was awkward and wrong. Still the strain held until Resar stretched out his hands to her. "And now we both know how wide that distance is. If I tried to make you do my will, it is only because of what I feel for you and how much I wish the future could be different."

Dara took his hands and then moved into his arms. "The future is what the Lady wishes it to be." She paused, then added distantly, "It is sehr-pei and we do what we must."

"Would you have it different?"

"I have stopped wishing for anything else. I accept things as they are but, remember, I wished for you."

"You have me. If we can't be together, so be it. Between us, it make no difference."

"None whatever."

"And we're together now."

"Oh, yes."

"Won't you be late with your packing?"

"It can wait."

The dawn light barely brightened the summer sky, separating object from shadow, color from darkness. Birds rose in chattering flocks, moving like erratic clouds out over the fields and meadows in search of food. The aromas of breakfast, wood smoke, and fresh animal dung blended in air that had, even now in midsummer, a crisp tang to it. By the main gate, the travelers gathered in a small group. Their mounts were restless; filled with rich grass and eager for exercise they stamped and sidestepped and pulled at the reins. Like the animals, Dara was eager to be off: she had developed a distaste for good-byes. Given her preference, she would simply have ridden out with only memories for farewells. She understood, however, the need most people had for the emotional catharsis provided by a leave-taking. So she waited.

Around them, a small crowd assembled quickly. There were new mothers with their husbands, grateful for the

Lady's grace upon their household, servants ready for
some small excitement to vary the daily routine. Lekh was
there, managing to look both proud and subdued at the
same time. Callain arrived, warmly dressed, to thank the
Dames graciously for all that they had done to aid her and
Highfields. She was at her best being the Great Lady; it
was the job that she had been born and raised to do.
Oddly, her actions over the past days had reassured Dara
that she truly wanted the marriage with Resar and would
work hard to make it successful. Perhaps her concern and
attention could reassure her husband as well. Callain spoke
well, blending sincerity with just the right degree of emotion. The group listened politely and the approval of the
other listeners was apparent. While she spoke, Resar moved
methodically around Dara's mount, checking the tack down
to the last piece, pulling on buckles and tightening straps.

Through it all, Dara gave the correct responses and
made the right gestures, at the same time wishing that it
could be finished. The sun rose higher, warming the air
slightly and giving light to a gloriously golden day. She felt
as edgy as the animals. Eventually Callain finished, the
farewells were complete, and the time for departure arrived. Gratefully, Dara prepared to mount when a disturbance rippled through the small crowd, which then drew
apart. In through the gap strode Sandy.

People moved away from the courser automatically, leaving him a clear path to Dara. For his part, Sandy showed
no awareness of any of the people around him. They may
as well not have existed. Straight to Dara he walked and
stopped before her. Then, to the audible amazement of
the crowd, Sandy reared and placed his forepaws on Dara's
shoulders. She looked directly into his large, intelligent
eyes and sensed the struggle inside him. Opening her
senses to "read" his feelings, she found raw turmoil and
comprehended his dilemma only too well. Sandy wished
to remain with her from here to wherever else the Lady
sent them. Yet, at the same time, he had another more
compelling duty. The new child that lay, as yet unnamed,
in the Children's House, was Sandy's responsibility. The
heir was his to guard and protect, his to accompany, his to
guide and teach. Dara reflected that the baby would even-

tually inherit wealth and power. With that burden ahead of him, he would need all the wisdom and strength he would find in his youth to rule it well as a man. Boy and half-savage hunter, they would make a formidable alliance, one that would bear watching over the years. And still, he yearned to go with Dara and she ached to keep this one friend with her.

Dropping back to all fours, Sandy turned his head and gave a loud commanding call. Before it was finished, another courser stalked through the crowd. All could tell by color and size that this one was a female and they drew back further. The female carried something in her teeth and, as she approached, Dara saw that it was a cub, or kit, of whatever the young of the species was called. It was curled in a motionless ball of fur and remained immobile until the female put it down on the dirt in front of Sandy. Then it sprang into miniature shape and raised its head defensively. The female stood guard over her young, stiff-legged and with the ruff of fur at her neck bristled out. She fairly radiated distrust and anxiety. People increased the space around her, respecting the unpredictable violence in a female with young.

Disregarding this display, Sandy went calmly to the cub and picked it up in his teeth where it automatically curled back into a ball. Without hesitation he deposited the little animal at Dara's feet and she understood. After all the turmoil, Sandy had reached a decision: he would stay here with the human cub and fulfill his self-appointed duty but he was giving a part of himself to go with her. That the cub was his own she had no doubt. It would be her duty to protect it and raise it properly, as he would do for the newborn heir. Dara felt suddenly inadequate. She hoped that she had enough patience and understanding to earn the trust Sandy was placing in her.

For a moment she looked down at Sandy and the cub, too moved to act. Then the cub uncurled and voiced a soprano hum that was far closer to being a chirp. Dara laughed, then stooped to lift her new charge. Her hands had not quite reached it when the female lunged for her. Sandy instantaneously stepped in front of his mate so that her strike spent itself abruptly and futilely against his strong flank. His message was obvious and the female backed away, angry but obedient. Dara picked up the cub and it curled into its defensive position again. It was about the size of a puppy and heavier than anything with that much fur had a right to be. Underneath all the fluff, however, she could feel muscles that were already very like a coiled spring. She handled it carefully but still the cub remained a featureless ball of fur. Then the female gave a terse sound and the little one twisted almost out of Dara's grip. With another squeak it went for her hand with teeth long enough and sharp enough to cause damage. Quickly Dara shifted her hold so that she grasped him safely by the back of the neck and his teeth bit on air. He chirped unhappily and she smiled. Raising this one would not be easy. But, then, few things on Khyren were. The satisfaction was knowing that the rewards were worth the price. She would go on working and paying and enjoying. It was what she was here to do.

With her free hand, Dara untied the flap on one of the saddle pouches and tucked the bristling youngster into it. Then, with a last squeeze on the hand for Resar and a wave for everyone else, she led the way out of the compound and up the trail to the pass.

POSTSCRIPT

Rakal lay back gratefully on his bed and smiled. His time behind the Sunburst Door was done and he was ready for the next phase. In his delicate hands he clasped the liquid crystal rod that would, when keyed properly, reveal the identity of the next Triarchal Master. Rakal regretted only that he would not see their faces when Estavin's name appeared. It was certain that Estavin had not the ambition of the other two men and was pious besides. Well, perhaps the Brotherhood would be better off with more piety and less ambition. Dedication to the Teachings and devotion to the tasks at hand were more productive in the end than political infighting.

Besides, Martus and Restobor had failed. For all their clever plans and subtle maneuvering, the Order was still unpenetrated and Nashaum lived on. Rakal laughed lightly. With the camaraderie of the very old, he was glad that she had outwitted them. All three men still had much to learn, oh yes. The problems would now be Estavin's to solve. May he find solace and direction in prayer for he won't get them from the other two. Or much in the way of assistance, either.

Then there was no longer time for thought as the capsule he had swallowed earlier dissolved and a massive dose of Extract suffused him. For an instant, his body was filled with radiant power and he became translucent. Then his consciousness broke up into myriad, glittering golden motes that rose on the Beetle's wings and carried him blissfully toward the long tunnel to the realm of Sah-Charis.

Anne McCaffrey
vs.
The Planet Pirates

SASSINAK: Sassinak was twelve when the raiders came. That made her just the right age: old enough to be used, young enough to be broken. But Sassinak turned out to be a little different from your typical slave girl. And finally, she escaped. But that was only the beginning for Sassinak. Now she's a fleet captain with a pirate-chasing ship of her own, and only one regret in life: not enough pirates.
BY ANNE MCCAFFREY AND ELIZABETH MOON
69863 * $4.95 _____

THE DEATH OF SLEEP: Lunzie Mespil was a Healer. All she wanted in life was a chance to make things better for others. But she was getting the feeling she was particularly marked by fate: every ship she served on ran into trouble—and every time she went out, she ended up in coldsleep. When she went to the Dinosaur Planet she thought the curse was lifted—but there she met a long-lost relative named *Sassinak* who'd make her life much more complicated. . . .
BY ANNE MCCAFFREY AND JODY LYNN NYE
69884-2 * $4.95 _____

GENERATION WARRIORS: Sassinak and Lunzie combine forces to beat the planet pirates once and for all. With Lunzie's contacts, Sassinak's crew, and Sassinak herself, it would take a galaxy-wide conspiracy to foil them. Unfortunately, that's just what the planet pirates are. . . .
BY ANNE MCCAFFREY AND ELIZABETH MOON
72041-4 * $4.95 _____

Available at your local bookstore. Or you can order any or all of these books with this order form. Just mark your choices above and send the combined cover price/s to: Baen Books, Dept. BA, P.O. Box 1403, Riverdale, NY 10471.

Trouble in a Tutti-Frutti Hat

It was half past my hangover and a quarter to the hair of the dog when *she* ankled into my life. I could smell trouble clinging to her like cheap perfume, but a man in my racket learns when to follow his nose and when to plug it. She was brunette, bouncy, beautiful. Also fruity. Also dead.

I watched her size up my cabin with brown eyes big as dinner plates, motioned her into the only other chair in the room. Her hips redefined the structure of DNA en route to a soft landing on the tatty cushion. Then they went right through the cushion. Like I said, dead. A crossover sister, which means my crack about smelling trouble was just figurative. You never get the scent-input off of what you civvies'd call a ghost. Never thought I'd meet one in the figurative flesh. Not on Space Station Three. Even the dead have taste.

What was Carmen Miranda doing on board Space Station Three?

CARMEN MIRANDA'S GHOST IS HAUNTING SPACE STATION THREE, edited by Don Sakers Featuring stories by Anne McCaffrey, C.J. Cherryh, Esther Friesner, Melissa Scott & Lisa Barnett and many more. Inspired by the song by Leslie Fish. 69864-8 * $3.95